Eva's Music

Eva's Music

PATRICIA CHUTE

Doubleday & Company, Inc.
Garden City, New York

*All of the characters in this book are fictitious,
and any resemblance to actual persons,
living or dead,
is purely coincidental.*

167-89

Library of Congress Cataloging in Publication Data

Chute, Patricia.
Eva's music.

I. Title.
PS3553.H88E9   1983   813'.54
ISBN: 0-385-18133-7
Library of Congress Catalog Card Number 82-45934

Eva's Music

*This book is dedicated to
the spirit and memory of
Jane Davison*

1

As I cleaned out the drawer of a bedside table in my mother's room in our summer house, I came upon a letter written to her by my father just before she died. That they both clearly anticipated her death is certain; I don't know that they ever talked about it with each other. The letter was mostly about small family matters, a sweet but unremarkable communication, typewritten, but scrawled across the bottom, in his bold hand, was a postscript about me: "Hasn't Eva been wonderful. There can't be a better daughter in heaven or earth." My mother penned her response: "On earth, to be sure. I'll check heaven."

For days I carried the letter around with me. I thought of mailing it back to my father, he was always so glad to come upon anything she had written, but then decided, no, this one will be for me.

My mother used to say that in everyone's life there appear certain critical moments, sink or swim times, she called them. Last spring, when I began to feel my world spinning, I don't remember deliberately choosing to swim, I was not like Scarlett O'Hara, raising her fist to the air, vowing never to go hungry again. Alas, no. Rather, by following a visceral, instinctive course of action, instead of a more reasoned, practical one, I seemed to find a new kind of energy, and indeed I did swim, although perhaps with more of a free style than I had bargained for.

It is hard to imagine that just one year ago, almost to the day, I was sitting in Cambridge, finishing my second season at the Amory School of Music, where I had enrolled as an unpromising but eager student of the harp.

A heat spell hit New England that first week in June and seemed to focus deliberately on eastern Massachusetts. For two days we were cloaked in thick, dull air and ninety-degree temperatures, sort of like Washington, D.C., in August. My red hair seemed to stick to my head and form tiny ringlets. My rehearsal that morning, a quintet for harp and strings, felt as if it had been conducted in a soup bowl. I sat on the concrete balcony of my fourth-floor apartment that June day at high noon, watching the haze over the Charles River.

Two letters had come that morning. Crisp, important-looking envelopes with my address neatly typed. I put them both on a table. I don't think I have a cowardly nature, but they both looked so formidable and menacing, compared to my usual mail, that I was almost afraid to touch them. So the letters rested there, fallen against each other without design. I sat immobilized in a nearby chair; the thick atmosphere seemed to cause objects to shimmer slightly, and as I continued to stare at the table, the white envelopes seemed to move, to undulate, almost as if they might dance.

I got up finally and picked one up; I chose the one that seemed to stick out with a touch of urgency. Though the return address was that of a fancy Boston law firm, I knew the source of the letter was Cal.

Calvin Bainbridge is his full name. He's tall, athletic (an oarsman), and possessed with a kind of bossy charm. We'd been together for about eighteen months, a time that produced long periods of cracking high spirits and constant activity, interrupted by short days of uncertainty, melancholy, and then a return to the old tempo of laughter, sex, teasing, and vague assurances of love. He's a bit of a prankster, Cal, leaving rubber bugs all over my apartment, setting my clock radio for three in the morning, tying a cow bell to my bathrobe. And now I sit holding his communication to me via a lawyer, a man I've never heard of. It reads:

Dear Ms. Wiltshire:

I am writing to inform you that my client, Mr. Calvin Fosdick Bainbridge, has retained our firm as counsel in the matter of your pregnancy, and any claims you may wish to make on him at this time or any time in the future.

Mr. Bainbridge has stated that he does not wish to enter into a legal union with you, and that he has made this clear to you. Nor has he been able to persuade you to terminate the pregnancy. Therefore, at his behest, we are enclosing a release, also called a waiver of claim, for your attention and signature. In this document, you are asked to renounce all financial claims on Mr. Bainbridge, his family or any future heirs he may have.

Should you wish to retain counsel in this matter, you are urged to do so. We look forward to hearing from you.

Sincerely,
R. Hadley Welch, Esq.

It startled me to see my pregnancy referred to in print. I was used to talking about it, certainly, as Cal and I had talked of nothing else in the past three weeks, but to see it all written out gave it an additional reality.

I paced my little balcony. It was easy to picture Cal, angular, breezy, his hair flopping over his forehead, full of smiles, which I knew covered a touch of melancholy, a hint of self-doubt. He helped me carry my harp so many times, in and out of the elevator, into the car, down the stairs; "Worse than an eight-man shell," he grumbled. My fun Cal, whom I curled up with, our legs looped over each other, as recently as a month ago, whom I had driven to the dentist to have a wisdom tooth out a mere two weeks ago, who claimed, occasionally, to love me—this was the Fosdick referred to in the letter?

I looked at it again: Calvin Fosdick Bainbridge. His name stood out from the typewritten paper like neon on snow. I'll tease him about that Fosdick, if we ever get back to teasing again, which doesn't seem likely. Cal doesn't tease when he's scared.

I looked at the waiver. But I couldn't bring myself to really read it. This menacing waiver, I guessed, is more a return of fire than a legal necessity, because Cal has no money. His decent but small headmaster's salary, an heirloom or two tucked away in a drawer, but beyond that, very little. I, on the other hand, thanks to my father's successes as a theater producer, have a bit of money, a small bank account fed from time to time by Wiltshire Productions, record royalties, or other such nuggets. Cal ruefully remarked to me one night, "You've got *my* trust fund." New England's good families traditionally back their children with quiet money, but Cal's father, a somewhat dreamy portrait painter, died leaving debts. Cal's financial state made him impatient, used as he was to traveling in moneyed circles, and it both rankled and fascinated him to see me float by, without apology, on my father's newly acquired dollars.

I stood before my icebox, a glass of juice in hand, and tried to breathe evenly and slowly. In the eye of a storm, there is a quiet pocket, a chance to think clearly. The overt purpose of this waiver of claim, to protect Cal from my greed or ill-will, had to be put aside. The real implication of this letter, the painful truth, I made myself say, is quite simply that I have lost him. I have lost Cal. I have lost him both ways: If I change my mind, bow to him, proceed with the abortion, though he may return to me afterwards, too much damage will have been done. Despite his lighthearted exterior, Cal cannot stand to be defied, not even for short periods. And I again will have proven myself an amiable marionette, molding and adjusting my designs to the will of others, a role assigned to me early. Little Eva, my father used to call me.

On the other hand, if I hold on course, have the baby to which I feel such a connection, he will hate me, Cal will. That's what he is saying in this letter; see how I will begin to hate you, I will cut off from you, speak to you through my lawyers, punish you for not doing what I want in *this* way. It was a bleak prognosis.

I slumped into a chair, one of two that I owned in that under-furnished apartment. The second letter waited for me on the table.

I already suspected the contents of this other one. It can only be bad news, because if the test report had been good, Opa would have called, I thought as I stared into the heat. My father was unable to speak of anything that wasn't "cheery"; so it falls to the doctor to give the dark verdict. The letter from Cal's lawyer held some curiosity for me; this other one made my stomach turn over. Why are these things happening at the same time?

> Dear Eva:
> I have tried to reach you by phone over the last few days; you must be a busy young lady.
> Your father has asked me to communicate directly with you and James and Adrian about your mother's new tests, completed June 2nd. The news is not encouraging, I'm afraid. Despite the considerable dosages of chemotherapy given your mother under Dr. Junot's supervision last March, I regret to report a spread of the cancer cells into the larger intestine and the liver. Surgery may be possible, and we will offer your mother additional chemotherapy treatments. She is now considering the best course of treatment with Dr. Junot.
> Your father hopes that you will communicate any of your concerns directly to me. I would certainly encourage you to do so.
> I am sorry the news couldn't be better.
>
> Cordially,
> Dr. Emory Kellogg

There it is. I am sorry the news couldn't be better. Good old Dr. Kellogg. A spread of the cells. A reoccurrence, the word I dreaded most. I leapt from my chair as if someone had put a pin in me. No point in trying not to cry. I felt prickles on the back of my neck. Tears sprang from my eyes. "That's a mean God up there," I whispered.

I felt drained of energy, yet I crossed the room like a panther. What must Mother be thinking now? Does she feel that this is just a setback, or does she see it as the end? What a bummer, my brother James would say. What a bummer.

She is competitive, my mother, she is handsome and competitive, she likes a good fight; if she can see this as a good fight, then she'll dig in. Most of all, I ask myself, is she afraid? I am.

I closed my eyes.

Mother used to say, "Thank God for Little Eva, she's so adaptable." And my father called me his Little Ray of Sunshine. And now, I wonder, is Little Eva so adaptable, as Cal, uptight and practical, hounds me to get an abortion? And in the face of this

news about Mother, what am I going to produce for my father by
way of little rays of sunshine?

Nonetheless, he will expect it, the stiff upper lip, the looking on
the bright side. He wears his own good cheer like a shield in front
of him. How is he going to keep it up now?

Opa, my name for my father since childhood, is an exuberant
man, in constant motion, full of bear hugs and encouraging
pinches and quick telephone calls. Though volatile by nature, I
think he's always saved his earthiest, most affectionate responses
for me. My older brothers fared less well. Adrian, scholarly and
surly by temperament, spent years of almost constant warfare with
Opa, and James, though more cheerful, was "unable to perform"
in any school of any sort and made a habit of taking off with the
family car and ending up in places like Idaho. The drama of
James's comings and goings, and the mood of *mano a mano*
created by Opa and Adrian, caused a fair share of disturbance and
tumult in our household.

However, my parents consoled themselves, they had me, Little
Eva. Cooperative, cheerful, and even quite amusing. And when
Opa called me Little Eva, or his Bright Light, or other such en-
dearments, I felt a warmth and connectedness between the inside
and the outside of me. Yes, a kind of identity has been fused
through the years by his picture of me as the radiant one. Two
brooding brothers and one sunny sister. Two troublesome boys,
one good girl. The rhythm was set. Little Eva was rooted early.
What course now, in face of these two letters, these harbingers of
ill wind, this dual disaster?

I threw cold water on my face. Try and take them one at a time.

It occurred to me as I stood in my bathroom that this was the
wrong time for me to be fighting with Cal. I need him to be—I
hesitated as I searched for the right word—I need him to be my
friend. Yes, to that degree, I must get him back, try and disarm
him, ask him to hang in with me, at least for the moment. It
seemed a reasonable objective.

I thought, I'll call him and tell him I'll sign that damned
waiver of claim, or whatever it's called. That should please him.
Then maybe he'll be nice again. I dialed his school.

Walnut Country Day lay nestled in one of Boston's greener

suburbs. Cal was the darling of the parents, possessing, as he did, the correct social credentials, reasonable administrative skills, a ready smile, and a sense, with the parents, of shared aspirations for the students; yes, the right schools later on, encouragement of sports and competitive instincts, and an unspoken attempt to keep the tacky and confusing world of the outside far from their door. Cal had been the science teacher when the headmaster, an older Mr. Chips type, suffered a heart attack at a hotly contested soccer game and was forced to step down. Cal stepped up, while trustees congratulated themselves on being able to find a replacement from within the school, a young man so very much their own sort.

"Walnut Country Day School." It was Joan Tuttle, admissions director and tennis coach, as well as Cal's assistant.

"Oh, hi, Joan. It's Eva, Eva Wiltshire."

"Hi, Eva."

"Is Cal there?"

"Well, he has parent conferences every Friday morning." There was a touch of surprise and contempt in her voice reserved for those who didn't remember this all-important fact about Friday morning.

"Oh yes, of course. Could he call me when he's done?"

"Well, he goes right into a luncheon meeting after that," she replied with an air of efficiency.

"Well, could he call me . . . after that? I'll be home."

"I'll tell him. Are you coming to the baseball game tomorrow? We play Dudley. I haven't seen you at any of the games recently."

"Well, that's true. I've been rehearsing for our final spring concert the last couple of Saturdays," I lied.

"I think we have a pretty good chance over Dudley."

"Good, I hope so. Will you give Cal the message?"

"Sure thing. See you soon."

Oh no you won't. "See you soon, Joan."

Even when Cal wasn't particularly busy, he pretended to be, so he probably wouldn't call back for quite a while.

I longed for a mindless task to plunge into, like cleaning a closet.

I wondered: Should I telephone Opa, maybe that's what I

should do. Or maybe just get on a plane and fly to Mother's side. Or is that too dramatic? Maybe I should try and call James in Vermont. Or maybe I should try and reach Adrian in Kenya, not exactly around the corner, but then again, he probably has Kellogg's letter too.

Another "should," this one more serious: Should I reconsider the abortion, in light of, in light of—what? New information. "Events have conspired," I hear myself telling the nice counselor at the women's clinic where I went two weeks ago at Cal's insistence, "events have conspired . . ." "It's your choice," she will say emphatically. Could I creep back there and say, "It's different now, my mother might die . . ." "It's your choice," she will say again. My choice.

A ring, shrill and persistent. I jumped up. It's probably my mother, I thought, feeling sweat form around my wrists. I'll tell her that I have the letter and that I'm coming home right away, as soon as I can get there.

"Hello." The tension in my voice made me sound frightened.

"Hello, Eva." Cal. Not Mother. Cal. "You called me?" Wary, guarded, he sounded very much like someone not on my side.

"Oh, Cal, hi, I'm so relieved it's you—"

"I've been in parent conferences all morning."

"I was nervous that it might be my mother—"

"Eva, I've only got a minute now."

"Cal, I'm scared. The doctors in New York gave Mother some new tests and the news is bad, there's been a reoccurrence, the cells have spread."

"I'm sorry to hear it. These things are mean. Very mean." His voice betrayed genuine concern. He liked my mother.

"I'm trying to figure out what to do now. I could try calling James in Vermont, but I don't really feel like it. Maybe I should just go right home to Riverdale and see her, but I'm not sure."

"I believe you have some business to take care of here first." I could sense him beginning to draw doodles, fidget. "Did you get Welch's letter? You should have it today."

"I got it this morning. What is all that about?"

"It should be clear." He was crisp: "I hope you've read it carefully. Did you?" Dear fellow, he did not quite succeed in his posture of businesslike exchange; there was a touch of pleading in his tone.

"Well, no, not exactly."

"Well, please do, and if you want to get a lawyer, that's fine."

"You make it sound like a divorce." Silence. The doodles were almost audible. What I had said seemed true, and he knew it.

"Why are you doing this?" I sputtered. "What's the lawyer for?" I heard him sigh. I could not cope with Cal, never could really deal with him, he reduced me to incoherence as no one else ever had, and even though I tried to think clear, graceful thoughts, I blurted out, "Who is this Welch, anyway?"

Cal was always pleased when he could describe someone's credentials, college, family background (Groton, Harvard, they are from the North Shore and play a lot of tennis) so I could tell he was relieved to focus on my question.

"Hadley Welch's family are the Boston-Salem Welches, he keeps his boat up at York Harbor, I knew his younger brother, Jack, at Harvard. Hadley's a senior partner over there at his firm, so I was pleased that he even bothered to take the case, instead of handing it off to an associate. He plays good squash."

"Case? Are we a case?"

"Look, this is a . . . sort of routine thing. You're the one who's doing this, Eva, insisting on going ahead with the . . . whole thing." He just couldn't bring himself to use the word baby. "Please just read the damn paper and sign it."

"I looked at part of it. It's not much fun to read."

"Few legal documents are." He was silent.

I reached for a new subject. "Your name looks funny all written out. Where'd you get the Fosdick?"

"My mother was a Fosdick."

"Sounds like some sort of outer space figure. A Fosdick. You know, like R2D2, a martian, a fosdick . . ."

"Quit kidding around, Eva." I remember a time when he might have laughed at that. He loved funny names. "Let's get back to the waiver. Why don't you read it this afternoon, and if you want to get a lawyer, I can recommend—"

"I don't want a lawyer." Though I managed to speak firmly, I felt as if I were spinning, almost queasy. "I'll sign your paper, Cal.

I don't want anything from you, you know that. Do you really think I'm going to hold you up for money?"

"I don't know what you'll do, Eva. I have lost confidence in your judgment."

"You're trying to sound like a headmaster, that I'm-not-mad-just-disappointed business."

"I haven't time to argue now, Eva. I'm going right into a meeting."

I reminded myself that I had hoped to disarm him, to woo him back in some way. I took a deep breath.

"Well look, I'm sorry, I don't mean to argue. Everything seems to be happening at once. Could we talk about this later tonight, when it's not so hot? Come over at around seven or so and we'll scare up something to eat."

"I'll come over just to pick up the waiver." He chose his words carefully. "Those are the conditions, just to pick up the waiver. I won't stay. I've got a lot of planning to do. Commencement is next week."

Commencement. Next week. Of course. Cal did well at such rituals, striking just the right tone, generous about giving credit to the faculty, getting all the trustees' names right.

"Commencement is pretty important, I guess."

"It is for me. These ceremonies have to go well. I'll come by around seven. Just for a minute."

"See you then."

I hung up and paced the bedroom. I had failed to woo him, failed to amuse him. Instead I got mad at him and failed to reassure or impress him with my decision to sign his waiver. He is not moved by my mother's condition, nor, more to the point, by mine. This round, I told myself, is his.

II

Cal leaned against the rail of the balcony and looked up and down the Charles River with a tense mariner's pose, squinting, shading his eyes against the setting sun, peering far off into the horizon. He looked everywhere but at me.

"So you're not going sailing in July after all?" I asked.

"No, I don't think so. Too many administrative duties; like hiring a new math teacher for the seventh and eighth grades."

Cal had arrived at my apartment with his hair combed, a "prepared to be pleasant" attitude, and a sheaf of documents for me to sign.

"I am truly sorry to hear about your mother." He sipped on his drink and continued to scan the horizon. "Life is unfair."

"I knew the news from New York would be bad. The minute she said 'more tests,' I knew we were in for it."

"Have you told your parents about your—condition?" he asked uncomfortably. He had yet to use the words baby or pregnancy.

"No, I'll do that next week. As soon as this concert is over, I'll go back to Riverdale." My quintet for harp, flute, and strings was to be performed the next evening, the final spring concert. Today in rehearsal, I played unevenly, even sloppily, but no one seemed to notice.

"Does it occur to you, Eva, that this is surely not the moment to heap additional problems on your parents? Your mother needs you to be well."

"I intend to be well."

"An illegitimate child may not hold much charm for them. Have you thought of that?"

"Yes." I smiled, trying to catch his eye. "But it isn't as if I set out deliberately to disturb them. It was an accident, this baby."

"Yes, an accident." He did look at me now. "For which there is a perfectly good remedy."

"No. No abortion, Cal. We've discussed this." I spoke gently, although I silently braced myself for another round with him. "I haven't changed my mind."

"You're crazy. Absolutely crazy." He grew slightly red in the face but was trying to control his anger.

"Oh, Cal, it's strange that these two unreasonable things have happened at the same time. But the fact that Mother might not live makes me more sure than ever. I never wanted an abortion and more than ever, I don't want it now."

He leaned toward me. "Eva, look, Eva, some things you can't control, like the fate of your mother, but the other one you *can* control. Don't confuse them. You don't have to have this baby."

"I know." I circled him now, more agitated than I wanted to be, feeling hot, even though the evening had cooled off. "Cal, I look forward to having the baby. I don't want to toy with things. Life is too precious."

"Jesus," he cried, "you sound like someone out of a right-to-lifers' group. Your head is in the clouds, Eva. Now think about this." He advanced toward me. "What will it be like for you with an infant in a pushcart, and no husband *or* mother to help you?"

"I'll be all right, Cal." The image of me with a pushcart left me momentarily confused. It seemed to suggest someone selling fruit.

"I think it's irresponsible," he snorted. "Irresponsible."

"Cal, here is something I think about, something I remember with total clarity: My cousin Trudy was pregnant with her little boy, Neddy, when was it, seven years ago, I guess, and she didn't really want to have a baby, then at least. She almost had an abortion. I talked to her about it for a long time. She decided to go ahead and have the baby, to complete the family, but she came close, ever so close . . . and if she'd done it she wouldn't have had Neddy. I know how close she came to having Neddy pulled out of her on the end of a suction tube. He wouldn't exist if that had happened. I think about that little boy, and I can't do it. I just can't do it, Cal."

He shook his head and shot me a weary look. "You don't even know who's in there," he said, waving vaguely toward my stomach.

"Well, I'm going to find out," I replied.

"You're going to be *alone*, Eva. If your mother isn't going to live, your father is hardly a diaper changer, your brothers are useless, Trudy won't help you because she's too busy making speeches, and you are not going to have me—have you thought all this through?"

"Everyone is alone up to a point, Cal. I have friends. I feel the rightness of it in my bones." I tried to catch his eye again, but he was back staring at the horizon. "I'll be a good mother, Cal. I'm able-bodied."

"Able-bodied! I can't believe this," he snarled. "Able-bodied has nothing to do with it, for God's sake, Eva."

"But it is my choice, Cal. The counselor at the abortion clinic said that many times. It is my choice. It keeps ringing in my ears. It is my choice. Why should I have an abortion to please you?"

So sudden was his fury that Cal seemed to puff up like a rooster, to hunch his shoulders forward, to gain in height and girth. The fact that I remained calm only seemed to turn his exasperation to rage. In an effort not to explode, he seemed to be making a wheezing sound through his nose. He held on to his drink with both hands, as if it were some kind of weapon. I stepped back from him.

It occurred to me that my stance in this must represent the ultimate defiant act for him, against the institutional world where he was so firmly grounded, where women moved with men's permission, children were regarded as bearers of standards, rules of conduct were unspoken and therefore not negotiable. In a world where a good sport was honored, I was being a bad sport.

He approached me, until we were face to face, almost squared off.

"You may be able-bodied, Eva, but you're not married, and that's going to be your problem." He strode off the balcony, back into the living room. "And you're not going to marry me!" he shouted, and with that picked up his briefcase, held it high in the air, and called "Here!" as if he had just caught a football.

I followed him. "You know I don't want to marry you, Cal, now or ever. We'd have a terrible marriage. I really don't want anything from you."

He opened the briefcase and tossed two or three wads of type-written paper on the table. "You've got something of mine anyway, Eva. You've got my child in there. It makes me nervous. Can't you understand that?"

"Yes, I think so."

"Who knows what you might do, what irresponsible act may occur to you next. How can I protect this child?"

"By being my friend." The answer came easily. "Be my friend, Cal, and be its friend. Share in some of it. Any part you want." And then as an afterthought, I said, "You can do it." I said it the way one speaks to a child who is learning a new skill. "You can do it."

He stood rooted by the chair, seeming to hold his breath, as I held mine. He looked at me for a brief second, allowed a moment of temptation, then shook his head. "Let's get these papers signed, I'd like to get everything cleared away." Cleared away?

I felt suddenly as if the air was thin and still, as if I might suffocate. He sat down and handed me a document, done up in a blue legal-size folder.

"This is the waiver of claim. You say you've read this? Did you get a lawyer?"

"I don't want a lawyer."

"You're prepared to sign this one then?"

"Sure. Is there more than one?"

"Yes, now please read this other short document. This is about the business of where you will live." He handed me something.

"I beg your pardon? I don't understand. Where I will live? What does that mean? Why does that require a legal document?"

He sighed, adopted a patient tone. "We discussed this, you remember. We said that it would be better if you did not live in Boston or its environs."

"Yes, I don't want to live in Boston or its environs."

"Well, all right, Hadley Welch felt that it is better to get everything down on paper. You know what I mean, I assume."

"No."

"Look, Eva, I'm trying to be reasonable. But I have certain principles, and I'd like them protected by whatever means the law can offer me." Cal shifted in his chair. "This document just says, in summary, that you agree to live one hundred miles outside of Boston."

"One hundred miles? And what if I should choose to live in Providence, Rhode Island? That's not quite forty-five miles. You must be kidding, Cal." I felt my jaw drop, almost comic-opera style.

"Indeed I am not kidding, Eva. Oh, I suppose I could change it to read eighty miles, or seventy-five miles, but I want to avoid bumping into you and"—he signaled vaguely—"and whoever, on the street."

"Cal, we're not going to bump into each other on the street!"

"We might!"

"Well, Cal, then you can just say hello, and I'll say hello, and neither of us will die from it."

"Don't mock me, Eva. It's not that easy."

He rose and started to pace. "Look, I can't spend my life worrying that you'll move back to Boston, or might be married and living here. I don't want to be walking down the street with one of the trustees from the school and see you coming up the street with a pushcart!"

That word again. "Pushcart?"

"Whatever they're called. Read this thing, Eva. It's not a big deal." He picked it up. "It just states that you agree to make your domicile at a distance of one hundred miles from Boston, or we can make it seventy miles if you want. It's a clarifying document, that's all."

I felt the blood rush to my head; surely this man who sat on my one other living room chair, who had enchanted me for months, was not saying these things. "We can make it seventy miles if you want—" I looked at him incredulously, and as I did I could feel the controls slipping from me. I exploded. "Cal, what are you saying?" He looked up, startled. "Get out, Cal. Take your clarifying document, and get out."

All efforts at staying calm were abandoned.

"Eva, control yourself."

"I *am* in control. I am willing to sign a waiver, so that you might relax a little, but do you really expect me to sign some legal document restricting where I can *live?* What if I want to live on the Vineyard?" The room began to spin.

"Well, I suppose that would be all right." He was stunned by my anger and continued to stare at me. "Look, calm down." He seemed almost apprehensive. "I'll talk to Hadley Welch about fixing this so the Vineyard would be okay."

"This is the way you deal, Cal, this is the way you are. Fix it up so I can live on the Vineyard? Who do you think you are?" I felt hot tears coming on in a rush.

"I'm trying to act responsibly, Eva. It's a difficult situation."

"Good for you. Now get out of here. Take your blue folders and don't contact me again." I was dizzy, but my anger carried me and kept me from toppling over.

"I'm not moving from here until that waiver is signed." He planted himself by the doorway, feet apart and firmly on the ground, somewhat like a goalie, and glowered at me.

I gathered the little blue folders from the table and lunged for him, pushing the papers toward his chest. We grappled with each other like beginning wrestlers. The papers dropped and as Cal shoved me away in an effort to pick them up, I moved around behind him and opened the front door. We must have resembled figures from the Keystone Kops movies, in our bumbling fury. As Cal recovered the papers, he gave me a withering look and tried to knock me aside in an attempt to slam the door shut, but for a brief minute he lost his balance. I now felt like Joe Palooka, with a strength born of suppressed rage and two gin and tonics. I moved back from the doorway and, using all of my weight against his shoulder, literally bounced him out the door. I slammed it shut, threw the lock, and braced myself against it as he began to pound. "Open the door, you dumb unwed mother!" he shouted.

Thus ended our attempts at conciliation.

III

It is time now to speak about my harp, my sultry companion for the last ten years. How did an instrument so bulky, so grandiose as the harp find its way into my unpromising musical life?

My original attraction to the harp was born somewhat awkwardly during my first semester at Sarah Lawrence College. My roommate, a lanky girl with a thin ponytail trailing down her back, named Pauline Turkel, remarked often, and with considerable envy, on my abundant red hair.

"You're lucky," she said. "All I have is this stringy-looking plain hair. You've got knockout red hair. All you need now is a harp, and you'll look just like someone from a Raphael painting." The image appealed to me.

Soon after college began, a women's consciousness-raising group was hastily formed in our dormitory, and a first meeting was called one cool October evening to "share past experiences and talk about future ambitions." The advance billing gave me an absolute chill, but I decided to go anyway. We gathered in a plain, disheveled room on the first floor, coffee machine bubbling, old magazines strewn on the floor. The meeting was presided over by a bushy-haired woman who taught anthropology at the college and who introduced herself as our "facilitator."

Talk of past experiences proved rather lean, to my surprise: traditional references to a Princeton man, or to a year spent abroad, reflections on a summer working in the inner city. All rather subdued. But when the conversation (dialogue, according to the facilitator) shifted to the subject of future ambitions, the session came to life. Hands flew up, cigarettes were lit, interruptions were constant. Future ambitions burst forth like so much popcorn. Among our group were future doctors, bankers, choreographers, welders, ranchers, executives of every stripe, social engineers, sculptors. At the suggestion of the facilitator, we went around the room, ambition by ambition, and I made myself small against the wall, hoping they would skip me. I had no ready answer. It wasn't that I lacked ambition, I just had never wanted to be anything special. I just had no ready answer.

"We've heard from just about everyone in the room, except for you, Gwen, and . . . is it Eve?" the facilitator said.

"Eva." Going around the room, a particular dread of mine in childhood, was bad enough, but to have my name botched up in the process gave me additional anguish.

"How about it, Gwen? Do you have any thoughts about your future?" Our determined anthropologist was trying to draw everyone out, and Gwen and I had eluded her. All eyes now focused on the dreamy Gwen. She was dressed in a faded Indian shirt; a shawl with long strings was draped around her shoulders. Her tiny glasses seemed to hide her eyes entirely. Although wispy, she did not seem to lack confidence. After a long moment of near agonizing silence, she drew herself up.

"I plan to become a nun," she announced.

Spontaneous murmurs of awe and approval filled the room. A nun! No one had come up with anything as original as that! A new value! A new category! I hoped that in the climactic nature of Gwen's announcement, they might forget about me. But the clamor soon died down.

"How about you, Eva?"

All eyes turned to me. How could I top a nun! I took a deep breath. The words came from some inner source, altogether unidentified. I heard myself speak: "I'd like to become a harpist. I'd like to play the harp."

A nun and a harpist in the space of one minute! The room buzzed with excitement. From the peaks of the corporate ladder to the highest vistas of the spirit. Vice-presidents to nuns. The meeting had been a wild success.

When I was nine or ten, I had been treated to the inevitable piano lessons, which in my case proceeded adequately from year to year, but without a hint of any progress. James and Adrian had each failed miserably at the piano, miserably but decisively, so that at least they were allowed to quit. Not so Little Eva. I could stumble through four or five Christmas carols, I could push out a minuet or two, or render an Irish jig with a certain bravado, but never, after the second year of lessons, did I improve my skill (if it could be so described), expand my repertoire, or, God forbid, practice.

Mother said to my father, "Do you think Eva has music in her?"

Opa replied, "Everybody has some kind of music in them. I think Eva's music may not necessarily find its way to an instrument. Or a concert hall."

"I think we should keep trying," Mother resolved. She tried. I didn't. It was finally decided that I needed the stimulation of a new instrument, and the flute was chosen, mostly because it fit into my tote bag. After eight months, the flute teacher wrote to my mother, "For the third time in a row now, Eva has come to her lesson with gum in her mouth, which she secretes in her cheek while playing her flute. One cannot play the flute with gum in one's mouth. Clearly her heart is not in this." I was allowed to quit.

Now, in my freshman year of college, stuck with my lofty image, spurred on by my roommate's vision of me in a Raphael painting, without a hint of ability or a place of instruction or the instrument itself, I decided at least to give the harp a try. In the minimum, I could chew gum during the lessons.

After much effort, I managed to rent a harp from a retired musician, Mr. Vasly, who happened to live near the college. The instrument arrived balanced in the arms of Mr. Vasly's two burly nephews and was installed in my room at Wigglesworth Hall. I must confess that I found the presence of the harp in my room to be a mixed blessing. As I had hoped, my stock with my peers went up about 100 percent. I did sit upon occasion at the one window

of the square, low-slung room that I shared with Pauline Turkel
and played at playing the harp with considerable abandon. But an
instrument of that size, standing just taller than I, with its
magnificent, delicate frame, has to have lofty space and a sense of
reasonable order for its surroundings. Imagine my horror at returning from class one day to find Pauline's dank leotard draped
over the prow of my harp. Of course, the instrument was rented,
old, chipped, and, if you will, a harp over the hill, but it was not a
clothesline, and Pauline's inability to remember this caused us
continuing problems. She was always apologetic, aghast to find me
unhooking a pair of knee socks or a towel from my harp, but
never, in that first year, did she find her way clear to actually
mending her ways. Our friendship did not survive the harp-
clothesline crisis.

In addition, the presence of this somewhat grandiose instrument and the necessity of its being by the window (largely for
effect, although I claimed to need the light) so crowded my side
of the room that there was absolutely no space for my desk.
Therefore I did my papers and reading on my bed and, when typing was necessary, in the bathroom, where a table of appropriate
size could be cleared. (College rooms are not planned with harps
in mind, my father remarked.)

Through the college music department, a teacher was found for
me, an angelic middle-aged Frenchwoman named Mme. de Quersize, who gave me an hour-long private lesson once a week in New
York at Hunter College, which she pronounced Unter. Now all
those wasted years at the piano finally paid off, for I could read
music (sort of), I had a reasonable orientation toward the upper
and lower clef, and a little sense of the use of foot pedals, although those of the harp are infinitely more complex than those
of the piano. In the beginning I had difficulty inverting the
knuckles of my fingers, pressing slightly downward as Mme. de
Quersize insisted, but after the first six or seven lessons, I developed the necessary calluses and began to respond to the instrument more naturally. I felt the urge to actually play it instead of
just hugging it. Fortunately for me, the harp is one instrument
which is quite rewarding from the beginning. Unlike screeching
violins, agonizing in the elementary-stage sounds, the harp just

waits patiently to be stroked properly, but doesn't drive the learner insane during the first birth pains. Therefore, untalented as I deemed myself to be, I could get off a short C-major Bach minuet, transcribed from the piano, after the first two or three months.

And so, as I traveled into the city for my 4:30 lesson every Thursday, I felt a sense of near exhilaration. To begin with, I had captured a tiny corner of that madly artistic Sarah Lawrence community for myself; I was the only harpist on campus, and I was none too quiet about it either. But far more important was the simple fact that I loved the harp. I loved looking at it, I loved touching it, cleaning it, tuning it endlessly, running my fingers over the strings, plucking at one or more than one at the same time, and when progress permitted, actually playing a piece of music. The harp rested on my shoulder (it now occurs to me) somewhat the way a baby does—lightly, but unmistakably a presence.

To my parents, I think, came a sense of an investment that had finally paid off.

A highly informal little chamber music concert during my junior year at Sarah Lawrence, in which I had a lengthy solo, moved my father in the direction in which I had been nudging him for some months.

"All right," he agreed after the performance, as he sipped lukewarm punch, "go get yourself a decent harp for your very own. No more renting."

"Oh, Opa, thank you!" I hugged him.

"How much is this going to cost me?" Opa was used to shelling out, but he liked to be warned.

"There are a couple of nice ones at Wurlitzer's for about seven thousand."

He sighed. "It's a lucky thing I've had a pretty good season. Go get one then. But don't drop it."

There are two parts of a harpist's life. One concerns music—the lyrical side of the coin. The other concerns logistics. The transporting of a harp is in many ways much harder than playing it. An average harp weighs about eighty pounds—eighty pounds distributed over a considerable frame, an exquisite triangle linked on two sides by some forty-seven strings, made of steel and sheep gut, varying in length from four feet to four inches. In other words, the weight is everywhere but at the center, where it should be; to move a harp is always a two-man job. I once actually succeeded in lifting the damn thing by myself, but then I couldn't go anywhere with it because I couldn't see to move. The pale lacquered wood frame of my first very own harp was smooth and laced with an intricate inlaid floral pattern which made it seem even more celestial and in need of special regard. I grew so sensitive to the possibility that some boob might smack into it with a can of paint, or besmirch it with a Magic Marker (or allow a peanut butter and jelly sandwich to rest in the curve of its upper frame, as Pauline Turkel had), that I covered the harp at all times with a massive, quilted made-to-order cloth. This of course caused the instrument to seem even bigger than it was and the room even more crowded.

For my lessons in New York I played on Mme. de Quersize's harp, and as I improved and actually began to play pieces, I was asked to participate with other Sarah Lawrence musicians in chamber music efforts in other parts of the campus. So I scared up one or two willing friends, and we would weave from room to green room to auditorium to living room balancing our burden between us.

One might sensibly ask, why not just leave the thing in a central place, like the main auditorium, practice there at quiet moments, and, as the lightning of a performance strikes, just sit right down and play. You with the biggest instrument, gather the others around you. Why bother with all that hauling? Ah me, at the risk of sounding foolish, all I can say is that when my harp was not in the room with me, not only did I fear for its safety (a legitimate concern), but I missed it. I missed having it near me. I liked to uncover it and look at its undulating frame just before I'd go to sleep. The tallest point, the front of the frame, seemed to move upward with such promise that I often imagined that it was a high diving board, yielding a graceful swan diver (probably me) every few minutes. The strings caught the light of a sunset and seemed to bounce signals to me. The curved arch made me feel cared for.

The logistical reality, however, was that I had allowed this piece of furniture into the center of my life and I could not take it any-where without asking (nay, begging) someone to help me carry it. When I went home for vacations or for holidays, my mother would drive the station wagon up to the door of my dormitory, with our gardener, Jerome, in tow, and we would all begin a process which is still an integral part of my life: loading the harp in and out of the car.

Immediately after I graduated from college, the harp came to rest on the enclosed sun porch in Riverdale, except, of course, on those occasions when I was asked to play a performance in a church, living room, or town hall. Then we would wrap the giant in its cover and inch our way out of the house toward the car: after the back seat had been flattened, we would slide the harp, which now took the form of a casket, gently into the padded back of the large Ford. Then we would breathe a sigh of relief—but just for a moment, as the unloading, the painstaking reversal, would soon be necessary.

After I'd been out of college for a while, goaded by an anxious social service fever, I decided that I wasn't going anywhere with my harp, whatever that meant. And so after a year of indecision, I decided to go to nursing school. I reasoned that I should pursue a career, a training that would *lead* somewhere. Nursing, I told my-self, would combine my nurturing instinct with a regular solid five-day-a-week (and alternate weekends) paying job. Playing the harp wasn't substantial enough.

In truth as it turned out, I liked the *idea* of nursing better than I liked doing it in fact. I had envisioned myself dressed in immac-ulate white, leaning over the sickbeds of young, sensitive men to whom I would minister. I instead, for the most part, sat in a dingy classroom on West 85th Street in New York, learning organic chemistry. Or I visited the wards, usually with a bevy of other trainees, which made me feel more like an eighth grader visiting a museum than like a committed, liberated woman in charge of her life. After two years, some stalling, I quit nursing and, like the wanderer come back to his first love, I returned to my harp. I remember walking onto the sun porch, seizing and hugging the beautiful frame, almost apologizing for my fling at nursing, and vowing to remain faithful.

I called Mme. de Quersize in New York and asked her to tell me honestly if she thought I could, by hard work and by stretching my talents to capacity, possibly make it as a harpist.

"Make it? What does that mean?"

"I mean, could I ever play on the stage, like a performer, in an orchestra maybe? I'm not sure myself."

"I think," she replied carefully, "that you will always be happy playing the harp. Make it? Well, we see."

At this point I decided I not only needed renewed determination and strong hands, but a new landscape.

New York can bury even the most aggressive young woman, which I am not, and having spent almost three uncertain years in a vast but ugly West Side apartment with two college friends as roommates, I sought a different tempo, a new, refreshing environment. Was I sure what I was doing? Well, not really. Mme. de Quersize suggested the Amory School in Cambridge, a small but rigorous training ground for aspiring musicians. It was not in the same league as the New England Conservatory to be sure, but it sounded just right for me.

"You can do as much or as little as you want," she said, "as long as you do it well." I was charmed with the prospect.

I left for Cambridge in my old Toyota station wagon, harp, clothes, skis, record player, a *Ficus benjamina* fluttering out the window. I had a little black book with some names to look up. My object in heading for Cambridge a week before the beginning of classes was to give myself time to find a nice apartment. I saw myself in a book-filled library, seated at a bay window overlooking Cambridge Common, enjoying a breeze from the river, or some variation thereof.

It is hard for New Yorkers to imagine that any place on earth can have the same problems as New York City. I was stunned to discover that, just as in New York, it was impossible to find a place to live in Cambridge. Holed up at the Holiday Inn, I spent one week chasing down leads that led nowhere, or scaling four flights of stairs to a cramped flat with nothing to recommend it except that no one was in it. In desperation I decided to try one of the fancy newer apartment buildings that bordered the banks of the Charles River.

It wasn't my first choice, and it would cost a fortune in rent, but remembering my harp, I had to admit that a building with an elevator was appealing.

The on-site agent of the Riverview Apartments looked at me with suspicion.

"I'm sorry," he replied. "There are only two vacancies, both very expensive."

"That's all right. Let's have a look." I was determined not to close my eyes in the Holiday Inn one more night.

"I have a fourth-floor apartment, three rooms and bath. How much space do you need?"

"Enough for me and my harp."

He eyed me with an air of condescension. "Are you a student?"

"Yes, I am."

"I don't know if a student . . . would be happy here."

"I don't have to be happy," I replied evenly. "I just need to be housed."

And so it came to pass that we landed in the most un-studentlike, un-Cambridgelike apartment—bare, efficient, arid, un-amusing. But, I reassured myself, there was my harp, my fine companion and easily the handsomest piece of furniture I could afford. We had each other.

IV

The Amory School is near Harvard Square, in an old stone building, and most of my classes took place on the second floor, where a practice harp, belonging to my instructor, sat waiting for me every Tuesday and Thursday. History of Music and Harmony were also taught there and recital workshops were in the two first-floor studios.

As I enter the building every day, a whoosh of sound encircles me, a constant discordant series of notes, like sounds from a zoo played on a fast tape. Me-he, ma-ha, may, me (singers), ripples (piano), thumps (horns), burp-squeal (reeds), eeeeeek (violin), and, of course, from the administration office, the telephone. Circular, engrossing sounds, with pockets of quiet in each empty classroom. A world unto itself, the Amory School continued to emit disharmonies—from eight in the morning until nine at night, seven days a week (open on Sundays for practice)—throughout the invasion of Afghanistan, the taking of the hostages in Iran, and double-digit inflation. I found being there very reassuring.

Every Tuesday evening from October through December, the School offers a series of public recitals, an opportunity for its students to bring music and their performance skills to an audience of anyone who will listen. Cambridge's music-loving population usually yielded seventy or eighty people at these evenings, many of whom were students, because it was free. I, of course, had played few recitals of this sort before, and never with much confidence, and so my first test at the Amory School, scheduled for mid-November, left me wildly nervous. The harp is so big, so prominent, people expect so much from it—and when the delicate, effervescent sounds emerge, everyone leans forward, listens harder (for mistakes, too), and is bound to be disappointed.

Although it was unnecessary for me to bring my own harp to this first recital, as the practice one was in place and would have been fine, in a panicky moment I decided that I must have my own instrument. Someone else's harp would mean bad luck, it wouldn't feel right, it would be like borrowing a stranger's sneakers for a tennis match. And so, at four in the afternoon, having gotten the harp into my car (with assistance), I stood stationed on the sidewalk in front of the school lying in wait for some sucker to come along who would help me, perhaps a fellow student. Having cased the building quickly and found no takers, I scoured the street again. Finally I saw a tall figure approaching, hair over his forehead, carrying a briefcase. He'll have to do, I told myself, or I'll be late for rehearsal.

"Excuse me. Can I ask a favor of you?"

The man looked doubtful. "Sure. You want me to sign something?" Cambridge was petition conscious.

"Well, no. I have to carry my harp into the school and I can't find any other students to help me."

He smiled now, and I noticed that he looked much younger than I had first thought. "I haven't carried a harp in weeks. Sure, where is it?"

We pulled it out of the back and set it upright on the sidewalk while I brushed off the cover. (Why was my car never as clean as my mother's?)

"You play this thing?" he asked.

"I do. I wish I could just take it around on my back and never have to bother anybody, but you can see why I can't."

"Yes, indeed. Are you any good?"

"I beg your pardon?"

"Can you play this harp at all?" He smiled now, a teasing grin.

"Well, I sure hope so. I've got a recital tonight."

He looked puzzled. "Oh, so you're really good?"

"It's a student recital. It's not quite the same thing as the Boston Symphony." We were standing by the harp, looking at each other carefully.

"You look like someone who should play the harp," he observed. "Has anyone ever told you that?"

"Yes. Yes, they have." He was almost handsome, this handsome stranger who reached now to get a good grip on the harp. I noticed a strong chin and snappy blue eyes, as we lurched toward the school building, into the auditorium, and up onto the stage. We were playing a series of Debussy dances that night, for harp, flute, and strings. Five players, sixty minutes of anxious music, missed cues, nerves. I began to dread it.

"What time?" He stood now at the corner of the stage, his coat slung over his shoulder.

"What time—what?"

"What time does your jigger start?"

"The recital? At seven."

"Good." He nodded at me as if we had just concluded a significant agreement.

"Oh, you're not thinking of coming, are you?"

"Yes," he said, in a matter-of-fact manner. "I'll be here at seven."

"You'll what?" I was aghast. "Oh no, you must not come." I faced him and tried to look forbidding. "I can't imagine why you would want to come to a dreary little thing like this. Debussy dances. You don't care about Debussy dances, do you?"

"No."

"Well, why would you want to come then?"

He put on his jacket, straightened his shoulders, and brushed the hair out of his eyes. "My name is Calvin Bainbridge. I teach math and science at the Walnut Country Day School. I'll be in the front row." He smiled once more and left.

"Dear God," I prayed silently, "let me get through these dumb dances, keep my fingers strong and fast, keep my feet on the right pedals, and keep Mr. Bainbridge at a teachers' meeting at the Walnut Country Day School."

No such luck. No such luck, my brother Jimmy used to say. There he was, promptly at seven, parked in the third row, his hair combed, looking fresh and pink. I, for my part, was wilted and disheveled. The afternoon rehearsal had been discouraging and the three doughnuts which I ate before the performance sat like lead in my stomach. My music stand fell down, I missed one cue, came in too soon twice, and felt that all the pieces were being played too fast.

As any harpist will tell you, a harp performance is a competition for the eye. All players have to look at their strings, and no amount of accuracy of feel is a substitute. In addition, unless you've memorized the score, which I never managed to do, you've got to follow that score, resting in front of you on your music stand. Finally, the conductor is meant to have the eye of all players, or in the case of chamber music, the first string sets the tempo, so that's a *third* place you've got to look. This is all okay if you're playing a small instrument. But I found myself, on this grisly November evening, peering sharply around to the left to catch the nodding profile of the first violin, switching around to the other side to follow the score, curling around to the right to watch my fingers on the strings; and each time I looked anywhere, *anywhere*, I saw Mr. Bainbridge. He smiled and nodded, even had the chutzpah to wave a couple of times, like Granny at the school play. I wanted to sink through the floor. As we limped through the final dance, I thought, I'll get rid of him as soon as this is over. I'll just say three words to him, thank him for helping me earlier, and go right home and get into the bath.

No such luck. No such luck, Jimmy.

"Well, wasn't that grand," he said as I approached him. "You played fine."

"Oh, I'm afraid I didn't. I missed a cue and came in early twice."

"Sounded fine to me."

"Thank you for coming," I responded in a ladylike manner. "I didn't know you were interested in music."

"I'm not." He stretched slightly and put on his coat. "Now why don't we drop your harp back to wherever you live, and then go over to my club and get a beer and a sandwich."

I felt spent, unable to muster anything like the proper Yankee get-up-and-go which clearly came so easily to Mr. Calvin. He was

attractive, with his straight features and lanky frame. He reminded me of a large bird, a hawk or a raven.

"Well, tonight I'm afraid that I am really exhausted, but perhaps some other night."

"Nonsense. What you need is a bloody mary. They make great
ones over at the club." He took my arm, guiding me back up toward the stage. "You'll feel restored in minutes, I promise you.
Here, put your harp's coat on and we'll go."

I felt then that he was stronger and more determined than I
was, and I feel it now. Neither of us that night had any idea of
what was in store for us; our major objective, as we struggled out
of the auditorium, was to bed down my triangular giant in the
back of my car and take it home to its apartment.

"What club are we going to?" I asked.

"Just a little club I belong to at Harvard. No big deal. You'll
have fun," he promised me. He was right. We had fun, more or
less constantly, for the next few months, through one spring and
then another.

Did I ever really know him? Well, I thought so, but innocence
as to any future we might have, prevented me from asking hard
questions. I was taken with him despite the unconscious feeling
that we were surely mismatched. We had fun, not despite our
differences, but because of them. I was his New York girl friend,
daughter of a commercially successful theater man (always suspect), a little exotic. He seemed the perfect Boston beau, as we
dashed off to watch the famous Head of the Charles boat race, or
the Hasty Pudding Show, where he knew everybody. Of course we
also had bad moments, when he considered me too "flaky" (often
right), or not the ideal partner for Walnut Country Day events
(usually right about that, too); then he would drift off into an
austere cocoon for several days. But we always got back together,
over some event such as a ski weekend, when six or eight people
were needed to share a house. It was nervous fun, jittery but robust, which we managed to keep up for close to eighteen months,
until that fateful June. Never once did he complain about carrying my harp: I think it was one of the things he actually liked
about me.

The house was quiet and had the look of recent, carefree abandonment.

They're not here. They're not here, how can that be?

Our house, large and busy, with a kind of disjointed elegance, loomed like an ark in front of me—an empty ark. Mother's station wagon was gone from the garage, the New York *Times* rested against the front door. I used my key.

I stood in the hallway, expectant, like an actor, waiting for someone to enter. Not a sound.

They must have gone to Martha's Vineyard. They often went to the island on the spur of the moment. Mother had a passion for the Vineyard and much preferred the simple house they owned there to the elaborate one in which I now stood.

I felt let down. I had expected something, a tableau of some sort, with her lying down, pale, on a couch, and my father nearby, brave but anxious.

I flopped down in Mother's study for a few minutes to catch my breath. Like a bed which has just been left in the morning, the room had a left-over warmth and motion, a sense of having been filled until very recently.

I dialed their number on the Vineyard.

My father answered. "Hello."

"Oh, Opa, it's me, Eva."

"Hi. How was your concert?"

"Fine. I'm in Riverdale. I came to see you."

"Well, that's lovely of you," he chuckled, "but we're not there."

"Yes, I can see that. How come you went to the Vineyard?"

"Mother felt like it." No other explanation was ever needed.

I plunged in. "I got Dr. Kellogg's letter."

"Yes, well, indeed. I asked him to write to you directly." He sounded somewhat gruff. Another pause. Clearly he did not intend to say another thing about the contents of Kellogg's letter.

"Is Mother feeling okay?" That seemed harmless enough.

"She feels fine. Here, just a minute, she wants to talk to you. But look, Eva, if you can stand the drive, why don't you just turn around and come on over to the island for a few days? You could be in Woods Hole by seven, and catch the seven-thirty boat. Here's Mother."

"Hi, Eva dear, it's so lovely here, not that awful heat. Please come on over. I hope you will." Her voice was soft, clear. I could see her, twisting her hair on top of her head, her red hair, like mine, her shoulders wrapped in an old beach coat they kept on the hook near the kitchen door.

"Sure," I replied.

"Darling, do me a favor. Look in the tan bag in the hall and see if you see my striped beach shoes."

"Okay. I'll bring them if I do."

"Also, Eva dear, be sure I turned the hose off in the garden. You know I sometimes forget and leave it on all night. We left in a bit of a hurry."

"I'll check it."

"One more thing, will you lock the upper part of the lock on the front door? Daddy says we mustn't be so cavalier."

"Okay."

"I'm so glad you're coming. Can't wait to see you."

"Okay. Me too."

Hardly the words of a dying woman. Cheerful, immersed in detail, upbeat. I began to pace the hot little study. Could it be, just maybe, that she is going to be all right, that she is going to beat this thing, that I read too much into Kellogg's letter? Were we being too dire? She did not sound sick or feeble just now as we spoke. She seemed just like any tired woman at the end of a long day who has forgotten a few things.

Although I had every reason to be tired, I now felt an extra stimulation, a kind of high, a mood totally at odds with the weather and what my circumstances suggested.

Iced coffee glasses littered the living room. I took them to the kitchen, emptied the dishwasher, and made some fresh orange juice. To a glass of the juice I added some lemon peel, a touch of club soda, and a slug of vodka. I had always heard that pregnant women liked to eat odd things at odd hours, pancakes at two in the morning, but thus far I was holding at a simple screwdriver. As the ice chipper, a relatively new kitchen toy, rattled on, I began to feel cooler.

This house in which I grew up, this kitchen in which I had first been kissed, the little downstairs bathroom in which I found that I too was going to menstruate like all my other friends, this house, which for one brief period I pretended to dislike for its opulence, now seemed intensely familiar to me. Endless numbers of rooms, comfortable old chairs, good rugs, solid fireplaces, wide halls, a garage chock-full of bicycles, lawn mowers, sleds, and three cars. It is a house that may have begun with formal ambitions, but which we reduced to homeyness very quickly. Big enough to contain our unequal but volatile temperaments, cozy enough to encourage intimacy, but with plenty of room to hide, it is also a place where it was easy to get yourself found. A kind of exuberance exists here. After all, what house had five pianos and but one piano player (Opa), whose skills were admittedly limited. Yes, in Opa's large living room sit two baby grands, curled around each other like the backsides of a couple of cats. Mother's living room contains a spinet, given to her by Opa for no known reason, which is dubbed The Virgin, because to the best of anyone's memory, it has never been touched. An old upright of my grandmother's was installed in the children's playroom for the purpose of our lessons, which were for the most part a failure. Off my parents' bedroom is a sleeping porch, never used, which houses another piano, presumably to accommodate my father should he rise from his bed and wish to try out a tune or something without taking time to go downstairs. Plenty of pianos.

My father, known as F. Lawrence Wiltshire on the marquees, is an immensely successful producer of Broadway plays and musicals. Was his name a household word? He always said that that depended on what household you were in.

Although he keeps a fully staffed downtown office, much of the early preparation for his productions takes place in our large living room. In his study, off this living room, three telephones rest available to connect him to the outside world. His preference for working at home meant that auditions, particularly meetings for potential financial backers, at which songs are played and scenes run through, were often conducted here, while we tiptoed around, or tried to listen to our beloved television programs "quietly."

"No one sings worse than songwriters," observed my mother dryly, as one of these late working sessions was winding down. My mother, amiable about music although happier with the written word, always knew just when to go to bed. "This looks like a long one," she would remark dryly as she headed upstairs.

However, she has her side of the house, her lair, if you will, and although it is a good deal more subdued, the living room to the left of the entrance hall (my father's is to the right) has its share of excitement. My mother holds court in this smaller, rather shabby room lined with books and periodicals to a small circle of New York literati. Some are former students, aspiring or successful writers, people connected with publishing, upon occasion an intellectual who has lost his way and come to her for counsel. People bring in chapters, galley proofs, rewritten articles, potential screen plays, or tales of their trip to Europe. It is not unusual to find my mother having a quiet dinner on trays in *her* living room, in company with a couple of earnest writers, musing about this year's Prix Goncourt, while across the hall one of my father's working sessions is winding up and about to take off. Although she receives in the left-hand living room in our house, her study upstairs where she does her writing is rarely entered, never invaded. Her book reviews, considered too sophisticated for us, are rarely read at home; her essays, mostly literary criticism, are admired more for their existence than their substance. "Isn't it remarkable what your mother manages to get done with all the racket in this house?" my father might say, holding up a recently published piece. She seems to sit at the center, while the rest of us dance in and out around her. But what she reads, what she writes, and, I must conclude, much of what she thinks, she guards jealously from the tempestuous surrounding of our household. The interests of my parents, although not automatically at variance with each other, have produced a somewhat bicameral atmosphere in the house.

Walking around, I noticed how swamped we are with photographs. On every wall, each mantel, the walls up the staircase, in the bathroom, hang recorded memories: Opa with everyone imaginable, from Joe E. Lewis to Julie Harris, a picture of Eisenhower at his desk with a slight smile, inscribed, "To Lawrence Wiltshire, with warm regards," Daddy with his Hasty Pudding reunion pals, Daddy with Mayor Wagner, Steve Sondheim, Dr. Jonas Salk, Joan Fontaine, Mary Martin. Pictures of awkwardly grouped family occasions, Adrian scowling, James hiding, Eva smiling, and photos of Mother, mostly on the Vineyard, one with Mildred Dunnock, many on the beach or at family picnics, a picture of Adrian graduating from Harvard in academic robes, Adrian in Africa in shorts and a ripped T-shirt standing next to his Piper Cub airplane, with an inscription from Opa underneath which reads, "Barefoot Boy with Cessna of Tan," and James with tennis racket, without tennis racket, with tennis cup, mostly without a smile.

James, lanky, crooked smile, distressed look, yes, James suffered the inevitable squeeze of the middle child. James who suffered endless conferences with well-meaning teachers, principals, and counselors, James who just didn't have the right attitude, James who left his school books on the lawn overnight in the rain, James who played tennis when he was supposed to be getting extra help after school. The fact that I loved him and tried to cover for him didn't help either. Even when I offered to do some of his homework for him, he just shot me that glazed, baffled look and slipped further and further behind.

But he could play tennis, as these pictures show, and play very well. When James was about twelve, Opa, who played tennis like a duck, offered to "take him on," little realizing that his son was a truer descendant of Pancho Gonzalez than of Lawrence Wiltshire. When they returned to the house, flushed and winded from their match, I remember James wore a look of triumph rarely seen on his face, never in evidence in these photographs.

Another picture had us all lined up like so many Indians on the porch on the Vineyard house: Mother, center and handsome, James on one side of her, me looking cutesy on the other, and Adrian and Opa at the opposite far ends. Were they not always at opposite ends?

Another picture of Adrian holding a conch shell, a faraway look on his face; he might have been twelve at the time.

As a young boy, Adrian was often isolated because it was assumed that he liked to be alone, to read, or to make out his lists of things. I myself have somewhat doubted this assumption, for I remember his lonely eyes and an essential shyness which he covered with a surly demeanor. James and I did play with him, of course, but not very often; and always the rules had to be his. He was the king of the castle, the head of the fort, the owner of the store, the oldest. He got to walk on the top of the fence in Riverdale, while James had to make do on a lesser level.

Because of his extraordinary quickness and genuine fascination with everything in the out-of-doors, Adrian could identify birds, trees, rocks, every kind of fish; he knew all about rivers, lakes, reservoirs, ponds, oceans, and waterfalls.

That Mother thought Adrian gifted, of special intelligence, was demonstrated constantly, unceasingly, and still is. We were admonished to leave him alone with his collections, be quiet when he studied, not to move his shells or feed his fish.

After years of special treatment, of course, Adrian came to expect nothing less. "Who touched my butterflies?" he would snarl at us as he examined the kitchen table, which held his pins, paper, formaldehyde, and other paraphernalia of his collection. "No one. We didn't, honestly." Neither James nor I would dare touch anything of Adrian's. "No one is to touch anything on this table," he would announce with supreme crankiness.

Needless to say I always preferred James, with his sweet vulnerability and rakish smile. In an unspoken policy we always stick up for each other. Adrian always has had Mother to stick up for him. Adrian flew through the Fieldston School, Collegiate, and Harvard, where he graduated cum laude in anthropology (having exhausted botany). Whenever he came home from college, the household was put on a kind of alert, as if to anticipate (perhaps to encourage) the inevitable clash with the other great personality in the house, our father.

It always seemed to me that Opa and his oldest son got off on the wrong foot and never got back to the right one. I used to think they were just born to fight. They argued, squabbled, "raised their voices," jockeyed for favor with my mother, positioned themselves in a contentious atmosphere and drama, which is still being played out to this day.

Opa represented Entertainment in Adrian's mind, a profession slightly above sales or advertising. Many of my father's theater friends were, perforce, glamour-pusses and jokesters, whom Adrian considered shallow. That they were often funny and satirical was lost on him. In most important senses, he shared the attitude of Opa's father (whom he never met) toward the theater and its principal forces: it was simply not the work of grown-up men.

My father, for his part, could not bear anyone who was not cheerful.

"Try smiling, Adrian, it won't hurt," he goaded, as Adrian sank deeper into his bird book, scowling.

There was only one bond, one tenderness for Adrian: Mother. Theirs was an empathy of the intellect, based on their admiration for each other's quiet, scholarly pursuits, in contrast to the noisy, philistine contribution by the rest of us. Theirs was an empathy based on love of the Vineyard before the great onrush of tourists, when its tranquil, intoxicating landscape captured their spirits and imaginations, while the rest of us were getting in and out of the car, taking tennis lessons, and talking on the long-distance phone. Theirs was an empathy sealed with the emotion of a supremely nurturing mother for her firstborn.

And it shows quite perfectly in a small picture of them both, hanging off to one side of the living room display wall, a photo probably taken by Opa, of Mother and Adrian on the beach, bent over a horseshoe crab which Adrian is holding, Mother's head almost touching his, their absorption total, their relaxation and harmony in sharp contrast to the silly, lined-up look of the rest of us, awkwardly sporting rackets and field-hockey sticks, looking sheepish.

I stood in the middle of the living room now, feeling encased and protected by the house. Yes, it was intemperate and full of bravado but I was glad to be there at this moment. I thought, Perhaps just by our sheer bulk, we'll ride it out. Whatever threatens us, we'll beat it. There seemed to be power in the excesses of the house, these photographs, the walls which had been witness to our past vitality.

I splashed cold water on my face and set off for the Vineyard.

VI

The drive from Vineyard Haven, where the ferry lands, to our house in Chilmark, a distance of about twelve miles or so, seemed particularly cool and clear; a release from the heat, the smell of salt air, a sense of breaking away from the mainland—no wonder Mother loved it here. And no wonder she sought its comforts now.

Will she look different? Will she look different because those disastrous cells are loose in her? I guess that nothing will look different and yet everything about her will be cast in a different light, a light reflecting our own apprehensions.

I wonder now how to tell them about my pregnancy and the upheaval with Cal. Should I wait? Wait until we have talked about Mother's tests, absorbed that horror? And then present this as a sort of—well, antidote? How to balance the timing of news of life and news of death? Compounding the dire word about her health with a showstopper like mine could either darken the drama or possibly distract from it. Yes, it could distract them from the apprehension, the dread of what is in store for her. Give another problem. Another focus.

Perhaps I could talk to Mother first. She was, in her way, more reasonable. No, I cannot count on that reasonableness now. Her life is threatened. Her reaction cannot be predicted.

And Opa, so affectionate, and in his funny way so eager to please, could he be counted on for at least a stolid neutrality?

On reflection I realized that neutrality was never Opa's scene, and certainly not when his Little Eva was concerned. His Little Ray of Sunshine with an illegitimate baby? No, it didn't look good.

My father is a social conservative, despite a certain flair acquired through years of being in the theater. Illegitimate children have no part in his structure. It didn't look good.

After I arrived, we sat on the porch, Mother, Opa, and me, looking southwest toward the ocean, picking up the occasional honking of geese. Mother was sorting strips of yarn for her needlepoint by the light which shone through from the living room. Her glasses masked her eyes, her fingers seemed busy and tense as she separated the colored yarn.

"I think we should rebuild the shed," Opa announced. "It isn't even a shed anymore, it's more of a lean-to. Maybe James or Adrian could prop it up a little."

"We've been propping it up for the last ten years," I offered.

"Just leave it," said Mother. "One day it will fall down, and the problem of the shed will have solved itself."

Opa stood on the porch, surveying his property. The land overlooked a pond, and beyond that lay the ocean, visible as a thin strip along the horizon. Open fields led down to the brush and then onto a rocky beach, owned by the town. It was a good quarter of a mile away, the ocean, but we could smell it, that wonderful briny smell, particularly at night.

My mother looked tired, and Opa's nervous concern and constant leaping to his feet to get her things clearly made her more so. For the rest of that first evening, and through most of the next day, we all just chatted away about housekeeping details and island gossip. Not one word was spoken on the subject of her tests. The one or two times I was alone with Mother, however fleetingly, I couldn't seem to say anything. Was it cowardice? Or was it the result of years of letting Opa control the mood? By indirection, Opa established boundaries of what could or could not be discussed. Now his mood was consciously lighthearted, even though his face reflected tension. He never left Mother's side, hovering over her like an anxious gull.

That evening I decided I would finally have to break this pattern by leading with my own headline. And so after dinner, I told them that I was pregnant and that I'd decided to have the baby, in a manner which I hoped did not give it all the coloration of a soap opera. I told them about Cal's reaction and our final meeting. After registering surprise, Opa said, "My, my, Eva, times have changed. In my day, if a girl got pregnant, her parents collared the young man and marched them off to the altar, and that was that."

Mother looked worried but continued to work her needlepoint. If I had expected fireworks, ultimatums, or whatever, I was mistaken. They asked predictable questions, gave me correct and understandable warnings, but on the whole treaded lightly on me. I did not trust this response.

No, it was all too refined, too pallid, this evening, given the cast of characters. After an hour or so of talk, conducted in quiet tones, Opa rose and proposed that we all go to bed early, as we had had a long day (which we had not). This seemed a further ominous sign; I interpreted it as his wish to discuss my predicament with Mother alone first, sharpen his teeth, and come back to me claiming a united parent front. My final recollection of this muted evening was that Mother, on bidding me good night, smiled at me, a smile of—dare I say it?—merriment.

Although my room was on the other side of the house, I could hear the timbre of their voices, a kind of buzzing across the summer air as I went to sleep.

In the morning I dressed quickly. My father was on the phone to London, talking about the rights to a play that had just opened there, so I tiptoed about, putting breakfast together, trying to find my favorite cereal. Mother appeared, looking as if she had slept poorly. She fixed a grapefruit, announced that she had a great deal to do that morning, and seemed to remove herself rather hurriedly.

After breakfast, Opa said, "All right, Eva, now let's sit down and discuss this baby business further." Actually, we were already sitting, my father and I, in the living room, with its faded slipcovers and air of loose management. Mother had gone out, to visit friends, she said, and thus allow our private confrontation—the idea being, I suppose, that she would be back later in the morning to pick up the pieces and offer her more reasoned judgment after our storm. The sun that morning was strong, almost insistent, and it seemed to spotlight us; bright patches caught and followed us like theater lights.

My father is a handsome man, balding slightly, of medium height, with fine features and a million-dollar smile (not showing that morning). His ability to relax was never equal to my mother's, and he was not particularly at ease on the Vineyard anyway, having not much of a penchant for old clothes and bad weather. His tailored, almost prim choice of clothes, compared to my mother's faded, loose-hanging garments, betrayed him easily as an outsider, or the one who just-comes-for-the-weekend-while-the-rest-of-us-are-down-here-for-the-season look. This morning he looked particularly pulled together, even taut, with brick-red pants and a navy blazer jacket; he held a cup of coffee, moving it from hand to table, never drinking it. He began:

"It often happens that young women in this day and age find themselves in your situation." He seemed to nod vaguely toward my stomach. "And they become seized with a particular fantasy, something they may have heard, or seen in a film, and they lose their sense of balance. Their judgment is off, emotions take over. You know what I mean, I assume."

"Not quite," I answered honestly. He seemed unwilling to expand, so I said, "I don't think I've lost my sense of balance. Actually, I feel . . . well balanced." I tried not to seem cheerful, since I knew that would enrage him.

"Eva, let me tell you something." Opa leaned forward, as if he were going to whisper. "We all think the world of Cal, as you know. But if you don't want to marry him, no one can force you to, obviously. But I don't think you have fully appreciated what it will be like to bear a child alone, take care of that child alone, and not be able to share those responsibilities with someone."

"I have thought of that. I really have. I have thought about the practical side of this. And, I assure you, I will get help. I will find people to share these tasks with. James will help me, I think. And after all, I'll probably marry someone eventually. Don't worry, I'm not by nature a martyr."

He leaned back, sighed deeply, gave me the look of the tired professor, shook his head. "What are you by nature, Eva? You're not a martyr, which I accept. What are you? Tell me."

I sat up in my wicker chair. It was not an unfair question, but my clearheaded, trust-me responses were of no use at this moment. He had thrown me a curve. What are you by nature, he had asked.

"Well, I haven't got a really clean-cut answer for you. I have always seen myself as a mother, but then I have also seen myself as a lot of other things too. I'm not being evasive, it's just that I'm not altogether sure."

Opa got up from his chair and peered down at me, like a magistrate. "Well," his voice rose, "until you find out, goddamnit, until you find out what or who you are by nature"—he paused to glare at me—"you will not proceed to have an illegitimate child. Is that clear?"

I shook my head. Here it is, delayed from last night. His true anger.

"And," he went on, raising his arm in the air for dramatic emphasis, "if you solve, to the best of your ability, the question of who you are and what you are, my dear, you can have eight illegitimate babies if you want!"

"Hardly," I managed to murmur.

"When you are able to answer the simple question, who you are by nature, then you can proceed to do whatever you want."

I felt a touch of impatience. "Oh, come on, Opa. If I were a wilting bride of twenty, with a husband and tiny baby, I wouldn't be able to answer that question either, but it would be all right, wouldn't it, to have children, legitimate children then, without understanding my exact nature—because I had a husband."

"A husband is not a small matter. You would have the support of a husband, yes, and you'd be grateful for it."

"Husbands don't automatically understand their true natures either. I'm not so sure that the support is guaranteed."

He sat down, banging his coffee cup on the table. This was an improvement over the days when he used to bite his cigarette, a habit terminated since he gave up smoking. "This is irresponsible, Eva. Utterly irresponsible. The fact remains, you're proceeding on a whim, a fad of some sort. I don't understand it myself, some ludicrous idea you probably got at Sarah Lawrence College. We shouldn't have sent you there, I told Mother at the time. I thought everyone there looked wacky."

"Don't blame Sarah Lawrence." Poor Sarah Lawrence.

"Who should I blame?"

"Don't blame anyone. It's just a baby, after all. A baby that you might come to love."

"I have no objection to babies, Eva. Don't paint me with that brush." He leaned back in his chair. "This whole thing reminds me of those letters one reads in the newspaper. You know, Dear Chit-Chat, I got pregnant and I want to keep my baby, and everyone's against it, signed, Maureen C., age sixteen. Or it sounds like Vanessa Redgrave, defying convention."

"But I'm neither one of those types, Opa," I pleaded. "I'm not a helpless teenager or a worldly actress. I just want to keep this baby growing inside of me because I feel very well about it. Of course, I'd rather have a husband that I loved, but I really do feel that I know what I'm doing."

"Well," he snapped, "if you know what you're doing, then return to Cal and straighten out your relationship and get this baby off to the right start. That would be mature, it seems to me."

I felt that I was losing ground. "We shouldn't be married, Cal and I. It wouldn't last. It would be a terrible marriage. You and Mother have a good marriage. I used that as an example to follow. Besides, as I told you last night, Cal won't do it."

"Cal is a decent young man. His father was two classes ahead of me at Harvard. I intend to call him, arrange a meeting with him, and discuss this whole thing in an open manner."

"Oh, no you don't," I heard myself shout. "Don't you dare. There will be no meeting. We've met, believe me, and there is nothing more you can do. Please stay out of it." This was all worse than I had imagined. The ultimate nightmare, it seemed to me, was Opa, Cal, and Hadley Welch sitting down to negotiate about me and my baby. "Cal can get very mean."

"I always thought he was charming."

"Charming people can also be mean. Cal can't stand people who don't do things his way."

"What does Cal want? What does he want you to do, really?"

"He wants me to have an abortion."

He gazed out of the window for a minute. "Well, given both of your circumstances, that seems reasonable to me."

"But it does not seem reasonable to *me*. You see, I don't *want* an abortion. I look forward to having the baby." The sun, which had been shining on my shoulder, now rested on my feet. I looked down at those feet, cloaked in old espadrilles, and followed the line from the arch of my foot to the anklebone. It occurred to me that these feet, on which my attention was now fixed, might be my only hidden resource. I could, after all, walk away. Take my stomach, still flat, get up on my feet, and walk away. Walk *out*.

"Eva," he said, in a low, somewhat menacing tone, "I will say this: You cannot give a baby back. You are proceeding on this ludicrous course, from which you will have no appeal. Do you understand that? You will have no appeal of this decision."

"That's fine. I'll make it work, Opa. I will. I've always loved children. I've loved the children in our family, like Neddy."

"You're not having Neddy, please remember. Don't romanticize this, Eva. It's a responsibility."

"I want the responsibility." I paused to find his eye. I needed to look at him directly. "I have never had any real responsibility. Never in my twenty-six years. It's time I did. I feel it in my bones. Trust me."

He looked momentarily respectful, if not exactly moved. "I trust you, as you know." He fidgeted. "But have you given any thought, in your single-minded preoccupation, with the situation of your mother's health, and how this might affect her?"

The situation of your mother's health, he had said. The first real reference to it. I sighed with relief. We were, after all, going to talk as adults, not as stern father and wayward daughter.

"Oh, Opa, I have, believe me."

"Well, she's very upset."

"Is she? I know she's worried about how I'm going to manage, but is she really against it?"

He rose and looked down at me again. "How can you, at a time like this, willingly take a course that would upset her?"

Checkmate.

He began to pace. "On Monday we go back to New York for one of those dreadful chemotherapy treatments. She needs you at a time like this, Eva, to be . . . what shall I say? Unencumbered." He looked at me now almost beseechingly. "News of this sort, however you may see it, is not what a sick woman needs."

I took a deep breath. "How sick is she? Can you tell me?"

He went on as if he hadn't heard the question. "Surely you must know that a person's mental and emotional state is a significant factor when physical health is threatened. That you should add to her worries at a time when she needs to feel strong and resilient is an act of uncommon selfishness." He repeated, "Deep, uncommon selfishness."

What followed was a silence that made me feel cut in half. I could have no response. Anything I might possibly say would seem only to pit myself against her, a dying woman. He was right, of course, if he had assessed her reaction correctly. I could not stand to be the one that upset her last months. I said nothing; I felt paralyzed.

He pressed. "Can you still get an abortion? Have three months passed?" He spoke quietly now.

"I guess I could."

"Don't you know?" His tone was edgy. Opa liked his facts sorted out, presented without ambiguity. "Let me call Emory Kellogg in New York, see if he can find someone, and you can fly up tonight. I know that you are disappointed, Eva, and you have made a decent case for yourself . . ." He went on, but I didn't listen. A picture came before me, of my mother's smile of the night before. Yes, she had smiled, I was sure of it. She had smiled; what did it mean?

"I'll talk to her." I began to feel some energy return.

"To whom?" Opa looked puzzled.

"I'll talk to Mother. Let me see what she really thinks."

He banged the coffee cup down on the table again. "You will do no such thing!"

"Why can't I talk to her? She's an intelligent, lucid woman. I'm going to ask her to tell me why I can't proceed with this baby."

"You'll upset her!" he shouted.

"I'll take that chance. She's stronger than you think."

"Eva!" His voice shot out like a bullet. "You have a moral obligation not to introduce problems into her life at this time."

We were both on our feet now. "The problem has been introduced. I'll find her. Where is she? Whose house did she go to?"

He approached me like a tiger, his head thrust forward. "I don't intend to tell you. She needs rest, not a big scene."

"Two can play this game, Opa. I'll find her." I felt the blood rush to my face, and I reached for my bag with my car keys. "But I promise you this, and I swear to it. If she wants me to go ahead and get an abortion, I'll do it, I will, and I'll never refer to it again. But I'll hear it from her first." I took my two feet, with knees shaking, out of the house and toward my car.

I felt a sudden wave of nausea; a shallow nausea, but it caused me to stop, lean for a moment against the car, and close my eyes. I suppose there are worse things than throwing up in your own driveway, but I couldn't think of any at that moment, so I took short quick breaths and hoped that it would pass. I also hoped that my father wasn't peering at me from a window. I didn't want him to witness any sign of my distress. It had to be caused by a combination of nerves and morning sickness (midmorning sickness), but I preferred that it be my secret. I'd only had one such bout before.

After a minute or two I climbed into the front seat of my Toyota, not quite as before, but feeling somewhat better. There's nothing like a rutted Vineyard dirt road in the spring to make a stomach that is turning turn faster, but I started off anyway.

The land surrounding the town of Chilmark is hilly; the roads, particularly the one to Gay Head, undulate up and down and around like a roller coaster. Green, yellow-green, blue-green, the meadows leading down to the ocean seem to dance with green. The scrub oak and pine dot and punctuate with dark green, the marshes hugging the inlets are pale but robust in tone, a shade of lime. I noticed the clusters of day lilies just coming out, bent over stone walls, buffeted by the breeze but sturdy, having been stationed in that same ground for years. We'd been given a near-perfect day.

As my old Toyota lurched out into the main road, I tried to

figure out the shortest route to the houses where my mother might possibly be. Visiting could also mean shopping, so I included the Menemsha food store and the summer-only Chilmark Store on my route. What else was there? Was the little library open?

"Has Mother been here by chance?" I called from the car to Martha Duffy, an old friend from New York who was just getting settled in her cottage.

"No, but I wish she'd stop by, Eva. I want her to read a letter to the editor that I'm sending to the *Times*. It's about time that someone protested this business at Lincoln Center." Martha Duffy was a permanently indignant lady, and rather than get sucked into whatever business this was, I waved merrily and called, "I'll see you then, thanks anyway."

I made seven more stops, including the stores. Her Ford jeep was new as of last year and easy to spot, but I couldn't find it anywhere. Could she have gone back to the house, could we have crossed each other's paths? As a last resort, I decided to try her favorite beach, Squibnocket, and if she was not there, I'd go on back home and seek a private interview with her under different circumstances. Maybe Dad was right, maybe she needed rest, and she certainly shouldn't be having to clear out of the house so that we could shout at each other for a while. After all, she was a sick woman, a woman with cancer that had recurred; she was due a certain deference.

The sun made patterns as I rode up Squibnocket Road, jigsaws, playful patterns, cubes of light, patches that seemed to suggest that this was all very funny indeed. That my mother's life should be threatened and all I was prepared to replace her with was, what?—a tiny baby.

There was her jeep at the end of the small parking lot.

I parked next to it and, feeling nervous, stopped to run a brush through my hair. I felt as if a cold collar had been placed around me.

Now we would surely have to talk about her health, her cancer, the spread of it, the threat of death. I was almost afraid of hearing her say anything on the subject. When anyone else referred to her cancer, like Dr. Kellogg, it still seemed a speculation. What she

said would be definite, or I knew it would certainly be interpreted
as such. She would be the final judge.

I started down the beach, and as I rounded a pile of rocks, I
spotted her, she saw me, and we waved. She was wearing a floppy
pink hat and an old cotton dress which I had seen her wear constantly over the years.

I thought to myself, Look at her quickly now, just for a minute,
as she sits reading, in profile, quiet and erect in this perfect tableau. As of this moment, she is still just my mother, reading,
watching the gulls. After we talk, it will never be the same. For
then she will be my mother who has cancer, who is sick, and who
may never get well. At that moment she waved again.

My mother is not considered beautiful, but rather handsome.
We both have red hair, she and I, a soft color, frothy and curly,
more orange than red. My father calls us his Renoir girls. Although I inherited my mother's hair, the rest of me is his, square
jaw, small nose, wide smile, the look of a cheerleader.

But my mother, hair piled high on her head, with her heart-
shaped face, pronounced nose, and wide-set eyes, looks like a
duchess. A duchess with freckles, she used to say, for freckles dotted her cheeks and hands. Although her looks were painted in
somewhat bold strokes, and her dress was unconventional at best,
she had a serene demeanor, which provided a necessary balance to
my father's rather manic high spirits. As I approached, I noticed
that she was sitting on an old towel which read, "Buy Narragan-
sett Beer."

"Hi," she called. "Well, who won? Any knockouts?"

I plunked down beside her. "It was a decision. And you're the
judge."

"That's what I figured." She smiled. "Did Opa play a good second act?" We referred to his gradations of temper in this manner,
the second act being the most dramatic, the first being the wind-
up, and the third revealing a slowing of resources due to exhaus-
tion. (My brother Adrian specialized in second-act scenes with
Opa.)

"No, not really. Just a first act."

"Well, all right. What a gorgeous day, Eva. There should be a way of storing up days like this, to be reused in March.. It's hard to focus on problems on days like today."

"I know, and I feel awful. I shouldn't introduce—"

"No apologies. We've got two problems, yours and mine. Here, sit on this windbreaker, the sand is cold."

"Well, all right. I guess it's not as warm as it looks." Mother stuffed her magazine into her tote bag. "*The Atlantic* is improving," she announced. "That new man has brought in some good people." I shivered slightly.

"Eva, have you absorbed the essence of Dr. Kellogg's letter?"

"Well, I've been somewhat afraid to, I guess."

"It's hard for you. But I must ask you to be tough on yourself now, and face facts without—I was going to say without flinching, but I take that back: you may flinch, dear girl." She shot me a quick smile, but I could only stare at her. "But for my sake, do you hear me, for my sake, we have to talk very openly and we can't back away from the truth. You are the only one I can ask this of."

I took a deep breath. "Tell me then, without backing off. What is the truth?"

She replied, "I cannot live. I think I've got a year, if I'm very lucky."

"Oh, please don't say it that way!" The words were out of my mouth before I knew it. Tears were there before I could stop them. "You are going to fight it, aren't you?"

I gazed at her, aware of how miserable I looked, how I must disappoint her with my lack of control. But she removed her glasses and I could see now that she too had tears in her eyes.

"I will fight it, in my own way," she replied quietly. "And you, Eva, you must help me."

"Of course, I'll do anything." The ocean seemed to dance in front of us in an almost vulgar manner, to bop up and down and close in on us, noisily, sloppily. I wished it would go away.

"I'll be going down to New York on Monday to begin another chemotherapy program. Silly word for it, program. I'll be back in five days. I'm only doing it as a concession to Daddy and Emory Kellogg. I know it's useless. But I'll go through with it."

"You might gain time." A hint of nausea, a feeling of seasickness crept back over me, but I fought it, fought it so I could listen and find out what she wanted me to do, how I am to help. "You must try and gain time." My voice was flat, toneless.

"Yes. It's true, and I might feel better for a bit too; apparently this type of treatment I'm to take is less punishing than the kind I took two years ago. But it means leaving the Vineyard, which I hate to do, particularly now."

Once more I felt myself losing the tiny foothold of control I thought I had. "Are you sure?" I cried. "Are you sure that it's all so certain? Have you consulted other doctors?"

"Yes, we have. They all agree. Even Emory, the most optimistic man in the world, says a year if we're lucky."

"It's unfair! That's a mean God up there!" I put my skirt up over my face. "A damn, mean God, that's all I have to say."

She laughed. "Now I've thought of a lot of things in this past three weeks, but I don't think I hit on that one. Dear Eva, try and be brave."

I didn't say anything.

"Because the others won't be able to, in the way that you will."

"You mean Opa?"

"Yes, Opa, and also James. I don't know as much as I used to about Adrian, over there in Africa, but he is very attached to me, despite the distance that he's chosen to live from us."

"I know. I tend to forget about Adrian sometimes."

"Well, we mustn't do that. He must be included, in everything."

She lit a cigarette; the breeze had died down and she leaned forward, under her hat, and managed to light the cigarette after several tries.

"Should you be smoking?"

"Well, I don't know why not. I don't have lung cancer. That's about the only kind I don't have, by the way. Your father is already driving me crazy, poor man, with his nervous concern. Every time I get up he asks if he can get something for me, if he can help me. His face is bathed in anxiety. He is so inexperienced with this kind of thing."

"Daddy has no—psychology, if you know what I mean."

"Absolutely. Your father does not really know how to pretend

very well. You would think he would, being in the theater, but he
is oddly unsophisticated about things like this. The whole texture
of his life has been constantly upbeat, good cheer, occasional ex-
plosions; you know how Daddy is. He has no well-developed
equipment to help him deal with what is happening to me. I feel
almost worse for him than I do for myself. If I had the courage,
I'd just wait a few weeks, and then take some sleeping pills, and,
what can I call it, release him. He can do so many things, Eva,
your father is such a gifted man. But honestly, I don't think he
can cope with my dying."

"But what can you do? You can't send him away."

"He won't leave my side, darling, even for a few minutes. I
urged him to go to London and settle this business about the play
he wants to bring in, but he said he would do it by phone, and
that was that. We're going to drive each other crazy." A few dark
clouds had formed, hiding the sun, and it seemed cold.

"Do you want me to stay here, and be a third?"

She looked me straight in the eye. "Yes. Please. Please do. Stay
with me, with us, stay for, well, all the way through. Be a third,
yes, a buffer, an ally. I would be filled with relief if you would.
Oh, Eva! It would be wonderful if you would do that."

"Of course, of course," I almost screamed.

"It's a lot to ask. I hesitated to ask, Eva, but . . ."

I was shaking now. "I'm pleased, I'm glad to, I'm relieved. Of
course! What do you mean, you hesitated?"

"It won't be fun. These things are ugly and burdensome. Particularly in the end."

"Well of course, but we can try, in our way, to sort of make it
fun. We'll think of things to do. Remember that I did go to nursing school for two years, and although I didn't learn much, I
could sort of tend to you. Then you won't have to have a fleet of
nurses, or maybe you won't even have to go to the hospital." I
babbled on, excited now by the thought of the pivotal role I
would play. Then I felt her reach for me. She hugged me, my
mother did, like a swimmer finding a life raft. Head on my shoulder, she breathed a tumultuous sigh and after a minute let go.

"Thank God for you, Eva. I can only tell you now, now that
you yourself suggested this kind of help to me, that I prayed that

somehow you would stick with me, maybe give me a little nursing when I needed it, but spare me the paraphernalia of dying. Isn't that the word, really? Paraphernalia. Be assured, darling girl, that I'll try not to impinge too much on you, we'll have a support staff at every turn. You must believe me, Eva, when I tell you that I have accepted the cruel thought of dying, but I cannot stand the thought of being sick. I'm a little like Daddy in this regard. I am not good at handling sickness. I can't stand hospitals, the smell, the tubes, the rented TV. But poor Opa, if I am at home alone with him, with his sweet, agonizing hovering, sitting in that huge house in Riverdale, and then the inevitable nursing staff—oh, I dreaded the whole thing, Eva! I dreaded it more than dying." She pulled a sweater over her shoulders. I was tempted to say, Shall we go home and get out of the sudden cold, but I checked myself. This is a woman who knows when it's time to go home. Besides, she was talking so fast now, I couldn't interrupt her.

"I'm also apprehensive for James. He's just now getting a real start in his place in Vermont, it looks as if it's going to go. This will be so horribly upsetting to him, and I think he's fragile, Eva. Still, I see it from time to time, just those old flashes of impetuousness. He gets terribly excited, and yet other times, he's just as cool as the next fellow."

"He still gets pretty jumpy."

"And Adrian. When I think of Adrian, and all the theories I had about him: he *was* brilliant, hostile, smoldering, introspective, all that, and now I have come to think that all Adrian is, is just a little nutty."

"Just a little nutty!" I had to laugh. She was, of course, quite correct. But she would never have said that before. Everyone, even Mother, was a little bit afraid of Adrian.

"Yes, he's nutty, and, as you well know, he and Opa don't get along very well. When he gets Dr. Kellogg's letter, he's likely to come and stay for six months and bring his new wife, and, as much as I love him, when he and your father start to argue and all . . . well, it's a nightmare."

I was pleased at these revelations. I'd always been sort of jealous of Adrian, but of course Little Eva would never say so.

"Yes, darling, Adrian is going to be a bit of a problem, but I can't tell what kind yet. And Uncle Bob and Aunt Polly, such bores. And they'll feel they have to come around a lot. Another nightmare is that I might have to spend my last breath talking to Aunt Polly. Well"—she took my hand—"we'll handle it. We'll handle it."

"You have loads of friends who aren't bores."

"That's true. We'll sort out the bores as best we can. I have some writing I really have to do too. Now or never."

She took out an orange and began to peel it. "How frightfully luck reverses itself, Eva. It is a simple fact that everyone is vulnerable. Here, have an orange section. Good vitamin C."

I felt a creeping excitement now, a feeling of mission, direction, importance. She had chosen me to lean on, not Opa, or Adrian, or one of her zingy friends. I suddenly wanted to know practical things. I asked, "Do you feel pretty much all right now, these days, I mean? Do you feel like eating?"

"Well, I feel okay, darling, but I do have stomach pains, and my skin itches, and I have some lower back pain, and well, I'm glad to get to bed at night. My appetite's okay. Kellogg says the treatments will make me feel closer to normal, for a while."

Clouds had bunched together right over us, and the temperature seemed to have dropped ten degrees. "We'd better go soon. Daddy will start to fret." She gathered her beach towel and tote bag. "I mustn't forget my *Atlantic*."

"Mother . . ." We stood now facing each other.

"Yes, Eva dear?"

"What about the baby? Can I have my baby? Opa said that if it upset you—"

"Oh, Eva, I'm sorry! I was so absorbed in myself that I forgot about your . . . baby." She stopped for a minute, as if searching for the right words. Then she said, "As one who looks death in the eye, I'm not about to give advice that stops the life of another. Godspeed. Godspeed, Eva. Godspeed."

The clouds suddenly suggested rain, as we moved quickly toward the cars.

"I'll follow you home," she called.

Ah, yes you will, Mother, we're a team now, and we've never been a team before. We'll cope, we'll support each other's follies, even final follies. We'll calm the men, sustain life. We'll take each day as it comes.

VII

I took a plane back to Cambridge a week later to keep my doctor's appointment, try to sublet my apartment for the summer, and spend a little time with my harp.

When my harp was with me, I took it for granted. Often I would ignore it for days, occasionally (dare I say it?) allowing a pair of my own mittens or a piece of the newspaper to rest in its exquisite dipped prow. (But only when the harp was covered, of course.) When I was away from it, I developed a case of separation anxiety, particularly acute at night. And so I gave the instrument a little hug when I got back to the apartment, played a few chords, a couple of quick runs, while I tried to figure out how to manage the next two days.

I decided to store most of my clothes with my neighbor in the apartment building, a man named Curtis LeMar, who was an interior decorator. Soon I was the soul of efficiency; I arranged to rent my apartment to a young law student, pushed my few pieces of furniture around to make the place seem more ample, and made one more attempt to call Cal. I felt his presence in the empty apartment, and when the doorbell rang at one point, I jumped up, assuming it was he. But it was Curtis instead.

"How you could live without furniture is beyond me," he said, waving his arms.

"Modern purism," I replied.

"No, you just didn't settle in here ever, did you?"

"I guess not."

"I'll keep an eye on the place for you. By the way, your cousin Trudy called when I was in here the other day watering the plants. Did you ever reach Cal?"

"No. He's sailing in Maine, I think."

"Fine. Good place for him. He should stay out on his boat forever."

Curtis and Cal had met a few times, and as Cal loathed homosexuals, and Curtis loathed "Yankee retards," the encounters had been awkward at best. Curtis had warned me about Cal: "He'll never marry you or anyone else. He's most comfortable with his dog, believe me."

"But he doesn't have a dog," I protested.

"He will," Curtis said.

It was Curtis who had spirited me from the apartment building one night when Cal threatened to drag me to an abortion clinic by force. It was Curtis who had lent me garlic salt; Curtis who watered my plants and lent me furniture for my one lone dinner party of the past two years.

"Is there anything I can do for you?" I asked, as I pushed my clothes into his closet. "After all, you've been my savior on more than one occasion."

"No," he said, looking at me squarely. "But answer me this. Are you sure you want to have a baby at this point? When are you going to have any fun? Of course, I can't stand children myself."

"I'll have fun. Don't worry. Children are fun." I gave him a squeeze. "Thanks a lot. Thanks for baby-sitting with the harp. I'll come back and pick it up in a couple of weeks."

The women's clinic where I had first registered (over Cal's protests) was crowded and hot, but I waited my turn for the doctor in a ladylike manner. Finally I was summoned by one of the harassed young Gyn-Obs, who weighed me, took a short (very short) history, prescribed some iron pills, told me that I was a little over three months pregnant ("You're past the first trimester"), and that I was fine.

"I feel terrific," I told him.

The night before I was to leave Cambridge to go back to the Vineyard, Mother called to report that Adrian had suddenly appeared in the driveway just a few hours before, wandering in in a nonchalant manner, as if he'd just been down to the end of the road for the mail. He was accompanied by his African wife, Inoye, who walked four or five paces behind him, in the tradition of her tribe. He wore khaki shorts, a faded blue jacket with beaded strings hanging off it, a straw hat, and carried a backpack. His shoulder-length ponytail was tied back with a scarf, and for one moment, Mother said, my father had claimed not to have recognized him.

"He looks quite marvelous in his way," Mother went on. "I hugged him, embraced Inoye, and stepped back to look at them, and thought for just a minute that they were characters from a movie. God forbid, of course, that Adrian give us any warning."

God forbid. Adrian lived by his own rules. Nonetheless, I had to admit, I was glad he was there. Adrian created currents, powerful currents, of which, I now realize, I was the eventual beneficiary. His troubled relationship with my father, born of the world's oldest rivalry, caused Opa to turn to me for comfort and relief. "Good thing I've got *one* level-headed child," Opa would say, giving me a squeeze. Opa would surely need his Little Eva now, pregnant or not, with the prospect of a long visit from Adrian looming. So it was with considerable interest and some pleasure that I listened to Mother's account of his arrival.

I made haste for the plane, feeling light-headed. The doctor had said I was fine, but he didn't really know how fine. My breasts were swollen, which didn't displease me, my whole body seemed to be in a state of change and alteration. After my first feelings of droopiness, I had hit a high energy level, a return to the pace of a good field-hockey player. I felt luminous, and yet, as I looked in the mirror, all I saw was me. Just the same me as before. As yet I had no stomach, not even the slightest swelling that I hoped for, no movement there. But I was ready for it, ready for the loose maternity clothes, for the look of ripened fruit that I had seen on so many pregnant women. Yes, I thought to myself, whatever it is, I'm ready for it.

Adrian was whittling on a piece of wood when I arrived. "Hi," he called casually. He looked as though he'd been sitting there rocking in his chair all of his life, or perhaps more significantly, he looked as though he might stay there for the *rest* of his life. Inoye, tall, beautiful, was sewing. Opa was on the telephone. Mother was resting. Such tranquillity!

Adrian had been ten when Opa bought Mother the Vineyard house. He was fascinated by the up island beaches, the dunes, most particularly the Gay Head cliffs, with the huge runs of color, terra-cotta, yellow, and gray. He took up shells—in truth he became obsessed with shells—and by the time he was fourteen, had collected and classified almost all the important shells to be found on the island. (This collection, altered not one inch, stands in three bookcases in the Chilmark house right now.) "Adrian is going off to find some things on the beach, so leave him alone," I'd been told.

I came to suspect that it was actually Mother who wanted to be alone, and she invested her desire in Adrian.

When Adrian grew to manhood, it became clear that what he really needed was his own continent, far from his arch rival and his mother, a place removed from the requirements of a university or of government research, someplace which seemed dramatic, exotic, and took him far from Riverdale. Therefore, when a modest, underdefined project in East Africa was offered, he had had the wit to seize it.

What he did over there was never clearly established, and my private guess was that the financing of his project petered out early and he just stayed on, continuing to look at all that interested him, moving from place to place, keeping voluminous notes for future publication, as yet unconceived. During this time the money allocated him from Wiltshire Productions kept him in gas for his Land Rover, for forays into different parts of the continent, and in wine. Adrian came home once a year, stayed until he'd had enough of whatever it was he was seeking, then flew back, without much explanation either way. I felt that he was now somehow lost to us, or more lost to us, than when he had lived here. But he was clearly happier.

Then one day a letter came, with a one-sentence announcement:

> Last month, I married Inoye Awayke, a Masai descendant, who lives in a village outside of Mombasa.

He then went on to complain about his jeep, which had broken down three times in as many weeks, causing considerable problems, all of which he described in detail. He concluded with what could only be described as a halfhearted invitation to come over and meet the bride.

Well, we didn't exactly catch the next plane out, but soon enough we organized ourselves to pay a visit to Nairobi. That is, Mother, Opa, and me. James refused. "What do I care who he marries?" James shrugged with elaborate indifference.

This was just two and a half years ago, in December. Two days after Christmas we boarded the flight to London, where Opa was to conduct a little business, see a play that interested him, then on to Nairobi. I was out of nursing school, and as yet unenrolled in music school, between engagements, as it were, so I was pleased for a break in the void.

We landed in Nairobi at two on a hot January afternoon, expectant, well combed, and prepared to embrace Adrian's wife in our most welcoming fashion. ("I don't mind having a black daughter-in-law, do you, Elizabeth?" asked Opa, without conviction. "Not at all," replied Mother, a bit too stoutly.) But we were up for it, as James would say, we were up for it. "I'm just glad that Adrian has found a partner in life," concluded Mother. "But I *am* curious."

But he was not there at the bottom of the ramp as we alighted, nor was his partner. We passed through varieties of lines, desks to stamp passports, craning our necks for him, but no, no Adrian, no Inoye. "Perhaps his jeep broke down again," offered Mother hopefully.

We arrived by taxi at the hotel expecting to see Adrian in the lobby, waiting apologetically, his trembling bride at his side. No such luck. We all decided to take a nap, a fitful two hours or so, then we paced around for a bit, and finally sat down to a gloomy dinner in the elaborate palm-treed dining room. Our mood was passive, watchful, punctuated with brief sallies of exasperation by Opa. ("Adrian has no sense of other people, no sense of responsibility toward the world.") As our coffee was served, we heard a shout, and there was Adrian, beaming at us from the doorway of the dining room.

"Hi there," he called, as if spotting us at a church fair. "There you are. I'm glad I finally caught up with you." He wore a dark smock, a scarf tied around his forehead, and a newly sprouted beard, giving him something of the appearance of a pirate.

"Well, Adrian," spoke Opa, "we were wondering where you were."

"Well, I'm right here, just looking for you!" he cried with obvious glee, as if we had been somehow trying to elude him. He gave Mother and me good-sized hugs; Opa got a thump on the back. "Inoye is in the lobby." Adrian was now as exuberant as he had been surly. "Ho, ho," he cried.

"We must go and see her at once," said Mother. Abandoning coffee, we filed out of the dining room, past the tables, to meet our new sister, like first communion children approaching the altar; quiet, single file, nervous. The lobby of the hotel suddenly seemed flat and motionless, without a hint of commerce, luggage, or travelers.

They sat in a row, beautiful in composition. The patterns of their dresses, the shape of their heads blended together in tones of blue, brown, and mauve. They were harmonious in deep mahogany skin color, long necks, beautiful smiles. "Here we are," cried Adrian. "Inoye brought her three sisters, her mother, and her grandmother," he explained.

We approached each other like competing bands at half time; one row moved forward, the other followed, we stood drenched in introductions and smiles. Then, at Adrian's instruction, we sat in a circle, while he filled the air with anecdotes about how difficult his day had been, the heat, the ever-ailing jeep, poor roads outside of town, etc.

I searched each face until I found the one I thought I remembered, or hoped, was Inoye. Very pretty, straight nose, yes, I prayed that that was Inoye. Whenever Adrian stops talking, I vowed, I'll go up to her and say something nice to her, if it *is* her. Welcome, sister, to our intemperate, fond family.

Opa sat in paralytic silence, but Mother, in an unusual change of roles, was the fluid one, playing conversational Tweedledum to Adrian's Tweedledee.

"Oh really," she cried, "Adrian, that sounds quite fascinating." The ladies murmured a kind of approval, a high, sweet giggle, but said nothing. An hour or so of this and even Mother wore down. Soon she skillfully released us all, claiming a most understandable headache, and we all rose to bid our opposite numbers good night. Adrian promised to come for lunch the next day, show us around town, and then take us to his bride's ancestral land, "sometime next week." Opa reminded him that sometime next week we'd be back in New York. "Oh, yeah, right," he replied. They left, moving toward the jeep and into the night like a gentle herd of llamas. "Good night," we called.

"Which one was she?"

"I know. The one across from Mother."

"No, that was a sister."

"The grandmother sat next to Adrian."

"That was the mother."

"Inoye was the one on the end, I'm sure."

"What end? We all had to sit in a circle."

"I know which one she was."

"Well?"

"I'm not telling," snorted Opa, and stalked off to bed.

And thus Adrian increased the mystery surrounding him. We left Nairobi two days later with a slightly better identification of his bride, who smiled often but never spoke a word through two more meals; we learned something of the city of Nairobi; but little new about Adrian or the forces which shaped his life.

And so it was with considerable curiosity that I arrived back on the Vineyard, the day after my doctor's appointment. Inoye would surely add charm and mystery to our little group, Adrian would at least divert Mother, and perhaps, in his offbeat way, he might prove an ally to my cause as well.

Adrian and Inoye were lodged on the second floor, and I could hear their voices at night, lilting and melodious, but for the life of me I couldn't make out what language they were speaking. Sometimes it sounded like plain old English—Oh yeah, sure, right—and then the next minute sounds that seemed utterly unrecognizable would emit from the upper floor. As of day number three Inoye had spoken no English (to us, at least), or to be precise, she had not spoken at all. Not that she was not responsive; she smiled, a wide, luminous smile, she made lovely little wheezing sounds of recognition, she giggled as before, a high, merry giggle, and most important, in fact a saving grace, she looked sharp, oh so sharp, as though she understood everything. Her presence was, oddly, quite soothing.

Adrian filled the void in conversation by a pattern of what my father called constant comment. He examined every corner of the house, made elaborate suggestions for repairs (no volunteer he, however), drew up lists of those vegetables he thought should be planted, told us, in exquisite detail, how he liked his food cooked (Inoye was, fortunately, the producer here).

At night, after dinner, he took up African economic and political life, something of a sure thing for him, and we listened respectfully.

"The white leadership says don't move too fast, but they don't understand the African mind set. The Africans want their country back, that's all. They want to make their own chaos. Tribal loyalties transcend political alliances."

"My impression is that the British did a pretty good job," remarked Opa, tactlessly, I thought.

And so they were off. Squabbling, bouncing up and down in their chairs, interrupting, jockeying for position, just the way they had ten years ago. Mother went to bed, Inoye smiled, and I just wandered out onto the porch and tried to find a pattern in the sky that interested me. I missed my harp. It was at a moment like this, with everyone yammering away or preoccupied, that I could sit down and play for a half hour or forty-five minutes and feel, somehow, restoration of balance, a quiet at the end of the day.

I thought about Cal again, about his boat, the *Sprite*, about the time last summer, just this time, July, when we were utterly free, without a trace of responsibility, when our biggest decision was which bathing suit to wear or where to put in at night. Dear Cal, son of New England, encased in his mold, cold yet charming, tough and wistful, terrible and wonderful. I folded my hands and prayed to the open skies: Help me not to miss him, help me not to miss him.

"Well, some people would say that you're nuts, absolutely insane, but I myself think it's wonderful." Thus spoke my cousin

Trudy, calling this time from Cincinnati, Ohio, where she was appearing as a panelist at a national women's rights conference. "Yes, I think it's marvelous, you couldn't possibly have married Cal, and I think the fact that you're going ahead with the baby, going it alone, is—well—noble."

"That's a new word to apply to me, noble," I replied.

"Well look, Eva, self-determination has many colors; your decision is part of the new freedom that everyone in the movement is concerned with. Many women want abortions, but, well, you're going ahead with the baby, that's your choice. You may be part of a whole new idea."

"What new idea?" I was always a pace or two behind Trudy.

"Well, you know, single women who don't want to marry, but want to have children, and so go ahead and have the baby."

"I think that's actually an old idea."

"Well, I guess so, but I think it's being done more and more."

"God forbid I be part of a trend."

"Well, you know what I mean, Eva. How do you feel?"

"Fine."

"Does anything show yet?"

"No."

"Well, be patient, it will soon enough. With Neddy, I looked like I had a watermelon tied in front of me after five months. How is Aunt Elizabeth? I'm almost afraid to ask."

"She's pretty much okay right now. The chemotherapy for this month is over."

"Oh, good. And is Adrian being a menace?"

"Adrian is exhausting, but he's very attentive to Mother, and I think she's very happy that he's here."

"And what's her name, Inowe?"

"Inoye."

"She's so striking. If only she'd say something."

"I kind of like her the way she is. We've got a lot of big talkers around here. I like her."

"Well now, Eva, I'm going to be here for three more days, then I go to the Coast for a week, then I'll pick up Neddy in Iowa, and after that perhaps we'll come for a visit."

"Good."

"And if for some reason I get tied up in New York, maybe I'll just send him down."

"All right, I'd love to have him."

"And I'll send down some of my old maternity clothes, too. I think I still have a couple of cute things."

"That's nice. I can't seem to bring myself to buy anything."

"Eva, I'm sure you've thought this all out carefully, from every vantage point." Trudy was clearly winding up for a final plenary statement. "And I'm sure that you've really explored your motives and all."

"Well, I don't know, not in the way you describe."

"And you are surely aware that there are still some people who will consider you a bad girl, an outcast."

"Well, my father's not too hot on me these days."

"Never mind, Eva, you do what you want. It's your body, your life."

"Well, that's true."

"I'm sure that having this child will help you in the process of self-actualization."

"Oh, Trudy, come on."

"Yes, Eva, this will bring you in closer touch with yourself."

"I sort of thought it would bring me in closer touch with someone else."

"Well, of course, but as you find the courage to go through with this, you will develop self-esteem."

"I have self-esteem."

"Well, look now, I have to go. I think you're doing a marvelous thing, Eva. Really I do. I'll call you when I get back from the Coast. Okay?"

"Okay, see you soon."

Was I doing a marvelous thing? Was I wonderful and was I going to develop self-esteem? I was shaking when I got off the phone. I honestly preferred my father's "see here, young lady" type disapproval to Trudy's purple praise. I'd always been a bit out of step with Trudy anyway. We grew up together, the way cousins do, an uneasy alliance, competitive yet dependent, safer perhaps with each other because we were related by blood, but on edge, pretty much on edge. Trudy, the one with the ideas, with stage presence, outspoken, rebellious. Eva, more hesitant, athletic, the funny one. We were locked together by family, time, and balance of temperaments, although I thought we might well come unlocked if she insisted on putting me in the forefront of a new trend. And yet I counted on her.

"How was Trudy?" asked Mother, looking up from her reading.

"Euphoric."

"Isn't she always euphoric?"

"Except when she's depressed. She wants to come for a visit."

"Well, we might be crowded, particularly if James comes, but we can squeeze her in somewhere."

"She won't come, I'll bet, she'll just send Neddy."

"That's fine too."

Mother was quiet today, stiff in the lower back, and I thought she looked quite pale. "Would you like me to take you somewhere, to Baldwin Beach or something?" I asked.

"No, darling, thank you, I'm fine." She closed her book. "Do you think Adrian's having a nice time?"

"Sure. You know Adrian has developed the knack of always having a nice time. He just takes what he wants from each situation and leaves the rest."

"That's true. I just want to see him happy."

"He's happy."

In fact Adrian's presence caused a noticeable regression in our physical household. His shells, placed gingerly in shelves and bookcases during his absent years, were back out again, on tabletops, on the porch, next to the sink; his mounted butterflies and attendant equipment resurfaced, nuggets of sea glass appeared in ashtrays, on the telephone table, fishing rods lay across the porch, a horseshoe crab shell left by accident on the couch, and who but Opa should sit on it. No, the house reverted quickly to a kind of casual laboratory for him. Mother seemed to take particular pleasure in the return of Adrian's memorabilia.

"Addy, dear, is this starfish a new one or an old one? It looks like one you had years ago."

"Yeah, that's an oldie. Here, I'll stick it somewhere. They've spotted some baby sharks off South Beach. I'm going to go take a look." And off he would go for a couple of hours, binoculars dangling from his neck, Inoye following, and then he would come back, hands and pockets full of more castoffs from the ocean.

I could not tell whether he was fully aware of the seriousness of Mother's condition, but so quick was he to anticipate her needs, so deft in his attentions to her, that I figured he must know. Unlike Opa, who leapt nervously to his feet every time she moved, Adrian skillfully, pantherlike, seemed to anticipate and solve little problems before they came to light.

"Oh, Addy dear, thank you, I was wondering where my glasses were." And she would smile at him, a smile of quiet familiarity.

When Mother and Opa were out one day, and we others were sitting on the porch, Adrian repairing a fishing rod, Inoye weaving, I nerved myself and said, "Adrian, because you have Dr. Kellogg's letter, I guess you know what to expect where Mother's concerned." He looked at me, as if to encourage me, but he didn't say anything. After a moment, I said, "You know she is going to die."

He seemed to stretch his neck for a moment and rub his chin. Then he said, "We're all going to die, Eva. Mother is just going to die sooner than the rest of us. In Africa, death is honored, and ancestors are worshipped." He stared straight out at the horizon, then took his binoculars to scan the nearer pond. "Couple of egrets out there."

This is the best he can do, I told myself, this is perhaps all he can do, and I vowed not to bring it up again. While I was at it I figured I'd throw in the chaser, the after-dinner mint. "Also, Adrian, in a different category to be sure, I'm pregnant. I'm going to have a baby."

"Good," he replied with a pleasant, serene smile and went back to his egrets.

This was the only exchange we ever had on either subject, ever.

Another effect of Adrian's first few days was that Opa returned to New York for a week, to Mother's relief, and perhaps also to his. In fact, my mother seemed, all in all, quite happy. Her first round of chemotherapy had not produced the hair fallout of two years ago, and although she felt temporarily ill, her recovery was quick and she was back on track and perhaps even a little better. Opa's time-bomb explosiveness with Adrian had relaxed a little;

the presence of the gentle Inoye put them on their better, if not best, behavior. They continued to argue, of course, but without the hideous personalization of the past, and I began to wonder if this was not their way of loving each other.

Although Adrian was exhausting to have around, he was also re-assuring. He took the jeep to be repaired, he brought in the wood for an occasional evening fire, and most important, he brought a smile to my mother's face, more a smile of recognition than of laughter. Inoye took over most of the cooking, somewhat out of necessity, to accommodate Adrian's eccentric palate.

With another man in the house, Opa felt he could leave, and we all took him to the airport in a cheery mood. Only he, for once, did not seem cheerful. His attitude toward me in these last couple of weeks was one of reservation and muted censorship. A couple of times I thought I actually saw him put his nose in the air at the sight of me. Much as I tried to coax a warmer response from him, I failed. "Be good, everybody," he admonished as he headed for the airplane. Yes, he looked sad, my father did, bur-dened and sad. Too much had happened too fast, even for a high roller like Opa. His contentious son was in full residence, taking his place as principal aide to my mother; his wife and life's true love was irreversibly sick and dying, a threatened loss of incalcu-lable dimensions; and last, and surely least, his antidote, his Little Eva could no longer be Little Eva, because growing inside her was another, littler Eva. Dear, dear Opa. If I could have allowed myself to do so, I would have wept for him.

VIII

The third week in July I went back again to Cambridge, this time by car and ferry, for the purpose of picking up my harp, which I had stored, along with a great deal else, at Curtis's. I was glad to see it again, and I played a quick Debussy dance (ever popular) while Curtis sipped iced tea. As he helped me angle the harp into the car, Curtis mumbled, "I hope this is the last time I have to do this."

"I can't guarantee it," I replied.

The ferry ride back was quite rough, which was unusual, and I could feel the harp's discomfort and mine too, for that matter. Lurching up the long driveway to our house, another rather bumpy ride, I noticed my father standing on the porch, talking to a young man. Both were smiling. I was relieved to find a possible harp carrier, as my father was poor at this, and whoever it was Opa was talking to looked vigorous. I was well aware of my habit of immediately judging men as potential porters, instead of lovers or tennis partners as did most of my friends.

"Hi," I called, approaching with a smile.

"Eva, this is Bill Diamond, who has done some arrangements for me and may do some more. Isn't that right, Bill?"

"That's right." Mr. Diamond smiled at me, turned back to say something to my father, then returned his gaze to me.

I saw nice teeth and a halo of hair, as he looked down at me from the porch. I shifted, noticed an oncoming hole in my espadrilles.

"I'm only playing at Stella's four nights a week, and I can put in some time for the rest of the summer," Bill Diamond said.

"Good." My father caught my eye. "What do you want, Eva? Do I have to carry in the bloody harp?"

"Is Adrian around?" Adrian had never touched my harp, the question was one of ritual.

"I don't know, he was in Gay Head this morning."

"May I help you?" spoke Bill Diamond.

"Well, thank you. It's right over here."

"Well look, Bill, I'll call you in a week or so, and if I don't, please ring me. You have this number."

"Yes I do."

"Fine, then." My father headed into the house, very much the producer.

What a funny, innocent face he has, Bill Diamond, he's coming toward me now to help with the harp.

"Where is it? Your harp?"

"In the car." We stood close to each other for a minute.

If only he were taller, he's really only about a forehead or so taller than I. Cal was a whole head taller, or so he seemed.

What do I care anyway, I told myself, I've got an ungainly complication, and he looks like that kind who already has "somebody."

His unblinking stare caused me to shift again, but it wasn't until I had the harp shackled to him that I could stare back, for then he was taken up with the business at hand, oozing the thing from the car, moving it up onto the porch. He has a quite angelic face, perhaps it's just the proximity of the harp and his halo of hair, but he has a face you could easily touch, and I found myself shamelessly wanting to lean over and push his hair back from his forehead.

"In the living room?"

"I guess so." It was not clear where my instrument was to rest, so we just left it dead center.

I spotted a gold earring in one ear, which gave him a quick

demerit in my book. No earring for me, I murmured to myself, and I thanked him.

"How long have you played the harp?" He was near me now, and I could almost feel the perspiration from his shirt.

"Well, almost ten years."

"So you really know how to play it then."

"No." I smiled slightly.

"It's a complicated instrument. What do you like best about it?"

"I think," I replied, without hesitation, "I like hugging it the best."

He gave a short laugh. "I'll take you for a ride on my motorcycle sometime."

"That would be nice," I answered. We walked toward the driveway. "Thank you again."

The motorcycle, black and fierce-looking, with its motor that went *rat-tat-tat*, carried him off down the road with dust billowing.

He looks like someone's brother, I thought, he has that expression of open curiosity, simple, not like *my* brothers, of course— Adrian with his spooky look, James with his disjointed gaze. No, but a man at ease in the world.

"Nice fellow, eh?" Opa appeared from nowhere.

"Yes. Yes he is. How's Mother?" I didn't see her anywhere, which always made me a little nervous.

"She's asleep. She seemed tired today, and I hope she'll sleep right through dinner, or let me take it in to her on a tray."

"I'll bring it to her."

"No, I'll do it. I can make an omelet."

"See if that's what she wants first."

"I already know she likes omelets."

"But she may not want it tonight, Opa. Ask her first. Do you want me to?"

"Please don't wake her. I'll do it, in an hour or so. Why don't you just sit down and play me a nice piece on your harp. Your eight-thousand-dollar harp."

I played poorly, but he didn't know the difference. A quick Bach fugue, then a short contemporary piece that a friend of mine at Amory had written. Opa looked bored, for which I couldn't blame him. He was used to fifty-five-piece pit orchestras. I hugged my harp. I was glad to have it back.

"Who is Bill Diamond?" I asked.

"He's a good jazz piano player, and an occasionally successful songwriter. He's over in Tisbury for the summer. Got a job playing at that good club in Oak Bluffs. He's a fine chap. He's going to work up some arrangements for me on this musical that I'm trying to bring in from the West End. If I can ever get them to send me the score."

"How old is he?"

"I don't know. Early thirties. He worked for me on *Starry Nights*. Very quick to get the point, very professional. Now, Eva, there's a nice fella for you to go out with and have a Coke with sometime."

"Well, yes, he seemed nice enough."

"Of course, if you weren't pregnant it would be a little easier; I would invite him over for dinner to get you two started, but what can I say now, eh? Come on over and meet my daughter, she's three and a half months pregnant and getting plumper, but you'll love her? Huh?" He was starting up, but I didn't let him get mad.

"Just say that you would like him to take your fat daughter out for a Coke sometime."

"Well, what *are* you going to do when you start to look like a kangaroo? Tell me that?"

"I'm going to just look like a kangaroo, that's all. Besides, I'm hoping to also look beautiful."

"This whole thing is absolutely preposterous. But"—he held up his hand in a gesture of elaborate restraint—"I promised your mother that I wouldn't talk about it. Where are the eggs?"

"Eggs?"

"I'm going to make myself an omelet."

"I'll make you an omelet."

The next morning as I was shopping at the casual Chilmark food store, I spied Bill Diamond trying, without luck, to stuff groceries into his motorcycle saddlebags. His hair was blowing around his face, and he looked grumpy, but I approached him anyway.

"Hi, want some help? I'm good at that sort of thing." He looked up. "I'm Eva Wiltshire, we met yesterday."

"Right, I remember. Well, okay, hold on to this," and he handed me a four-roll package of toilet paper and some celery. It was clear to me that he would soon run out of ideas of how to squeeze this large grocery order into his saddlebags, so I said, "Look, if you want, I'll drive your groceries over to your house. I don't mind. I don't have all that much to do."

"No, that's okay, Eva. Now give me the celery." The celery fit, but out popped a bag of oranges in exchange, so after a few more attempts he said, "Okay, to hell with it. We'll put this in your car and you follow me." He started his motorcycle and I drove behind him, toward Tisbury. He has a nice back, I thought, nicer than Cal's.

We were slowed by the usual rutted road, but stopped eventually in front of a small, low-slung contemporary house whose only distinguishing feature was that a huge man lay across the front steps, sound asleep.

"That's Bob," Bill Diamond announced, as we stepped over the hulk with the groceries.

"Well, okay, that's nice of you, Eva. Now leave your car here and I'll take you for a ride on my motorcycle, just like I promised."

"Well, what about *my* groceries? Could we take them home first? I just have butter and my mother's apples."

"Sure, of course." He smiled. "Let's get all the damn food in place, yours, mine, Bob's, Mrs. Wiltshire's, then we'll go for a swim. We'll go to Gay Head. You can grab your suit when you're at your house."

I looked at him carefully. He didn't look quite so young after all, and he seemed less cherubic than yesterday, more seasoned. I noticed creases at the side of his mouth, a scar on his chin. From the kitchen door he unhooked a tattered bathing suit. "We're off."

We stepped over Bob again, and I was tempted to ask, Who *is* this, but a kind of rhythm had been set, one of forward motion, not a lot of questions, which I was glad for. Early morning clouds had begun to blow off and it looked as if it might be a clear day after all.

We left my food package at home, with a quick word to my mother, stuffed my suit and Dr. Scholl's sandals into those over-worked saddlebags, and took off on his motorcycle. "Do you like walking around the Gay Head cliffs? Lot of tourists," he called back to me.

"Yes, I love it. I don't even see the tourists."

"Good for you."

Good for you, he had said. Good for you. Good for you, Bill Diamond, said I to myself, for taking this pregnant Cinderella out for a ride, out of our taut household, out of myself, out of my cramped, crummy car, out into the air. Without much effort, I moved closer to him on the motorcycle, and I could feel his back muscles shift as we sped toward Gay Head. The road is curvy, with a series of short little hills in quick succession. I felt like I was on a roller coaster.

The cliffs at Gay Head stand out facing the ocean like a rugged old man staring down an adversary; high, proud, gnarled, riveted with bumps and crevasses. When you stand at the top, where the road ends, looking down that steep drop, past strips of clay colors, you get a fleeting sensation of feeling almost imperial. The light-house sits at the uppermost peak, a venerable old beacon which has guided in many a lost ship, signaling light through both storms and gentle nights. Now it is surrounded by a roped-off area and a sign reading, "Do Not Deface."

We walked around, neither of us saying much, smiled at each other as a group of pink-and-blue-clad tourists filed out of their bus and then started down the cliffs. There is a logical descent, a path of sorts, but we took an alternate route, stopping often to look out at the ocean, toss a stone over, to look at each other, or to pretend that we weren't looking at each other, to pick a wild flower. The beach at the base of the cliffs is narrow, rocks jut out, and we jumped over all we could, landing often in the shallow water, helping each other over less than perilous obstacles.

"Pretty nice, eh?" said Bill Diamond. "Are you ready for a swim?"

"I'm ready."

We scampered up again, up the obvious path this time, as we couldn't pass through to the swimming beach but had to re-mount the cliffs and walk over a blacktop road to the south side. We jumped behind a couple of rocks to change our clothes.

The ocean water, high, bounding, dancing, looked to me like a mad gray-blue swirl. I'm such a chicken about cold water, but on this day I plunged in with Olympic speed and vigor, so that my tiny expansion, that hint of things to come, wouldn't be too closely observed. Glacial. The ocean was glacial. I felt almost faint for a minute.

Bill Diamond swam toward me, although no one can really swim much in these waves, they're too rough. He allowed himself to be tossed toward me, and with his hair matted down, his curls flattened by the water, his teeth seemed to stand out, his nose and forehead glistened, and he looked stark, almost menacing.

What do strangers do in the ocean to guard against unwar-ranted intimacy yet not appear uncongenial? We allowed the waves to carry us, short runs toward the shoreline and back out again. We circled each other playfully, exchanged a word or two about how cold we were, and just floated. Floated because there was not a single requirement of either of us but to give in to the ocean's rhythms, give up any pretense of looking attractive, and let time pass under a clear sky.

When we had had enough, we made our way back to the sandy part of the beach and let the wind dry us. Numb, braced, we were protected from the cool breeze by our body temperature, and as we strolled away from the rocks Bill said, "I feel like I'll be warm for the rest of my life."

"Me too. We don't even need towels."

"Do you ever dig for mussels or clams?"

"Sure."

"We'll do that sometime," he said, looking at me with a soft nod.

I wonder if he's going to kiss me. I wonder if he's going to do something. He's oddly unflirtatious, this man, no winks or nudges, no intimate asides or phony playfulness. No, he's a plainspoken fellow. Good for you. We'll do that sometime. Without the flirta-tious tentacles out, he seemed more self-assured, more potent. He caught me staring at him, smiled, and nodded, as if to say, I see you staring at me, and I'm staring at you too.

After a few minutes the wind came up and we lost our invincible feeling about staying warm forever, so I found my way back to my rock and changed into my clothes.

I wondered, What do I look like? Without a mirror I felt lost for a minute. I don't want to be the fairest of them all, or any of that, I thought, but I just want to see if I look human. If I might look nice enough for this lovely man to want to kiss me. And, lo and behold, what should I find underfoot at that very moment but a piece of mirror, pink, dirty on one side, but a small triangle of a piece of mirrored glass. I picked it up and it revealed me to be red-eyed, red-nosed, with dripping hair. Oh to hell with it, I thought, and tossed the piece into the bush. Maybe it won't matter.

He was waiting for me, without impatience, but he was standing in a way that reflected attentiveness, even urgency.

"Okay?"

"Okay."

As we started up the road toward the motorcycle, the wind seemed stronger.

"We may be getting some kind of front in here." He walked backward up the hill, looking at the sky.

"Oh, it's always worse up island. More changeable." It was colder.

"Put this on." He took an old sweatshirt from his saddlebag, found another faded sweater for himself. The motorcycle looked monstrous, almost like a horse.

"Come to my place," he said, looking at me directly. "Please."

"Yes. Of course. But will what's-his-name be there?"

"Bob? I'll get rid of him." We got on the motorcycle, without another word. I felt hot and cold at the same time, both numb and excited.

Minutes later we pulled up in front of his house, freezing, sticky with ocean wetness, jangled by motorcycle noise and motion. After he turned the engine off, we stood still for a moment, to adjust to the quiet. To my relief, Bob was nowhere in sight.

"Hold on." Bill went into the house first, while I stood outside the door like a country cousin, waiting to be made welcome. A minute or so later, he came out. "He's split. Nowhere around. Come on."

He held out his hand and drew me inside. We stood in a chaotic kitchen.

"Are you all right now?" he asked quietly.

"Yes, just cold."

"Come on. Come in here. Messy bedroom." He closed the door.

I was afraid my teeth might start to chatter. He kissed me and we fell immediately onto the rumpled bed, more like tired children than consenting adults.

"Take those clothes off, Eva," he urged. My teeth did start to chatter. "I'll make you warm." He reached for me and I moved toward him without hesitating.

He seemed solid and sweet as he held me and kissed me and put his face in my stomach; we made love gently as if we'd known each other for years. He was returned to a kind of innocence again, unlike his sharklike appearance in the water. I felt dazed as we reached for each other, but alert enough to notice the earring again. It did not last long, a simple folding into each other, a touch of urgency, the need to go on. It all happened easily, the natural order of things.

Then, against my conscious will, I fell asleep.

IX

The car felt like a little hot box as I drove down the bumpy dirt road from Bill's house toward home. I caught a glimpse of myself in the car mirror. I thought, I look so dreadful that I almost look beautiful. To be figured out later.

The breeze through the car window cooled me. And if someone asks, What did you do this morning, Eva? I will have to reply, I've made love to a near stranger, that's what. I couldn't seem to remember all that I wanted to about the last couple of hours, but I had a clear memory of Bill leaning over me, loving me without effort, and of my own desire just to lie with him.

Does he do this often? I wonder. Bed down with women right and left, just bring them along home with a bag of groceries, and —no, I know he doesn't. He just isn't that type, he's too guileless. No, he had focused on me in an instinctive, uncalculating way, I'm sure of it.

I wonder what will happen now.

I lurched up the road to the house at top speed. The plumber's red van sat in our driveway, reminding me that I was supposed to call him earlier in the morning about the downstairs bathroom. Mother had beat me to it.

"Am I late?" I flew in the door, flushed and breathless.

"Where have you been?" Mother sounded cross. "That silly little hospital gets crowded at around five o'clock. I don't mind having a blood test, but I don't much like to have to wait to have a blood test." She was often irritable about matters to do with time these days.

"Did you have lunch?" I asked.

"Yes, Inoye and I made a salad."

"I was going to make grilled cheese sandwiches."

"Well, now that it's two-thirty, why don't you just forget about that. Unless you want one yourself. Did you have lunch? I hope that young man bought you a sandwich."

"I don't want anything. Why don't we go then."

We were off to the Island Hospital and a swing through Vineyard Haven for some new porch furniture.

I felt disoriented. Since I had slept, however fleetingly, it now seemed like morning again; since I had been to bed, however unexpectedly, it should surely be night time; the last thing it felt like was two-thirty in the afternoon.

"James is coming at the end of next week. I don't know how they'll all fit in on the second floor. But perhaps, Eva, if James doesn't want to be up there with Adrian and Inoye, you could change rooms with him, just for these few days so he'll feel more comfortable." That translated out to mean that Adrian and James were always on edge with each other, James didn't know Inoye, he was a mess maker on a grand scale, and how could they all be happy sharing a tiny bathroom? Little Eva in the pinch, then. I agreed.

My mother now focused on us all in a different way. She wanted to hear constantly, repetitively, that we were happy, that our lives were settling down, that we were all getting along with each other. "I think James is going to be fine. I just wish he had a nice girl," she said at least once a day. "I think Adrian seems happy, don't you, Eva? I'm so glad Daddy has decided to go into production with this London musical. He'll be diverted and happy for a while."

And what she thought about finding a niche for me, the prospective unwed mother, she didn't say. Perhaps, knowing that I would be with her all the way, she saved me for later. Or could it be that she figured that Little Eva might just be all right on her own?

I looked at her as we drove along, searched her face in a quick moment for any signs of despair. I had sometimes observed her staring out of the window with a vacant, wistful look, but now, today, she seemed fine. The chemotherapy had caused her a certain puffiness in the face, but she did not look like a dying woman.

"I've begun a journal of sorts, Eva. Just jotting down some things. It isn't important, not a candidate for posthumous publication, but after I'm dead you may want to read it."

After I'm dead. After I'm dead! "Well, all right, of course," I mumbled. How can she say "After I'm dead" as if she were saying "after Thanksgiving," or "after the play closes"? How can this be happening, I wondered. How can we all let this happen?

"Opa should look into my journal too, when he's able. He already knows how much I love him, but this will further remind him."

"Okay."

"What's that young man like who took you to lunch?"

"Who took me to lunch? I didn't have lunch."

"Billy somebody."

"Oh. He's very nice. Yes."

From "after I'm dead" to Billy somebody was more than I could absorb, still dazed as I was from my extraordinary morning. I left Mother off at the hospital entrance, so she could start the blood test process while I went to park the car. All I wanted to do was go back to my room and close the door and think a little about Billy somebody.

"Do you want to come over to Stella's tonight?" he said. "We play starting at about eight-thirty or nine. Would you like that?"

Would you like that? "Yes. Sure, I'd love to come."

"You know where Stella's is, don't you? In Oak Bluffs."

"Yes, I know where it is."

"Okay, that's wonderful, I'll look for you. I'd pick you up, but maybe you wouldn't want to stay till one or so."

"I'll drive. That will be fine."

"Okay, Missy, see you there."

"Who's Missy?"

"You are."

The phone had been off the hook when I walked in the door with Mother and the new porch furniture, and Adrian said, "Some dude for you, Eva." When Opa announced, seconds after I hung up, that he'd take us all out for dinner, I saw my opportunity for a little solitude and begged off.

"Opa, Bill Diamond plays the piano, isn't that right?"

"Yes, he plays a fine jazz piano. Good musician."

"I'm going to hear him tonight around nine."

"Well, that's nice, Eva. Billy Diamond's a nice fellow." He gave me a reproachful look, that if-you-weren't-pregnant-you-might-be-able-to-enjoy-yourself look.

Adrian had cut his hair, changing from the Daniel Boone look to the June Allyson look, pigtail off, replaced by bangs and what I guess was once referred to as a pageboy. Inoye, a generous wife, giggled longer than usual when he, or his coiffure, made its debut. She herself had taken up American staples such as apple pie and ice cream, and appeared to have gained a few pounds as a result, only adding to her allure.

So as they lined up to go out to dinner, Mother in a long, out of style Marimekko dress, her hair piled high on her head, Opa in his usual master-of-ceremonies brick-red pants and navy blue jacket, Adrian with his pageboy and dashiki, Inoye in a purple and blue headdress wrapped tight around her head, they made quite a picture, driving off in the jeep. So relieved was I not to be in that parade, not taking my place with them as The Daughter, so thrilled was I to be by myself for an hour at least, that I put on a Carly Simon record, poured a glass of white wine, and sang with her "Anticipation." Anticipation.

Stella's had the look of an old-fashioned grange hall, a square room with tables and chairs and the music makers at one end, set up on a slight platform. I had expected something more intimate and sultry.

I slipped in and sat down at a corner table, thinking not to interrupt Billy in the middle of a set. (Now that I was Missy, he could be Billy.) He was in shirt-sleeves, hunched over the piano, and it was dark enough so that I figured he wouldn't see me.

"Hi there," he called, full voice, looking up and smiling.

"Come over here. This is Hank Duranti on drums, Ace Dukenney on guitar, Eva Wiltshire, and Bob you already know."

How did I know Bob? Bob, looped over his bass, smiled too. Bob! The sleeping figure on the front steps! Bob, awake now, standing up. "Hi," I said to the giant, "you don't know me but I know you."

"Right," he grunted.

"Order yourself a drink, Eva, and tell them I'll sign for it, and we'll be done with this set in a few minutes." They were winding up (or down) on an old tune which I finally recognized: "There Will Never Be Another You."

I sat nearby with a glass of wine and watched him. Now it was really okay to stare at him, forty or fifty other people were doing the same thing.

He moved in and out of periods of concentration as he played. At times he looked like a surgeon, focused and intense, his shoulders bent forward; then, a minute or two later, you might think he was at a barbecue, turning the spare ribs, looking around, talking occasionally. He has a handsome head, Bill Diamond, but he doesn't look like a musician, not like the bespectacled, frazzled string beans who sat for hours at my father's piano, or the haunted, exuberant rock people. He doesn't look jaded, I decided, that's what it is. I expect musicians to look jaded. And yet, from that little platform came live music, fast, upbeat, energetic, all his.

He seemed to play effortlessly; it's his thing, that's all, I told myself. While other people produce steel, soap, or legal briefs, he produces music. The man who this morning seemed more like a boyish backpacker, with his short frame and broad shoulders, the man who made love to me so sweetly and without artifice, he was transformed now to a man seated at work, serious, handsome, indoors, at his piano, making these sounds, dominating the room, wooing me in a different way. Between numbers, or while Bob took one of his endless choruses on the bass, Billy stared out ahead, glassy-eyed, intense, listening without appearing to, adding a chord here and there, waiting to come back in. He looked over at me once, smiled. I'll be there in a minute, he seemed to say. As he came toward me at the end of the set, I felt myself blush. A schoolgirl blush, even at my age.

"Now, Missy, did you get something to drink?"

"Yes." I leaned toward him. "You . . . you do wonderfully."

He smiled. "That's nice of you to say. You do wonderfully too. Here, sit next to me." I moved over from the spot across the table to sit right next to him. "Tell me, what do you think of Bob now that you see him standing up?"

"Not exactly Tiny Tim, is he? And is he at your house all the time?"

"I share the house with him. It's his house too." He looked at me with a smile this time, reading my thoughts. "Maybe we'll rent him out for a while at the West Tisbury fair, as the local giant. Don't worry, Bob's a good guy, but there is a lot of him."

I looked at Billy closely and remembered, in a rush, the morning, remembered his holding me, moving inside of me.

"Do you have any other girl friend?" The question rushed out of me, unscheduled.

"What?"

"Do you have any other girl friend? Someone else."

"I had someone else until this spring."

"Is that over?"

"Not completely."

"Will who that is ever come here?"

"No. Never." He grinned now and reached over and pulled my nose.

"I don't mean to sound like the FBI. I don't usually do that." I didn't either. This time I was just too curious. The room was filling up, a kind of pale yellow look came over the place.

Billy leaned forward. "Sometime I'll tell you about my uncle Charlie. He could really play the piano."

"Oh, tell me now."

"Too many people. I have to play again in a few minutes."

"I bet it was Uncle Charlie who taught you to play the piano. I bet you never had to take piano lessons the way we all did."

"That's almost right. You see, my uncle Charlie had a stroke, and all he could do is sit there and he wanted me to entertain him."

"So you just up and learned to play the piano?"

"Yes, sort of." He nodded his head slightly and smiled.

"I thought that only happened to Mozart."

"No, that's not what happened to Mozart. That's what happened to Art Tatum, though."

"Who is Uncle Charlie?"

"My mother's brother. He's dead now. He used to play real good ragtime piano and show tunes and all. He worked in a hat factory but he played at night and on weekends in a pit orchestra. Because he and Aunt Minnie had no children, he gave me and my brother all the love and attention he might have given to his own sons. My father was different, he was a baseball fanatic, he wanted us to be baseball stars. Guess what his nickname was; go on, guess."

"I can't."

"Try."

"Tell."

"Baseball Diamond." He shook his head.

"I don't think that's so bad."

"You would if you were Baseball Diamond's son. My dad actually played in the minors for a while, but he didn't really make it there, so he scouted for a while for the New York Yankees. He did know some of the big wheels in baseball, he was sort of a baseball groupie, he went to everything with his pals. My brother liked the game, I didn't. We were both good, but he liked it, so I figured I was off the hook, so I'd put in my time and then go home and play my records, or run over to Uncle Charlie's house and listen to him play the piano. My father was an Irish drinker and the kind of guy who thinks music is for sissies, so I took my best records over there, 'cause I thought he might smash them or something. Uncle Charlie would talk to me about his old musician friends, how he wished he could give up working and just play the piano all day and night. He was a member of the local New Jersey musicians' union, and each year he said, 'This year I'm going to do it, this year for sure.' "

"Did he ever do it?"

"No. Jobs playing were hard to get and it meant he would have to travel a lot, and, no, he had a stroke when he was sixty and he lost all movement on his left side. He could just move his right arm a little, and walk a few steps. So Aunt Minnie had to sort of drag him, but the poor guy couldn't really speak any more, so he'd watch TV, they put him in front of the TV. Christ, I knew he couldn't stand it, so I'd go over for hours on end and put on his favorite records for him, Fats Domino or Louis Armstrong. Once when I was over listening with him, he made me sit down at the piano, and he kept making little sounds, moving his head, he was saying, Now you play like those records."

"Just copy the sounds? How could you do that?"

He leaned back and smiled at me. "I don't know. I fumbled around, picked a few things out, I had a pretty good ear. And he would nod or wave his right hand when I got a passage right here or there. And then when I screwed up or something, or stalled, he'd take his cane and whack it against the table. I can still hear the sound now. Bomp."

"It sounds like a great time." I could only recall my arid lessons, enforced, humorless, certainly without a hint of human warmth. "So then what happened?"

"Aunt Minnie, who had no music in her but could actually read sheet music, Charlie would call her in and they'd get out the sheet music, and she'd put the chords together for me, so I'd fool with the sheet music for a bit. And yes, I got so I could play some things, and I loved it so much. Minnie and Charlie and that sheet music and the records were my lessons. When I went away to college I took a course or two, but it wasn't fun, no show tunes like we used to play, and I kept hearing Charlie playing 'Sweet Lorraine' while this guy was talking about counterpoint. Uncle Charlie died that winter anyway so I just stopped. Isn't it funny, he died in front of the damn TV set. I just wish he could have gone out listening to Pee Wee Russell or Duke Ellington or someone like that. It was awful."

"How people die is no small matter." I watched him closely. He looked clear-eyed, almost luminous. "Did you keep playing after that?"

"No—my dad started to hound me about trying out for the summer farm team for the Yankees. After my freshman year, I thought about Charlie, and how much I loved him and how much I hated my father, and how Charlie had protected me from my father all these years, and I thought I'd better arm myself. I

wanted to try the piano again; after all, I loved those times banging around on Charlie's piano. So I enrolled in a music program
up in the Berkshires. My father was furious, and refused to pay for
it, which I knew he would, so I went to Aunt Minnie and she
took a thousand dollars from the little life insurance money Charlie had left her, and she handed it to me, and she said, 'You keep
this money, you don't ever have to pay me back.' I'll never forget
it. No one had ever just given me money. Ever."

"Did you pay her back?"

"Aunt Minnie developed bad arthritis and she's in a nursing
home now which costs a thousand dollars a month, and I pay for
that."

"How can you . . ."

He leaned back and smiled. "How can I afford to? Well, I had
two hit records, in seventy-six and seventy-eight. I made some
money on the first one, 'Tollgates,' and a grotesque amount on
the second, a little rock piece called 'Without You.' "

"Oh, I know that song! Sure I do! They played it on the radio
all the time." I knew he wrote music, but I hadn't yet connected
Billy to a real song.

"Hi, Billy, how're you doing?"

A man and woman, both in dark glasses, leaned over the table.
"Hi. Fine."

"Are you playing soon?"

"In about one minute."

"Right."

They disappeared back into the crowd.

"Who's that?" I asked.

"I don't know." He shrugged.

" 'Without You.' I love that song. I can hear it in my head
right now."

He nodded in that funny way again. "Now, just sit here, Missy,
for a bit while we play another set." He touched my shoulder and
got up and summoned Bob from the bar; they ambled up toward
the front.

Stella's was getting crowded now, noisy, and beginning to look
like a smoke-filled room. The wine had gone to my head and I
wished I could just step out and get some air the way we used to

at dances, but the door was blocked by the crowd. Billy had started to play again, unbothered by the increase in traffic, and I tried to listen but my thoughts drifted to Uncle Charlie, to my mother, even to Cal. Yes, Cal would have liked this place, although it would have been in the slice-of-life department to him; but he would have recognized it as authentic. A new group of people had just come in, living it up from the cabin cruisers that docked in Oak Bluffs. Stella's was beginning to make me feel like Alice in Wonderland—that I was getting smaller and smaller while everyone else was huge and booming. So I managed to get up after Billy had finished a long rendering of "Midnight in Moscow," and I picked my way over to him. "I'm going," I said.

"This is when it gets a little rough. I'll walk you to your car."

"What time is it?"

"I don't know." He seemed disgruntled.

"I feel like I've been up for about three days."

"I'm not surprised."

We walked out of Stella's and up the side street toward my car. "I'll be thinking about Aunt Minnie all night," I said.

"Don't think about Aunt Minnie," he said, "think about me." And then he kissed me quickly.

"Tell me, Missy," he said, "does this happen to you often, how we met and what we did today?"

"It happens to me never."

"Good night."

"Tomorrow?"

"Tomorrow."

As I drove home, I thought, When do I say to this dear man, nephew of Uncle Charlie, star of Stella's, a prince among men, There's someone else's baby growing inside me.

Billy called the next afternoon and said, "Wait while I put the phone on the piano, and then you listen, okay?"

A series of tumbling sounds followed, a crashing down of the phone. "Are you there, Eva? Hang on."

A roll of blurred chords came forth, a little melody that I could make out, with more crashing thumps. "Well, what do you think?

It's a song I started this morning called 'You at Noon.' How do you like it, Missy?"

"Fine. I like it fine."

"Well, I'm going to work on it some more."

"What are you doing, Billy, besides writing the song? I'd like to come over."

"Well, why don't you? Do you want to go for a swim?"

"I want to do just what we did yesterday. Everything."

"So do I."

"Oh, good."

I was surprised at my own forwardness; it had certainly not been my style in the past. I would never have invited myself, so to speak, not just from shyness either, but possibly, it occurred to me, from a certain lack of confidence in the result. But from Little Mary Sunshine to the modern *Cosmopolitan* girl seemed somehow the easiest of transitions. Why had I taken so long to hit my stride? Or was it not actually just my own pace, but the accelerated tempo of moving *with* someone; his and mine together. I found a loose-fitting dress and jumped into the car. Soon, I knew, I'd have to tell him about the pregnancy. But not just yet.

For the first time in my life I moved with a dazzling, sustained energy. I had a sense of the tiny force of the baby growing, expanding, cells multiplying inside me. But although I was housing something in there, I was also encouraged by it. I had a constant vision of a small ball curled up inside of me, prodding me on, giving me energy. "Don't stop now," the energy seemed to say.

I lost track of time and sequence during the next weeks, but I remember clearly a feeling of chunks of time out of time for Billy. Always enticing, always ending in bed, always at odd hours. No routine was established, but I tried as best I could to spend mornings and early evenings with my mother, particularly as Opa was in London, and Adrian and Inoye, feeling a touch restless, took several day-trips to naturalists' points of interest.

"I'll come to Stella's tonight later on if you like," spoke the new me.

"Fine, wonderful. We'll go back to my place afterwards."

Then at two in the morning we'd arrive back at his house and proceed immediately to scale a ladder up to the roof, where Billy had created a little nest for us by dragging up a mattress and quilt.

"I always go high up when I want to feel safe. No one can see us here, but we can see everything. What was that song the Drifters sang, 'Up on the Roof'?"

"The Drifters didn't say it was cold."

"Nonsense. Cozy on down here," he said.

And for the next hours we would make love again and again. The sky was bright, and it was all much lighter than I imagined the out-of-doors to be at night, and I felt completely uninhibited by the glow. He encouraged me, and I felt almost drunk with him and bold, as I kissed him and held him and kissed him again. I began to wonder if I didn't have a touch of moon madness, lying there on that mattress with the moon and stars above me. "I am swept away, I am swept away by you," I told him. He laughed and held me under the quilt. Then, at the first hint of dawn, I would head home, not tired but spent, ready to snatch a few hours' sleep before my mother and I met for breakfast. I felt on an almost constant high.

"You look pretty this morning, Eva," Mother said as I made her tea. "Being pregnant makes you look quite luminous. Opa told me the same thing when I was carrying you."

She looked sunken, far from luminous now, and I felt a dull ache in my throat as I looked at her. She had been the bearer of children too; now it was all so decisively over for her. As I began to puff outward, swelling gently and slowly, she now went into the reverse course. Diminished, paler, hunched forward.

"It is remarkable that you manage to look so nice, considering that you stay up all night. Mr. Diamond must be good for you."

"He is."

"You have to tell him that you are pregnant. Have you?"

"No. I keep putting it off. I know I shouldn't but in a way it's a sort of race against the clock, because, after all, it's just a summer romance, and summer is two-thirds over, and in the fall he'll just —go off."

"He doesn't look like the kind who will just disappear to me," she said. "Does he live in New York?"

"Well, musicians live a lot of places, but yes, he lives mostly in New York."

"We're going back to Riverdale in the fall, Riverdale being only twenty minutes from the heart of New York City."

"But he has a whole different life."

"Eva." Mother looked at me, not unkindly, but with a sure reproach in her eye. I felt my breath come short.

"I know. Oh, dear God." I jumped up. "I should have told him right away, but it all seemed so lovely, and it still does, and I don't want to ruin it."

"Is that fair to him?"

"No. Of course not. But then, if I had told him right away, we certainly couldn't be having this kind of summer, could we? No matter what his reaction, it would be different."

She nodded. "Still, better tell him soon."

I looked at myself carefully in the mirror as I stood naked after a shower. My stomach continued to carry a slight rise, nothing startling, and now I definitely lacked a waist, my breasts were swollen as before, but no, it was still within bounds, for the moment. Almost four months and still holding . . . If I could just wait a couple of weeks more without telling him, then, I vowed, I would take what was coming to me, absorb his wrath and hurt, compensate somehow. Just a couple more weeks.

"Are we having a summer romance, Billy?" I asked as we snuggled under the quilt. "Would you say we are having a summer romance?"

"I don't know. Summer romances always remind me of couples in canoes in the moonlight."

"What is it then?"

"Let's just wait and see. I'll rent a canoe for you if it would make you feel better." We moved together a little more closely.

Around the middle of August Mother went back to New York for another chemotherapy session, which I knew she dreaded and which we all dreaded for her. Opa was coming back from London and would meet her in New York.

"Let me come with you," I offered. "I can drive the car."

"I can still drive a car, Eva," she replied briskly. "Your chance will come for all that." As she left in the jeep, I wondered to myself if I would be that brave, so free of complaint, without panic.

James came down for a week soon after that. I picked him up at the boat. He appeared more jittery and disheveled than usual, his hair seemed to stand straight up, his face was flushed despite the reasonably cool day.

"How's Mother?"

"She seems all right."

"Christ, Eva, how can this be happening, can you tell me?"

"You'll be reassured when you see her, Jimmy. She looks okay. Almost okay."

He shot me a wild look. "None of that matters, Eva. How she looks one minute or the next doesn't matter. You know that. The point is, she doesn't have a chance. That's the point. I don't see how you can all be so calm about it."

"I'm not calm on the inside, James, but I am trying not to panic on the outside."

He ran his hand through his hair. "How does she keep from going crazy?"

"I don't know, James, but she's not desperate. That's all I can tell you. Quieter, more withdrawn maybe, but not desperate. I think she has accepted her fate, which is hard to believe, and she's been quite happy for the last few weeks. It's helped to have Adrian here."

"That turkey."

"I think what she wants now is for us all to be settled."

"I'm as settled as I'm going to be." He leaned back against the car seat.

"Have you got any new girl friends?"

"You too," he snapped. "Mother's asked me that about six times. Let me ask you something. How can you be pregnant and going out with some new guy at the same time?"

I felt a quick tightening in my stomach. "You ask hard questions. I'm going to solve that all soon. Pretty soon." I turned up the hill, past the bustle of Vineyard Haven, toward the greenness of Chilmark.

"Jimmy, how's your place going?"

"Going pretty well."

James's place, as he called it, was an eighteen-acre estate in Vermont. With money advanced by our father, James had bought a sagging old estate for a good price four years ago, and with his two partners immediately installed four indoor tennis courts and six outdoor tennis courts. Ten miles of cross-country ski trails were cut, the main house restored, a bar added in what had been a drawing room, and they began to advertise expensive tennis vacations, winter and summer, everybody welcome, but particularly those who read *The New Yorker*. We all held our breath for the first year, agonized through the fissure with one of the partners, watched, relieved, as our father dug deeper into his pocket to buy the fellow out, held our breath again as the plumbing broke down in the main house and a fuse blew continually on the lighted indoor courts, but breathed a sigh of relief as a group of people here and there took up the place, and at last James announced quietly, "I think it's going to go . . ." He had a distinct style, James, and was of course a terrific tennis player himself (he took charge of all the classes). But as a manager, a manager of anything, he certainly was unproven.

"Yes," he said, "I'm actually making money. Not a lot. It's going to fly though, Eva. I think we're going to make it."

If I could have kissed him and still driven the car I would have done so. His triumphs had been few in a household which tended to blossom with successes. "Good for you, kid."

His face was flushed with excitement now. "We're building a little place to change clothes down by the outdoor courts. A kind of Japanese-style thing. I'm naming it House of a Thousand Tennis Balls. I ordered the sign yesterday. It's cool."

"House of a Thousand Tennis Balls?"

"Right. Do you like it?"

"Well." I wanted to be tactful. "Sort of. I guess. I'd like to see it first." I rushed on. "Then I'll know if House of a Thousand Tennis Balls is a good fit."

"Sometimes I go down there at night, just by myself, when everything's quiet, and I just sit there, have a joint, look at my tennis courts and feel like some real peaceful Japanese guy. Serene and peaceful."

Japanese serenity in southern Vermont. Well, why not? "That sounds like a good scene. I could use a bit of that serenity myself."

The traffic in and out of the house seemed to increase during those weeks in August. One morning, without much notice, Inoye decided to go back to Africa. Apparently she missed her mother and her sisters. We all hugged her and kissed her as we saw her off at the boat.

More people came in for drinks, Opa drawing his associates, including Billy, more closely around him as he went into the initial stages of production for his new show. The house lacked a piano (by design), so no backers' evenings were launched, but he was more his old self and evidenced more of the high energy he could call upon when he was in production. Mother seemed pleased. As per request, I moved up to the second floor when James came, next to Adrian, but I missed the familiarity of my own room and cozy bathroom with its long mirror. After three nights of this, I simply announced that we were reswitching. James could cope with the second floor, I was resuming my station on the first floor.

"I don't like it up there," I told Mother.

"Well, darling, James is only staying a few more nights."

"Well, fine, then he can manage upstairs."

James and I stalked past each other on the stairs as we moved our stuff.

"What do you care where you sleep, you're never here at night anyway," he said.

"I care."

"Don't fight, children," Mother called.

"Okay, okay."

Billy and I sat on the beach. "You bring your harp over to my place soon and we'll make up something nice together."

"The harp doesn't go well with a jazz piano."

"We'll try things. We'll record some things and play them back. We'll see. I can play anything you know, waltzes, polkas, old show tunes, sonatas. Not just jazz."

"I can only play very straight stuff."

"You limit yourself too easily, Eva. You don't know yet what you can do. Try, and I'll find some piece we can start on. You'll learn something even if it's terrible."

"What if it's terrible?"

"We'll still be friends."

"You promise?"

"Absolutely."

The next night Billy was off from Stella's, so we hauled the harp over to his place, found a spot for it near the piano in his disaster of a living room, which was piled high with sheet music, old porch furniture, and a Sailfish which lay serenely across one end. I had to stand on the Sailfish to open the windows.

"We'll begin with a little joint, to put us in a receptive mood," Billy announced. "Here you go." I hadn't smoked grass for quite a while so I was glad for the chance, surely it would relax me for this unpromising musical session, so I inhaled with pleasant anticipation. "Adrian smokes this in his room all the time, but he never offers any to me," I told Billy. "Adrian looks tough," he replied. After a minute I began to feel super charming, that everything I said was immensely clever, my traditional response to grass.

"All right, let's just start with something, any old thing, Missy, play 'Mary Had a Little Lamb.'"

"Okay, but this isn't nursery school."

"Go on, let me hear it, 'Mary Had a Little Lamb.'"

"Mary Had a Little Lamb" for the piano and harp was amusing enough, but we were going nowhere with it, so then I proposed "Down by the Old Mill Stream." "Oh right," cried Billy, "Uncle Charlie used to play that." But it proved a poor choice. We bounced off "Yesterday," even worse, several tunes from oldies like *Carousel* and *Show Boat*, tried a fast "Clair de Lune," took a break, during which we agreed to have solo time. That proved to be one hour and a half for Billy and ten minutes for me. After that we put on some of his old records, things he had written that hadn't taken off, a couple of which I secretly thought were better than "Tollgates" and "Without You." Bob came in at one point, took one look around, and left immediately. We tried a few more grotesque duets, and ended up with a fairly zingy version of an old Charlie Parker tune, "Straighten Up and Fly Right," which was made bearable by the fact that we alternated choruses, his longer and more rambling, mine short and whimsical. It worked.

The evening was capped by a trip to the roof, which had to be recapped as it started to rain, so we ended up downstairs again, in the messy bedroom, half clothed, disheveled, supreme.

I asked her, "Let me do something for you, won't you?"

She put down her paper and smiled. "You're my ally, Eva. In a sense you're doing everything for me."

"But I wish I could, I don't know, rearrange your pills or drive you somewhere, or cook something for you."

"I drive myself. You don't know how to cook and neither do I. So come on, we'll take a walk to the end of the road. Bring the binoculars, maybe we'll see a bird or two."

We ambled down the dirt road, the sun at our backs.

After a minute, Mother said, "I am surprised, aren't you, that I don't have more—what shall I call it—distress. Here I am, riddled with cancer, just walking around, tending to my business like everyone else."

I winced inside whenever she talked that way: "Here I am, riddled with cancer," or "after I'm dead." I lack sangfroid, I guess. But whenever she did insert those words into conversation, which she did only with me, I just tried to move along without missing a beat.

"Chemotherapy has a positive side," I said stoutly. "You may feel like hell when you're taking it, but in between bouts, you do wonderfully. Today, for instance, you look fine."

"Thank God, Eva. Thank God."

She really didn't always look so great, but more important, she was equal to most of the challenges of the moment—a picnic on the beach, Adrian's presence, the uncertain behavior of the first floor bathroom, trips to the market, an occasional concert.

We stood at the end of the dirt road now. "I'll walk over to the Chilmark Store. Want me to get you anything?"

"An apple. Find me a perfect apple, Eva."

I headed for the Beetlebung corner, the little hot spot at the meeting of South and Middle Roads, a beautiful but tense little intersection on which rested the Community Center, the library, the post office, and the ever so casual Chilmark Store. If it's the perfect apple she wants, by God, I'll find it for her.

I came in one night around two only to find my mother sitting in the living room with a single lamp on, casting her face in a harlequin-like shadow.

"Hi. Why are you up?" I whispered.

"Oh, just a sleepless night, Eva, a bad sleepless night. I don't like the new pills they gave me, and then tonight your father and Adrian got into one of their awful quarrels."

"About what?"

"Oh, it's hardly worth recording. Who knows what these things are about really? It just left me with the sinking feeling that they're just never going to get along, ever. That despite my best efforts, I have put them in some kind of adversary position. I just don't know, Eva. Adrian is dear to me, but he is so arrogant, so . . . unyielding, and you know I have tried to tell this to Opa, but he doesn't listen. He just goads Adrian on, he picks on him, he brings up subjects which he knows will set him off. Why, I don't know. Why don't they just talk about the weather, these two men?"

"They'd probably argue about the weather, too."

"Well, that's right. But because they have no common ground, really, no feel for conciliation, there is no way for them to resolve an argument. Adrian storms out of the room, Opa rails after him even after he's gone. I don't so much mind *that* they argue, or even those fights, but just that they don't know how to resolve anything. They don't know how to make up."

I had rarely seen her in such despair.

"They are not children, you know, Eva. Daddy is sixty, Adrian is thirty-one. Are they going to do this for the rest of their lives?"

"Oh, they'll wind down. The third act, you know."

"No. They're too competitive."

I was sitting opposite her, on a little bench, but close to her. For the first time since the spring she actually looked sick; her eyes did not seem to be in the same place as before, they were sunken and lower on her face. Although puffy from the chemotherapy, she still looked thinner. I found it quite alarming to look at her and got up to get an apple from the dining room table. "They may not remain competitive forever," I answered. I had long avoided this one piece of confrontation with my mother, the essence of Adrian and Opa's rivalry, because I felt it to be a genuine blind spot on her part. She understood the surface symptoms of it but had always failed to perceive the depth of the competition, that Adrian and Opa both loved her in the same way, the same sweeping, all-pervasive way; that Adrian had to go to another continent to find a wife and would stay there rather than share Mother with Opa. I myself never believed that Opa and Adrian disliked each other, but just that they could not control their rivalry for her. But it did not seem fair to trespass into these murky waters at this time. The sight of her further convinced me of that on this evening.

"Eva, I'm afraid that after I'm dead, Adrian will just never come home again. He'll just fold into Africa and disappear and we'll lose him completely. He could, you know, just remove himself from your lives, without me here to keep him coming back. Daddy will feel terrible and he won't know what to do about it. If they are always at such a logjam, what will bring them together?"

She asked: What will bring them together? How could I answer, Your death will bring them together?

"It will be all right, Mother, after a while. I won't let Adrian disappear, I promise you. I'll keep up with him."

"He's always liked you."

"Well, no, he hasn't, actually, but maybe he will."

"How can you keep Adrian in touch with Opa and James, however?"

"Well, I'll have regular family reunions." It felt like a terrible answer to me, but it seemed to please her.

"What if Adrian just says he won't come?"

"He will."

"He's very able to say no, you know."

"Well, then we'll have the meeting in Nairobi."

"And what if James won't come?"

"He will."

"And what about Opa?"

"Oh, he always goes to things, it's just what he does when he gets there that's questionable."

"Oh, dear God, I can see it now. What if you're all sitting here or in Nairobi, and they sort of start up the way they do . . ." But she was smiling. "What will you do then, Little Eva?"

"I'll just knock their heads together."

"Bravo, child." She paused for a minute. "I'm going to bed now." She rose, poured herself a glass of water, wiped her face off with a damp cloth, looked at me again, and smiled. "Good night, heavyweight champion of the world."

I was suddenly exhausted. In fact I felt a bit dizzy, as the day had included an endless trip to Vineyard Haven for supplies, a long session with Billy, and a hot trip to the beach. Nonetheless, I found some white paper napkins on the dining room table, took a lipstick from my bag, and composed two similar notes to Adrian and Opa. "You two guys just goddamn well get along," I wrote with my lipstick. I put Opa's in his Docksiders by the door, and Adrian's under his door. A poor beginning is better than none, I told myself.

Adrian announced a few days later that he wanted to drive out to the Grand Canyon, "just to have a look around," and that he wished to take Mother's jeep. Secretly relieved to have him out from underfoot but still in the country, Mother agreed. My father, not so secretly relieved, gave his blessing ("Well, Adrian, that sounds very enterprising") and a large check. Adrian, true to form, accepted everything without blinking. He just stuffed the check in his pocket, picked up his fishing rod, put his hat on, waved to us, and drove off as if he were just going to Sears, Roebuck.

"You spoil us, Opa. Why do you spoil us all so?"

"I'm damned if I know," he replied.

I recorded this all to Billy and mentioned particularly the check business and the ease with which Adrian pocketed the little blue folded paper. "He fights with Opa, and then turns around and takes a wad of money from him."

"What do you do, Missy?"

"I don't purposely fight with him, for one thing," I said a trifle defensively.

"But you don't refuse a check from him, do you?"

"No, but it's not quite the same thing. I get a regular amount quarterly. Not a huge amount either."

"Pretty much the same thing, Missy. You're all on the dole."

"Oh, come on," I snapped, "that's not so unusual."

He was technically right, in that our father was our common source and our only source, for that matter, but I had always thought Adrian to be in a different category, since he was supposedly a trained anthropologist and he had a wife and all. But I hesitated to pursue the fine points of these distinctions with Billy since there was no way I could come out of the conversation looking anything but pampered, in his eyes.

"What are you going to do when you grow up, Eva?" he asked, continuing to prod me with a touch of merriment.

"I'm going to be a mother," I replied guilelessly.

"Oh, man, that's wonderful," he laughed, with some admiration, I thought. "No executive ladder for you, eh, Missy?"

I looked at him carefully, as I so often had. I suspected that under this informal style and gold earring (mercifully removed) lay a man of considerable convention and propriety; he would probably not seek a modern, fast-track career girl, nor would he be pleased with an already-pregnant girl friend. Just a couple of more days, I told myself, then I'll tell him. End of fool's paradise.

But why doesn't he see it? I wonder. I looked at myself again toward the end of that last week in August; the gentle swelling seemed to have moved upward, to include anything that might have been my waist; and from the profile came an unmistakable thrust forward that seemed to say, Here I am, I will not be hidden anymore. I took another look. Well, at almost four and a half months, what else should I expect. You look pregnant, Little Eva, you wanted this baby and now you've got it, right up front where it's supposed to be, for everyone to see.

For two days after that I was seized with hideous, irrational doubts, visions of myself alone with a deformed baby, or a child with problems, speech problems, a twisted foot, a cleft palate. Nightmares about being unable to cope, having an agency take over because I couldn't handle things. It could happen. My mother said, We are all vulnerable, it could happen. I knew that these were conventional nightmares, but I could find no sense of detachment, no way to protect myself against these fantasies.

I said to my mother, "What happens if this baby turns out to have a problem, be retarded or something?"

"You'll learn to cope. You'll learn to handle it," she replied, looking up from her typewriter with a gentle smile. "By the way, Eva, there is a box of baby clothes on the third floor in Riverdale, all of your things and the boys'. You might look for it when we get home."

"Was I a good baby?"

"Perfect."

Trudy called, "just to check in," she said, and I spilled my anxieties out to her.

"I think this happens to everyone, honestly, Eva, I remember the same thing when I was having Neddy. Just hold on. Everything will be fine."

"Oh, I hope so, Trudy. I just hope my mother lives through the whole year that the doctors promised her. Even if she's not all that well, just the fact that she's here will mean something."

"Remember, you'll be taking care of her too. You're the nurturer."

"Oh, I can take care of any number of people," I replied, my confidence returning. "I just need her to be there." I do need her to be there. Cal was right.

"I ran into James and he said you were having an affair with a piano player. How do you manage that?"

"I don't really manage it. I just let it happen, I guess."

"And he still doesn't know you're pregnant?"

"He will tomorrow. Tomorrow I will tell him; I am so dreading it, Trudy. I've waited too long."

"I thought that would happen. You were always a procrastinator of sorts."

"A procrastinator of sorts. I hope that's all I am. Oh, Trudy, at
first I thought it was just a summer fling, in a few weeks he'd go
back to the city and . . . and . . ."

"And what?"

"Well, then I would never have to say anything about the
baby."

"Do you love this man?"

"Well, I don't know. Yes, I guess I do. I'm sorry I don't sound
more clear-headed on the subject. What's up with you?" I needed
to change the subject so I wouldn't continue to sound like a dope.

"Fantastic news, Eva. I'm onto something so great, I'm not
sure I can talk about it." Having filed this disclaimer, she went
on: "I've been offered a twelve-week TV contract, starting in October, to go to six major cities to discuss women's issues on an
hour-long panel show, with the top feminist leaders in each city.
They want to do a two-hour special on regional differences.
They've got almost all the sponsors lined up, and a nifty producer
named Al Levinson—have I ever mentioned him to you? Well,
he's a very aware, very sensitized man. I, of course, thought we
ought to have a woman producer, but I got nowhere with that, but
anyhow, Al and I can relate to each other, and the special will be
aired sometime in January, after the Christmas hysterics. I'll be
the moderator, anchorwoman, and they may actually make me a
coproducer, if I can work well with Al. It's a marvelous scene, I
can hardly wait."

"That sounds super, really."

"Now of course, if I can just figure out what to do with Neddy,
I'll be okay."

"Can't you get a baby-sitter. Maybe a couple?"

"Not for twelve weeks, I don't think."

"You'll be gone the whole twelve weeks, no breaks?"

"Yes, little ones, here and there." The covert suggestion hung
in the air. "What are you going to do in the fall, Eva?" Trudy was
moving in.

"Well, we'll all troop back to Riverdale, I guess."

"I see."

I didn't bite. I've got my hands full, I love Neddy but how on earth could I take care of him now? "Look, I'll be back-up if there's a crisis." I offered that, at least, to clear my conscience.

"Well okay, Eva, I've lost eight pounds and I look like a skinny witch. It's kind of fun."

"Soon I'm going to begin to look like a whale, Trudy. I don't know whether it's going to be fun or not."

"Now don't lose your courage, Eva. You're doing what you wanted to do."

"I know." Before we got started on courage and nobility, I changed the subject. "Look, Trudy, if you really get stuck about Neddy, call me back and I'll talk to Mother and we'll try and figure out something. I have to see how she is first."

"Oh, Eva, you're an ace, really. I'll be there for you when you need me. Which you will."

"Yes, I will."

Yes, we could probably absorb Neddy in the big swampy house in Riverdale, find some way of getting him to and from school. I'd done it once before when Trudy was pressed into service in Los Angeles, making a documentary film on women who worked in factories, for which she won an Emmy nomination. Absorb, absorb, why not?

Curtis called minutes later to report that the tenant in my Cambridge apartment, that earnest law student, had been arrested in a cocaine bust.

"You may have trouble collecting the rent, my dear, since the poor fellow is in the slammer. He was quite a dealer, that guy. I'll send you the clipping."

"Oh, damnit, Curtis, I wish I could get rid of that place, particularly since I'm going to have to change doctors when I get back to New York anyway, and there is no earthly reason for me to go back to Boston after that, except to see you, of course."

"Never mind that shit."

"Do you know of anyone who would like to sublet that place?"

"No, but there is such a thing as a real estate agent."

"But I don't want to have to haul all the way up there . . . just now."

"Look, Eva, you're so dumb, just write me a letter authorizing me to rent the place for you, and if anyone is fool enough to take it, I'll send the papers down and you can sign them."

"Oh, thank you, Curtis. Is this fellow's clothing still in there?"

"Yes, along with all his many law books. Cocaine and all, the place looks better than when you were living there."

"Oh, I'm sure," I replied. "Curtis, do you ever see Cal?"

"Heavens, no, why on earth would I ever see Cal?"

"Oh, I don't know. I just wondered."

"Don't give him a thought. I'll let you know what happens about your apartment."

The final call of the morning was from James, who reported that his little changing shed, named, in fact, House of a Thousand Tennis Balls, had burned to the ground when a couple of grass-smoking teenagers had snuck in there with a kerosene lamp and succeeded in turning on and torching the place within minutes.

"For Christ's sake, *I* just got the place built," James cried. "These fucking kids. Kerosene lamp in a place like that, what the hell, how can anyone be so dumb?" We passed the phone back and forth, Mother to me to Opa. "Did you have insurance, James?" "Yes, but it will take me a year to get it settled, everything up here is so slow, and we really used the place. Stupid, goddamn kids." "Well, I'll advance you the money to rebuild it, and you can pay me back when your insurance comes through." "Well, thank you, that might be very helpful, Dad." "Meanwhile, rope the place off."

Balm applied to the wound, James calmed down enough to report that the weather had been perfect (a tennis camp in the rain is a disaster), the place was full, and the staff doing well. "But I wish to Christ there weren't so many dumb kids in the world." The voice seemed a far cry from the teenage James, who used to hide his grass in the piano and smoke in many corners of the house, including the walk-in linen closet.

The net effect of these three phone calls, following as they did within minutes of each other, was that I moved away from my worries about the health of the baby, put aside my catastrophic fantasies, and replaced them with visions of a cocaine bust in my apartment, the House of a Thousand Tennis Balls in flames, and Trudy on nationwide TV.

By this last week in August, the pace of the summer seemed to hit a crest. I had been keeping the oddest of hours and continuing my attention to Mother and our household. I was in constant, bouncing movement, either at Billy's, at Stella's, or on the beach, darting to town, making breakfast as if I hadn't come in at four in the morning, running to the airport to pick up Opa, then back to Billy's, up on the roof. Up on the roof.

I felt like a bird in flight, sensing that cold and migration are near, but hesitating to light, to break the soaring curve.

In that spirit then, that night at ten, when everyone had gone to bed, I got in my car and headed for Stella's. Traffic seemed to pass me close and fast, corners on the road seemed sharp, and I felt that I was speeding, even though the speedometer read a sedate thirty-five miles per hour.

The streets of Oak Bluffs were crowded and I had trouble finding a parking place, so I ended up leaving the car on the hill overlooking the harbor, and as I walked back toward the main street the wind seemed cold and mean. An ill wind. It seemed to say, Summer is over, and so are a lot of other things. Tomorrow I'll tell him. Tomorrow for sure.

Stella's was jammed, and I found a faraway corner table and slipped into a chair with relief. Billy was playing, but the noise was such that I couldn't hear much from my distant perch. Just not a good night to be here. Too much clamor, he's way over there, and I'm way over here, he didn't expect me, we have din and distance between us. I watched anyway.

His hair seems to float above him, his shoulders move up and down almost like a slow-motion dance, and when he looks down at his hands, at the keyboard, pensively, and hits a passage he likes, why he just smiles. That was fine, he seems to say. What is it, I wonder, that is so very alive about what he does, about his music, that he can do it and smile at the same time. I struggle simply to transfer the notes on the score in front of me to the strings of my harp. Not Billy.

He looks wonderful. Comfortable in his own skin, a natural man.

I took a napkin and found a rugged tube of lipstick from my bag, and in my new favorite method of communication, etched him a message of tenderness and foreboding: "I love you. Eva." I got up and handed it to the waitress. "Will you take this up to the piano player, please?" "Sure. A request?" "Yes, a request," I said, and let myself out of Stella's into the chilly air.

That night it was so cold that I couldn't sleep. I tried putting on a sweater, tried and failed to find another blanket; finally I went up to Adrian's room to steal his, but his bed had been stripped. I saw a light flick on in the living room and went downstairs.

Mother moved about rather aimlessly, as if she weren't sure whether or not she should sit down.

I spoke softly so as not to scare her. "Hi. It's just me. I was looking for a blanket. I hope I didn't disturb you." She stared at me, waved her hand slightly, but didn't answer. "I got so cold, Mother, that I thought I'd try and find a blanket or a quilt." She was wearing an old, faded bathrobe, which she pulled around her closely.

"Well, it is cold, all of a sudden, isn't it? Look over in the closet next to my bathroom, Eva." She sounded hoarse.

"All right. Why are you up?"

"Well, I'm not sure. Couldn't sleep."

"Can I get you anything, Mother, shall I make some tea?"

"No thanks." She stood in the center of the room now and seemed to shiver.

"Are you cold too?" I asked.

"Yes, a little."

"It was so warm today, around noon, why do we all of a sudden get this cold?"

"There is no sun without shadow. 'There is no sun without shadow, and it is essential to know the night.' Albert Camus said that, Eva." She moved toward the window. "Get a quilt, and try and sleep now. Good night, child."

XI

"You should have told me." He clenched his fist.

Billy sat at his kitchen table, motionless. If only he would move, I thought. Move toward the icebox, get up, open a window, do anything. He is like granite in front of me, held in position by hurt and anger.

"And what if I love you? Did you think of that? What if I've come to love you?" His voice was quiet and anguished. "Eva, you kept your secret too long."

"Keep loving me, can you?" I felt frightened as I asked the question, frightened that he would say no, no, no.

But he looked at me with a slight smile. "Well, of course. But it's just different now. Very different." His head was tilted off at a funny angle, but still he didn't move. "Let me see. Take that dress off and let me see."

Obedient, I took off my loose dress and underpants and stood before him, feeling awkward. He shook his head and closed his eyes for a minute. "I just never saw it. Never suspected. I like that round stomach. How the hell am I supposed to know what a pregnant woman looks like?"

"You weren't supposed to know. It doesn't look that different."

"Oh, but it does now." He smiled again slightly and nodded in that familiar way. "It sure looks different now."

I dressed quickly. He got up from the messy kitchen table and started pacing, tugging at his faded shirt.

"You lured me, Eva. You went for me in a big way, and god-damnit, you misrepresented yourself."

"I misrepresented my situation, Billy. Not myself."

"Well, whatever the hell it is, you didn't come clean."

"No. No, I didn't."

"And see now, we've been together now, and it's a good scene, I'm involved with you, and now you're suddenly unavailable to me."

"But I'm not! I'm *not* unavailable, Billy, not at all. It's just that I'm going to have a baby. It doesn't mean that I'm unavailable to you."

"Put yourself in my place, Eva. I feel tricked. I feel hood-winked."

I covered my face with my hands. The room started to spin. I know I have hurt him and it's much, much worse than I thought it would be. "Oh, please take that word back. I didn't trick you. Please, that can't be right."

"Okay. Let's just stick with hoodwinked." He set his jaw.

"Billy, if I told you about the baby at the start, we would not have had this kind of time together. It's been almost pure, in a way, and I've never had that with anyone. And we've had fun and staying up all night with the piano and all, look, it all started so quickly, and kind of took off, I didn't expect anything like this that first day I took your groceries home. Then, I just couldn't give that all up. I was greedy, I guess." I moved back in my chair and took an old towel from the table and started to fold it, back and forth on my lap. "Greedy, yes. But not tricky."

"Okay," he said. He stopped pacing and seemed to light near the doorway, still staring at me.

"Put yourself in *my* place," I went on. "I knew we had a month before it would all become clear anyway." The kitchen seemed tiny, airless, and I felt clumsy and oversized in it.

"I think," Billy said, "that you decided to have yourself a fling —or whatever—before motherhood. I think you must plead guilty to that."

"In some sense I do, yes, men do that all the time, by the way. Shore leave. But I love you too, Billy. I told you so."

"Did you think about me at all, and how I would feel?"

"Of course."

"And?"

"And I decided to take the chances. At first I thought we were having a summer romance—"

"And that I'd go back to New York at the proper moment."

"To that other girl friend, possibly."

"That's over. And *then* what did you think would happen?"

I tried to take a deep breath but was capable of only shallow puffy bits of air. "I thought, Billy, that there would be a price to pay—and there is." We were both quiet, and I felt an odd sense of relief that I had managed, somehow, to say what I meant. I never could simply say what I wanted to with Cal, I always would wind up sputtering and feeling overwhelmed for some reason. Even with Opa, I had spent most of my life telling him what he wanted to hear. Now, with Billy, when it mattered most, I had managed to say what I mean. Well now, Eva, let the chips fall where they may.

Billy sat still, staring out the window, his brow furrowed, his eyes remote.

"It's only a baby, Billy. I sometimes say to myself, when I feel a little besieged, It's only a baby."

He shook his head again. "I don't think I can compete with a baby, Eva. Another man, yes, I can do that. I've done it before with some success. But I don't think I can compete with a baby."

"Why compete, Billy? Babies are small, and they sleep a lot. Sure they're cute, but—"

"No, Eva." He stood up now and faced me. "It's not the size of the child that I'm talking about. It's just the fact that it's there. I suppose it's simple jealousy. But a woman with a child must be shared. For years." He went to the icebox and took a can of beer. "I hardly know you in some ways, Missy. But in truth, from this moment on, no matter what, you must be shared—by me or anyone else." He moved back toward me now, waving his beer can. "*And* it isn't even my baby!" He kept on walking out onto the porch and sat down on the steps.

Now it was my turn to sit frozen. I wanted to follow him, to put my arms around him, to continue to plead my case. But I simply couldn't move. No, it isn't even your baby, Billy. I sat in a kind of stupor for a minute, and then I heard his tape deck play-ing, an old Joe Cocker tune, "Cry Me a River." It sounded loud and angry. I'll sit here, I'll be calm, I thought. I'll wait for him to come back in. And most of all I won't cry. Joe Cocker can cry himself a river, but I'm going to stay steady.

He appeared in the doorway. "Look, Eva. I have nothing against children. In fact I kind of like them. And I also think you've followed your best instincts in going ahead with this baby. I think that's fine, I really do. I can see you with a baby, see you holding a baby, I think that part is fine." He seemed less taut now, he looked less stricken. "There was a little extra erotic qual-ity to you, I just sensed it. Maybe it was because you were preg-nant."

"Maybe it was because I was with you."

He looked at me now, almost tenderly. "You'll be a good mother. I can see you with a baby, I really can. You'll be a good mother." He walked over to the window and stared out.

"When you say, 'You'll be a good mother,' it sounds almost like a dismissal. Like you're putting me aside. Don't dismiss me, Billy. Even to the honorable category of motherhood."

He moved back to the table and sat down. "Now look, Eva. Try hard to understand this. Forget about whose baby it is and all that, and think about the way we live. A baby, a child, is not within the pattern of my life. Not now at least. And maybe it won't ever be. But it is within the pattern, the context of your life. Very much so. You come from a world of station wagons, music lessons, big Christmases. It's a world which can absorb your baby. You're doing something which may seem unconventional, but it's probably very natural and correct for you. And you will be a good mother, Missy, for lots of reasons. Among other things, you've had a wonderful mother of your own."

"I won't have her for long."

"Look, my father was a bully, and my mother was a profes-sional martyr, and I couldn't wait to get out of the house. But when I'd come home, and Mother would start this number about settling down, here's a nice girl here and a nice girl there, I felt cold in my stomach, Eva. Cold in my stomach."

"You don't have to settle down with me, Billy."

He flashed me a quick smile and reached over and touched my arm. "Well now, Eva, I know, but here you are, or there you will be, with a baby, and you will find yourself, despite yourself, despite everything you say, looking for a husband."

"I will look for someone to love, but then, I always have."

"A husband, Eva. When your baby comes, you'll want a husband. You'll want someone to take the car to the garage, to empty the garbage."

"No, I'll do that myself."

"The hell you will." He was on his feet now. "I'm a musician, Eva. Not very successful yet, I've got some good songs to write yet, but essentially that's my world. My mother once asked me how I could stand the hours, and I said, I love the hours, the worse the better. I don't care when I sleep. I work nine to five maybe, but my nine to five is at night; and it feels fine to me. I had a girl friend once, I was with her for two years or so, and she wanted to marry me. And I sort of wanted to marry her too, sort of, but not enough. She got tired of my evasiveness, for which I don't blame her, and she said, finally, that I was one of those fellows who couldn't make a commitment. That was her big word, commitment. I told her, 'Look, I have a commitment, it just isn't to you, that's all. I'm committed to my music, wherever it takes me.' It was cruel of me, maybe, but it's true, I have that commitment. You know, I hear music all the time, Eva, even when I don't want to. Music was my way out, when I was younger, out from under my family, and it is my way up, because without it I don't have a dime. And it's also my way inside myself, it's what I hear when I'm alone. It's all I have."

"Is it all you want?" I looked at him carefully and held my breath for the answer. He waited a long minute.

"No. No. I also want love. I also want you."

"I wrote you a note on a napkin last night."

"I got it." He smiled now, his slight, funny smile. "I love you, Eva. I love you madly. Do you know who said that?"

"Duke Ellington."

"Duke Ellington is right."

"I grew up in a house with music too, you know." I felt a return to normal breathing. Through this last hour, I felt as if I dare not

take a proper breath, as though I might lose everything if I
breathed properly.

I asked, "Do you think we love each other in a way that sur-
vives trouble?"

He leaned back in his chair, almost relaxed. "Trouble?" He
squinted. "Well, Missy, this isn't really trouble, is it? You said
your old boyfriend, what's his name, Cal, saw it as trouble."

"Well, he hated the impropriety of it."

"Well, I'm not in his shoes, but I don't really see it as trouble,
and certainly not as impropriety. My mother would have. That
was her bag, everything had to be genteel. The way I see it, trouble is a fight that doesn't finish, a bad vacation, missed connec-
tions, selfishness. I think we're just on different paths, that's all.
You can love someone and travel a different path. We have, as
you pointed out, had a great summer."

"Do you want it to end? Can't the paths meet? I know I'm
sounding like a soap opera."

"Well sure, I guess that's what paths are for, to bring you into
a larger place. But they weave, they're not on a straight course,
and maybe we should just each follow our own for a while. You're
a fine girl, Eva, and I go for you, and you know I really do. It's
hard to get used to the idea that your girl is pregnant with another man's baby. I'm not sure I can—get used to it. Or that I
should."

"Yes you can! Billy, forgive me, if you can, for not telling you
and all, for my greed about the last few weeks. But I'm going to
be greedy some more, now." I went over by the window and stood
next to him. "Stay with me. Stay for the next little while, at least.
Hang in with me. Even though we're on different paths."

We were close to each other now, and I could feel the rhythm
of his breathing. "Well, it's hard to imagine just walking away
from you," he said.

I sighed with relief. He won't just walk away from me. I wondered in a quick flash if I was afraid of being alone.

"Eva, I can't sleep with you anymore. You can understand that.
I can't lie in bed with you knowing that you're pregnant with another man's baby. How can I do that?" He looked pensive, almost
defiant.

"Well then, can we find other things to do? Other nice things to do together?"

"Oh, come on now. What do you have in mind, picnic, a clambake?"

"There are loads of other things." I tried to think of something, but I could only think of picnics and clambakes.

"Billy, you don't stop playing at Stella's for another three weeks, and in just about two or three weeks Mother and I will head back to New York, so there's some time left here. It's too cold to go up on the roof now anyway."

He stood back and looked at me, a look of tenderness and resignation. "Summer is over. Maybe the summer romance should be over too."

"Summer winds down. Let's let the season carry us awhile."

XII

The nights turned even colder but the middle of the day remained clear and hot; I wondered if that was a sign that, yes, summer *is* still going on and therefore summer's exuberance will last too. But it was not to be.

Opa came back for ten days, much of which he spent on the telephone. There were the traditional snags in production plans, but he seemed to take them with a new kind of frustration, almost an ill-will. "Goddamnit, I thought I could count on Len Meyer, and he's failed me twice. We've got money problems galore, and I can't get Martin O'Keefe until October thirtieth, which is going to be mighty late, although MCA said he'd be available on the fifteenth. I obviously can't trust Al Lawrence at MCA anymore."

Mother soothed him as best she could, and he admonished her, without conviction, not to worry, that he had everything under control. Still he clearly didn't have quite the nerve and sangfroid at sixty that he had possessed in quantities at a younger age. Mother seemed to be hunched forward in a slightly more pronounced way, and I noticed that Opa could see this, but he didn't say anything and I certainly knew better than to ask. He continued to hover around her, between bouts of telephone calls, proofreading something she was writing, insisting on taking her for her blood test (which I would have been glad to do), with a certain grim forbearance on his face. He had always been of the faint-at-

the-sight-of-blood school, and a trip to the Martha's Vineyard
Hospital made him jittery.

"Do you want me to take her?" I asked, in an effort to be
helpful.

"No, I'll do it."

"I don't mind."

"I don't either." Back and forth we went, vying for position as
first helper. When he was there, I let him win.

"Eva," he said one morning, "why don't you go into Edgartown
and get yourself some more—suitable clothes? You look a little
swollen."

He was right, of course. I have always hated shopping of any
sort, but I could see for myself that something had to give.

Edgartown lacked a Lady Madonna or any other maternity
clothes shop, so I pieced together from regular stores a few loose-
fitting tops, another wrap-around skirt, and a waistless dress.
What I really needed at this point was a skirt with an elastic
panel in the front, instead of those few shapeless garments; they
had the net effect of making me look like an egg-shaped camp fire
girl. Opa, at least, commended me for trying to "do something"
about my appearance. "Well, a little better," he said.

Adrian reappeared around the middle of September. This time
he brought back with him, in order of size, a moose jaw, fossils
embedded in rocks, bone particles from a mountain goat, many
rock samples, and some dried clay, all of which he left on the dining room table.

"That looks interesting, Adrian," Mother murmured.

"Are you going to leave it all there, Adrian, so we can have it
for dinner?" asked Opa, smiling. Unsmiling, Adrian removed his
treasures to his room upstairs. He seemed moody and restless
without Inoye. I screwed up my courage and asked him, "Addy,
how long are you staying?" "I dunno." "Don't you miss Inoye?"
"I do." "Well, look Addy," I advised sympathetically, "go on
back. Really. You don't have to stay. Come back whenever you
want, of course, but after all, everything is more or less stable with
Mother for the moment." He gave me the first warm look that I
can remember in recent times. "Well, I might go back to Nairobi;

but you'll have to let me know what's going on. I don't like sitting around Riverdale, but I am available. All the time."

He was particularly solicitous to Mother for the next two days; they stayed up late one night, talking. Then with a touch of sadness he cleaned out the jeep, bid us farewell, and left for Africa. I thought Mother looked teary as he got on the ferryboat to the mainland. "I'll be back," he called.

I didn't see Billy for a few days after our big meeting at his house, but he did call, odd, purposeless calls.

"Missy."

"Oh, Billy. Hi."

"Missy, I don't see any picnics or clambakes coming our way, so do you want to go to a concert in Edgartown?"

"Oh sure." I might have asked who or what was playing, but in fact I didn't care. It had been close to a week since I'd seen him and I felt jittery and longed for him. "I'd like very much to go," I replied.

The concert proved a change of pace for us, as so much else was changing pace—a chamber music evening at the Old Whaling Church in the center of Edgartown. It was a beautiful, crisp evening, the air smelled of fall. I wore one of my new, definitely pregnant dresses. Billy was quiet and sweet, but remote. He needed time, he said, to get me out of his bloodstream. "I've got you under my skin," he said.

"That's a song by George Gershwin," I answered.

"That's a song by Cole Porter," he replied.

He didn't kiss me; he didn't touch me at all. He kept his distance with grace. I was seized by a desire to bury myself in him, put my arms around him, and kiss him, all of which I resisted.

A couple of nights later, when he was off from Stella's, he invited me over to his house and played some songs he had written. The evening was agreeable but careful. I wanted to kiss him more than ever.

For the first time in a long time, I grew tense and moody. I couldn't seem to read, and listening to records caused me to think more of Billy, and yet I wasn't calm enough for reflection. I tried to play my harp a little, but with disastrous results. My fingers seemed to have glue on them. I began to busy myself with uncharacteristic tidying.

"What are you doing, Eva?" asked Mother.

"Just cleaning my closet."

"Whatever for?"

"Well, I guess, because we're going home soon."

"When you're done, come proofread this piece with me. I want to get it up to New York by Monday."

"Can I do it after I clean my car?"

"Sure. Why clean your car?"

"I don't know."

"Opa is taking us out to dinner tonight. We might go to the Homeport and try some lobster."

"I don't like lobster."

"Well, you have something else then, my dear," she replied evenly, and went back to her work.

I called Trudy. "How are you doing?" I asked. I could hear New York in the background.

"Well, I'm frantic, of course. I have to have new clothes, and they keep changing the schedule on me. Now I'm supposed to go to Dallas first. It's crazy."

"How's Neddy?"

"Well, I've got a couple who are going to sit with him. I'm not quite sure about them. I think they smoke pot."

"You smoke pot too."

"That's different."

"Well, if there's a problem, let me know."

"How's your piano player?"

"Well, he's fine. But he wasn't pleased when I told him about being pregnant. I still see him, but it's obviously different now. I don't want to lose him. I have come to love him, Trudy."

"Well, maybe you haven't lost him."

"For a while, I'm afraid. Maybe forever. He's going back to New York next week. There's some girl there, and he might well take up with her again. I don't know."

"You didn't really expect him to stay there and hold your hand, did you? You said it was a summer romance."

"Yes, well I guess not." Although Trudy irritated me at times,

she could be very bracing, and I felt safe in appearing melancholy
with her. "Trudy, I don't think musicians and babies and families
make a good mix, do you? I think Billy just may not want any of
that. With his odd hours and all."

"That's nonsense. There are no rules. Tom was the most perfect picture of a father and husband you can imagine, reliable, stable, all that, and two years after Neddy was born he shot out of
there like a bat out of hell. There are no rules. Perhaps you'll
meet someone else."

"I don't want someone else."

"I mean eventually. There's a price for what you're doing, Eva.
I guess you're beginning to see that. There is no sun without
shadow. That's a quote from Simone de Beauvoir."

"No, it isn't. Albert Camus."

"Since when are you such a know-it-all?"

I called Billy.

"I long for you," I told him. I longed for our nights on his roof,
his face close to mine, for his arms and shoulders, for his music,
for his smile.

"Yes, Missy, I know."

"I can't sleep."

"Be a big girl now. Go out and look at the stars, then go in and
climb into your nice bed, and go off to sleep. Count sheep if you
have to."

"When do you go back to New York?"

"Next Monday."

"Are we going to see each other when we're both back in the
city? Just for little events?"

"I guess so."

"Billy, can I ask you something?"

"Sure."

"Are you alone? I mean right now, you sound as if you were
with someone."

"Well, as a matter of fact, I am."

My stomach turned over; I felt the color drain from my face.

"Yes," he went on, "Frieda is here."

"I see. Frieda is that girl from New York?"

"No, Frieda is a dog from Vineyard Haven."

"Oh." Relief flooded my system. "You mean a four-legged mammal?"

"My guitarist, Ace Dukenney, gave her to me to keep while he got set up on the West Coast. Then, supposedly, Frieda will be flown out there. I'm sure she's with me for life."

"How do you plan to keep a dog in New York?"

"I haven't figured that out yet. Go to sleep now."

Rain, overcast skies spotted with patches of sunlight dominated the final days of September. The surf still smelled wonderful to me, but the scent of jasmine bushes, along the path to the Lucy Vincent Beach, was gone. Dusk came early. Someone told me that we lose almost two and a half hours of daylight between August and September.

The summer population thinned dramatically, the number of cars in the beach parking lots dwindled to almost nothing, except for a slight surge on the weekends. (Tensions around boat reservations remained.) On the road to Vineyard Haven, a slow turning of leaves away from green to autumn could be seen, and the meadows turned pale and scruffy. High winds caused the ocean waves to seem more tumultuous than ever. Rose of Sharon bushes, large and grown wild on the island, lost their flowers. The air was light and cool and promised swift change.

XIII

"Eva, come here and talk to me. I have a new plan." Mother seemed worried this morning, the sleepless nights showed on her face, her eyes seemed saucerlike and unfocused. "I love new plans," I told her truthfully, since anything coming or going seemed interesting to me now.

"I have to go to New York on Wednesday for more tests. God only knows what more there is to learn about me, but it will only be for one day. I don't want to have to stay overnight," she said. "I'd like you to go with me."

"Of course. And then are we moving back to Riverdale?"

"No, darling. I want us to come back here, to the island, you and me. And I would like to stay here through the fall. I want to be here, well, through Thanksgiving, if possible. That's my new plan."

"Oh. But what about all you have to do? I thought you wanted to get some work finished, and you had people to see . . ."

I tried hard to conceal my disappointment. New York City in the fall held some real magic even for me, a non-New Yorker; I had pictures in the back of my mind of occasional meetings with Billy, a favorite Chinese restaurant that I wanted to take him to, a concert here and there. So much for all that.

"I can work here, and I'll see people when we get home. Fall is the most beautiful time on the island, I can't allow myself to miss it. You don't mind, do you?"

"No, I like it here in the fall too," I replied, mustering as much enthusiasm as I could. "But don't you think you ought to be near the doctors?"

"Good God, no. I want to be as far away from that gang as possible. They don't offer me much these days. If I have to fly down I will."

So much for the doctors. I wondered what new responsibilities this might bring to me. I doubted if the local hospital had sophisticated treatments available for this kind of gravely ill patient, although they could do some things on an emergency basis. But what if she got suddenly much worse?

"If I get much worse," said Mother, "we'll go home. I don't plan to get worse, however."

"Good." I couldn't help smiling. "Now, what about Opa? He won't like this."

"Well, he certainly won't say he likes it. But Opa is starting those backers' evenings, the house in Riverdale will be ablaze with activity, the phone ringing every two minutes, and all that crowd from his office will be there, and he, poor dear, would feel that he has to try and be quiet, or whatever, which is not possible, and in this case, not necessary. I'm fine here. He's got a momentum to these productions, you know what it is, Eva, there's a sort of warm-up period, then the assembling of things, the backers, then the pace picks up, and it all sort of spirals upward. There's a rhythm to it all, you know."

"Yes, I do know." I recognized the upward spiral pattern, although for me the metaphor was more of a boat in a storm finding its way to safe harbor. As a young girl, I remember thinking of a boat tossed around (the show, with Opa at the helm), slow clouds gathering, thunder and lightning (opening night), and then the downpour (the critics), and finally, safe in harbor (a long run). Mother's upward spiral was better.

"He will feel that his wings are clipped with me lying upstairs resting. His exuberance will be dimmed. But Eva, it's not only for Opa's production that I want to stay here. I so much prefer the Vineyard anyway and always have. The fall is relaxing, more so than summer, I think. Opa will come down for snatches here and there; that will be good for him too. How about it?"

"Well, it sounds fine. I want to do whatever you want to do." I
added, "If the doctors say it's okay."

"The doctors are just there when I need them, that's all."

"True, but they can do something important—they can add
time."

"I'm not even sure they can do that, Eva. Or to be clearer,
they've already done it. No, I think whatever happens to me for
the remaining days of my life is more or less up to me." She drew
herself up, shot me her special duchess-on-the-throne look, and
opened her newspaper.

She is quite beautiful, my mother. Her hair has thinned, her
eyes are sunken, her face is puffy, her shoulders hunched forward
slightly, and those same old clothes, but oh, what charm in that
smile, what clarity in those eyes, what splendor in her hair, red
and gray, sitting up on her head like half a melon, disheveled,
wavy. Her glasses seemed like the most fashionable of ornaments,
tortoiseshell, with a string hanging off the ends. She wore three
large rings on her thin fingers (Opa's testaments), a cigarette
dangling from her left hand. And those beach shoes; those same
two-hundred-year-old beach shoes, faded, molded to her bony feet.
That morning she wore a once-green dress which had aged to a
near yellow. (My mother's old clothes made other people's old
clothes look new.) Everything seemed intricately woven, perfectly
assigned to her.

And so it was arranged, over Opa's protests, that we remain on
the Vineyard for the next six to eight weeks. Opa would be down
often, James would come for a week somewhere in there, and
friends who were *selected* (her word, not mine) would visit.

Of course, it made perfect sense for her to choose to see whom
she wanted to see, in her preferred setting. At Riverdale, with its
elaborate traffic pattern and charged atmosphere, she would not
have the proper amount of control. Trudy's mother, Aunt Polly,
provided enough deterrent to keep Mother on the island for
weeks.

More and more now I felt the changing pattern of her absorp-
tions. First she had needed to feel satisfied that we were all happy
(enough), that we were on some reasonable course, that we were
going to be all right without her. Now her preoccupation fell to

righting her own house: careful use of her time, work that needed
to be completed, with family and chosen friends, in a place where
her spirit was nourished. Details of living were still of vital concern to her—the new porch furniture; which fish store was better,
Larsen's or Poole's; people to be met at the boat; Vineyard details.
But the scale was smaller. The grandiose atmosphere of Riverdale,
which she loved and was indeed partly responsible for, was now
too overwhelming. The Vineyard house, informal, muted, modest
in its demands, was a place where she could withdraw on her own
terms. We all agreed privately that she was absolutely right to
want to stay.

The New Plan left me suspended, hanging behind on the summer island while everyone else went ashore. I looked decidedly
bulky now, yet still not quite at the point of that clear, insistent
frontal bulge that I had seen on other pregnant women. I felt a
slight longing for the comforts of Riverdale. But we had signed on
for the whole trip, my mother and I, no matter where, no matter
what.

Billy delayed his departure to New York in order to try to make
arrangements to avoid the miserable prospect of taking Frieda
back to the city. The owner of Stella's, a large, friendly man
named Angelo, agreed to keep Frieda for a ten-day grace period,
while Billy tried to figure out another holding pattern to avoid
taking this large and easily frightened creature into his small
apartment. He said he knew some people in the suburbs who
might cover for him for a month. All in all, he was quite generous
about the imposition of Frieda into his life. "You can't say no to
a good lead guitar player," he explained.

The night before he was finally to leave, he came over to the
house. He left his motorcycle toward the end of the driveway, so
as not to disturb Mother with its *rat-tat-tat*.

"Have you got a beer?"

"Sure."

He eased into the most comfortable of our sloppy chairs, allowed his head to rest against the back, and closed his eyes.
"What did you do all day?" he asked.

"Well, I just drove from one end of the island to the other,
twice. Doing errands."

"I really can't think of a better place to do errands. If you have to be pregnant, you might as well wait it out in nice surroundings."

"New York still might have been fun."

"Eva, maybe fun is something you shouldn't expect for the next little while."

"You're right, I guess. But I still think I'd just as soon be there. It's still the Big Apple." I tried not to sound wistful but didn't succeed. "I love it here too," I added.

"In the morning you hear song birds, in the evening you hear geese. I'm very conscious of what I hear. In New York you mostly hear traffic. There's something very fitting about your being here, watching over your mother, waiting to become a mother. New York's no place to do that."

I smiled. "You've convinced me."

"Look, you have a chance to do something unique now." He leaned forward, almost urgently.

"What, tell me?"

"Talk to your mother. Talk to her about everything and anything. You've got her to yourself, more or less. Ask her things. Ask her why Adrian is such a lulu, for instance."

I laughed. "I'm not sure she knows. Or may not want to tell."

"I'm sure she has an idea or two. Find out. You won't have this chance again."

"All right. I will. Let's build a fire. I think it's pretty cold in here."

The fire warmed us considerably, and we pulled the pillows from the couch to get close to it; I assumed my mother was asleep, as she had been going to bed quite early these last few days, saving her strength for when Opa was here. "We better whisper," I cautioned.

"Now tell me something," said Billy. "Do you ever read some of the articles she writes?"

"Sometimes I proofread the pieces with her, and yes, I look at them, but I guess I don't really sit down and read her stuff carefully. She used to do a lot about French writers and all, and we were always led to believe that these things were too erudite for us."

"What was she working on the other day, the piece you were proofreading?"

"Well, that was something for *The New York Review* called, let me think . . . 'The Self-Confessors: Intimacy as Heroics.'"

"Doesn't sound so French hotsy-totsy to me."

"It was all about people who write books about their operations, or their descents into hell, with drugs or whatever, and how they are made into literary heroes."

"Well, if I were you, I'd read a few of these things and ask her about them. I speak as one whose mother did crossword puzzles and read Dear Abby."

"We read Dear Abby in this household too."

"Ask her about her work, Eva. In a year or so you won't be able to." He leaned back against the pillow. "Have you got another beer?"

He looked ruddy and handsome and tired, Billy did. It was hard to imagine him in city clothes, waiting for a bus or hailing a taxi.

"Billy, what does your apartment look like?"

"What do you mean?"

"I mean, what do you see when you walk in the door?"

"Oh, Missy, my apartment is charmless, characterless, on a noisy corner of West 104th Street, up three flights of stairs. Is that what you mean?"

"What do you see when you first walk in the door?"

"A piano."

"Are there any pictures on the walls?"

"Yes, a couple of pictures of the Stones, one of Joe Cocker. Not paintings, posters."

"Does it have a fireplace?"

"No, for Chrissake."

"Where is the bedroom?"

"Where is the bedroom, she asks. My dear, it's right next to the so-called living room. My mother gave me some hideous furniture, and Minnie gave me Uncle Charlie's piano, and I bought one white couch, as every New York apartment has to have a white couch. Frieda will probably end up sleeping on it unless I can come up with something else. No oriental rugs, Missy." He

smiled. "It's not artistic either. The sole advantage of that apartment is that it's mine."

"You own it?"

"I bought it after 'Tollgates,' when I had some cash. The place
does have wonderful light. That's about all."

"And what are you going to do when you get back to the city?"

"Well, I'm going to try and get a couple of demos made of
some songs I wrote this summer. Remember 'You at Noon'?"

"Oh yes," I replied.

"And I might have to go to California for a bit. First, I'll see
where I can go with those songs, and I'll finish the tapes for the
score your father asked me to do. And my agent, Al Donnelly,
wants me to play a gig at some uptown place for four weeks. But I
don't think I'll do that. I don't like that every night deal."

"It's just that I can't quite imagine you in New York. How you
are there. I'm only used to you here."

He held out his arms and I went over to him and crawled in.
"Oh, Missy, I'll be back. I'll be back in fact in ten days or so, to
pick up this dog, and then I'll try and come up once in a while.
I'm not walking off the face of the earth."

"It feels like you are."

He gave me a little kiss on the forehead, then got up and
walked toward the fireplace. "Mind if I put on another log?" He
was fidgety, I felt he wanted to tell me something, but I was quiet
(for once) and let him find his words. At last he said, "What happens to me for the next little while is not important. It's what
happens to you, Eva. You've got to prepare yourself for, well, for
just about everything. Birth, death. I have a sneaking suspicion
that this hasn't all quite sunk in with you yet."

"I tend to practice avoidance politics."

"Well goddamnit, don't do it anymore, baby. Look things
squarely in the eye. You're going to be caught badly in the end if
you don't."

"I know that, Billy, I really do. Everything seems suspended,
because of Mother's situation—"

"Oh no, don't use that as an excuse, Eva. You can still make
plans, you just have to be prepared to alter them. Where are you
going to live, for instance, when this baby is born?"

"Well, I guess in Riverdale, for a while . . . until I'm not needed."

"You'll probably always be needed; watch out for that. Do you want to take a place of your own, do you plan to stay around New York, are you going to come back here?"

"I don't know."

"Well, Eva, you'd better think about it. You've come from a world where things are done for you. Now you're going to be on your own. Are you ready for that?" I felt like someone caught without an answer in a classroom.

"Billy, I promise you, I'll get ready for it."

"Well, that's encouraging, Eva." He smiled, and nodded in that familiar way. "I'd like to leave with the feeling that you're paying a little attention to practical matters."

"Billy, you must understand that while my mother's alive my first thoughts have to be for her."

"But you don't know how long that will be."

I repeated slowly, "I don't know how long that will be."

"There's a chill in the air, Eva. Summer's over."

We sat by the fire for another hour or so, close together, remembering pleasures and funny moments from the past. The light cast by the fire made us look pink and innocent; we whispered, except for when we forgot to, as my mother slept in an adjacent room. It was late and an early boat awaited him in the morning, but Billy seemed reluctant to go. Although we sat whispering and giggling like happy campers, I felt a singular dread, an apprehension, as if I were about to be cut off from vitality, from blood supply. Let him go soon, I thought to myself, while I am still able to appear buoyant and self-contained.

"Look, Billy, if there is a crisis about Frieda, I suppose I can take her for a while."

"No, I wouldn't do that to you."

"It's a bona fide offer."

"No. I'll leave you with something else though, Eva. Let me go get it. It's out in my motorcycle. Then I've got to leave."

I stood in the kitchen, waiting for him to come back. Stars dotted the sky, the moon cast a bright glow over the meadow, it all looked like a stage set, like the opening set for one of my father's best musicals, *Starry Night*, which ran for three years, a wonderful story about some sailors in the Mediterranean, and yes, the boy gets the girl in the end. How will my scenario end? I whispered to myself, Please, dear God, don't let him just wander away from me before I've had a good crack at him. Let girl have a *chance* to get boy in the end. I still felt the knot in my stomach.

"Here you go, Missy." He seemed to be holding a square box, like a tool kit.

"What's that?"

"It's a tape deck. Now you just cozy up with this in the evening, and push this on button here, and you'll hear some mighty fine music."

"Oh, I see."

He held it up to me, a twinkle in his eye. "You didn't expect a family broach, I hope."

"Mercy, no."

"Here you go, kid. I'll just leave it right here on the kitchen table."

"Please put your arms around me for a minute, Billy. You can even kiss me." He kissed me and I felt every part of him up against me, his tongue on mine. His hands held my face.

"Hang in there, Missy." He held me for another minute. Then he was gone. Seconds later, I heard the motorcycle move down the driveway.

I sat without moving at the kitchen table. Now he was off to New York, to his apartment on 104th Street, to Al Donnelly, maybe to his old girl friend, to his world, and though he promised to be back and surely would be, it would never be the same. I wasn't able to find the energy to move. Even though our parting had been graceful, as things are with Billy, I still couldn't seem to put it behind me, get up, and go about my business. I've got you under my skin.

The light in the bedroom went on and I heard Mother stirring, heard her cough a couple of times, and the faucet run in the bathroom for a minute. I held my breath. Don't let her come out, I prayed, for one of her little night walks, of which she had had many recently. I just wasn't up to it. "Why are you up so late?" she would logically ask. "Why are you sitting there?"

Mercifully, she returned to bed, I heard her cough once more, and the light went out. I still didn't move.

The tape deck, looking now like a tin suitcase, seemed to say to me, Get up, push the button, see what Billy wants you to think of as great music. Quite typical of those egocentric musicians to leave a tape deck, surely of his own songs, as a parting gift. Well, let's see. I rose, gripped the thing, poked the fire for its last remaining hot coals, and went to my room. I undressed slowly, put a T-shirt on under my nightgown to ward off the chill, I wove my hair in a pigtail (a habit, not a necessity), and caught a glimpse of myself in the mirror. Do I look like someone's mother? No, ma'am. At least not yet.

I pushed on. Nothing happened. Could I have pushed the wrong on? Then I heard a twinkling sound. Yes, of course. That's me, on the harp! Then the piano, yes. His piano. And then the harp again. "Straighten Up and Fly Right," back and forth, first me, tweaky, frail, accurate, then Billy, taking off in response, straighten up and fly right. I let it run through, then pushed rewind and played it again. My harp, overshadowed by the rambling, thumping piano, still seemed independent and clear. It was coming through. Let me come through that way for the next little while, I whispered. Maybe I can even straighten up and fly right. I'll have those loud vibrant choruses of Billy's to listen to and maybe that will help. I punched off. Time for quiet.

I got into bed and pulled my legs up so that the upper part of my thighs touched my good-sized stomach. It was a harmonious sensation and made me feel circular, like a slightly oblong ball. I put the tape deck next to me on the pillow, pulled the covers up over both of us and, aware of how absurd I looked, closed my eyes. I'd done this often as a little girl; in moments of doubt, fear, I'd pull the blankets up over me and shut the problem out.

Tomorrow, I thought to myself, tomorrow I'll come out fighting. Tonight I'm taking cover.

XIV

"I don't see how you're going to manage alone." Laura Campbell, an old friend and classmate, leaned back in her porch chair, pulled her jacket more closely around her, and shook her head at me. "After all, Robert and I had each other, and we agreed before the baby was even started that we would share in all the responsibilities. We shared everything. We were very supportive of each other; it helped our relationship. That's what parenting is all about."

"Is parenting a real word?" I tried not to sound irritable.

"Well, it's a new word, sort of, but yes, it's a real word, there've been books about it. Did you read *Parenting: Sharing the Joys?*"

"Certainly not."

"We read it, and the book was very helpful to us. We figured out a schedule that worked. Of course Robert only taught part-time, and his department head was very nice about it. Paternity leave, it's called. It's the only way to do it nowadays."

"I feel pretty far removed from paternity leave." Laura was annoying me, but I still was interested in hearing from a new mother. I had begun to feel that I was entering foreign territory ill-prepared. "Go on," I said. "Tell me about your schedule."

"Here's what we did. Robert taught on Mondays, Tuesdays, and Thursdays. I would get up with the baby on those days and get him all changed and Robert would give him the bottle and that awful Gerber's stuff. Then I'd take over for the morning until he got back, usually around one-thirty. Then I'd speed over to the office for the rest of the afternoon, and try and get home by five or so. Then, depending on if the baby took a nap or not, I'd take him for a quick walk and pick up some groceries, while Robert corrected his papers, or whatever. Then on Wednesday, Friday, and Saturday, we'd sort of reverse it, I'd go in the morning, and so on."

"And what did you do on Sunday?"

"On Sunday, we'd try to spend as much time together with Ben as possible, both of us, we'd go to the park. It's important to do things as a whole family, as a unit. Sometimes we'd take him on our backs. It's worked out very well."

"I'm tired just hearing you talk about it." I was giving up any pretense of good humor and descending into crabbiness.

"I'll tell you something, Eva. It brings you closer together, it really does. Robert and I did not always relate that well to each other before Ben was born. By understanding what was going to be involved from the very beginning, we avoided what could have been some real crises. You know, Robert is quite isolated, in many ways, and doesn't, or hasn't always expressed himself very openly. But through this year, neither of us felt victimized, we both respected each other's professional needs. After all, why should women suffer deprivations professionally, and have to bear the baby too! Right?"

"The next thing you're going to tell me, I bet, is that you've arranged to have Robert bear the next baby."

"Well, it would be fairer, wouldn't it?" She did smile. Dear Laura, the girl who used to chew her pigtails, a gifted but unsmiling tennis player who had a crush on my brother James for years, Laura now sat with me on this crisp October afternoon in Chilmark, looking very handsome in her slacks and tweed blazer.

"How's the baby?" I asked.

"Who, Ben?"

"Yes, Ben."

"Fine, wonderful. He has a very good relationship with both of us."

"An equally good relationship? With both of you, equally?" I shifted my bulky frame in the deck chair, trying not to scowl.

"Well, actually that's very interesting," replied Laura, and started off on what seemed like a twenty-minute answer to my set-up question. I stared off toward the meadow ahead, now past its autumn prime, and thought to myself, How am I going to manage? Who the hell am I going to *relate* to? Since Billy's departure some weeks back, I had made myself repeat, over and over again, There, he's gone now, so don't get used to the idea of him, don't imagine that he's really here. Billy is the kind of man who, when you're with him, makes you feel that you'll always be with him, one way or the other. I had been invaded recently with images of myself having the baby alone on a mountain, sort of like Ingrid Bergman in *Stromboli,* or driving myself to the hospital in the middle of the night, and then suddenly Billy would be there, at the entrance to the hospital or struggling up the mountain after me. No such luck, Little Eva, I cautioned.

". . . And anyway, it really has worked out very well, Eva." Laura smiled.

"Was Robert present at the delivery? I'm a little nervous about the whole business."

"Oh, of course, he did all the exercises too."

"What exercises?"

"The breathing exercises, and others too, stretching the abdominal muscles."

"You mean at the delivery then, Robert . . . was there the whole time?"

"Absolutely."

"What did he do all that time?"

"Why he just breathed along with me, just the way we did in the class. We just breathed together."

"For four hours?"

"For eight hours."

That did it for me; I proposed that we go inside and join my mother, who was awake from her nap. Nostalgic as I might be for a loved one to be with me at the climactic moment of the birth, the thought of someone panting alongside of me for eight straight hours caused me to think that, after all, I'd be better off alone. I resolved to be better humored with Laura.

We had plenty of visitors during October. Opa was in and out but managed to spend a good part of the month with us. However, he said that in November his production was going into preliminary rehearsals, and he counted on me to keep things going. I thought to myself, Only *she* can keep things going; I am just a kind of caretaker, manager, or perhaps the social director on a cruise ship. Mother was at center stage, she caused the forward motion.

Thus far she had held up pretty well, although now, toward the end of each interval between chemotherapy treatments, she seemed in considerable pain. Nonetheless, she provided the momentum of those days. The spacing of visitors to the summer house was something we did together. The choice of who, and how long, was hers.

"Let's ask Rudi and Myra for Tuesday and Wednesday, rest up on Thursday, and pick up the Keppels on Friday night."

"That sounds fine," I agreed, like a true secretary.

She went on: "And we mustn't forget to call Aileen Thompson, she's such an old friend. Maybe we can squeeze her in toward the end of the month."

"James is coming next Monday for a week."

"I haven't forgotten." She smiled. "I haven't forgotten anyone."

In her mind were distilled the memories that counted, and from them, the people she most wanted to see—the former student who rose to be literary critic for a New York magazine, the now-retired publisher of her first collection of essays, a couple of old theater friends, some of Opa's gang who had sort of moved over to her through the years.

Although it was a hectic time, measured by the number of trips to the boat and the size of the bills from the Up Island Market, it was oddly uncomplicated. People who came knew what they were coming for; to say good-bye before the fact. To see Elizabeth Wiltshire, very ill, yet somehow at her best, in her favorite place. Short visits, careful agendas, yet, to my mother, visibly satisfying.

"Ted Greenspan is really a marvelous fellow, and such a good writer. He still hasn't quite learned how to finish things, how to bring his work to term, so to speak. I told him that, gently, last night, and he seemed to get the point," she mused. It was a time when everyone seemed to get the point; a busy but clarifying time.

I felt too that no matter how silly my role in all this seemed (she called me Eva's Taxi Service), I was doing right by her.

Meanwhile my figure continued to balloon outward, giving me something of the appearance of a kangaroo. When Mother had gone to bed, or was taking a nap, one or two of the "old friends" cast of characters would corner me.

"When is the baby due?" asked Aileen Thompson, a backer of many of Opa's plays and an old friend of Mother's.

"January."

"I can't imagine why you're doing this, Eva. Why didn't you get an abortion, for heaven's sake. Do you want to have an illegitimate baby?"

"I want to have this baby. I don't think of it as illegitimate."

"You don't, huh? Well, everyone else will, I assure you."

"We'll survive."

"People still look into each other's background very carefully, despite the fact that social standards have relaxed a little. If it's a boy it may not be as serious, but if it's a girl, she might not be invited to some of the best dances."

"We'll survive that too, Aileen, either way."

"I know you will, darling, I'm just worried about you."

"Don't worry about me."

Ted Greenspan, disheveled, bespectacled, loyal, said, "I'll find you a husband, Eva. I know a lot of very nice guys, I really do."

"Oh, that's all right, Ted, that's very nice of you, but well, I'll be all right."

"You can't live in New York, alone, with a baby."

"I may not live in New York."

"Where else is there to live?"

"It's a big world, Ted."

"I'll find you a husband anyway."

Dorothy Keppel, cigarette holder, dark glasses, teeth clicking. "You're insane, Eva. You know that, don't you?"

"Well . . ."

"You're insane, but no more so than the rest of the population."

"I actually don't feel insane."

"Neither do they."

Mother liked to take walks, when her strength permitted and the weather was good, so we'd drive to Squibnocket or South Beach without boots on and squoosh on the sand. On a clear day, at midday, it felt quite warm. We picked a few rose hip blossoms and toyed with the idea of making jelly. The wind blew up occasionally, gusty, a little cold, but not mean.

Opa was concerned that the house was cold, which it was, and since it was not possible to go through the serious effort of really insulating the place ("An energy audit is hardly what we need at this point," noted Mother), he bought several room heaters, which he placed strategically around the house, in the bathroom, by Mother's desk. We tripped over them and their cords at least twice a day, causing Mother to remark crossly, "I'm not going to die of cancer, Eva, I'm going to die tripping over one of these bloody heaters." When Opa left, we put them back in the closet and threw an extra log on the fire.

Billy wrote a short letter once, and he did call occasionally, but he sounded far away, caught up in an entirely different world. Once he sent me the score of a song he had written, with instructions that I try to play it on my harp, which I did, but it didn't sound like anything. Different paths, he had said. It felt very different to me. His promise to come back and pick up Frieda had not materialized by the end of October. I ran into Angelo, the dog guardian, on the street in Vineyard Haven one day, tugging Frieda along on a makeshift leash.

"Any word from Billy?" he asked.

"Well, he says he's coming down soon," I replied.

"Not soon enough," Angelo snorted.

The fall foliage, never quite the peak experience on the Vineyard that it was in Vermont, came and went quickly, "like a show with mixed notices," Opa remarked.

I took my vitamins and went for solitary walks. As I trudged along the misty South Beach, my sweater wrapped around me, I tried to imagine just who, just who was really inside me; what matter of infant is it whom I've signed on for? If I had a boy, a boy like Neddy, I would feel some kind of confidence. After all, I had played soldier with him, built sand castles with him on this very beach. But a girl? A girl presents new challenges in this day and age, I reminded myself. A girl named—what? Another Elizabeth? I shuddered as I thought of the timing of all of this. The possibility that Mother might die first, leaving me unsupported in the birth of this baby, caused me to pull my sweater tighter around me. How could these two things be happening at the same time? Yes, I reminded myself, I had knowingly chosen this course. One fights death with new life.

I headed home and decided to attempt to sort out and organize a few of Mother's old newspaper articles and essays and try not to think too much about what lay directly ahead of me.

"I'm putting these articles in groups by the year they were published, is that okay?" I asked Mother.

"Oh, darling, for goodness' sake, throw all that stuff out." She waved her hand, duchesslike, from the armchair.

"No. Opa would be mad if I did." Whether he read all of her writings was in question, but he would never allow anything to be thrown out, particularly now. "I want to read them too."

Stacks of magazines, typed articles, rewritten, untyped articles, clippings, all had been pitched in the bottom of her closet for almost twenty years. At night, after Mother went to bed, I sat in her armchair, poking through the boxes, reading what caught my fancy.

I asked her, "How come you sounded so angry in some of these things?"

"What are you reading, darling?"

"Well, the pieces in this folder, dated around the mid and late fifties." I held it up for her to see.

"Oh God. That was just after the McCarthy era. We were all mad then. Young and mad."

"You seemed to be mad at everybody."

"It just spilled over. Look and see if you can find a piece I did criticizing Eisenhower. Daddy was furious at me."

"Opa liked Ike."

"So did I later, when I met him."

"All book reviews and columns from nineteen fifty to nineteen sixty are in this blue manila envelope," I announced.

"All right darling, just as long as I don't have to look at any of it."

"Are you sure you don't want to?"

"I'm afraid it will make me nostalgic. I can't afford that now."

One day as we were cleaning up after the last round of visitors, Mother said, "Where do you think you're going to live when the baby comes? Have you given it any thought?"

"Yes," I replied a bit untruthfully. "Well, maybe I'll just stay in Riverdale for a while."

"For a while, of course. But you'll find that unsatisfactory in the long run. Maybe even in the short run. Opa runs quite a show there."

"Oh, I know. I'll have to just get my bearings."

"I've thought about it a bit," said my mother, taking off her glasses.

"And?" I knew she had been storing up something for me.

"Well, Eva, there's no single place that doesn't have advantages and disadvantages. But I think you should try and live in a place that nourishes your spirit. I admit that's easier said than done, and I can see why it might tempt you to go back to New York, because, after all, you cannot cut yourself off from the activity of a lot of people. But I'm convinced that you must primarily look for a place that appeals to your inner landscape, where you like what you see and smell. A place which gives you clean energy."

"I keep thinking that I should be near other people, people I know."

"Yes, but go to a place where you like to wake up in the morning. People will find you. I promise you."

"Trudy said I could come live with her, but that seems crazy."

"That would be crazy. You'll end up sitting with Neddy all the time. Although it was nice of her to offer." Mother had quiet reservations about Trudy, considering her a quick study and a publicity hound, and I could see that she might well be right about such a living arrangement with Trudy for any length of time. "She's a port in a storm, though," I added.

"That's right," replied Mother, "she's family."

Trudy called once, from Dallas, full of peaks and valleys, as she always is, euphoric about her TV panels, worried about Neddy.

"Eva, will you call him?"

"Of course."

"He sounds wistful, and that couple, dear as they are, seem a little flaky to me. He did say they were nice, but that they never go to bed."

"I'll call him. Don't worry."

In that spirit, I phoned Neddy in New York the next evening. "Hello-o-o." The sitter, with a somewhat theatrical rendering of hello.

"This is Eva Wiltshire, Trudy Carmichael's cousin. I'm calling from the Vineyard just to see how Neddy is."

"Neddy. Oh, Neddy is wonderful," she breathed. "Neddy is one of the most marvelous children I've ever known, so bright, so sensitive. In fact I was just saying to Hugh the other night, we would be very lucky indeed to have a child like Neddy of our own."

I shifted. Something was awry. This excitable response smelled of drugs.

"Well, I agree. I love Neddy and always have. Tell me, what do you do . . . I'm sorry, I don't know your name."

"Christine."

"May I call you Christine, then?"

"Oh please do, of course, I wish you would. I can't stand my last name, and I'm not even going to tell you what it is, but I love Christine and I hope everyone will call me that."

"What do you do, Christine? I think Trudy said you were a writer."

"Yes, I am a writer. I've had one book published, a novel, and I'm sweating bullets over another. I don't know why people write; sometimes I think it's a form of masochism, really."

"And what about—Hugh?"

"Hugh is a psychologist. Group therapy."

"Christine, has Neddy been all right in his mother's absence?"

"Neddy is so happy. So wonderful to be around. Neddy is a most unusual child."

There was the kicker. This woman was clearly completely spaced out. Neddy is cute, but he is in no way unusual. I felt my arms and back muscles tighten. If Neddy is in trouble, I must be cautious.

"Tell me, Christine, has he been getting to school on time and all?"

"Of course, do you think we wouldn't get him to school on time?" Her voice was high, shrill. "Do you think we're irresponsible? I mean, after all . . ."

"No, of course not. Kids are sometimes slow in the morning, that's all."

"Not Neddy. He does everything perfectly."

"Has his grandmother been to see him?" Aunt Polly was a nervous, daffy, but devoted grandmother.

"Yes, and she's coming again tomorrow. They're taking him to the zoo."

"They? Mr. Wiltshire too?" Uncle Bob could be a strong man in a crisis.

"I really don't know," she replied irritably.

"May I speak to Neddy?"

"Of course, of course, why shouldn't you?"

My mind raced. Bob Wiltshire, my father's younger brother, wouldn't recognize marijuana or cocaine if he sat on it, but he could be counted on to detect suspicious behavior and act firmly. He and Aunt Polly could keep Neddy for a day or two, while Trudy winged it home to straighten things out with dear old Christine and Hugh. If . . . if . . . it was still just a hunch.

"Hi, Eva." Neddy's voice was eager, breathless.

"Oh, Neddy dear, are you all right?"

"Yes, I'm fine."

"What are you doing now, Ned?"

"Watching 'The Brady Bunch.' "

"Do you like your sitters, answer yes or no."

"Yes."

"I'm so glad. They sound very enthusiastic about you."

"They never sleep," he whispered. "They're always awake."

"They must sleep sometime."

"Well, once in a while."

"That's unusual, Neddy, but people have different habits, you know. But they're nice to you?"

"Oh, yeah."

"What are you doing in school, Neddy?"

"Indians."

"I see." I could see him, with his teeth sticking out, eyes wide, and the cowlick on the top of his head, which sent strands of hair straight up into the air; we called those wisps his "Pluto."

"Neddy, are you going to see Grandma tomorrow?"

"Yes, she's taking me to the zoo."

"All right, honey boy, go back to your TV and I'll see you soon, maybe very soon."

"Can I visit you?"

"I hope so. We'll try."

I called Uncle Bob Wiltshire in Summit and tried to convey my concerns to him in some detail. Aunt Polly went into a tailspin, insisting on roaring in there that night with the police, but Uncle Bob's cooler head prevailed. He had not planned to go on the zoo expedition, but now he agreed to cancel his golf game and go along.

"What should I look for, Eva? They sound very nice on the phone, and Pol says they're very presentable-looking."

"Watch for a wide-eyed, glassy look and excitable talking. Now, maybe just tonight she had a bit of marijuana and was feeling the effects, and after all that's not dangerous."

"Mighty hard to understand, though, why responsible people would smoke something like that with a young boy in the house."

"Neddy has told both his mother and me, on separate occasions, that they never go to bed."

"And what does that mean?"

"That they may be on something stronger, like cocaine."

"What is this world coming to, Eva?"

I broke in quickly, to catch Uncle Bob before he started in on that track. "Observe the state of the apartment, Uncle Bob. Really case the joint, and scrutinize them, as you would a company applying for a loan."

That struck the right note, and Uncle Bob Wiltshire, now pointed in the right direction, took the bit in his mouth. "You can count on me," he vowed. And I did. We agreed that he would call me with his conclusions right after they'd been to the apartment, and we'd make a decision then.

I called Trudy immediately in San Francisco and was told that she was filming, so I left a message for her to phone me at whatever hour she came in. I felt queasy. Maybe I am creating a problem, put off by a verbose, flaky writer, who might have a heart of gold. But that staying up all the time . . . it sounded suspicious. Cocaine is dangerous, Neddy is precious, it is a chance I have to take.

At four in the morning Trudy called, and we had a hysterical exchange, in which I finally managed to calm her and get her to agree to do nothing until Uncle Bob returned a verdict. We all planned to stay by our phones the next morning, with a series of contingency plans. I sensed that, if it became necessary, Neddy would end up with Mother and me on the Vineyard, as Aunt Polly could never absorb him for more than a day (all those antiques), and Neddy didn't like it there much himself.

Again, I pictured his face, his Magic-Marker stained hands, his pants which usually hung low on his tiny frame. I can entertain him, it might be fun, and Mother didn't seem to mind the idea. I tried to get back to sleep.

What if I have a little boy who looks just like Cal? What if every time I hold the child I feel like I'm holding Cal? I have to remember, as James had warned, that I'm not having Neddy. In my fantasies, all babies were like Neddy, round, button-nosed, bald, and all children were like Neddy, bright, whimsical, with his Pluto.

Mother and I paced around most of the morning waiting for the phone call from New York. Mother had always been generous toward Uncle Bob (partly because Opa wasn't), and she had always admonished us to be "extra nice" to him, presumably because of the cross he had to bear in the person of his idiotic wife. "It's no wonder Trudy has taken off on this feminist tract," remarked Mother. "Anything to put distance between herself and her mother." Aunt Polly was a traditional upper middle-class housewife, who specialized in shopping.

At eleven-thirty the phone rang. "Well, as far as I'm concerned, that couple is as high as a kite," Uncle Bob announced. "They were perfectly nice, you understand, but the woman, Mrs. Pringle, talked excitably the whole time, and the man just seemed to stare. We stayed quite a bit, just to be sure. Pol discovered that Christine Pringle's mother went to the same boarding school Pol did in Washington. Now isn't that something? From a nice family, too.

The living room was cleaned up, but the kitchen was a mess.
Worse than Trudy."

"Where is Neddy now?"

"He and Pol went to the zoo, and I'm in my lawyer's office."

"I recommend that you simply call Christine at the hour you
were going to return Neddy to her, and tell her that you're taking
him to Summit for the night. Nothing more."

"All right. I don't know how long we can keep Neddy. You
know how nervous Pol is."

"I'll call Trudy in San Francisco now. She said last night that
she'd get on the next plane if it looked like there was a problem.
She was very upset."

"Well, as far as I'm concerned, there's a problem, Eva."

"We'll let Trudy deal with Christine and Hugh. You keep
Neddy happy for the next two days, and then if Trudy wishes, she
can send him here to me for the next couple of weeks, while she
finishes her TV project."

"That's nice of you, Eva," said Uncle Bob, clearly relieved.
"But what about his school?"

"He can skip school for a couple of weeks. He's studying Indians. I'll tutor him about the Gay Head Indians. Don't worry, he
won't miss a thing."

And so it was that two days later I flew to La Guardia Airport
in New York to meet Trudy and Neddy, and to bring Neddy back
with me. Dazed, bleary-eyed, they had the air of refugees. Trudy,
usually elegant in her designer jeans, looked like she had been
caught in a snowstorm. Neddy's Pluto stood up even more than
usual. We hugged each other wildly.

"Oh, Eva, imagine, they were so highly recommended to me,
she's such a good writer, he's a psychologist, they seemed so nice."

"They *were* nice. They just liked cocaine, that's all."

"I just grabbed those clothes of Neddy's, I don't know what I
have here. Please take him to Brickman's and get him what he
needs, and send me the bill."

"Don't worry. I'll take care of him."

"I know you will." Trudy began to cry, Neddy began to cry, so I
began to cry. Why not?

"I don't know how to thank you, Eva, but I'll find a way."

"It's okay. Go get your plane now, quick."

Trudy was off, hair flying, back to the Coast.

Neddy and I had some time to kill, so we headed for the snack bar.

"Well now, you see," I told him, "you're going to get to visit me after all."

"Boy, am I glad I didn't have to stay at my grandmother's," he said, sipping his Coke.

"Neddy, your grandmother loves you, but she is very nervous. And those sitters, Christine and Hugh, they liked you too, but your grandfather didn't think they were the right people to take care of you."

He paused for a minute, pointing his straw in the air. "They were queer," he proclaimed. "Eva, you know what I was wondering?"

I braced myself. Clearly this was a moment when he might want to reveal some of the concerns he'd stored up over the last weeks. I leaned forward. "What, Neddy, tell me."

"Do Indians wear underpants?"

"What?"

"You know, the Indians we've been reading about in school, in the pictures they just have this cloth around them, and I was just wondering, did they have to wear underpants?"

"Well, actually, Neddy, I don't think Indians did have to wear underpants."

"Okay." We ordered more french fries and some ice cream. Neddy, though clearly exhausted, seemed to be enjoying himself.

"Ned, if I ever write a book I'm going to call it *Do Indians Wear Underpants?* That's going to be the title."

He smiled. "You write it. I'll read it."

XV

November wasn't substantially colder than the previous month, but it rained a lot, mostly in the mornings, and the road to our house began to sog up and develop the traditional parallel ruts and soft spots. It wasn't exactly bleak; just a betwixt and between time, not cold enough to seem like winter, yet the fall colors and clear days were certainly over.

I watched my mother carefully to see if the presence of a peppery seven-year-old child in the house was disturbing her. The first morning Neddy fell off the back of the couch, to no ill effect, but she seemed more easily startled by this than she would have been a year ago. As we installed Neddy up in Adrian's room, Mother whispered to me soberly, "Please be sure, Eva, that Neddy doesn't touch any of Adrian's shells." That seemed a near impossibility to me, so I transferred him immediately to James's room, with its dank tennis clothes smell, where he seemed equally happy. One day, I vowed, we're all going to have to stop being so afraid of Adrian. Not only for our sake, but for his.

Neddy bounced around the house like a Fresh Air child. He built a fort in the corner of the living room, I took him for walks on the beach, we outfitted him in Vineyard Haven, and I bought him a book on Indians. Mother dusted off an old Parcheesi set, dating back to my childhood, and she and Neddy played every evening after dinner. On balance, she seemed pleased to have him; we both needed the slight relief from each other that a third force, even a small one, provided. Our guests were thinning (by design) and I was quite pleased to have his company as we spun all over the island, doing our chores.

On the way home from the market one day he asked, "If Aunt Elizabeth is so sick, why doesn't she stay in bed?"

"Well, she's not really that sick."

"Just medium sick?"

"I guess so."

"She walks funny sometimes."

"It's because she's stiff, and she has pains in the lower part of her back."

"Even if she's going to die, I still like her."

This seemed such a pure thought to me, so free of artifice, so innocent, that I told it to my mother. She smiled. "I'm fond of Neddy," she said. We made a pretty good trio.

But our trio was soon to become a quartet.

On November 7 Billy left New York for the Vineyard, to deal with Frieda and visit me. He stopped in Woods Hole to pick up his motorcycle, which he had stored there, and made a dash for the late afternoon ferry to the island. We'd had some rain and fog that week and the boat was delayed, so Billy got to the island around dusk.

There is a sharp curve on the road to Chilmark, just past a graveyard entering Tisbury. Many times I'd rounded it too fast; down a slight hill, sharp curve, up the hill again. The road was rain-swept and slick as he headed into this curve. The motorcycle skidded, managed to stay up, and angled for just long enough to turn itself around to face in the opposite direction before it keeled over on Billy, pinning his right leg underneath the front wheel. Had he been going faster, he would have been thrown off; in this case his caution proved damaging. He lay beneath the front of the bike, his shoulder twisted, his right hand bleeding badly. His predominant fear was that an oncoming car would simply run over him.

"You can go in now."

I moved numbly toward the treatment room door. There seemed to be two figures lying on tables, separated by the traditional sheet curtain, and in my haste I headed for the wrong one, a young boy with some kind of head injury. "Excuse me," I murmured.

Billy called, "Over here, Missy."

He looked slate gray, his hair matted now, his eyes bleary. I wanted to kiss him. "Are you all right?" I asked, aware of how dumb it sounded.

"Well, I've been better." He managed a slight smile. "They're going to take another x-ray in a while. My shoulder feels numb but what hurts the hell out of me is my hand. Look at it, will you, just unwrap it and tell me if all the fingers are there."

I gently removed the loose gauze bandages. The skin on his knuckles had been almost completely torn away, bone showed through in two of the fingers, clearly a great many stitches would be necessary, but I replied, "Everything is there. You've just had a bad trauma to the skin, but it will heal."

His face seemed to contort. "I had a nightmare that I lost my hand and couldn't play the piano."

I stroked his forehead. "You'll play the piano."

My brief stint as a student nurse seemed to give me a bit of confidence as I spoke. "Your hand may be a mess now, but you'll be playing in six weeks," I told him.

"Oh, Missy," he murmured, focusing on me for a minute. "You've gotten a lot bigger there in the front."

The doctor in charge that night was a revered old Vineyard figure, Dr. Horton, whom I remember seeing a little through the years, as we paraded in and out of his quarters with swollen bee stings, earaches, and in Adrian's case, a fishing hook embedded in his leg. I cornered Dr. Horton in the hall. "I'll stay and help with him," I offered. "I did go to nursing school, I can take a blood pressure and other things."

"Are you this fellow's wife?" he inquired.

"No. A friend."

"Well." He looked at me carefully, with a hint of recognition. "Okay, I can use you, I'm short-handed tonight. Change your clothes, wash up, and then we'll bang his shoulder back into place. That will be very painful. Then you can assist me as I sew up his hand, which will take at least an hour or two. I can't put his leg in a cast until the swelling goes down."

Billy was soon transformed by morphine and a solid whiff of oxygen into a muted but cheerful young man with vastly improved color. In my green nurse's dress, bulging from the front, I leaned over and kissed him. "Oh, Billy, I love you anyway."

"I hope so," he murmured, "big, fat nurse."

"Should I call your parents, Billy? Or your brother?"

"Oh Christ, no," he groaned. "Those are the last people I want to see."

"Perhaps later."

"No, no, Eva; I really have no family, not in the way that you do. My mother drives me crazy, my father and I dislike each other, and my brother's a fool."

"Well, if you want to," I offered stoutly, "you could borrow my family for the next little while."

He smiled. "Just you. Only you."

Opa seemed enthusiastic about Billy's moving to our house for a couple of weeks of recuperation.

"You need a man in the house, in case the car gets stuck in the road," he announced to me on the telephone, "and Billy Diamond seems very reliable to me."

"You must understand, Dad, that Billy has a cast all the way up his right leg, his shoulder is in a strap, and his hand is completely bandaged," I replied.

"He has a head on his shoulders though," he said, as if somehow the rest of us didn't.

"Now you know that Mother is coming up a bit early for her chemotherapy," I said, switching to the dreaded subject. "She's in pain even though she's doubled her Darvon."

"I'll meet her right on time and whisk her in there. Does she seem all right apart from the pain? She's very clearheaded on the phone."

"Yes. She's being brave though."

"Is the house warm enough? It seemed warm to me last week, but now it's colder outside."

"We're warm enough."

"Ask Bill Diamond to be sure the doors are locked at night."

"Okay, Opa. See you next week." Who did he think had been locking the doors all these weeks?

Billy was installed in my room and I took Adrian's. Fresh from two nights at the Martha's Vineyard Hospital, he did look something of an apparition, slumped forward on his crutches, pale, his hand and fingers bound up like an astronaut's glove. One-legged pants revealed a three-foot cast. Again I watched my mother to see if this newest intrusion upset her in any way, and my conclusion was that it didn't. They talked a little bit every morning, Mother and Billy, mostly about Vineyard matters and household details, such as the need for more firewood, and occasionally he got her to laugh. She had withdrawn somewhat in the past two weeks; she said less and yet did not seem to be busy writing anything. She did read and took short walks, but she moved around the house with a new caution. She's fading, I thought, my heart sinking. She's fading and I'm getting fatter, which one of us is going to meet our deadline first? She seemed to be pulling back, confining herself, saving her strength for Opa's visits and calls. More than being put off by the presence of Neddy and Billy, she didn't seem to notice them. She did make an effort, however, for the nightly Parcheesi game.

So Billy rounded out our household, odd group that we were. No one was more pleased to have Billy there than Neddy. Here was a broad-shouldered man, with a twinkle in his eye, who actually had time for him, and in addition had a three-foot cast to add to his dowry. Neddy drew pictures on it, wrote the names of all his friends, added Scotch tape where he felt it was needed, and looked up, in rapt admiration, to a man who had been "smashed up" while on his motorcycle. Billy enlisted Neddy to help him carry things around and to serve as an aide in all matters of dressing, as Billy did not have the use of his right hand. Neddy responded like a child in love. "Want me to get something for you, Bill?" "Well, sure, why don't you bring in another log for the fire." Billy taught Neddy how to use a tape deck, Neddy taught Billy the rituals of his Star Wars Action Figures. It was a fair exchange.

We sat up, Billy and I, after the others had gone to bed, and huddled by the fire.

"I think I prefer you *not* pregnant," he said one evening, after looking me over.

"Well, Billy, I don't intend to stay this way. I felt the baby kick yesterday. A solid kick. That's got to be a good sign. It will only be seven or eight weeks now. I hope."

"You'll have a baby all your own then, Eva. It's hard to believe; I still haven't . . . taken it in, I think." He looked momentarily wistful.

"Don't take it in, at least not right now, Billy. Let's just hold the moment. I'm beginning to dread things to come."

"Your mother seems remote, not like she was this summer."

"No, and she was pretty fine in September and some of October too. She's getting worse, that's all. Little by little now. Maybe after next week's treatment she'll be better."

"I won't stay long. I'll hobble out of here in a few more days."

"Oh no, Billy, I love it that you're here. Neddy's happy, Mother certainly doesn't mind, and Dad is ecstatic because he thinks you're the only one who knows how to lock the door."

"Was I supposed to lock the door?"

We drank a little wine, those chilly evenings, since there wasn't much else to do, and we both were intermittently uncomfortable, particularly Billy, who couldn't really get much sleep with his eight-pound cast. So we sat up, listened to a little music, hugged each other when possible, and got sleepy as the fire burned.

I said to Billy one evening as we sat huddled by the fire, "Where is your motorcycle, by the way? Did someone haul it off?"

"It's in the repair shop in Vineyard Haven. I called about it this morning."

"Badly damaged?"

"Not as badly as I was."

"Then are you going to get a new one?"

"No. The alignment is off, but it can be fixed."

"I still think you ought to get a new one. They'll never be able to get it back the way it was," I said with authority. "Repairs of that sort never really work, I don't think."

Billy shifted his cast leg, gave me a quizzical look, and sighed. "It costs too much to get a new one. In addition, Eva, I didn't have any medical insurance, no group plan or whatever. So I'm really in the hole on this one. I'm not sure quite how I'm going to pay for it all."

I was puzzled. "Why don't you have medical insurance?" A rudimentary thing to miss.

"I just don't, that's all." We stared at the fire. How could he not have some kind of insurance? How did he not have some firmer link to his family? Why was he so—at large?

"Eva, do you want to know something that's been on my mind?"

"Okay." It sounded ominous, and I shifted closer to the fire.

"After the baby is born, and other things are settled, what are you really going to do?"

"Well, I—" I started to make a quick response, but he held up his hand.

"Wait," he said, holding me with his eye. "I know you're going to be a mother. I know you will have the responsibility of—whoever this is. But beyond that. I don't want you to use the baby as an excuse to slip back into your father's fold."

"I'm not in his fold."

"Well, whatever you call it."

"I don't call it anything," I responded with a royal sulk.

He looked uncomfortable, and I decided to let him squirm a little.

"You're a trust-fund girl." He looked at me now with a slight smile.

"What's that?" I asked, knowing full well the answer.

"Women with money. Often spoiled, but not always. A real estate guy out in Aspen told me that these women were a solid, recognizable type, particularly to real estate people, I guess. But they're very glad to have them. So is everybody, for that matter. I knew a couple of real fun gals out in Aspen, real good-looking, a pile of money, flying around here and there. In the beginning I guess it's fun."

"Well, why is it bad?"

"It isn't bad, Eva, it's just that because they've never really had to earn anything, then in a funny way they never have to pay for anything. I think it leads to a kind of funny, repetitive existence. You know, after a while they attach themselves to a tennis player or a cause or something. High class drifters. How else can I say it?"

"Do they ever attach themselves to a marriage or a career?"

"Oh sure. Of course. But the temptation is there just to go from event to event, because, well, everything is paid for."

I drew in my breath. Not a minute ago I had thought of *him* as a drifter, unconnected to his family, unprotected from common accidents, now came the not so veiled suggestion that I might be such a type.

"So you think that I might be"—I waved my hand vaguely— "like them?"

"Yes. Might *get* to be."

"Really. It's funny, I was just wondering if you weren't a bit of a drifter yourself."

"Of course. Of course I am. But I have objectives, in fact I'm overrun with objectives sometimes. Obsessive even. Look, it's not a stylistic thing with the trust-fund girls, because their style is attractive. I just don't think it holds up, that's all. Problems come from being underutilized. You have the freedom that money brings, Eva, but there's no power behind it."

"Power? What does that mean?" I tried not to get angry. Macho business.

"In your case, I think you have to learn to earn your own keep. Right now you are on your father's payroll."

"Payroll is not the word!" I jumped up and put a log on the fire with exaggerated urgency. Payroll indeed.

"What is the better word? Who supports you? You're twenty-six."

"Well, of course *he* does. But it doesn't come out of his pocket directly. We get a regular amount, every three months, and it's not all that grand, believe me."

"And it comes from . . . ?"

"Wiltshire Productions."

"Ah, Wiltshire Productions, the great tit on which everyone sucks, you and Adrian and the other one, James."

"Billy, I think you're just jealous."

"That's a logical thing to think, Eva." He smiled. "I don't have any money and I've had to hustle, but struggle is the best thing I have. It gives me a sense of fight, a feel for limitations too, and God knows, at times a sense of foreboding. But also a sense of power, of possibility. Of independence."

"I feel independent from Opa. After all, I defied him on this baby."

"But I don't think you would have had the baby without the dough to back you up."

"Maybe not. But then again, maybe I would have too. But it's true, without Wiltshire Productions, I'd have had to work earlier and harder, and yes, it would have been different. Of course."

"Independence is as independence does. You should go out and find yourself a job, any job. But try and support yourself."

He dropped his leg, encased in the cast, back on the floor and came toward me. "It's better than being a trust-fund girl, Eva. I know them. I watched them. I lusted after them, and admired some here or there, but it's no life. Looks good at first, but it's no life."

"The next thing you're going to tell me is that the best way to learn is from adversity. I can hear it coming." I flopped back down on the couch, in the spot just warmed by him.

"That's just what I'm telling you, Eva."

"Billy!"

"Take my word for it. You know what Kurt Vonnegut said, 'You have to learn to paddle your own canoe.' "

The mention of my beloved Kurt Vonnegut took the sting out of the argument. Paddle my own canoe, eh? I found it hard to stay mad.

After a minute I said, "I'm not sure why anyone would pay me to do anything. Oh, I'm good at helping out, and I suppose I could give a harp lesson to some unsuspecting type, but—be paid for it?"

He leaned toward me now, looking rumpled, calm. "Have you ever tried?"

"Not in the way that you mean. Never because I had to. But I will. At some point." I looked at him directly.

"It's fun. Hard work is fun, Eva. It certainly causes the blood to race a little."

"I thought sex did that."

"They're not unconnected." Billy leaned up against the stone fireplace now, looking serious and a little taller than he actually was. "Paddle your own canoe," he repeated.

"I don't like this sermon."

"It's not a sermon, Eva. It's a warning."

"I like a warning even less." We were silent. Of course, it was natural, it had to be that he would find the exposed nerve, my principal area of doubt, and pinpoint it like a precision dart thrower. What does it mean to be independent? Isn't feeling it enough?

I had often longed for the clarity of a single ambition, a sense of mission or a skill that showed itself early. That makes it easy. When the dust settles, I'll figure out something, somehow I will. Billy is irritating but he's not wrong. Paddle my own canoe. All right, I'll paddle my own canoe.

I decided to press my own inquiry. "Billy, why does your mother drive you crazy, why do you and your father dislike each other, and why is your brother a fool?"

He was ready. "My mother drives me crazy because through no fault of her own she cannot stop talking. My father dislikes me because I haven't done what he wants, and my brother's a fool because he's a sporting goods salesman who lives in San Diego and plays volleyball on the beach all day."

"You're very hard on them."

He shrugged. "You wouldn't like them, Eva. You think you would, because I've seemed so rough on them, but you'd hate an evening with them."

"I might not."

"Believe me."

"Do you ever call them up?"

"Once in a while."

"They must be okay on the phone. It's not like a whole evening."

"My mother's okay. My father keeps asking me when I'll settle down, all that crap." He seemed to shudder.

"Does she love you, your mother?"

"She thinks she does."

"Then is she glad to hear from you?"

"I suppose so."

"I'll make a deal with you." The wine had gone to my head but I spun on. "You call her up, this woman who can't stop talking through no fault of her own, tell her what happened to your leg and all, and listen to her for whatever length of time she wishes to talk."

He roared, "What are you selling tonight, motherhood, charity, dial-one-you-love?"

"As one who is about to lose a mother, maybe a little of all three."

That seemed to sober him. "What's the rest of the deal?"

"You do that," I went on, full of my own craft, "and I promise, after the baby is born, I'll find a job."

He paused for a minute, looked at me carefully, gave me a slight smile. "Okay, Mary Worth, I will now keep my part of the bargain, and you damn well keep yours."

He hobbled off toward the telephone, turned to look back at me, and growled, "Now don't you listen, damnit. You find a long symphony, stick it in that tape deck, put on those earphones, and don't take them off until I'm done." Taking a pillow from the couch, a blanket from the chair, he awkwardly made himself what appeared to be a makeshift bed, kind of like Neddy making a fort. He glared at me until my earphones were in place, then dialed. It was nine forty-five.

Beethoven flowed through my system. I wished Billy could flow through my system. As I started to doze off, I felt a sudden quick ripple of motion inside me, in my stomach, not a kick this time but a turning over. Okay, I'll turn over too. I shifted position, closed my eyes, and dreamed of open fields, of summer. I turned occasionally to check my captive, who was hunched over the phone, propped up on pillows, looking bleary-eyed. I thought about taking Neddy to Menemsha tomorrow to watch the fishing vessels come in; I reminded myself to call James; I remembered the rooftop of the summer's romance, and I thought, We're still holding, still holding.

At ten-forty he stumbled toward me, and I whipped off the earphones. He looked drunk.

"How was she?"

"Fine, fine. I'm exhausted. We went through the whole accident knuckle by knuckle. Christ, how long was that? Must have been an hour."

"Almost."

"I hate to think what the phone bill will look like."

"Never mind," I said grandly, "we'll let Wiltshire Productions take care of it."

He had the grace to smile.

Trudy called breathlessly to say that she'd been delayed by more filming and could we "hold on" with Neddy for another week or so.

"Of course," I answered. "We're not just holding on, we're thriving."

"Oh, Eva, you have such a marvelous life, really, all that good air, here I am tearing around from city to city, unable to get my breath." I let her wax on for a bit. When she wasn't working she was frantic to do so, when she had an assignment, she was then "too tired to talk," although of course she always managed. But I sensed that she was more or less happy, that she had found her pace. "I have to hang up now," she said, winding down, "it's time for my meditation."

"Meditation? I thought that was a fad that had come and gone."

"I'm not interested in fads," she announced. I let that one go. "Talk to you soon."

Mother came back from her treatment in New York feeling perkier (her word). She looked better too, not as pinched as before. Opa, she reported, was ripping right along in his rehearsal schedule and, to her surprise, he had taken on an associate for this show, in fact a team, a couple named David and Noel Larkspur (good stage names), and this duo was doing a lot of the things Opa hoped they would, important things, without pushing him out of the spotlight.

"Very smart of Daddy," said Mother, pulling her sweater around her. "They can take over, Mr. and Mrs. Larkspur, if it has to be. Daddy still has a constant assignment, a place to go at all times."

"He's never had an associate," I mused. "I wonder what it will look like on the program and in the ads and all?"

"F. Lawrence Wiltshire in association with David and Noel Larkspur present . . . whatever it's going to be called . . . It will be fine."

"And they're not the types who are trying to take over or anything?"

"Oh no. Apparently they're far too ambitious to make that kind of mistake. They want to begin out-of-town tryouts in February." She rummaged through her bag. "I have a ten-page letter from Adrian, which I haven't quite gotten through. He's planning to come home for Christmas. The mail is all stacked up at home. Opa forgot to send some of it down."

"Were you tempted to stay, once you were there, in Riverdale? It's so comfortable."

She looked out of the window. The sun was clear this morning, the meadow looked pale gray and yellow. "Another month," she said. "Another month."

With Mother's slight upturn in energy, we decided to make occasional expeditions, all of us, to Oak Bluffs for a movie, Edgartown for lunch, or Gay Head to watch the sunset, all this supposedly to amuse Neddy, but in truth we were all getting a little antsy and needed airing. The jeep remained our only transportation, since my car had lost its muffler.

With our various disabilities, it was not clear at first how we could best arrange ourselves in the jeep. Billy had to stretch out, of course, so he was awarded the entire back seat. Frieda, who had joined us a day or so after Billy's accident, was crouched in the very back. I proposed to drive, put Mother in the comfortable front seat, and squeeze Neddy between us, somehow. However, Neddy wouldn't squeeze. I had no lap to offer at that point, and I didn't want him jostling around on top of Mother, so Billy took him in the back for the first miserable trip, during which Neddy banged his head. So we had to rework the seating so that Neddy could be controlled in the front by me. That meant that Mother drove, which I wasn't sure about, but she insisted (plan two was her conception), and as I protested she reminded me briskly, "After all, it *is* my car." So Neddy and I shared the front seat, pressed against each other like sardines or, as he pointed out, "two sardines, one sardine with a watermelon in front." No seat belt could possibly pass over us, so we just mushed together and held on.

Something seemed to happen to my mother as she drove the car. I observed it at first casually, but then as a consistent pattern emerged, I watched with fascination. She would place herself in the driver's seat, turn on the heat, put on her glasses, and start lurching down our horrendous driveway. Then, as we reached the main road, I would notice a smile on her face, a look of anticipation, a keenness as she began to move down the road at a greater clip. She did not drive recklessly, but she didn't exactly creep along either. We bounced up back roads, grabbed parking places, moved like teamsters up and down South and Middle Roads. This had not been her style before. She seemed to take her health back again as she drove the car.

Having discovered this oil well of pleasure for her, I made a sort of social director's effort to see that we took an expedition at least once, maybe twice a day.

"We are now leaving for a trip to Menemsha to pick up the fish. Everybody aboard," I announced. Neddy scrambled for the car, Mother gathered herself up. Billy didn't much care for these trips in principle, but he sensed the onset of occasional cabin fever, so he hobbled out and hoisted himself into the back seat without protest.

One afternoon I announced, "We are going to Oak Bluffs to buy some liquor. Everyone in the car." Opa was coming down soon and he liked a full bar.

"Can I buy some more action figures?"

"Liquor. Not action figures, Neddy."

"A comic then."

"Okay."

Billy said, "I'd like to stop in Vineyard Haven and check my motorcycle if that's okay. They should be almost done with it."

"Fine."

"I'll drive, of course," added Mother.

"Neddy, you squeeze in front with me," I ordered.

"I want to be in back with Billy."

"Can we leave Frieda for this one?" I asked. "She gets too excited."

"We all get excited," Billy noted.

"Frieda may come too." Mother's decisive voice.

And we were off. A near Laurel and Hardy scene, the quartet
jammed in with the dog, lurching down the driveway for a big expedition.

Billy's motorcycle looked restored, and we all waited a few minutes while he talked to the repairman. "All set," he said, sliding
back into the rear seat.

At Oak Bluffs we bought liquor and other essentials, such as
comic books, potato chips, sardines, *DIRT Magazine* for Billy to
read about motorcycles, paper clips, Magic Markers, and yes, two
new action figures for Neddy.

As we wound our way home on that particular day, I glanced at
all of them and I thought I'd never seen three such happy faces.
Billy was happy because the motorcycle was fixed and didn't cost
too much, Neddy was happy because he was where he was, and
Mother looked happy because—dare I say it?—because she was
driving the car. "You seem to like to drive these days."

She shrugged. "It's fun."

We screeched up in front of Alley's store in Tisbury. "Jump
out, Neddy, and get me a *Times*," she ordered, "while I turn
around." I watched her turn. As she rotated the wheel, she had
the look of a mariner at the helm of a familiar boat; confident,
perhaps even cavalier.

She feels control, I thought, watching her. She feels power and
a return of control. She surpasses pain here, she is not sedentary,
she's moving forward, and for these few hours, she's team leader.
For we were a team, our little quartet, and at the wheel, she was
team leader.

Upon return from these forays, she often would withdraw
again, find her favorite chair, read the paper, stare out the window, wait for dinner, quiet, subdued, sick again. She seemed content to have things out of her hands. I noticed that she ate less
and less.

A persistent fantasy chased me during these days and seemed to carry me off; a fantasy that both embarrassed and sustained me. I dreamed that I was the Mother, Billy the Father, Neddy was ours and the oncoming baby was ours, and that my mother would live forever. In my reverie we did things that *Family Circle* tells us families do: we went camping, made cookies, redid the third floor. Of course the fantasy was full of holes, no mention of Billy's music, or my lack of it, no hint that this nuclear family of my creation might provide frustrations for me, no, it was a fifties fantasy, a backward glance. Sometimes as we all struggled in and out of the car, or made an effort for a reasonably cohesive dinner, I played at it, played Mr. and Mrs. Smith, baby due, mother visiting. While the fantasy was clearly regression in modern day terms, it came in mighty handy as the days seemed to get longer and now repetitious, and the future more uncertain.

The last vestige of the summer tourist crowd did finally disappear, inns, restaurants, and gift shops closed for the winter, antifreeze was administered to cars, serious L. L. Bean apparatus, boots, jackets, vests, appeared almost simultaneously all over the island.

Opa came down that third week in November, for what proved to be a cheerful few days. He and Billy talked at length about problems of the score for the show, Mother rallied nicely, even treated Opa to one of her jeep rides ("She drives like a teenager," he observed), and Neddy seemed entertained by his uncle Lawrence.

And what did I do? I just retreated to Adrian's room and sulked. Opa breezes in, now let him figure how to move that group through each successive hour. I just closed the door and stared out the window. After a while I caught a glimpse of myself in the mirror. Ah, there it is: the arrival of the great whale. I pulled my hair back and tied it in a bun, which added to the imbalance of my small face and huge body. I felt thick, stupid, and spent. I vowed to sleep the whole day.

"What are you doing, Eva?" called Billy.

"Sulking," I replied.

"May I come up and sulk with you?"

"If you can get up the stairs. I'm not coming down."

He had not tried those steep stairs before, but he was at the door in a minute. "Hi. Don't sulk, Missy."

"It's not like me, I know, but I'm kind of enjoying it. What do you want?"

"When your father leaves tomorrow for New York, I'm going to go with him. And Neddy too. Trudy called a little while ago, she's back in New York. Your mother took the call. So Neddy's to go home."

"I don't know whether to laugh or cry."

"Well, there'll be two less of us. Maybe that's better."

I shrugged.

"I wish I could fuck you," he said.

"What?"

"You heard me."

"I look so awful."

"No you don't. I like your sulky side." He smiled.

"Well, there's more where that came from," I said menacingly. He laughed and bumped back down the stairs.

So they're all leaving. After three weeks of care and custody, the boys are pulling out. Our jolly quartet is gone, the car rides won't be fun anymore, no more wine and hugging by the fire.

I went into the bathroom and threw water on my face. Same old face. Same small nose, eyes a little too close together, bold chin, pretty good teeth. Same face, different base. It's no time to drop the ball now, Little Eva.

Frieda was returned for more temporary custody to Angelo. As we drove back toward Chilmark after leaving her off, Billy said to me, "I may go to California in a few weeks, Eva. I'm going to make some recordings. By the time I get there, my hand will have healed, and I may have to just drag this damn leg around in a cast, but I can't let it stop me."

"How long will you be gone?" I felt too many leave-takings were going on, and this one didn't seem to really register with me.

"Oh, maybe a month or two."

"Well, we'll stay in touch with each other, that's all."

"We'll stay in touch with each other—and that's not all," he said quietly.

I stared out the window at the many bare trees, the stone walls, now without any hint of the summer's lilies; the scrub oak looked a little bent from the wind of the night before.

Better to let him go for a while.

Trudy was on the phone and ecstatic. "Oh, Eva, I don't know how to thank you. Neddy had such a good time, he seems so, so restored somehow. He told me everything you did, all those little trips, how you read his Indian book to him."

"He was fun."

"And Aunt Elizabeth wasn't annoyed by him?"

"She didn't seem to be."

"Would that my mother showed such forbearance."

"They're different types."

"God knows they are—different types. So how long are you going to stay down?"

"I just don't know, Trudy."

After she hung up, I took one of Adrian's huge jackets and wandered onto the porch. The temperature read just above freezing; the night was clear, stars covered every section of the sky. I felt both mammoth, bundled in this ridiculous coat, and microscopic, dwarfed many times over by the stars. I wondered, quite simply, how long we could last down here, just the two of us.

She was wearing another one of Adrian's coats, another huge, misshapen fishing jacket. She came out onto the porch noiselessly and stood next to me for a minute.

"It won't be long now, Eva. We'll go in a few more days, maybe a week. I'm almost ready."

XVI

We sat, in various stages of gestation, like hens perched in a row, but in this case the hens were all reading *Vogue* and *Bazaar*. Nine of us, counting me, some more swollen than others, all flushed in the face because the doctor's office was wildly overheated, though it was a warm first week in December in New York.

Mother and I had been back in Riverdale only ten days, and I felt a long distance from the quiet rustling sounds of the Vineyard. The sharp edges of trees without leaves, a pre-Christmas buzz of commerce, and overheated New York offices all bespoke the beginning of winter.

In this particular overheated waiting room, I sensed that all nine of us shared one thought: How much longer is this doctor, on whom we are so dependent, going to make us wait?

In fact, there were two doctors, in association, the clearly senior Dr. Robertson, a kindly and soothing obstetrician, a classmate of my father's, and Dr. Donell, his younger partner. On each of my previous two visits, I had drawn Dr. Robertson, who seemed puzzled by the fact that I was not married and spent an undue amount of time telling me what a great chap my father was at Harvard. This time I hoped for Dr. Donell, for a change of pace. I took another look around the room, checked out a new arrival, and plunged back into *Vogue*.

"All right, Eve. Come this way please. Second door on the left." The nurse summoned me and guided me down the corridor

to a small, pristine examining room. I undressed, put on the paper
smock, and got on the scale: One thirty-eight, up three pounds
from last time. The whale is gaining.

I was now experienced enough in this process to know that just
because I had been assigned to a little examining room all my
own, the doctor wouldn't automatically appear. This was only
Phase Two. So I kept my *Vogue* with me, lay back on the examining table, and continued my article on the "New Slim Look: Slim,
Muscular, Healthy." Long, lithe, athletic women floated by in full
color, in shorts, in gypsy dresses, in gold, in nothing, all resem-
bling Thomson's gazelles. Hold on, Little Eva, you who were neither particularly slim or muscular, your day will come. I closed my
eyes. Am I healthy? I always felt so. A predisposition to colds, a
broken ankle in field hockey, but in essence, yes, healthy (though
perhaps not quite in the *Vogue* way). Recently, surrounded with
my mother's decline and Billy's elaborately done up broken bones,
I began to wonder about my own constitution; perhaps it's my
turn now to have something go wrong, the lottery system.

"Hello, I'm Dr. Donell."

It's hard to manage much more than a smile when you're flattened on the table covered by a piece of paper, but being a good
proper girl, I stuck out my hand anyway.

Bespectacled, fortyish Dr. Donell, with a droopy mustache,
looked like an earnest sixties figure with a white coat. Instead of
his gynecological tools, I could imagine him holding a guitar.
"How're you doing, Eva?" Three points for him for getting my
name right. "Fine, thanks." He took my blood pressure, listened
for the baby's heart, consulted my folder for a minute, poked and
felt here and there, and then pronounced, "Looks okay, everything seems fine." He smiled, a nonprofessional smile. "No husband, huh?"

"Not yet."

"No hurry. Wait till you find the right one."

I felt a surge of warmth toward this virtual stranger. He had
taken off those silly rubber gloves and stood by the side of the
table now, his hands in his pocket, as if nobody was waiting for
him, as if he had nothing to do but talk to me. "Have you any
questions you'd like to ask me?"

I closed my eyes for a brief second and then plunged in. "Well, actually, yes, I was thinking . . . we've had some sickness in our family recently, and I just began to feel that this is such a risky business. Is there any way to tell if, well, if the baby is all right?"

He shrugged. "Did you have an amniocentesis?"

"No."

"You don't need one anyway. Have you listened to the baby's heart before?"

"No. But I'd like to."

"Let me see if I can find it again." He took a large stethoscope, placed the flat end in four or five places all over my stomach. I held my breath. A long minute passed.

"Here you go," he announced, handing me the stethoscope. "Put this in your ears and tell me when you get it." Like a Geiger counter, I thought as he moved the flat end back to where he thought the heartbeat was.

Horses' hooves . . . That's what I first heard, horses' hooves, in a fast canter, the heartbeat, thiddly-ump, thiddly-ump, fast, steady, strong. I laughed. "So fast, an accelerated heartbeat all right!" I remembered a little of that from nursing school. More horses' hooves, more fast drums. I listened for another minute. What a racket! What power!

I would have listened longer, but I felt some obligation to my sisters out in the waiting room. I could hear that pounding well after I returned the stethoscope.

"You can't tell me that's not a healthy baby," he said, putting the instruments away. "Do you feel better?"

"Sounded like the Lone Ranger," I said, a little giddy.

"That's all right, we'll deliver anything. Come back in ten days or so."

That first week we got back to Riverdale, Mother really did seem glad to be home; Opa's constant, loving presence, the warmth of the house, the clear physical comforts, faithful Louise, our cook for fifteen years, it all seemed to cheer her, to envelop her. But a few short days later, she made a decisive retreat to her room, coming down to the first floor only for small periods of time. Either she stopped trying to eat or simply could not. But it seemed to me that she allowed herself to get worse. The new important fact was that her base was now upstairs. She wrote in her journal, read a little, watched a bit of TV, but within ten days of her arrival home, she had a new look about her, a new frailty. Dr. Junot ran some more blood tests, changed her pills and diet somewhat, but said nothing.

I tried to take a hand in the eating struggle. "I thought you liked cream of wheat," I urged.

"I used to." She smiled.

"What about Maltex?"

"Even worse. Just give me some ginger ale." Each meal became a test, a trial. Would she eat, *what* would she eat, did she take any soup from the bowl just returned to the kitchen, did she continue to like Wheat Thins?

It was clear to me, even clearer than before, that the decision to stay down on the Vineyard for as long as possible had been a real saving grace for her. The atmosphere at Riverdale remained insatiably charged and jumpy, but oddly, not fun. Even when this house was quiet, it was noisy, circuslike.

At Aunt Polly's urging, extra help had been put on. It seemed to me that every time I went into a room it was being vacuumed. Opa reduced the phone calls as best he could, but they still came in a steady stream and at all hours. As well, Opa installed his secretary, Lucille, out in Riverdale, so that he could be "on hand." Visitors, uninvited, came by (mostly Aunt Polly), and since Mother was, after all, alert and generous, they were ushered in and out, at times ungraciously, by Opa and me. But we couldn't control for the bores now, as we had, and Aunt Polly, dear woman, did become public enemy number one.

"I already know that baby-sitter—cocaine story by heart," Mother sighed, "but she told it to me again."

"I'll tell her you're asleep next time," I promised.

"Then all she does is sit and talk to me," complained Opa, somewhat insensitively.

"Never mind, I'll see her," said Mother.

James came for a week and she seemed to rally a little. They went for drives (James at the wheel), she ordered some Christmas presents by phone, stayed downstairs a little longer.

"She looks terrible, terrible," James whispered to me, the first night he was home. "She seems to be *shrinking*."

"Urge her to eat," I replied.

Opa dashed around, rushing into New York and back, hovering; his one irritating preoccupation was that we hire a nurse, "to make her more comfortable."

"She's not uncomfortable, and she hates nurses." The nurse idea, I deduced, was to make *him* more comfortable. Every day we had a round on this subject, but I managed to stay ahead of him. She knew, and I knew, that the presence of a nurse would signal the beginning of the end. We simply weren't ready for that yet.

"A nurse would take the pressure off of you," said Opa one morning, trying a new tack.

"I'm all right, Dad, really. I have nothing else to do but sit here and balloon outward." (The sight of me made him wince.) We were already overstaffed, with Louise in the kitchen, the new cleaning woman, Jerome the gardener standing around waiting to drive to the grocery store or do other errands, and Lucille typing away in the study.

On December 14 I decided to send for Adrian. He wasn't due until the day before Christmas, but I thought it would not be fair to him to wait too long, to have her too weak to do anything with him, and besides, Adrian just might be able to persuade her to eat more, to come down more often. Opa was furious.

"Did I agree to this nonsense of sending for Adrian?"

"She likes having Adrian around, and maybe she'll eat more."

"You're acting like some sort of general."

"Preparation for life," I answered, a touch too breezily.

Billy said on the telephone, "I'm leaving for California in a couple of days. I'd like to come out and see you before I go. How about this afternoon?"

"Of course." I hadn't seen him at all since our return from the Vineyard, although we spoke on the phone a couple of times.

"How is your mother? Is she holding?"

"Well, not really. She's gotten worse since the Vineyard."

He arrived in a borrowed car later that afternoon, a windy, cold day. His shoulder strap was off, his hand unbandaged, he now only sported the cumbersome cast on his leg.

"You look better," I told him. "Less like a spaceman."

"I guess so." At first he seemed a bit subdued by the Riverdale excesses. "Do you really need all these pianos?"

"No, but you know my father." Oh, Billy, his Vineyard exuberance gone, all pulled together, he had the look of a young man scrubbed for a dance. He visited Mother for a few minutes upstairs, sat with me in the kitchen for a while, talked to Opa for a bit, exchanged a word or two with James, whom he had never met before.

"How's Frieda?" I asked him.

"Packed and ready to go."

"So you're taking her back to Ace Dukenney?"

"You bet I am. Cargo. One hundred and twenty-four dollars."

After an hour or so, I walked him out to his car, bundled up in an old fur coat of my mother's, as nothing else would cover me.

He pulled a piece of paper from his pocket. "Here are some addresses where I'll be." He looked at me directly for the first time all afternoon and I thought he seemed almost frightened. "Look, call me, call me any time; something's bound to happen around here pretty soon. Please call me and tell me."

"I will."

"I don't know how long I'll be gone, but probably not too long. California's no place for a man with his leg in a cast."

"Let me know too, Billy. Let me know what happens to you."

"Be brave, Eva."

"I am brave, Billy."

"Yes, by God, you are."

I waved to him from the driveway. What a picture I must have made, wrapped in that hideous fur coat, my hair flying, my face red from the cold.

I looked at the paper he gave me.

Ace Dukenney, 451 San Luango Drive, Santa Monica; Steve Markel, 6 Northstar, Venice, Cal.; Nina and Bart Stern, 3490 Topanga Canyon . . .

The names and addresses seemed so abstract, so remote, that I almost wished I didn't have them at all. These names seem to signal our distance, or different paths. Nina and Bart Stern . . .

For one short minute I wished desperately to be free and clear of this whole sideshow, to be slim and carefree and leaving for Topanga Canyon too.

"So that's the new boyfriend," James said as I came in.

"Yes, I guess so." Boyfriend seemed an odd word. "Do you like him?"

James shrugged. "I liked Cal better," he announced. James was not always helpful.

XVII

Yes, Adrian did it again. He arrived four days after my telegram, huge, silent, spooky, his hair now grown out from the summer, a pair of granny glasses perched on his nose, and a beard, all of which combined to make him look like an all-purpose mystic. But things with Mother took an upward turn from the minute he walked in the door. He seemed to lift her up, the way none of the rest of us had managed.

James took off for Vermont, promising to return for Christmas. Opa's rehearsal schedule was very demanding and he felt conflicted about his time. I looked so elephantine that Adrian must have decided to retire me on sight; so quietly, with a tactful and persuasive skill, he took over the care of our mother.

Each morning he made her breakfast, or what he hoped she would eat; Jell-O, Rice Krispies, tea, melba toast. When something didn't work, he made fast substitutions, whole wheat bread, oatmeal, chamomile tea.

Her mealtimes, previously a time of tense preparation and accounting, with all of us putting in our two cents' worth, became his bailiwick.

"You see, she likes corn muffins," he announced triumphantly, "without butter, that's all."

"Good, Adrian."

"And beef broth for lunch, and nothing else!"

The new dietician had a small score of successes in fact. "Nothing with salt on it, obviously," he said, glaring at me.

I didn't care; let him feel triumphant; she *was* perkier. Mother now came down twice a day, during which time Adrian enchanted her with his bag of anthropological goodies.

"Now," he said, leaning over her, "here are those stone rubbings I was telling you about." He spread out a series of the dreariest looking pieces of paper on which could be detected certain markings, oddly patterned.

"How interesting, Addy," she exclaimed. "And these are from Tanzania?"

"That's right. Now check this out . . ."

I'm now sure that if Adrian handed her a plain gray one-inch stone she would murmur, "Oh, how interesting"—a reflex formed over some thirty years, not to be broken now. Nothing he offered for her examination seemed remotely attractive or interesting to me, but what the hell did I know?

"That's just what I was wondering about," she murmured. "You think these really are fossils, you're sure?"

"Oh, absolutely," Adrian declared.

They were off on a pas de deux, oo-ing and ah-ing. Adrian, flushed in the face with excitement, Mother, her glasses dominating her thin face, encouraging him, as always. Let 'em fly, I thought, my nose a little bit out of joint. More power to him, he's made her smile.

Despite his well-known difficulties with Adrian, Opa trusted him too. He returned his martyred secretary, Lucille, back to the New York office and, seeing Adrian so much in charge, spent more time in town.

I decided to plunge into Christmas. A few packages of mail-ordered stuff were stacked up in the hall, looking sparse. By the time the week was over I had smothered the place in boxes, all sizes and shapes. We had planned to tread lightly on this most demanding of holidays, but somehow I just blew it. I bought everything in sight.

"Which one of these bathrobes do you think your mother would like?" asked the saleswoman at Saks.

"Well, I'll just take them both," I replied, "with matching slippers."

What was I coming to? Matching bathrobes and slippers?

More tennis clothes for James, fishing equipment for Adrian, haberdashery of all sorts for Opa, books that no one would read, I moved like a tempest through the department stores. I readily acknowledged to anyone who questioned me that I had lost control. They all seemed a little intimidated by me as I came through the door with my huge frontage, carrying more huge frontage.

In the middle of this frivolity, Curtis called from Cambridge to say that he had a taker for my apartment: "You're lucky to get anyone to rent that dreary place." I had almost forgotten about the whole thing.

"I can't budge from here now, Curtis. If I send you a power of attorney, could you complete the arrangement on my behalf?"

"Sure. Why not?" the dear fellow replied.

"I don't know if I'll ever set foot in Boston again," I told him a touch wistfully.

"Why should you? I'm thinking of moving to New York myself."

"Well, if you do, Curtis, you can always stay with me. That's a firm offer."

"That's nice. Where will you be living?"

"God only knows."

"Well, God only knows is a good address. I'll bear it in mind . . . I'll mail everything to you when the deal's done, which should be soon."

"Thanks a lot, Curtis. Really."

"Merry Christmas, Eva."

"Merry Christmas."

" 'Tis the season to be jolly."

"Jolly and quick. I just want it to be jolly and quick."

At the base of my huge stomach, a pulling, maybe once or twice, but enough to wake me. Must be the result of our enormous grossout Christmas dinner. Louise had staged a sort of last supper, with more and better of everything than ever. Could it be? How would I know labor pains?

I felt jittery. One or two of these tugs doesn't mean anything and besides, this is not supposed to happen for two more weeks. The clock read three-ten. I'll try to go back to sleep and let *it* wake me again if *it* is going to.

At four o'clock I got up, stood up, and walked around the room, watching for the time between pains: there was no rhythm to it now, only what I presumed to be the sporadic fits and starts of false labor. Back to bed, not to sleep, but to wait. It started up again a little before five, different this time, strong and regular.

Can this be happening two weeks early? Please let it be so. In my deadline race with my mother I was afraid she might win. Let the baby come now.

I paced some more. By five-forty it seemed to me (was I cheating?) that I had pains about every seven minutes. I tiptoed downstairs, sat for a few minutes among the wine glasses, dessert plates, and Christmas boxes that lined the living room. I waited for two more jabs, small short pains, then I dialed.

"The doctor will call you back," spoke the answering service.

I looked out the window at the still, pale-gray morning. Dear God, please don't let this be false labor, let it be true, true labor.

"Yes, Eva. Dr. Donell here." Did the phone ring? I was holding the receiver, but I don't remember hearing it ring.

"I can't really tell, maybe I just ate too much, but it seems to be about every seven minutes . . ." I hear myself babble on, almost incoherent, certainly repetitive.

"All right, come on in to the hospital, Eva. We'll just have a look."

I tore into James's room. "Jimmy, wake up. Will you take me to the hospital? I think the baby is coming."

"I thought that wasn't supposed to be for two weeks?" he mumbled.

"I'm lucky. I think I'm going to be lucky. Don't wake the others. We'll leave a note."

"Okay, kid." He shuffled to his feet.

"Don't stop. Don't stop," I said.

"Who are you talking to?"

"The baby. I'm talking to the baby."

Talking to the baby. And that's just what I did for the next eleven hours. I talked incessantly. I asked for more solid, well-timed pains, I spoke soothingly but firmly to the innocent baby: "Keep your head down just like a football player," I urged. I talked and laughed and blanched and held on to the side of the bed; I made atrocious jokes with Dr. Donell; I told the nurses more than they wanted to hear about my short time in nursing school. Constant comment, Opa would have said, constant comment.

"Why do you suppose the baby decided to come two weeks early?" I ask Dr. Donell.

"Eager," he replies. "Just eager."

I watch the clock, count the pains, try to breathe the way they told me, and pray, pray for a safe passage for whoever this was, for a good clean entrance into the world.

At three in the afternoon, dilated, exhausted, and still babbling, I was wheeled into the delivery room and given a spinal anesthetic, which froze me from the waist down. I could now only watch the light bulbs bobbing above, the stirrups, which held my legs, covered by a green sheet, two nurses scurrying about, and Dr. Donell's face, almost all covered with a mask which left his glasses to peer over at me occasionally. Everything danced in front of me.

"Now we have a head showing," he announces, voice muffled. "Only one or two more minutes, Eva."

The one or two more minutes becomes a blur of motion, noise, and pressure, strong pressure, which I feel despite the anesthetic. "What's happening now?" I feel a huge pull.

"Here's your little girl." He speaks calmly, holding up a bundle of flesh.

"Did you say girl?"

"You have a girl child. A lovely little girl. And she seems to have a touch of red hair."

I floated; for five days after the baby's birth, in my hospital room, I floated. I felt high, airy, submissive. I was pleasant, even joyful at certain moments, but pliant. I ate what was put before me, talked to almost no one, fed the baby when she was handed to me, read a magazine here and there, stared out the window.

And I held the baby Elizabeth and just lay quietly on my bed and let a cocoon form around me.

However, I did manage one assertive act; I wrote a note to Cal:

> Dear Cal:
> Yesterday afternoon I gave birth to a little girl, who will be named Elizabeth Wiltshire. She was two weeks early and weighs six pounds and six ounces, so it's hard to imagine what she might have weighed two weeks from now. She seems to have red hair and a funny face.
> I will always take good care of her. Any time you want to see her just let me know. Mother is failing and I will be in Riverdale for a while.
> On the birth certificate, your name is next to the word father.
>
> Eva

I wrote the letter with care. When it was all done, I didn't see how it could have been more bland, less provocative, and still contain what must be significant information to him. I wondered if in some part of Cal, some tiny part, he was moved and flattered by the thought that he had a daughter. Would he want to see her?

Baby Elizabeth, or Baby girl Wiltshire, as she was named on her bracelet, was scarlet in the face, her eyes were mere slits, and a few strands of hair seemed to stand straight up, and yes, it was pale red, our color, Mother's and mine. I looked at her closely, stroked her smooth skin, with its perfect baby smell, tried to get her to open her eyes. She was surely no beauty. Not yet, I said. I lay in bed with her on her every-two-and-a-half-hour feeding schedule at night, and I felt a certain contentment. No, it was not exactly what I had always had in mind, but here we were, just the two of us, not doing badly by day number three.

I wondered, what had all this been about anyway, this fandango of mine over these last months, my insistence on unwed motherhood? No, I was not "making a statement" (surely not!), as one of my college friends had suggested, nor was I leading the light charge away from marriage. It was about *her*, all this drama; about this wee little baby, who pulled on my breasts like a suckling pig, whose cry was more of a croak, but who was a breathing, gasping human being, a little girl who would some day dance, join the field-hockey team, bring innocence back to us. The new Elizabeth.

And the old Elizabeth? I talked to her on the telephone; she sounded hoarse. Her good cheer had a vague, unfocused quality. "I'm sorry," she said, "I'm sorry I can't come in and see you." "That's all right, for goodness' sake. I'll be home in two days." "Good. We miss you."

Did I miss them? No, for those few short days as I lay in my hospital room, I was relieved not to be there. Nonetheless, I forced myself to focus on balancing the requirements of the new Elizabeth with the requirements of the old Elizabeth. At the sound of Mother's voice, I felt an inner alert system come to life in me. How was she eating, did Adrian take her for a drive, has the nurse Phyllis, hired the second I was out the door, found a way to serve her without seeming a harbinger of death? How long can she last?

Despite these and other jarring thoughts (I had decided not to communicate with Billy), I found a new and convenient detachment for those few days at the hospital. The maternity ward swirled around me, but I just burrowed deeper into my cocoon. After my managerial high and my general bossiness at home, after that manic Christmas and my nonsensical babbling during those hours before delivery, now all I wanted was quiet, quiet, and more quiet.

XVIII

Six days after I came home from the hospital, Mother died. Six short, chaotic days, filled with baby sounds and smells, sleepless nights, more medication for Mother and the nurse to go with it. During these days I passed quickly in and out of her room, for she was in real pain and I didn't think she wanted me to stay long. I held the baby up for her approval, like a waiter exhibiting the wine for the evening.

"She's dear, she's very dear," Mother exclaimed before I whisked the child away; I had the impression somehow that she didn't want to hold the baby. Only once, when I held Elizabeth in front of her, did she really seem to focus on her. As Phyllis the nurse stood by, Mother stared at the baby for a long minute—an open look of recognition and warmth. "She looks like—us, Eva." She nodded then, to dismiss us. "That's fine," she murmured.

I myself felt like a disk on a tightrope running between two poles. Baby Elizabeth, shrill, tiny, vital; Mother, subdued, weary, eyes darting. Because of the trumpetlike quality of the baby's cry, her crib was placed in a guest room at the far end of the house. I raced between the two camps, bringing up iced tea for Mother, while readying a breast for the hungry baby. Now I regret, so regret that I didn't stay longer in Mother's room, didn't simply place the baby in her arms, despite Phyllis's hovering. But in truth I didn't think she would die just then. I felt we had another month coming to us, maybe more.

She left abruptly, by our measurement, but clearly not by hers. Ominous talk had begun about moving her to the hospital to "make her more comfortable," to which she replied that she was perfectly comfortable at home. The day before she died, Dr. Junot began to insist, gently insist, that more tests were needed. Mother stayed up later than usual that night talking to Opa, about nothing in particular, but she was calm. Later that night, door locked, she wrote our four notes, arranged them carefully on her bureau, changed into an old, more familiar bathrobe, swallowed exactly the correct amount of sleeping pills, lay back with a book, and allowed them to carry her off.

At eight forty-five the next morning, Phyllis knocked on her door and, alarmed at finding it locked, summoned Opa, who tried the door and then called Adrian. With one hard shoulder blow, Adrian knocked in the door; they found her serene and still, the book open beside her. The doctor later said she had been dead for about six hours.

I remember hearing the crash of the door, hearing what sounded like noise with an alarm factor in it, but my first thought was that it not wake the sleeping baby, who had been up three times that night. Upon hearing voices, I assumed that whatever it was, someone else was taking care of it, and I turned over and tried to go to sleep.

Minutes later the door was open and James stood silhouetted in the light from the hall. "Wake up, Eva."

"Please don't wake the baby," I murmured.

"Mother died last night." I shot up from my bed and stood before him, unable to form words. "Mother is dead, Eva. She did it herself. Pills. She just didn't want to go back to the hospital. She left us notes."

I ran from the room, past James, down the hall, past rooms on the right and left, up the two stairs to her bedroom. Opa stood at the door, pale, forlorn, looking as if someone had just hit him. Phyllis hovered nearby.

At first glance Mother looked as though she might be asleep. I felt her forehead. It was cold. Her face was alabaster white. A towel was tucked under her chin.

"It's all right, Eva. She was peaceful when she died," Opa said gently. "You did everything for her that anyone could possibly do. You did what I could not."

I looked at him, standing now at the bottom of her bed. His face was twisted and sad, his bathrobe hung on his shoulders as it might dangle on a hanger, rumpled, slack. He clutched his glasses in his right hand and a glass of orange juice in the other. "You did well by her," he said, with a slight smile.

I ran downstairs to find Adrian sitting in his shorts and a T-shirt, talking on the telephone to what I presumed to be her doctor. He paused, shot me one glassy look, and went back to the telephone. Jerome stood in the corner looking for all intents and purposes as if he might faint.

I walked back to my room and sat on my bed. From an envelope marked Eva, I withdrew the note she had left me.

> "Eva dear. It is time for me to sleep now. The baby Elizabeth is wonderful. Love her as I have loved you and I'm sure everything will be all right."
>
> Mother

P.S. Try and keep the boys together.

Tears. Tears. With my head in my pillow, I cried with no thought of stopping. I cried for Opa, just now so helpless, for James, for Adrian, whose toll in all this was hard to calculate, for myself, now cut off from her reassuring spirit, for the baby Elizabeth, who would not know her grandmother, and for my mother, who was, after all, only fifty-nine years old.

I was, of course, well prepared for her death in principle, absurdly well prepared, yet as I stood later looking out of the window at the cold and motionless trees and shrubs, I felt in a trance, rooted to the floor, as if my feet and legs were tied down with huge weights. Frozen there at the bedroom window, just staring, I half expected her to come into my room and say, "There, Eva, that went well, didn't it. I beat the hospital gang." She had been so alive on the subject of her death, almost chatty, it was her silence now that seemed so unnatural, so forbidding, final. I would now have to face the fact that I would never hear from her again.

For the next few days we all wandered around the house, addressing ourselves sporadically to funeral arrangements, taking phone calls when necessary, bumping into each other, trying to be nice. Adrian proved to be the strong man, taking care of details that Opa couldn't, dealing with the funeral director. Opa, for his part, was pretty good with the dozens of people who came by to call; James was a reasonable second to him, and I was useless.

Elizabeth had to be fed at three-and-a-half-hour intervals, an improvement by one hour over her schedule at birth. Breast-feeding her had been easy, but from the day Mother died everything went haywire, my poor drooping breasts didn't seem to remember what was expected of them, I lost track of the schedule, and the baby picked up the jittery atmosphere of the house and became erratically demanding, so my new doctor recommended that she be put on the bottled milk, Similac. I was therefore off the hook a little, since Phyllis had agreed to stay on an extra week or so to help cover the night feedings with Similac, so I could try to sleep.

Or so I thought. James felt like talking. James felt like talking at night, and not just a few idle remarks after dinner, but, "Eva, I want to tell you something that I think is really important, and I want you to pay attention." He would lead off with this at ten-fifteen, as I started for bed. He talked about his plans for Mountain Top, made some references to Mother, shared his thoughts on teaching tennis, told me about the tournaments he might enter in the summer, and on and on. What could I do? His need to talk seemed so urgent that I couldn't abandon him much before twelve-thirty or one o'clock, and if Phyllis covered the one-thirty feeding, I would be up again at five-thirty. Ah, well, it was a crazy time anyway, and if James needed me to listen, I'd listen. I felt like a limp rag, but I could listen.

Billy called from Los Angeles, where apparently there had been an obituary in the Los Angeles *Times*.

"I'm so sorry, Eva."

"She went out on her own terms, Billy."

"Not like Uncle Charlie." We had a poor connection, and he sounded another continent away.

"No."

"Now when is the baby due?"

"The baby is here, Billy. It's a girl. Named Elizabeth."

There was a pause. Then: "Good for you, Eva." (Good for you. Hadn't he said that before?) "I thought it was supposed to be mid-January."

"She came early."

"It's a wild time for you, Eva. You hang in there."

Some college roommates and Riverdale friends came by to see me. At that point I was moving on extra adrenaline, and I felt sort of out of it, but I tried to be nice.

The funeral and burial took place on January 10, four days after Mother's death, in a nightmarish procedure that was planned for family only but seemed to include fifty or sixty friends as well. On an icy day, we flocked into the chapel on the grounds of the local cemetery, sat solemnly as the chaplain in charge spoke the few usual remarks, prayers were offered, and Ted Greenspan droned on with loving, well-chosen words about Mother, all of which I tuned out completely. I sat between Opa, who seemed to be following it all with genuine attention, and Adrian, who looked contemptuous and ill at ease. Adrian was dressed like a shepherd, or so it seemed, with a long white and gray poncho, heavy boots, and a band covering his forehead which held back his hair.

"Don't you think Adrian could wear something like a jacket?" Opa had whispered as we left for the service.

"I don't think he has a jacket."

"Why does he wear an old blanket?"

"It's a poncho. I'd leave him alone," I advised, advice that Opa took, for once. Adrian had been cool as a cucumber in the past four days, dealing with all manner of practical details, and Opa was grateful.

James sat nearby in a ski parka, his ski hat clutched in his hand, tears streaming down his face. From James, I thought, we can always count on the most clear-cut, uncomplicated response to things, for which we should be grateful. Adrian and Opa were frozen and controlled, I sat between them in an amorphous, zonked-out state, only James felt the liberty to cry.

Burial took place at a nondescript site near the chapel, and we all huddled together, the wind blowing harshly around us, like sheep waiting to get back to the barn.

The barn in this case was the Riverdale house, where Aunt Polly had taken over the assignment of providing "a little something to eat." Friends and family returned back to the house from the funeral only to find a spread worthy of a Bar Mitzvah. "Who ordered all this food?" demanded James, surveying the rows of platters and fanciness. Aunt Polly had spared no effort here, and with Uncle Bob "helping out" at the bar, the event took on the hue of a cocktail party almost immediately. I am now convinced that people who are cold and sad plunge into food and liquor with even more zeal than everyday merrymakers. Adrian took one look around the room and walked out of the house, for which I don't blame him. Opa, surrounded by sympathetic and loving friends, strung tight with grief, allowed himself ten drinks, which safely put him away for the afternoon, for which I don't blame him either. James locked the door to the upstairs study and turned on the football game. I talked to Trudy for a few minutes, then went up to my room, first to check the baby, then to fade into the walls.

It has all happened too fast, I thought to myself, we needed a little more time. I looked at her note to me again; so brief, so clear, as if she's written a little memo, to be left by the phone. Could I keep the boys together? We were certainly off to a poor start on this day of her funeral, with Adrian taking off, James locked in his room, and Opa downstairs, plastered. Hardly the picture of a united front.

It was five-thirty in the afternoon, and I fell into a dreamless sleep.

I shifted up and down a bit during the night, but didn't really wake up until six o'clock the next morning. The house was quiet. The funeral goers had packed it in and left, Opa and the boys were surely asleep, the baby was covered for the next little while by the ever-cooperative Phyllis, so I threw on my bathrobe and went downstairs. For the first time in weeks, I had nothing to do.

The wind of the last two or three days had died down, leaving a pale stillness to the morning. Nothing moved. The big oak tree in front of our house looked like it was cast in iron. Occasionally a branch cracked, but it was too cold to snow. I wandered around, waiting for a sign of the sun. It felt strange to be alone.

I thought, Where is my mother? Why is she not here? I looked
out of the window with a childish expectation that she might be
coming up the driveway. Why is she over in a cemetery, under the
ground, when she should be here? We're all here, she should be
here. We've lost our anchor. What are we going to do without
her?

A quiet panic began in my stomach and moved up through my
body and arms until I felt I couldn't breathe. How will we get
along, four unlikely family members, without our center? And the
baby, now almost three weeks old, only three weeks old, all mine,
all mine to care for. Who will help me with this baby if you cannot, Mother?

I felt like a spinning top now, a frightened spinning top who
must move in order to keep from falling. I bolted upstairs, threw
on some jeans and a sweater, grabbed James's parka, raced down
to the kitchen to find the station wagon keys, left a note for
Phyllis, closed the front door behind me, jumped in the car, and
headed for the cemetery. Not to stay long, just a few minutes, just
a way of reassuring myself, of locating her.

The twenty-minute trip, through one small town and part of a
parkway, seemed to take no time at all. As I drove through the
gate of the cemetery, I lost my bearings and could not remember
from yesterday which way to turn. Everything looked alike. The
same little hills and crests, the same dots and slabs of gray lime-
stone, the same trimmed paths and paved roads. I thought it ludicrous but possible that I would have to sneak home again, having
missed her grave entirely. But I finally went back to the chapel
and carefully retraced our path of yesterday to the grave site
where we were all massed only fourteen hours earlier.

A lone figure sat by her grave, so complicated in his posture
that, at first, I couldn't tell that it was Adrian. He seemed to be
slumped forward, his arms wrapped around his head. He was sitting on an adjacent gravestone, facing hers, his legs drawn up
under his chin. Adrian. Alone on this freezing morning, doing just
what I was doing, trying, vainly, to get her back, to be where she
was. I turned off the car engine and sat without moving and
watched him. He shifted slightly, tugged his poncho closer around
him, and pulled what appeared to be a duffle coat over his knees.

How long has he been here? Could he have been here all night? No car was nearby. Could he have walked? He put his head up for a minute, stretched, and slumped forward, arms circling his head.

Oh, Addy, we never understood, even those of us who thought we understood, how you loved her, what the nature and depth of your connection to her is. Addy, so quick and steely in these last few days, almost beyond what was necessary, now here you are, huddled and shivering, looking like a rag picker, unable or unwilling to move.

At first I thought to spring from my car and retrieve him, bring him back to the house, talk to him, fix some coffee, be Little Eva. But something about his posture, sitting there on a small slab of stone, wrapped up so awkwardly around himself, caused me to wait. Maybe he'll straighten himself out and see me, and I'll go sit with him, and then we'll ride home together. I waited.

How cruel. She is there, underneath. Adrian is a few feet away, and I am again a few feet away, and yet we cannot say a word to each other.

Adrian shifted again, this time he moved his legs in front of him and reached in his pocket and pulled out some small objects. I couldn't see just what, but I guessed it might be some of his artifacts, some small gnarled rocks, which he turned over and over in his hand again.

He looked around again, but Adrian didn't see me because he wasn't looking for me, or anyone. He was in a world of his own, Mother nearby, the way it always had been.

I started the car, hoping the noise of the engine would not interrupt him. I drove off slowly. He did not look up.

XIX

"Eva, do you know where Mother kept my tuxedos?"

"No, I don't. Maybe in the closet outside the bedroom."

"I looked there . . ." His answer hung in the air, the unspoken part being "please come up and help me find my tuxedo." I waited.

"Please come up and help me find my tuxedo," he called.

I started up the stairs. "Maybe they went to the cleaner. How many tuxedos do you have anyway?"

"Two good ones, one ancient one. Ask Louise if she sent anything to the cleaner recently, will you, darling?"

"Okay. First let's look in the attic."

Another sample from our daily life: "Eva, Mother's old address book had the Cartwrights' number in it under C, can you find the old book without disturbing anything?"

"The green—"

"No, the red one, I think it's somewhere in her desk. Look, but please don't move anything."

That's exactly what he meant too, *don't move anything*. Now four weeks after her death, he allowed not one single object, not a Kleenex, not a nail file, book, or shoe to be moved. Her hairbrush remained by her bed, in the same place as the night she died. Vacuuming was permitted as long as the vacuumer didn't move anything. After Elizabeth and I had gone to bed, Opa often sat quietly in her room at night, although he slept in an adjacent study.

He was reasonably chipper, but confused about household maneuvers.

"Eva, the exterminator just called, to ask if he could make his regular visit tomorrow. But what on earth for? Do we have bugs in this house?"

"I don't think so. I've never seen any."

"Well, why do we have to have the exterminator then?"

"So that we can continue not to have bugs, I guess. Mother must have hired him."

"What shall I tell him? Should I tell him to come?"

"I guess so."

"Well, all right. I hope it's worth it." He seemed baffled, overwhelmed, at the prospect of a visit from the local exterminator, this man who had hired and fired the most expensive performers on Broadway, who lit up the New York theater, who got Billy Rose out of the bathtub to receive his calls.

"If Mother had the service, then there must be a good reason," I assured him.

Louise was not particularly helpful to him; she did cook up a storm, but she did not assume a more executive role, which I had hoped she would. Although she adored "Mr. Wilt," she was just as vague as he was about where things were, preferring to listen to the radio and play with the baby rather than chase around for his tuxedo. "I don't know why we need an exterminator," she threw in. "There's never been a bug in this kitchen since I came to work here." Not helpful.

The ongoing activity of his production and the preparation for the out-of-town tryouts kept my father on a very brisk schedule. Yes, Mother was right, she predicted that it would be a godsend, since his time was taken up and he was in demand.

"I'll be home late," he called from the door. "Want to join me for dinner in town, Eva?"

What no one could predict, least of all me, was the speed with which he incorporated me into the vacant role of his companion-aide-*bonne-à-tout-faire*. Perhaps it was logical. After all, I was *there*, the unwed mother, in need of shelter and warmth after the trauma of my mother's death, and he certainly provided me with safe harbor. In return, he saw me as a dutiful daughter on whom he could depend, wife without portfolio.

"We'll be six for dinner tonight, because the Larkspurs think they can get here after all," he announced. "I assume Louise is up to that."

"Who are the six?" I inquired.

"Ben Malina, Harriet Parker, Noel and David Larkspur, me and you."

Me and you! You and me!

Always sweet, at times deferential, he nonetheless did expect me to fill in, be the sixth or the fourth, find his tuxedo (which I did) and the Cartwrights' phone number (I did that too). I owed him something, surely, and since Adrian and James had more or less disappeared, we did need each other, my father and I. But my role as first substitute, filling in for Mother, made me very queasy.

In all fairness, I was quite comfortable at home. A neighborhood teenager proved able to give Elizabeth a bottle, Louise covered for me on short jaunts, I did accomplish an occasional foray to the movies and a shopping trip with Laura Campbell, but for reasons I could not understand, I was exhausted, much more tired than when I had real reason to be, just a few weeks earlier. Elizabeth developed a tiny smile and a more reasonable feeding pattern, which allowed me to sleep through most of the night. I set up a little L-shaped baby chair for her out on the porch and watched her reach for things and follow me with her eyes. It should have been a respite, this time; Dr. Donell, at my postpartum checkup, declared me "ready to roll" (his words). Where was I to roll to? And with whom?

At night I felt a knockout tiredness, coupled with a new kind of anxiety, a sense of falling into an abyss, sinking slowly into a mattress never to rise again. I had fantasies of someone coming and taking me away, forcing me to recast my life. Was it Billy? No, not really, just someone not unlike him, but without sex, an entity, a beckoning force. Someone who would cause me to resurface, take my place again among other young vibrant American women. Someone who would end my odd sabbatical.

Billy did call a couple of times but I was out, and he left a

number for me to call back in Los Angeles. When I telephoned, a
woman (Nina Stern?) answered.

"Is Billy Diamond there, please?"

"No, no, they've gone out." They?

I wondered to myself, Is it possible that I may never see him
again?

"This is Eva Wiltshire. Would you tell him I called?"

"Sure, Eve." A friendly enough voice.

They? Who is they?

And another question, just as good a one, who is we? "We'll be
there," Opa would agree on the telephone in response to an invitation. "We'll be there." He insisted that I go with him to lunch
in Cos Cob, to visit Aunt Polly and Uncle Bob, to a brunch with
the play's star on Gramercy Park. "It will be good for you to get
out of the house. And I need an escort." That was who we was.

As my claustrophobia increased I called Trudy. "I'm coming for
dinner and bringing the baby." I could see her, caught by surprise,
switching gears and turning her focus away from herself to her
troubled cousin.

"Of course. We're right here. Is everything all right, Eva?"

I dressed the baby and packed her in her port-a-crib and
grabbed a fistful of Pampers and an extra bottle of Similac. Traveling light was no longer possible, I realized, as I loaded everything into the car, that's gone for a while. Mother's station
wagon, which I had more or less appropriated, had developed a
baby orientation, with a backward-facing car seat, a lined diaper
bag to cover emergencies, stray rattles, a loose pacifier, and an
open box of Pampers floating around the back. Yes, I had quite
the look of a suburban matron, as I headed out of the driveway, in
my duffle coat and boots, the baby's car seat in the back.

Traffic was particularly dense and the snowfall of two nights
ago left mountains of plowed snow, capped with gray dirt,
along the side of the road in odd, careless chunks. The Express-
way seemed narrow and mean as I edged my way along, stopping
and starting, maneuvering for position. Elizabeth, who usually
slept through all car trips, was restive and made little peeping
noises. "It's okay, Elizabeth," I murmured without much conviction. The gray-blue dusk, the presence of all those strange shapes

of grimy snow, caused me to shudder. Headlights from oncoming cars seemed to dance in front of me, and I wondered, for a brief minute, why I'd left the sanctuary of Riverdale for the certain harassment of New York. Some people do well in this city, this Big Apple. Opa, for instance, would come home from the most tangled, racing, throbbing New York day fresh and pink and excited as a schoolboy. I had never been able to make that special tension work for me; in that sense, I was my mother's daughter.

Up to Fifty-second we went, across to Madison, one way on Fifty-seventh, circling around to the garage on Fifty-fourth, down two levels, a punched green ticket belched out from the time machine; I gathered my many parts. Back out on the street, headed into the wind, I felt like a frontier woman as I juggled Elizabeth's port-a-crib and my handbag, ladened with baby goods, my knit hat pulled down over my ears, my boots gooshing in the snow. I spotted Trudy's building in the middle of Fifty-seventh, white and gleaming ahead of me. "Onward," I whispered to myself, pulling my wagon.

Could I possibly move in with her? Mother had warned against it. Find a place which nourishes your spirit, she had said. Could 225 East Fifty-seventh Street nourish my spirit?

Trudy was more animated and authoritative than even I remembered.

"Of course, of course, Eva, you must move in here for a while at least," she said, as we finished dinner. "You can't sit out there in the suburbs, you have got to get back to New York."

"New York isn't so much the objective . . ."

"New York is a symbol then." Trudy looked like New York itself, glamorous in her slacks and little silk blouse, anklets and open-toe shoes. Oh to be chic, I thought.

"New York will stimulate you. You're beginning to isolate yourself, I can tell, you need to *see* people," she said, emphasizing the "see," a suggestion of more exotic activity.

"I've been seeing people."

"No, but new people, not those same old creeps from college and family friends. Single, attractive men."

"There aren't any single, attractive men in New York."

"That's true." She pushed her hair back with a flick of her wrist. She knows the score on this one.

"I was thinking that I'd try to get a job somewhere." I leaned back in my modular section of her modular couch and closed my eyes, braced for the logical answer.

"That's wonderful, Eva. What can you do?" What can you do? I drew in my breath. "Well, I'll just have to think of something." Period. I hoped that would end it for the moment at least.

"Look, Uncle Lawrence is going out of town with his show in what, two weeks? Why don't you just move in here, I'll sleep on the couch, which is very comfortable, you and the baby will take my room, of course I'll have to get in there in the morning, but you can see the room is plenty big. Neddy will love it. He's always wanted a little sister . . ."

I couldn't interrupt here—generous Trudy—but with each new enthusiasm, the option of moving in with her closed more tightly.

"I don't think it will work, Trudy."

"You're just depressed."

"No, I'm not depressed."

"What are you?"

"Paralyzed."

"Where do you want to go, Eva?" My father looked at me directly.

"I'm not sure. Just somewhere different for a little while."

"Well, I can understand that, my dear. Why don't you call one of those agencies and get a nurse for the baby, and we'll go down to one of the islands for four or five days."

We.

"I think the show can get along without me for four days. I will want to get back in time for those previews in Philadelphia, that's a tough time. Although the Larkspurs are taking hold in a nice way, I do feel I must be there—"

"Opa." I felt the color drain from my face. "Opa, I'd like to go by myself."

"By yourself?" He looked puzzled. "Would that be fun?"

"Probably not, but I'd like to do it anyway."

"Well, my dear, in that case, why don't you go to Bermuda, where at least you can call the Fergusons."

"I don't want to go to Bermuda. I don't like the Fergusons."

Opa sighed. "Where do you want to go, Eva?"

Another one of those basic, unanswerable questions. What can you do? Where do you want to go? I paused for a long minute and stared out the window. Mother said, Go to a place which nourishes your spirit.

"I guess I'd like to go back to the Vineyard. I think I'll just take Elizabeth and go to the Vineyard for a few days."

He shook his head. "I can't think that will be very restful, with the baby. Who's down there now, anybody? Will the house be warm enough?"

"Sure."

"You were just there, Eva, remember. Just three months ago. Why would you want to go back?"

"I like it there. Besides, I miss my harp."

He smiled. "You do what you want. You're a grown woman."

Three days later the grown woman and baby took off in a tiny airplane for a few days' change of pace on Martha's Vineyard. Opa drove me to the airport at White Plains. "Have fun, Eva," he said vaguely, giving the baby's cheek a little pinch. "I hope it won't be gloomy for you." We hugged each other. As I looked out of the tiny plane's little passenger window, Opa was standing by the door of his car, looking so forlorn that I wanted to shout out to him, "Everything will be all right, you'll see, everything will be fine." But instead I just waved elaborately. I could tell that he couldn't see me at all.

The trip on the airplane seemed a hideous sort of rite of passage, a rocky, uncertain, swaying ride, the little plane bobbing and weaving like a boxer in early rounds. I told myself as we lurched along that at least I was out of that house, with its certain comforts, its thousands of photographic reminders of every family occasion, its clear abundance, and the sweet, suffocating presence of my father. I thought about hugging my harp, about its taut, sparkling strings, which would need hours of tuning, about the gentle arch at its top, about those few familiar opening runs that I always play; I call those sequences my running water sounds, and I tried to hear them now above the plane. I thought about the house and that monstrous rut in the driveway we had vowed to fill when Billy, Mother, and Neddy were there. Plenty to do. There will be plenty to do.

Opa and I had agreed that this would be a good time for me to clean out Mother's desk, her Chilmark desk; piles of manuscripts and notes were left crammed in the drawers, and Opa was agreeable to some kind of ordering of that mess. (No such action was permitted at her Riverdale desk however.) I also vowed that now that Adrian was safely back in Africa and his principal protector was gone, I would remove a portion of his seven hundred million shells to a box in the basement. Lots to do.

We circled the island three times waiting for clearance to land. The sun set slowly but decisively over the western corner of the island, over the Gay Head cliffs and the nearby harbor of Menemsha. I could see Menemsha Pond, where James and I had sailed (or attempted to) and Squibnocket Pond, Mother's favorite. No little dots on the landscape, these bodies of water. Even from the airplane they looked big and spunky, with jagged shorelines and complex inlets. Lights came on in patches from the towns of Edgartown, Oak Bluffs, and Vineyard Haven. Elizabeth stirred. "This might be sort of fun," I whispered to her.

We came in onto the runway and plopped down with the ease and grace of a Frisbee. Rough beginning, smooth landing. I wondered if that might be a reasonable expectation for the next few days.

Island Taxi, a van loaded to capacity with luggage, four other passengers, and two dogs, deposited us an hour later (final stop) at the door of our house.

"You live here?" asked the driver.

"Mostly in the summer."

"Oh yes, I used to drive your father out here a lot. Is the heat on in your place?"

"It will be in a few minutes," I assured him.

The house seemed specterlike, no light on, and the moon cast an eerie glow through the thin clouds. We had left a light on on the porch, I remembered, but after all these weeks it had burned out and the darkness seemed particularly cold and mean. I shuddered and fumbled for the keys, while trying to hold Elizabeth. My disorganized packing consisted of two tote bags, rammed full of sweaters, boots, Pampers, and baby clothes, with my checkbook sticking out of the top. The driver of Island Taxi, a rugged man, looked uncomfortable as he clutched the bulging tote bags, waiting for me to get the door open. "Will you be all right here?" he asked, as I pushed through and managed to turn on a light. "Oh, sure, of course," I replied, with excessive confidence. "Everything will be okay as soon as I get the heat up."

The thermostat read fifty-five but I didn't believe it; the house seemed to crack with its own coldness. I pushed the instrument up to seventy. My harp stood with dignity in the corner of the living room, looking like a dinosaur with a bathrobe on. I gave it a little pat. Tomorrow, I whispered. Tomorrow.

We had left a fair amount of disorder, my mother and I. I remember now that we had had to dash for the plane last November, and I had promised to get someone to come in and finish picking up but never did. Normally I would have liked that familiar, relaxed disarray, but without Mother to breathe life into it, it seemed a sterile disorder, not the stuff of living. I reassigned things back to place where I could, but Elizabeth, who had slept through these last three hours, was now wide awake and required a full-scale effort, bottle, new diapers, a warmer sleeper, holding, and bouncing. The clock over the kitchen sink read eight twenty-five. If the heat was coming up, it was doing so mighty slowly. Elizabeth's nose was cold, a little icy button.

To combat a beginning feeling of panic, I went through the house and turned on every light I could find—in James's musty room, with a batch of Neddy's comic books on the bed, in Adrian's oceanographic PX. Both rooms looked muted, not brightened by the single light I managed to find. My own little cubicle, heretofore a bright and silly room with posters and summer trappings, seemed familiar but intensely out of season. A picture of a warm sunlit beach covered with Canada geese had come loose at one side and hung down across itself like wet laundry. My bathing suit dangled off a chair.

Elizabeth started to cry, not so much from the cold, I suspected, but from an unsatisfactory, hastily delivered bottle. I bounced her more vigorously. For the first time in my life in this house, I longed for a television set. When we were younger Mother decided that it was "unnecessary, where there are so many other things to do on the island," which was probably correct, but on this grisly night, when there didn't seem to be a damn thing to do but pace around, I longed for the blurry, reassuring sound. The kitchen was reasonably tidy; a few cans of S. S. Pierce soup sat on the shelf, but every time I put the baby down she howled, so I deferred the pleasure of dinner for the moment and continued to keep moving until the house warmed up.

A fire, I thought, I'll build a fire. Of course, a fire, a warm, glowing, noisy fire, that will seem like a person, and a true kind of light, not just these few yellow light bulbs. Why did it take me this long to think of it?

I let Elizabeth howl as I ran outside and rummaged through the shed near the porch for wood. The sky was clearer now, but the wind had come up and I hurried inside with my logs and kindling, imagining myself running along the moors as my blue-jean skirt billowed and flapped around my legs. As soon as I have a fire, everything will be all right, I reassured myself: a fire is company.

Under any reasonable circumstances, I can build a fire in my sleep, but on this particular night, I was a Brownie Scout, fumbling with kindling, too much paper, logs that crossed each other the wrong way, tiny bursts of flame that quickly dissolved into smoke. After a good twenty minutes, a modest, constant fire shone through the shambles. I hugged Elizabeth, gave her the rest of her bottle, and managed to quiet her. She gave me a faint smile.

"Dear little baby, be a Vineyard girl, like your grandmother," I advised her. "Be a lover of this island in such a way that you don't notice the thermostat."

I then remembered the heaters that Opa insisted on, rescued them from the closet, and placed them around the living room, which took on their red-orange glow. "We're camping, Elizabeth, camping in our own house." I rubbed her back and in a few minutes she fell asleep in her navy blue port-a-crib, snoring slightly, like a little bull. We were both warmer.

The fire gained energy. I thought of Billy now, of the hours spent sitting right here, so confident and silly. What can be the effect of California on this man? I wondered. Will he be susceptible to it, will he forget me, forget to come back? I had fun the few times I went to the Coast, but I retained a reasonable wariness of a place with no seasons, where nobody has a last name. (Hi, I'm Sherry, this is Dina. I myself couldn't just say, I'm Eva.) Billy may swallow it whole. A wish-you-were-here postcard from Santa Barbara last week revealed nothing.

With Elizabeth finally asleep, I wandered a bit more, toward Mother's coats which hung by the door, to their room, to her bedside table stacked with reading. Ah, and there is her second pair of glasses we spent so much time looking for in Riverdale! With some apprehension, I reached into the drawer of the bedside table, to discover a fistful of letters, bills, notes to herself, grocery lists. Mother may have organized her thoughts before she died, but not her things. I stuffed everything back in the drawer. Tomorrow.

With the old quilts I pulled out of the closet I made a cocoon-like bed for myself on the couch near the fire. This living room, which I had thought of as cozy, now seemed huge, empty, and borderless. I closed my eyes.

Where is the funny, tight little quartet of the fall? Neddy tearing through here with his parka over his pajamas, Billy bound up like one half of a Michelin man, still sexy in plaster and bandages, and Mother, her pale, luminous face, reading, right there in that nearby chair. Scattered. That's what we are. Scattered like tumbleweed on a windy plain. My momentary feeling of triumph at achieving a warm fire and a quiet baby slipped quickly away. I felt cold, untriumphant, and alone.

Mother is dead and will never come back; James and Adrian are at large in their different tracks; Opa is lost to me in a newer, subtler way, in that I can't any longer stand to be alone with him for any length of time; and Billy, doing who knows what at the other end of the country. Are they all lost to me?

Elizabeth had stopped her snoring and now slept peacefully beside me, her fist clenched. I watched her for a few minutes.

Elizabeth will get me through. Baby Elizabeth, who measures but twenty-one inches and weighs fifteen pounds. Elizabeth is nothing but innocence and need, but still an entity with her own forward motion and her own willpower. I will have to borrow a bit of her forward motion. For a while, that's all. I pulled the quilt around me.

There is nothing but open space in front of me right now. Wide open, yawning, open space; a terrifying void.

Elizabeth slept soundly. I lay awake for a long time, slept fitfully, and dreamed of summer.

XX

Dutcher Dock in Menemsha Harbor, a five-minute drive from our house, is a serious dock for fishing boats in the fall and winter, a tourist "must" in the summer, and a corner of the island which holds authenticity for me at all seasons. Standing in front of Poole's fish store, the day after our arrival on the island, Elizabeth and I follow the efforts of the harbormaster as he dispatches a smaller boat, the *Troubador*, and receives the *Lady Elaine*. The crew of the boat, six or seven men, looks cold and tired. In the summer they become a cause for awe and curiosity for the tourists, which is only faintly amusing to them. But now, in the winter, it's just the other crews, the other men, the people from the fish store, ready to weigh and cut up the fish, and the harbormaster—the winter family. Interesting how little they speak. It's a no-frills operation.

Sea gulls are everywhere. I note that the gulls and the men are both after the same thing: fish. Swooping low to check the wharf for fish parts, the gulls call to each other, soaring sideways as well as up and down. Dozens at a time hover over the incoming fishing vessel, the *Lady Elaine*, now docked and refueling and adding up its haul from an eight-day scalloping trip. Two of the crew are busy rewinding the massive iron scallop net back into its wheel. Elizabeth and I watch in fascination.

In the summer, of course, Menemsha Harbor is filled to capacity, the traffic in and out is quadrupled with big motor boats, long, sleek sailboats, hoping for a mooring, whalers, and day sailors, dogging each other and jockeying for position. Now it's quieter, quieter but by no means dead, just a lot less congested.

Up on the ridge just above the long wharf are tossed stacks of lobster traps, parts of nets, a few rusted oil drums, piles of painted lobster buoys, tossed up there but not discarded, the harbormaster tells me. Nothing in this day and age can be discarded. Holding Elizabeth, I pick my way past it all with respect.

I love the small inner harbor, past the dock, with its cluster of fishing shacks. Most of the shacks are lived in, and some are built so close to the edge of the water that I wonder why a couple of them don't just fall in. In front of the houses are small, rakishly pitched landing piers, with boats and fishing gear resting on their uneven boards; why don't these things slip off? Made of solid stuff, I guess. Some of these year-round residents know a good thing and rent their houses in the summer, so a fancier crowd can be seen in July and August. But not today. March is for the hard core. "We're not hard core, Elizabeth," I whisper to her, "but it's kind of fun to pretend." The sun came out.

Young men in huge slickers and rubber boots pound up and down the dock; one even winks at me. I wonder if there are more attractive single men in Menemsha than in New York. It's an entertaining thought. Must consult Trudy.

Everyone moves toward the one tiny open-for-business supply store, the central meeting place where gas, newspapers, peanut butter crackers, and all marine goods can be found. Adrian used to hang around here when he was younger. It's bustling today.

I observe that even with this considerable life and commerce, there still are more sea gulls than people on Dutcher Dock, by about four to one. The gulls seem to be on familiar territory as they light, unconcerned, near the doorway of the store, just walking down the center of the dock, checking for food, or just strolling. Time has bred relaxation.

The salt smell is everywhere; it comes in from the beach side, where Elizabeth and I wander, from the wharf, and from the Menemsha Pond, beyond the inner harbor, from the west, across Lobsterville Beach. The sun is now officially out. I am warm for the first time in days.

The summer advertisements flapped in the wind, little pieces of
yellowed paper pinned with thumbtacks to the bulletin board in
front of Alley's store.

> Will babysit while you're at the beach. Call Marcie.

> Baby-sitting, $3 per hour, experienced, call Lynn.

I seized upon one Mrs. Prescott:

> Will care for your child in my home. All seasons. Tisbury, call
> 555-3319.

On the telephone Mrs. Prescott sounded weary but reliable.
"Can you cope with a nine-week-old baby?" I asked.
"I like them best of all. They sleep," came the reply.
We drove Mother's jeep up and down back Tisbury roads, look-
ing for Mrs. Prescott's house. March leaves a deposit of winter
snow on the island, but not the piles of gray-brown drifts that I
was used to at home. The wind came up, buffeting the scrub oak,
causing the dust on the road to rise and billow. We slogged up
Old County Road, port-a-crib, diapers, Similac, baby chair. The
sun was trying to peek through.
"Just for a few hours in the morning, for a week or so," I told
Mrs. Prescott. The TV set shimmered in the back of the kitchen.
"I just need a few hours to myself."
"Sure." Mrs. Prescott smiled. "Kids can drive you crazy." She
was younger than I had imagined, with thin shoulders, her hair
pulled back in a ponytail. I tried to check out the house as best I
could; everything seemed disorderly, but in control. Piles of shirts
lay draped across the ironing board. African violets flourished
under a grow-light in the window.
"How many children do you have?" I asked in a further attempt to reassure myself about her.
"Two boys. Six and eight. Couple of bandits. There's no work
on the island in the winter so I watch other people's kids while
mine are in school."
I installed Elizabeth, propping her up in her seat on the kitchen
table. "I hope she'll be all right." I must have looked agonized,
because Mrs. Prescott laughed.

"Oh sure. Don't worry. You can call me Edna if you want to."

"Thank you, I will, Edna. Please call me Eva."

"Okay, Eva. Go and relax."

Edna! Eva! Human, grown-up contact! For the last five days my little girl and I had been at our pioneer best, coping with the jeep that wouldn't start, the heat that was whimsical, trash bags full of junk, that huge rut in the road; I am a camp fire girl at heart, and I was confident of my fortitude in the trenches. But who could I talk to? Elizabeth slept and gurgled. With no one to talk to, for the first time in my life, I felt the onset of sure craziness. Despite the constant sounds from the record player (Carly Simon, an old Vineyard hand, cried, "Jesse!") and occasional trips to the market or to Menemsha, I longed for an exchange, a real conversation, of which Edna had provided the first hint.

In addition, and perhaps more serious, I had begun to hate the house. Without Mother, it seemed lean and sullen; the rooms looked undernourished.

I have done what I came to do, I thought as I hauled the final trash bag to the jeep. I came back to the homestead for good, necessary reasons, I have cleaned out my mother's desk, and now I just want to get the hell out of this house. Question: Where could we go, little Elizabeth and I? Where were we going to live? Where could I break ground, my own ground? I almost asked the kindly Edna Prescott, on leaving, "Do you have any idea where I might go to live?"

Go and relax, she said.

I sat in the SeaView Diner in Edgartown. A cozy, overheated little sliver of vinyl and tin in the middle of a chilly clapboard town. Three women sipped their coffee at one end of the diner. I reached for the menu, typewritten, encased in plastic. On the top, in bold letters it read: Breakfast—6:30 to 10:30. Lunch—11 to 2:30. The clock above the coffee maker read ten forty-five. I sighed. So much in transition am I that I can't even qualify for breakfast or lunch. After a moment I took a pencil from my bag and marked on a clean napkin:

Decide: 1) Where to live
         2) How to live.

XXI

"Just the two of you?"

"Yes. Just the two of us. The baby and me."

"Well, all right," said Mrs. Bray, still a little curious. "I think we might have something."

Elizabeth and I sat nose to nose in Mrs. Bray's office, trying to look businesslike. I had installed the child in my newest piece of baby equipment, a pouch which hung across my front, a marvel of efficiency because it freed both my arms and allowed me to watch her as she dangled around my neck. The only trouble was that we didn't look serious, *couldn't* look serious, as we lumbered around town, Elizabeth looking more like a third bosom than a baby. Peering around to the right of Elizabeth's head, I smiled at Mrs. Bray. "I'd like to see whatever you have," I said earnestly.

"One small, partially furnished house, right here in Edgartown. More of a cottage actually. Over by Pease Point Way. It's been available for over two months now. The owner moved to the mainland to live with her daughter. It has a lovely porch. You could have that house for a year."

Mrs. Bray, a long-time real estate agent who probably knew every house in Edgartown, clearly had some reservations about the "cottage," but I must have seemed so suggestible that she decided to try it on me anyway.

"Of course, the heat isn't on," she said as we headed for her car, "so it will be a bit chilly."

"I'm used to that," I replied.

The cottage, tiny and clearly abandoned, stood on a side street about ten minutes from the center of town. Yes, it was sweet, despite the weeds growing up around the front and a desperate need for a coat of paint. Picture-postcard. Picture-postcard in distress.

A wisteria vine crawled across the door, draped like a poorly hung curtain.

"Wisteria. You'll get lovely wisteria in the spring," noted Mrs. Bray. "It may need a little cutting back."

I smiled. "I love wisteria," and I saw myself with pruning shears cutting it back, freeing the vine from its own entanglement, helping it to blossom in the spring. Now the vine all but blocked the entrance to the house, but still, I was encouraged. I hugged Elizabeth and held my breath as Mrs. Bray fumbled with the keys. We pushed our way in.

"First thing you see is the bathroom," she announced. "Some people don't mind that." A perfect period-piece bathroom, with fading flowered wallpaper, yellowing sink, and tub with claw feet met us head on, across the two-foot hall.

"Well, I'm kind of glad to know that there *is* one," I said.

"Oh yes. This house has everything," replied Mrs. Bray. That seemed to be something of an overstatement, but Mrs. Bray was a plugger. The narrow front hall led to a small bare room on the left, with empty bookshelves and a couple of mariner's charts of Vineyard waters, held up by thumbtacks. Plastic sheets covered the two windows.

"This room can be used for just about anything. It's a good place to take off your boots," she explained. An ancient record player occupied one corner. "The owner says that the record player goes with the house," she went on. I would gladly have exchanged that piece of the past for a good solid chair (to sit on while I take off my boots), but I said nothing. Partially furnished can mean just about anything.

"The parlor is here." Mrs. Bray, a gentle but fast-moving saleswoman, moved us to the next little room. "This could be lovely," she mused. "It has the flavor and spirit of an old New England parlor. Of course without furniture it seems a trifle inhospitable."

I could only nod. I wondered where the partial, of partially furnished, was.

"Well, I like it anyway, even without furniture," I finally managed. "But it's a little dark."

"Just a little dark," she agreed. The one window was encased in plastic, yielding a pale gray light. "Parlors were dark in those days," continued Mrs. Bray. "But look at this small, beautiful fireplace."

"Lovely. Does it work?"

"I don't think it's been used in some time," came the careful reply.

"The floors seem to tilt."

"Yes, yes they do."

"And the house is heated, I assume?" I felt I must be practical.

"The two small bedrooms upstairs are not." She smiled. "To live here will require a bit of an effort."

She opened the door to the right off the parlor with a touch of hesitation. "The kitchen."

Whatever spartan instinct had guided the owner in the first two rooms reversed itself dramatically in the kitchen. Pictures of Vineyard scenes, old calendars, posters of church activities covered every spot of wall space. An old meat grinder hooked onto the counter, the ancient stove and icebox were so closely rammed up next to each other as to suggest a merger; a broom closet, without a door, revealed dozens of brooms; there were coffee tins, a couple of teapots, cabinets chock-full of teacups, yellowing plates, painted vases, bread boxes, pie tins, and all manner of pots and pans, boxes of nails, hooks—the owner had clearly run out of gas just before the kitchen, in the "preparation for rental" department.

"Looks like a rummage sale."

"Before you decide, come look at the enclosed porch. It's relatively new."

Stepping out onto the porch was like stepping onto a dock after a day at sea. It was solid. A plain, large room, with a view that extended to a pond in the near distance (as well as some backyard trash cans), it was definitely from a more recent era. A clear-cut addition.

"Is this room heated?"

"Baseboard heating," she announced with assurance, "the best there is. The light in here is marvelous. The sun comes up here"—she made a sweeping gesture to one side of the room—"and sets here"—she pivoted back. "The real advantage of this place is that you can *live* out here." A day bed, covered with a madras spread, and one wicker chair filled in one corner and seemed very hospitable indeed. Elizabeth shifted.

My father always cautioned me "not to take the first thing you see . . ."

"I'll take it," I said. Mrs. Bray nodded warmly. It had been an easy morning for her. "Immediate occupancy, two ninety a month, one-year lease, no sublets."

Two ninety a month seemed a bit steep for this cottage of uneven virtue, but it seemed to draw me in, this little shelter, its chaos warmed me. The tilting floors seemed reassuring. They tilt, I tilt, we can both tilt together, I told myself.

"Will Mr. Wiltshire be joining you?" Mrs. Bray inquired.

"No. It's just the two of us."

I hugged Elizabeth, glassy-eyed, bouncing on my chest. "We'll make it work," I whispered to her. "You can learn to crawl right here on this porch. We'll make it work, just the two of us."

I looked around. A freezing, unfurnished shambles. Nonetheless, it promised protection.

Immediate occupancy proved elusive. Digging out the kitchen became the first priority. At this point Edna Prescott became a necessity instead of a luxury. For the next week I established a routine of sorts. We were up at the crack of dawn—Elizabeth's opening bleat came at about five-thirty—and by seven-thirty we were ready to tackle the world. I left her off at Edna's at eight. The drive from Chilmark to Tisbury at that hour, even in the murky month of March, had a sting to it. I developed a sense of myself as a pioneer woman battling the elements to make a new homestead. That reverie came to a temporary halt as I stopped by the Up Island Market to pick up whatever extra boxes they had. Then I headed to Edgartown, to cut back weeds, rip off plastic from the windows, to stake my claim.

Having spent most of my formative years in a house of monumental excesses, I found, as I moved out on my own, that I couldn't stand clutter of any sort. So I ended up stuffing most of the owner's kitchen into boxes and dispatching them quickly to the cellar. In addition, I scrubbed the joint from corner to corner, even polished the brass door handle. Having brought the place to an antiseptic cleanliness, I suffered a momentary crisis as I realized that we now actually had to *live* here; that we had to leave the familiar, memory-filled territory of the Chilmark house and put our bodies and souls into the uncharted waters of this place. Standing in the bare sun-room (my name for it) on an overcast day, I felt a decided chill. It seemed to me that I had just rented a tiny gray sloping shoe box, and for a year at that. I would have been pleased to cut and run, but my newly developed stoicism wouldn't let me.

I remembered my harp. How callous I've become, how obsessed with Ajax and Lysol and cleaning out desks and dealing with thermostats, how miserably domestic, I thought. I called Island Taxi from the drugstore, and with that same kindly driver who had deposited me at the door in Chilmark a little over two weeks ago, I sped back out to the Chilmark house, where I hugged my harp and carried it gently out to the van. I also managed to snatch a chair and lamp to play by, some firewood, sheets and towels, and the record player.

Reunion! We are three, in principal, I mused, as we bounced back to Edgartown, me, Elizabeth, and the harp. The cottage was improved by the noble instrument, alone at center stage on the porch. I plugged in the lamp and played a part of a Debussy dance before I had to run to pick up Elizabeth.

We moved in. The first night, we both slept on the porch, and I had a grim fantasy that we were trapped in a small barren rural hospital. Where are the charming settees, the curtains, the hooked rugs, where is the *cottage* of this cottage? The bright moon cast a warm glow on the harp, which looked large and human and gave me comfort.

The next morning I called Curtis LeMar in Boston. I am not a schemer by nature, but I did feel the need for a friend with a sure hand for interiors—which disqualified Trudy, James, Laura Campbell, Edna Prescott, and of course me. Some people know how to find or do the right thing for each room, but I remained stymied by the process, still a field-hockey player at heart.

"What do you want, dear?" Curtis was more brusque at his office than in his own living room.

"Would you like to come visit me this weekend?"

"In the dead of winter?"

"It's nice here."

"I don't believe it."

"Well, I've just rented this cute little cottage, and I thought maybe you might be able to think of how to make it look nice."

"Oh, Eva, you're not going to stay down there all winter, are you?"

"Yes. I like it."

"You're crazy."

"Let's assume that. Will you come?"

"All right. It's the only way I can think to get rid of all your clothes that are jammed in my closet. Read me the boat schedule."

The boat schedule. As I rattled off the departures and arrivals, I remembered the dozens of times I had rendered this information to Mother's friends as they prepared to make the pilgrimage to her last fall. Was it only six months ago?

"I'll see you at seven-fifty then. Is the place clean at least?"

"Clean to the point of obsession."

"Fine. Don't put up any fishnets or anything dumb like that. I'll see you Friday."

For the next two days we wandered around the quiet town, Elizabeth in her collapsible stroller, or what Cal had called a pushcart, stopping to pick up little things we needed, slushing through puddles in my boots. We watched the little two-car ferry move back and forth to the island of Chappaquiddick, observed with respect the symmetry and grace of the large houses on North Water Street, had ice cream at ten-thirty in the morning, poked in a few shops open year round. Edgartown had never been my bag, I thought it too stuffy and much too civilized. But on this winter day, I was glad to have its snugness, its orderly crisscross streets and sense of commerce. I wondered if I would be able to find a job here. As we walked up the main street, everything

seemed sleepy, laid-back, not very job oriented. Later. One thing
at a time.

Curtis arrived that Friday evening with two bulging suitcases of
my clothes and a large bottle of Mouton-Lafitte red wine.

"Open this immediately," he ordered, "while I look around." I
had no corkscrew, so I had to resort to his Swiss army knife.

"Alrighty, I see the problem," he said. "A little arid. Why did
you move here? Why did you not just stay in the Chilmark
house?"

"Too isolated. The house is at the end of a dirt road, with no
one nearby. I needed body warmth."

"I see. Can you afford this tumbledown place?" He waved his
arm around the room.

"Just barely. I am planning to get a job. What do you think,
Curtis? Can we fix it up?"

"I think so." He sipped his wine. "What's the child's name?"
he asked, peering at the baby suspiciously.

"Elizabeth."

"Thank God she doesn't look like Cal."

We drank his fancy wine, had a less than fancy steak dinner,
and laughed for the next three hours straight. Over what? I can't
possibly remember. I only recall the great release the wine provided, a feeling of giddyness, due to the fact that Curtis LeMar,
of the decorating firm of LeMar and Engel, was here to prop up
my bleak little cottage with a touch of finery, a finery that I
couldn't possibly have brought to it myself, that a helping hand
was sitting on the floor of my parlor, laughing and telling me anecdotes from his childhood while I sat listening, listening to the
voice of someone else, listening and laughing and feeling the simple pleasures of a shared evening.

"Now, Curtis," I said the next morning as I jiggled Elizabeth
into her sling, "I don't want it to look too done up, if you know
what I mean."

"Hardly. Just follow along behind me with your checkbook and
don't speak."

We hit the hardware store first, where we ordered five essential
storm windows. Then we drove to Oak Bluffs and found a reasonable kitchen table. We bought plain muslin curtains, two old

chairs for the parlor, one small table, three lamps, two medium-sized hooked rugs, and six rolls of dotted wallpaper. ("I don't think the owner would like me to put up wallpaper without her permission," I said feebly. "Don't be silly, that woman isn't dumb enough to come back here.") We found another wicker chair for the porch, a painted bureau, we ordered a new mattress for the upstairs bedroom, bought two cans of eggshell-white paint, and two bedspreads. ("I think I'm running out of money," I protested. "Nonsense," he snapped.) We got a mirror, a ridiculous painting of a sunset, and four new long-playing records. "You've got to have something besides Carly Simon," he said.

By six o'clock that night, I slipped the exhausted Elizabeth into her crib and opened a new bottle of wine.

"Don't sit down," he cautioned. "Plug in those lamps, put on a record, we'll start with the wallpaper. Now you'll really learn what a good day's work is."

Having released the demon in him, I could hardly collapse myself (which I was dying to do, influenced as well by the fact that Elizabeth woke every morning at about five-thirty). Curtis handed me a measuring tape. "Give me the dimensions of this room," he ordered. The room in which I could take off my boots was soon to become the baby's room.

From an airless square with two small crooked windows and a sagging bookshelf, it became a room worthy of the Laura Ashley catalog. I removed the mariner's charts with care just in case they had sentimental value for the owner, and with a damp cloth I wiped down the cracked walls while Curtis followed along behind me slapping on wallpaper, brushing it into place with a couple of strokes like a character from a speeded up silent movie.

Zip. Slap. Clap. I dared not wander away or even go for a drink of water.

"Quick, give me that brush," he ordered, standing on a chair with the final strip of wallpaper. "See, if you'd just painted this room white it would have been drab. And this dotted wallpaper covers all the cracks and holes and water stains. Remember, when in doubt, Eva, wallpaper."

I nodded.

"Now give me those curtains." We knocked the windows open

with a couple of hammer blows, just to be sure they actually did open, painted the window sills, and tacked up the curtains.

"Why don't we move some of the baby's stuff in now?" I asked. "It looks cute."

"First bring me in the smaller of the hooked rugs. And then start painting the bookshelf."

I could but obey.

The siege continued until three in the morning. Then a break was allowed until Sunday noon, when we took up brushes again and started to paint the parlor eggshell white.

"Now, my dear, this is a silly room, you see, and it must remain a silly room, particularly as you're going to live on the porch anyway. So we'll hang the sunset painting over the mantel, the mirror on the right-hand wall, put the two old chairs in front of the fireplace, the lamp is just a joke, it's so dark you can't see in here anyway."

Furniture seemed to fly about the room and land by prescription in just the right place.

"Oh, marvelous," cried Curtis. "Looks just fine."

"Maybe I could bring another comfortable chair from the house in Chilmark."

"No. Leave this room just this way, please. I may have one more thing for you to put in here. But don't muck it up after I go, Eva. Now, my dear, what sort of bedroom do you have in mind?"

"No bedroom, really, just nothing."

"I beg your pardon?"

"Just a plain room. To sleep in."

"Well, all right, I'll simply have to leave the bedroom to you. Remember your mattress will be here in ten days. At least let us take this bureau upstairs. One, two, three, Eva. Then we'll rearrange the porch."

Sunday swirled by at top speed, just like the strokes of Curtis's brush. By eleven that night, with the few lamps lit and the smell of paint cloaking the air, we sat in the two chairs by the fireplace. The house seemed not to have adjusted to its new-found gains, but to me the sense of overhaul was total. "The place doesn't look dreary anymore, Curtis."

"Of course not," he replied.

On Monday morning I took him to the eight-thirty boat. "Curtis, how can I thank you?"

"You can't possibly."

"Anyway, it looks like a place where people live now."

He pulled a manila envelope from his briefcase. "In that vein, hang this over the fireplace. I made it for you myself a few weeks ago, but forgot to mail it. Open it after the boat leaves, please."

Shifting the baby from left to right and back again, I waved and blew kisses as the ferry pulled out of the slip and moved slowly around the bend, headed for Woods Hole.

Back in the jeep I opened his manila envelope.

A red and blue needlepoint sampler, its little square stitches perfectly constructed, read:

AND BABY MAKES TWO.

I looked at it carefully for a minute, then held it up for Elizabeth to see. "That means you and me, kid."

As I drove home I thought to myself, I will keep this forever, this little square, this little comic square, I will never let it out of my sight. No matter what our numbers get to be, just two, or three, or whatever, I'll never be without this little needlepoint, with its clear reminder that I am not one. Baby has made two.

Elizabeth, punchy from her weekend, slept on in her car seat.

XXII

Opa said, "There are two messages for you, Eva. A letter from the Walnut Country Day School, that must be Cal, isn't it?"

"I'm sure."

"And Billy Diamond called. We didn't have your new number. Louise took the message. He just said he'd call back."

"Okay. Thank you. Will you send Cal's letter down?"

"Of course." Opa paused. "It's nice that your boyfriends, or whatever, are trying to stay in touch with you."

"That may be. I don't see either of them helping me with these storm windows."

"Eva, remember that nice fellow who lived in West Tisbury, Darren something, I think his name was, Mother had him do things around the house. Maybe you should look him up in the phone book and give him a call. It's nice to have someone who is handy."

"I'm handy."

"It doesn't sound like you're so handy."

"Opa, listen. I got a job this morning."

"You *did*? Well . . . what is it?"

"I'm the new breakfast cook at the SeaView Diner."

"You must be joking."

"No, no I'm not."

"And how did you come by this assignment?"

I took a deep breath. "Well, I've been going there quite a lot recently, with the baby, I'd just put her seat right on the table next to me, and I was having breakfast there the other day, and Helen, who runs the place, was complaining that she was too old to get up that early in the morning."

"How early?"

"Oh, six o'clock or so. And her husband, Al, has arthritis, and can't really cover for her, so she was thinking she'd try and get someone to open for her and cook the breakfasts until ten, when she could come in—"

"Eva, I don't understand. You don't know how to do anything like that. All I ever saw you do was pour a bowl of Cheerios. You certainly never cooked a full breakfast for me." He sounded plaintive.

"Well, come into the SeaView Diner and I will."

"Do you know how to make six omelets at a time?"

"Oh, Opa, please. In any event, I told her I was looking for a job, and I'd like to try it, but I'd have to bring the baby, and she said okay, as long as the baby didn't get near the grill."

"Eva, didn't I say that I was going to call Scotty Reston and see about the possibility of your working on the *Vineyard Gazette*, one of the best small newspapers in the world? You recall that?"

"Yes, but this just came up, and I thought I'd better grab it. The hours are actually very good for me."

"What are the hours?"

"Six-thirty to ten-thirty—A.M."

"What's good about that?"

"Elizabeth wakes up every morning at five-thirty. We can be there by six-thirty easy. It's a ten-minute walk from my house."

"What about the *Vineyard Gazette*?"

"To hell with the *Vineyard Gazette!*"

"Eva, please!"

I slept fitfully that night, had dreams of a huge, wide, fiery open pit, over which I had the job of turning a single-egg omelet, while dozens of onlookers jeered. So much for a traditional breakfast-cook nightmare. Elizabeth saved me by awaking at five-thirty sharp.

"Ever worked a grill before?" Helen peered up at me, eyes like moons over her bifocals.

"No." Honesty would have to be the best policy.

"Well, honey, a couple of rules. You've got to clean a grill carefully or it will start to smoke. Every hour or so, be sure you've scraped it down clean. Put a couple of drops of water on it every few minutes. Start your eggs here and your pancakes and french toast over here. Keep your plates right nearby."

I nodded.

"Your toasters you can do with your left hand." She pointed to a bank of toasters lined up next to each other like a small marching band. "And you mix your pancake batter in advance, a lot of the guys like pancakes, you know. Take your butter out of the icebox when you open, but don't put it too near the grill, or you'll have butter soup, right?"

"Right."

"Maureen will place the orders up here." She pointed to a metal shelf to the right of the grill. "She'll stick 'em up here with this magnet, and when you're working on an order, place it above you here." I began to feel dizzy. "And when the order is done, the pickup counter is right here. Okay, honey?"

"Okay."

"Let me tell you one thing." She leaned in at me. I held my breath. "Find your favorite spatula, the one you work best with, and hide it so no one else will use it when you're not working."

"All right."

"Maureen's a little testy in the morning, but she's a good gal, and real good waitress. She's got two kids of her own. Now, do you know how to light the grill?"

"Not really."

Helen shook her head. I was a bit more of an amateur than she had bargained for. "It's tricky. Turn the gas on, up high at first and then just hold it back to low, and hold it like this for a minute . . ." As she demonstrated the intricacies of the grill lighting, I noticed her hands. Big, gnarled, huge knuckles. Helen's face was broad, a vein stood out on her temple. Her glasses' chain dangled around her cheek. But underneath her certain swagger, I felt she possessed, if not a heart of gold, a sort of reasonable good will.

"What happened, your boyfriend walk out on you?" she inquired, the kitchen lesson over.

"Well, not exactly."

"Look, men are all takers, right?" she proclaimed, clicking her false teeth. "That's what they are. We got the nicest bunch of guys in here, eating breakfast every morning, same time, same place, right, but I know when they go home at night, they push their wives around a little, you know what I mean?"

"I suppose so."

"Lookit here. I've lived sixty-one years. I know what I'm talking about. Takers. Two-faced. Leave you in the lurch, right? Like you, right?"

"Well, actually, the baby's father—"

"Are you alone, or are you alone?" she rasped.

"I'm alone."

"Never mind, honey, you'll do fine. Now tomorrow, be here at six-fifteen, just in case you have trouble with the grill. Don't be nervous. In a few days you'll get the hang of this business. I can do it in my sleep. That's just the point. I'd rather be asleep. Call me at home if you can't light the grill."

That night Elizabeth developed a case of simple fussiness which resulted in her having to be held half of the night. She screamed, she croaked and bleated, and by one-thirty at night I felt helpless, as if we'd begun to move into the twilight zone, a short period of temporary insanity. Somehow I had managed to transfer to her my apprehension about the SeaView Diner. She's got *my* jitters, I thought as we paced up and down the length of the porch.

What am I doing with this child, at this hour, on this silly porch? Most other women are curled up with their menfolk, what am I doing alone with this baby? We continued to pace. I wondered, Who would take care of Elizabeth if I should die suddenly? Not Cal. Opa? Not James. Who? I hugged her.

By two-fifteen she had quieted somewhat. I looked at her carefully. She is beginning to look like Cal. Curtis is wrong, there is just a hint of Cal in the mouth and in its ratio to her nose. Just as long as she keeps the red hair.

"Dear little baby," I said to her. "It doesn't matter who you look like or what you do tonight, only please be good tomorrow morning at the diner. Sit in your chair and doze, play with your foot, watch your fingers, anything, but please don't cry." By quarter of three she was out.

At three o'clock, I looked out of the porch window and prayed, "Dear God, help me remember how to light the grill. Help me make passable eggs and pancakes." I thought about my mother. "Please, Mother," I whispered. "You who could never cook breakfast either, steady my hand."

A symphony in eggs and bacon. Rhapsody in Blue, George Gershwin's piece; mine would be called Concerto in Omelet, Pancake, and French Toast.

"You're right. That's really it," Maureen said, after my second day on the job. "It *is* like playing the piano. You've got to do a lot of things at once, and not stop."

"Every time the little bell above the door jingles, and someone comes in, I get all psyched, and think, Dear God, what are *they* going to want? I don't like to hear the bell," I said.

"You'll get over that. After all, we do *like* customers."

Maureen was a stocky, solid woman who counted her tips carefully. Though absolutely unsmiling, she was reassuring, and I liked her right away.

"Oh sure, I'll get used to it all."

"In fact, one sort of regular customer, that fellow who does the surveys, he asked who you were. These guys are used to seeing Helen. Things are looking up." She zapped some toast away from the pickup counter. She's fast, I thought. I've got to learn to be fast too.

Despite the "fellow who does the surveys," I was not much noticed those first mornings. The grill was well behind the counter, so I could make my mistakes quietly. A pile of lesser omelets, burned bacon, and charred french toast lay concealed to the right of my grill. I looked in vain for the perfect spatula, as Helen had advised.

My terror of not being able to light the grill was second only to my fear that Elizabeth, moving in new territory, would blow my ship out of the water by squawking all the time and force me to deal with her while on the job—along with fifty omelets and ten pounds of bacon. On the contrary, she proved to be an enchantress, gurgling and beaming at anyone who acknowledged her, amused by the clatter and movement, content in the baby chair; she smiled as Maureen called out, "Two up, two over, toast, sausage well done," while I braced myself and tried not to panic. In quiet moments, I held her and whispered, "You're doing fine, you're doing fine."

"Tomorrow you get paid," Helen rasped at the end of day four. "And if you continue to do good I'll raise you at the end of the month."

Tomorrow I get paid. I smiled in as nonchalant a manner as I could. "That's fine." Tomorrow I get paid. Here's looking at you, Bill Diamond.

Despite what I told Opa, my morning schedule at the diner had the effect of badly unbalancing my day. All excitement, if that is the word, was now skewered toward those early morning hours. By 10:40 A.M. we were back at home, my little girl and I, back from a hard day at the office, reeling with the tremors of the morning, in need of quiet and a different pace. By eleven we were ready for lunch, which we hit fairly hard, at which point Elizabeth fell immediately into a stupor of a nap. I have never been able to sleep during the day, so I practiced my harp, or read *Ms.* to see what my sisters who were climbing the executive ladder were doing, or I often just stared out of my porch window, searching Eel Pond for ducks. By three Elizabeth was up and ready to go, so we took walks, wandered through town, or drove over to the A & P in Vineyard Haven to pick up some groceries and watch the ferry come in. Dinner was served, *à deux*, to the accompaniment of the six-thirty news, which gave us a pale, violet glow as we sat on the porch hearing about projected budget cuts. I developed a brief fantasy during this time that I was taken up by a young senator, strong and handsome, who invited me to Washington to give him a hand in his legislative and fiscal ordeal; he fell in love with me and wished to take me to his bed, except for the fact that he never went to bed, or so he explained. It was not one of my richest fantasies, but it was lean times all around, I figured. By seven-thirty, maybe eight, I had the baby back in her little room, stuffed with Gerber's and milk and ready for sleep. By nine, having completed one more chapter from *Pathfinders*, I curled up under the covers. Not exactly Arabian Nights.

"How can you stand it?" asked Trudy.

"I can stand it," I replied.

Almost every night, as I lay quietly listening to night sounds, branches cracking in the wind, I thought about Billy. Dear Billy, so vivid to me, his face and body so real that I almost thought I could see him standing near me smiling. At times I felt his absence so sharply that I had to draw in my breath, catch myself for a minute.

In the early evening, just after putting Elizabeth to bed, I often found myself staring out the window, longing for him, longing for our quartet of last fall, Mother, Neddy, me, Billy. I knew how trite it was to sit at the window wishing I could turn back the clock, but nonetheless, nonetheless . . . It all happened too fast and I wished I were back there again.

I sometimes played a game called *Where is he now?*, a rather self-defeating little number I devised to pass the time. He was either 1) jumping into a sports car, 2) jumping onto a beautiful California girl, 3) riding a big wave (the least likely), 4) sitting by the piano in a sun-filled beach house (more likely).

Yet somehow, although I missed him quite fiercely, I did not miss hearing from him. Billy was a proven terrible letter writer and our phone calls were awkward. I guess on balance it was better to keep my fantasies churning rather than deal with the real answer to the question, What's he doing now? He said separate paths. Well, we were on them.

However, when I think back on this period, just after I started the job, I retain the feeling that it was actually a pretty good time; a little dull, yes, and lonely, but nonetheless a time of anticipation and elasticity.

The little house, although haphazard in appearance, proved perfect for me and Elizabeth, a place in tune with its tenants, lacking in symmetry but holding together. It would soon be time to prune the wisteria.

I loved Elizabeth from day one, but for her first two months, she seemed little more than Miss Baby, small, pink, expressionless. From the time we moved to the Edgartown cottage, she became a creature of parts and mood and, when closely observed, certain skills as well. Who else, I ask you, can chew on her foot and soil her pants at the same time? Yi yi yi, she called, her eyes following me. And a little smile, all hers, appeared, a kind of side smile, which Opa would have called a smirk had it crossed the lips of Adrian, but on Elizabeth it seemed angelic, a sign of perfect merriment.

"You ought to call her Betty," said Maureen after a particularly busy morning when Elizabeth had been at her best. "Or why don't you just call her Liz, you know, like Elizabeth Taylor?"

"It's too late, she has to be Elizabeth; I can't recycle on Betty or Liz."

"You could call her Betsy for short."

"She's Elizabeth." And so she was. Her hair was holding to the Wiltshire red-orange pattern. Only I had noticed the influence of Cal in her smile.

Cal. His note to me had been brief but nonbelligerent. "I am not good with babies," he wrote, "but when she's older, I'd like to meet her."

Fair enough. One day, that's what we'll do, we'll meet. Equipped with an explanation, most likely the real one, Elizabeth and I will go and call on him and present ourselves for review. Meanwhile it was just the two of us, and as of this moment no prospect of an intervening force, a father figure, a grandmother, or a favorite baby-sitter. Just us girls. In the words of the sampler over my fireplace, AND BABY MAKES TWO.

I was besieged by her, but not unhappy with her. I was rankled by her, but proud of her, as she sat, receiving, on the counter of the SeaView Diner. I was burdened by her, as I carried her up and down streets, in and out of the jeep, but her bundled closeness caused me to love her more. I was irritated at five-thirty in the morning to hear her squawk, but I needed her regular pattern to get me started. I was charmed by her too, as she called yi yi yi to me, and at five forty-five in the morning, I called back, "Yi yi yi to you, kid."

By the end of the second week at the SeaView I felt on easier footing. A decided rhythm emerged, as I shifted eggs and pancakes from the hotter to the warm side of the grill, as I snapped those toasters down, six and eight at a time. Instead of regarding each customer as a potential enemy, I began to smile and acknowledge an occasional compliment tendered to Elizabeth. "Yes, she's cute," I responded.

"I think that survey fellow wants to go out with you, Eva," Maureen whispered.

"You mean the one who always asks for the three-egg omelet?"

"Yes. The big guy. Twice now, he's asked about you. First he wanted to know if you had a husband. Then he asks me who's the father of the baby. You know, he's curious. Anyway, he wants his usual omelet."

"Coming up." I peered over the grill. He had dark hair, big jaw, glasses, the traditional plaid wool shirt. Solid.

He disappeared a day or so later, this nameless surveyor, and I found I was disappointed. I called him my three-egger.

XXIII

"I can come toward the end of next week maybe, just for a day or so. How's that, Eva?"

"Oh, James, that's great, please do, I sometimes think I'm going crazy here in the evenings."

"Okay. Can you put us up?"

"Who's us?"

"I'm bringing my girl friend."

"You have a girl friend? Who?"

"You don't know her."

"Does she have a name?"

"Yes, Laura Dash."

"Good name. Of course I can put you up. My house was crummy at first but now it's fine, and you can sleep on the porch, the warmest room. Opa says you've had a good season."

"Yeah. Too many people though."

"Now, Jimmy, you're in business. You mustn't resent customers."

"Some of these customers are real turkeys. A couple of days without tennis won't hurt me."

"How is the House of a Thousand Tennis Balls?"

"Rebuilt. How's your job, Eva?"

"I love it."

"You do?"

"Sure. Well look, James, let me know, anytime is fine—"

"Eva?"

"What?"

"Do you think about Mother a lot?"

"Yes. Particularly at night. Do you?"

"Yeah. I got stoned the other night and I thought I saw her, sitting in my room. Just sitting there. Reading."

"Sometimes I find myself asking her things, should I do this or that, as if she was still here. I was reading a book called *Pathfinders*, and as I went off to sleep, I thought I heard her say to me, 'Don't read that silly book anymore.' "

"Eva, I wonder something. Do you think she's anyplace but under the ground?"

"I think she must be."

"Christ, I hope so."

I figure that on an average morning we served up about fifty-five to sixty breakfasts, mostly to regulars, who were used to the steam and tempo of the diner; a few tourists from time to time wandered in toward the end of the morning, but the hard-core regulars hit their crest at around seven-thirty to eight in the morning, before shops opened and business began. For about an hour in there, at peak time, the place really jumped. Around nine-thirty, the pace slowed, and just as I began to loathe the sight of another egg, breakfast, with all of its rituals, ground to a halt.

"Take it easy," called one regular to me, a graying electrician who had been there every morning since I started.

"Take it easy," I called back.

Elizabeth developed a cold one morning and we had to stay home, so Helen was returned briefly to duty. I so missed the smell, the faces, and jangled nerves of the place that I bundled Elizabeth up and sped down to the SeaView for a quick late lunch.

"Was everything okay this morning?" I inquired of Helen, grumpy at the cash register.

"Sure, I guess so. You'd better get back here tomorrow, though."

The three-egger, as I called him, reappeared a day or so later and asked for his usual omelet. Pensive, tidy, his folded paper beside him, and alone.

"Now smile at him, go on," ordered Maureen, not a famous smiler herself.

"I can't," I protested from my station at the grill.

"Well, look at him, at least. He's a sexy-looking guy. His name is George McElroy, and he's some kind of biologist."

The same plaid shirt, firm, All-American good looks. On his face this time I thought I saw a kind of keenness, a look of anticipation, even at seven forty-five in the morning.

I threw some extra parsley on his omelet and put the plate up on the ready-to-go counter for Maureen. He looked at me and smiled.

In the last six months, I haven't had enough sex to keep a chicken alive, I thought to myself. Maybe it's time to smile back.

Maureen had his name wrong; it was John McElroy. He was good company at dinner, although a little heavy on the flora and fauna, and tireless in my bed where we had landed quite quickly. Yes, I felt a return to a reasonable balance, if not exhilaration, in my life. As we headed off to the movies, with Maureen's niece Betty serving as baby-sitter, logic seemed restored. Working girl, baby, boyfriend, movies, sex.

John McElroy was a giant, about six-foot-four, with broad shoulders and huge hands. My little cottage trembled as he stomped in at the end of a day and plunked down in the one chair that would hold him. The stairs shook as we tiptoed up to my bedroom, quiet so as not to wake Elizabeth. We undressed quickly because of the cold. He seemed vital and desirable, perhaps because he wasn't familiar. With genuine satisfaction and relief I turned away from him, finally, to try and catch a few hours' sleep before the five-thirty call. For a few brief nights at the beginning of a rainy April he was a welcome presence.

"James, this is John McElroy, my brother James."
"Pleased to meet you."
"Hi, how are you?"
"This is Laura Dash."

"Hello, how are you, Laura?"

"Fine, thanks."

"Want something to drink, John?"

"I'll get it, Eva." James was quick on his feet.

"Just a beer, thanks."

James looked different in the company of Laura Dash. The hair-in-the-face, baffled expression was replaced by a take-charge ease that had not been his in early years. I noticed John observing him carefully. James was indeed less good-looking than John, but he had a kind of rumpled charm. John McElroy, chiseled features, square jaw, seemed huge and sedate next to James, who flopped about, getting everyone beer, noisily munching potato chips.

And what to make of Laura Dash? If Brooke Shields and Martina Navratilova could be blended into one, you might have Laura Dash. "I lucked out," explained James with a grin. I liked her because she seemed to take to Elizabeth; the night before she had held her and bounced her while I produced a miserable vegetable dinner on my wok (James and his lady had gone vegetarian). Though she looked like a movie star, with her long hair, athletic build, and fluttery eyes, she could plainly be trusted. "I'll hold the baby," she offered. As I had once judged my fellow man by his willingness to carry my harp, I now saw everyone as a potential holder of the baby, and Laura was a "10" in that department. James looked at the child tentatively. To John, Elizabeth was downright suspicious. Laura cooed, "Yi yi yi."

James and Laura had agreed to baby-sit while John and I went into the village to one of the two restaurants open for dinner. "Back in a while," I called as we headed off, with rain coming down in a gentle drizzle.

"Wind is coming in southeast," John said. "The barometer is falling."

"Is that good or bad?" I asked with true innocence.

"Depends if you like bad weather."

A definite motif, that of draped seafaring paraphernalia, hung on the walls of the restaurant. My eye followed the lobster pot, to the telescope, progressed on to the round life preserver, to the pair of oars, crossed, all connected by fishnets and white rope. At the end of the line, so to speak, a lobster, the prize, shown in bright painted orange. I concentrated on this wall get-up. I tended to daydream as John talked on about ponds, algae, and winter draw down.

"You see, Eva, aquatic succession can seem complicated, although it's really very logical. Plankton, tiny algae and animal life, becomes so dense on the top of the pond that it prevents sunlight from getting through, and then growth and animal life, submerged, is often just eliminated, even though some small faunal life like frogs or diving beetles or some new insects appear on top of the pond."

"And that's what's happening over at Tisbury Pond?"

"That's right. The bottom of the pond has no life, so to speak, and soon the water depth is reduced, because oxygen in the water is so badly decreased. That's why we are going to have to cut through on the bank, and let some ocean saltwater flow in. Did you want to order?" He smiled, acknowledging the foot-long menu in front of him.

"Sure, what are you going to have?"

"Bluefish sounds good. I like to fish for blues. Caught a couple last spring."

"I think I'll stick to scallops."

"Anything you want." His bulk, so out of scale in my house, seemed to fit well in this comfortable, chunky restaurant, where the chairs were built for halfbacks.

"You could come with me next week to Nantucket, Eva. We're doing a project over there similar to the Tisbury Pond project here, but in some ways more challenging. You've been to Nantucket, haven't you?"

"You folks ready to order?" Our blond waitress towered over us.

"Sure. Okay." We reexamined the menu, unable to announce our choices without actually seeing them again, written out.

"Our special tonight is the crab meat Newburg, with cheese and wine sauce over chunks of crab meat, with bread crumbs, served with scalloped potatoes and sautéed green beans."

"I'll have the bluefish." John held his own under the fire of the nightly special.

"I'd like the baked scallops, please."

"Anything first?"

We searched the menu again. "Clam chowder, please."

"And for you, miss?"

"Stuffed mushrooms, I guess."

"We're out of stuffed mushrooms tonight." She smiled.

"Well, the chowder for me too, then."

"Alrighty." She beamed and swirled away, almost as if on ice skates.

"I like Maureen's no-nonsense waitressing, don't you, John, better than people who smile all the time, and don't really mean it."

He shrugged. "I guess so. She gets the order right, Maureen."

"She's terrific. She's been great to me. Whispering encouragement, spotting handsome men, covering my mistakes."

"Eva, how about it?"

"How about what?"

"Come to Nantucket with me. We'll be there about ten days, there's a great place to stay all set up for us. Did you say you'd already been to Nantucket?"

"Yes, a long time ago, my parents visited Nathaniel Benchley, and took me along."

"Who's Nathaniel Benchley?" He shifted, a touch irritated.

"A writer, a very funny writer. His son was the guy who wrote *Jaws*, which you know they filmed right here at Oak Bluffs, some parts of it anyway."

"Oh, right. Your folks are writers, you told me."

"My mother was a writer. She died at Christmas. I mentioned that to you."

"Oh, of course, gee, that must have been tough."

"Yes, it was. Still is."

Music oozed through the walls, glasses clinked, plates rattled, voices produced a stage "low murmur," and I had a sudden clear view of my mother, sitting near me, just for a quick minute, looking through the menu herself, glasses on the end of her nose, puzzled as to what to order.

"What about Nantucket, Eva?"

"Well, in principle, I like to go most places."

"You'd have an interesting time. Why don't you take a few days off from your job?" He leaned forward. "This pond is fascinating. Maybe you could hold the charts for us or something.

Some patience will be required." He gave me a little nudge. "Leaving next Saturday."

"I don't know quite what I'd do with Elizabeth, John."

He sighed. "Can't you leave her here? Get a sitter?"

"I don't honestly think I can leave her here, or anywhere, for any length of time. I could come for a day maybe, or I could put her on my back for a while, but I have a feeling that when she got cold and tired, and there was no crib to put her in, she might scream and disturb the plankton."

He didn't smile. "Well, that doesn't sound very possible, then. I was hoping you could get free. As to your bringing the baby, even for a day . . ." He rubbed his chin, his handsome, square chin. "Somehow, it doesn't seem very, well, professional. I mean, these men are trained biologists, specialists in their field."

"Presumably they have children too, biologists?"

"Sure, but with wives at home to take care of them."

Silence. The arrival of the clam chowder allowed us to look away from each other. I stirred, he fiddled.

"I don't mean to ask personal questions, Eva"—(oh, please, ask a personal question)—"but why did you have this baby, without a marriage. It seems kind of a queer thing to do."

"Well, I told you that I found myself pregnant by a man who I had been going with for a while, but couldn't dream of marrying—"

"Well, why didn't you have an abortion?"

"I really wanted the baby."

He looked puzzled, leaned back in his chair, and shook his head. "Why?"

"I just felt a certain rightness about it. It's hard to explain."

"You could have waited. You're not exactly old."

"But then it would have been some other baby, some other egg, some other child. Not Elizabeth. I really didn't want an abortion."

His eyes darkened. "A right-to-lifer?"

"No. Just a sense, I suppose, that I could do it, and after all, this constant talk about women's choices—this was my choice."

"Did your parents object?"

"At first."

"Funny business. Of course, I'm a zero population man myself. There are too many people in the world already." Now it was his turn to stare at the plastic lobster.

"Here we go. One bluefish?" She seemed to come out of nowhere, our waitress.

"Right here."

"And the scallops."

"For me, please."

"Enjoy your meal." She whirled away.

The music had been turned up and seemed to vibrate through the room. That great old song "Dancing in the Dark" rendered on a thousand violins, seemed to engulf me, make me want to dance in the dark.

"Do you know this song?" I asked John.

"No, no I don't."

"It's an old Arthur Schwartz song, 'Dancing in the Dark.' You see, I know all these oldies because my father loved these songs, and since he is a producer, we had those songwriters around the house. Arthur Schwartz was a pretty good friend actually."

"Don't you think you were irresponsible to bring a child into the world without a father?" He sat up rigid in his chair. I had been babbling on about dancing in the dark, and he was furious, three feet away from me. "What are you going to say, when she asks who her father is?"

"I'll tell her."

"She deserves two parents, don't you think?"

"Ideally. We don't always get what we deserve, maybe not right away."

"It was an arrogant thing to do."

I felt a shiver in my rib cage. "We are happy, Elizabeth and I, and we have hurt no one."

A large man, when mad, has a tiny, comic aspect, which I certainly did not mention at this critical moment, but John fumed in a way that seemed to make him seem more than ever like a wooden Indian; he was angry, but he didn't move.

"Don't you want to be free, Eva?"

"Of course, whatever that means."

"Well, for example, this weekend, I would have liked to take

you with me. It's a very interesting project, and Nantucket is one
hell of a beautiful place. But you can't go, because of your baby.
Now I can't imagine how anyone would—on purpose—allow himself, or herself"—he pointed his finger at me—"to be trapped with
a baby."

"I don't feel trapped. It's time you understood that."

"But you can't come with me at any point next week, can you?"

"No."

"Well, that's no way to live, is it?"

"Yes."

He clenched his teeth. "Look here, Eva, I want someone who is
free to come on my adventures, not someone who is tied to some
baby."

"Not some baby. MY baby."

He shook his head. "You should be able to come and go, ex-
plore your world, perhaps to join in bettering your world," he said,
poking his fork in the air for emphasis, "as I think I'm doing. I
am trying to understand nature's balance and keep man from de-
stroying it." He leaned back, satisfied.

"Part of the way of keeping nature's balance, it seems to me, is
that those of us who want to bear children, and will take responsibility for them, should do so."

Our contest was squared off now, on equal footing. I dived into
my scallops. My opponent ate nothing.

"You know, Eva, you're going to have a hard time. Getting a
man, I mean. Anyone who takes you on, gets the baby, too.
Right?"

"Right." This, I felt, was below the belt.

"I mean, she's cute and all, but you have no father to take her
away for the weekends, so when are you going to have fun?"

"I'm having fun now."

"I don't believe it. I think you're stuck. Just stuck."

I wanted to do like they did in old movies, dump a plate of spa-
ghetti down his front, or go the grapefruit-in-the-face route, but
flipping a bluefish in his lap seemed shy of the mark.

"You're just stuck," he repeated.

"There are all sorts of ways of being stuck, John. Such as fol-

lowing along behind some biologist, holding his charts for him.
That's a way of being stuck."

"I'll get someone else, Eva."

"I'll let you start now," I replied. I popped two more scallops in
my mouth, rose, folded my napkin, and headed for the door.
Shame not to be able to finish a good dinner, but all I wanted to
do now was to be clear of him, to be out in the air.

My exit, smooth and swift, was diminished by the fact that I
took the wrong parka and had to slink back in and make the exchange. I cast a sidelong glance at John, sitting quietly eating his
bluefish. Righteous biologist with bluefish. It would make a good
painting.

The rain had stopped. I walked quickly up the main street,
passing each little cross street at double time. Back to Elizabeth,
James, my slanting cottage. A briny smell filled the air. I saw the
house as I rounded my street, lit up, tiny, a beacon. I wanted to
dive in the front door and hug everybody, to reassure myself that
we were all intact, holding on.

"Hi, you guys," I shouted, much too loud for a house with a
baby.

"Oh hi." Laura stood in her leotard, by the fireplace. "Just
doing my exercises."

"Is the baby okay?"

"Yeah, everything's cool. How come you're back so soon?"

"The evening ended abruptly."

"One of those, huh?" She smiled.

"Where's James?" I asked, still on edge.

"In here," he called. James was on the porch, curled up in my
bathrobe, reading *World Tennis*.

"Was the baby okay? She didn't wake up?"

"Nope. Not a sound. She was good."

"Dear thing." I flopped down in the big chair. "What did you
think of John?" My routine question.

"Well, I think I like Cal better."

"Actually, so do I."

We raced back and forth in a pretend football game, James
throwing long passes which Laura and I received expertly. A

warmer Monday, with clear skies and a smell of spring, plus a wine hangover combined to cause them to forget the boat and Mountain Top, and stay an extra day. With Elizabeth in the backpack, we headed to South Beach, parkas open, hair blowing, the salty air tempered by a dulcit breeze.

"Okay, Eva, here comes a long one." James backed up, Joe Namath incarnate, and threw a perfect nonexistent pass to me which I caught on the run, with a slight jump.

James. He's the best of the lot, when all is said and done. He looked the perfect boy at that moment, sweater with holes, red cheeks, flying hair, his beautiful smile. My pal, my brother. He does not need to hold center stage the way Opa does, he is connected to the world the way Adrian isn't. A bit like Mother, James is, yes I see it now; he's like Mother in his touch. Same sweetness, a hint of mystery. Now if only he can find her confidence. Maybe Laura Dash will have a hand in that.

"Touchdown!" shouted Laura.

"Yi yi," Elizabeth called.

We headed up the beach toward Windy Gates, oceanfront property owned by the Baldwins, old friends. Trespassing undetected past other clumps of private beach property, past sloped cliffs of gray-red clay, leaving huge footprints in the sand with our boots, it seemed a longer walk than I remembered. Elizabeth bounced along, strapped to James's back, the first time I had ever seen her hanging on someone else. James. He'll do what he can, and it won't be much, but every once in a while he'll turn up and take a hand in things. I ran over and pinched Elizabeth's cheek. "Be nice to your uncle," I warned her.

Laura looked more like a model than most models; her jeans clung to her, her parka billowed around her, she leaned her tall frame into the wind, and her hair licked her face.

"How much farther?" she asked, unused to soggy beach walks.

"To travel joyfully is better than arriving, Laura," spoke James. "Did you know that?"

"No I didn't, creep. When are we arriving?"

Windy Gates, its tall cliffs buffeted and eroded by years of winter storms, the steps up the steep parts rebuilt many times, now shaky again, looked under siege. But how tall, how tough, so in flight those cliffs seemed, as we stood below. The beach absorbed the pounding of the surf, the rocks glistened as they were uncovered by the water. The sun warmed us, and I felt gleeful. "Jimmy, I bet no one has been down here all winter. I bet we're the first."

"Knockout place," said Laura. "Who lives here?"

"Roger Baldwin. Old friend of Mother's."

Laura looked around for a minute. "Okay, let's go home." She was a short-take girl.

But we'd been out for a couple of hours, so we headed back, the wind behind us now, pushing us gently back toward home.

"I'm starved," said James.

"I'm tired," said Laura. "What about you, Eva?"

"I'm practicing traveling joyfully," I replied, with a smile at my brother.

XXIV

"I wonder if you could run this ad," I asked the rumpled man at the front office of the *Vineyard Gazette*.

"Right over there," he answered, pointing behind him. I followed his directions.

"Could I get this ad in the next edition of the paper?"

Without looking up, a lean Grant Wood young woman rolled a piece of paper in the typewriter. "Read it to me."

"Harp Lessons. At my house. Edgartown. Beginners welcome. Call after eleven A.M., 555-2938."

She typed rapid fire. "All right, twelve words. That will be two seventy-five." She finally looked at me, gave me an encouraging smile. "Sounds fine."

"Do you think that anyone on the island cares about playing the harp?"

"No," she replied.

"Well, I'll try anyway."

"Absolutely."

"Thursday, the eighteenth. Eva, I will be disappointed if you don't come for the opening. Get a charter plane if necessary." Opa was insistent, I could feel it through the telephone.

"I think on Thursday I can get a regular flight, Air New England at two-thirty. How have the previews gone?"

"Martin O'Keefe's voice has not held up very well, but we've got some throat expert from Venezuela with him now. I don't know, Eva, you would think that I should be relaxed about these things after all these years. Why don't you come up a couple of days early?"

"My job, Opa. I can really only be away for a day."

"You mean they can't get someone else to cook breakfast for a few days at the diner?"

"It's not as easy as that. Here's what I'll do. I'll try and leave Elizabeth with Maureen for one night, so I'll go to work, get out around ten-thirty or so, take her over to Maureen's with the gear and get her to sleep, then I'll run home, grab my things, jump on the two-thirty flight to Boston, which is always late, then get the four o'clock shuttle to New York—"

"You'll never make it, Eva. You're not leaving yourself enough time to get home to Riverdale and dress—"

"Don't worry. I'll meet you in front of the Martin Beck Theater at six-thirty. Trust me."

"I trust you," he replied. "Or I've learned to. Good-bye."

I dialed Trudy.

"Hi. Are you up for doing me a favor?"

"Natch."

"Meet me at La Guardia next Thursday at five o'clock with a dress of yours that I can wear to Dad's opening, and shoes, size six and a half."

"Oh, Eva, I'm not sure I have anything you'd like."

"I don't care if I like it or not. Just something festive that covers me. I'll go straight to the Martin Beck Theater from the airport. Okay?"

"You don't have anything you could wear?" She sounded plaintive.

"Nothing. Zip. We don't dress for the diner."

"You know they're wearing some funny-looking things now. I don't know if I have anything—"

"Trudy?"

"Yes?"

"Remember Christine and Hugh Pringle."

"I'll be there."

And so she was. I made my plane connection in Boston with

ease and came running down the ramp in New York at 5:15 to find Trudy holding what looked like a prom gown in a plastic bag and a pair of silver boots.

"I have a feeling you're going to hate this." She looked unhappy.

"Nonsense, that's just fine, looks wonderful. It doesn't matter what I look like anyway as long as I show up. We've never missed an opening, and now, without Mother, Opa seems jittery, and anyway I'd like to see the show. Did you hear anything about the previews?"

"Someone said it looked pretty good."

We headed for the ladies' room, where I switched to a very pretty, totally uncharacteristic maiden's gown, of the sort that was currently in style. By five-fifty we were headed into New York. After the spare tranquillity of the Vineyard, the approach into New York made me feel like we were entering Rio at Mardi Gras. The taxi driver lurched from lane to lane at top speed. I thought of Elizabeth with Maureen.

"This taxi driver is really crazy," I whispered to Trudy, thinking of Elizabeth an orphan at five months. Where would she go if I should die?

"Just normal for New York." Trudy shrugged. "You've become a country girl."

We left Trudy off at her apartment and pulled up at the theater at six twenty-five. I emerged, looking like Scarlett O'Hara's country cousin (after the ball). Opa was waiting. He hugged me and whispered, "Right on time. Aren't you wonderful."

We went right into the lobby and entered into a round of what my grandmother used to call how-do-you-dos. Any opening, particularly a Wiltshire Productions opening, has a certain glamorous, freewheeling, cordial period before the curtain goes up, and I was swept into this one immediately.

"Jake, this is my daughter, Eva."

"How do you do?"

"Jake's with *New York Magazine*, the dance critic. Change of pace, eh, Jake?" Jake beamed.

"This is Lydia Despres." His lady.

"How do you do?"

"Eva, do you remember Hatti McFarland, toured for two years in *Starry Nights?*"

Hatti McFarland looked like Phyllis Diller. "How do you do?"

"Here's Paul Bell, with *Cue* magazine, how are you, Paul, my daughter, Eva."

"Hello."

"What do you think you've got here, Larry?"

"We only deal in hits, Paul. Martin O'Keefe is grand in this."

"Good luck."

"Henry, this is my daughter, Eva, Henry Joseph. Henry stayed with us on the Vineyard a few summers ago." A nice-looking fortyish man smiled at me.

"Nice to see you again, Eva."

"I remember you," I said, thrilled to recognize someone. "You carried my harp. Do you remember?"

"How could I forget. What are you doing now, Eva?"

"Living on the Vineyard with my daughter."

"Your daughter. I didn't know you were married."

"I'm not."

He shook his head. "Divorce is tough. I've just been through one myself."

"Eva dear, I want you to meet Merle Wallace, our new press director."

"Hi."

Merle Wallace looked like he hadn't slept in a week. "Hi. Your father was afraid you wouldn't make it."

"I made it." Opa and Merle went into a moment of intense whispering.

"Larry?" A high female voice.

"Grace Mortimer." Opa was on his toes. "You remember Grace Mortimer, don't you, Eva?"

I couldn't quite place her, but I embraced her warmly anyway. Oh, Mother, why aren't you here to get me through this charade?

Grace Mortimer was talking to me about the last time she had seen Mother, looking so healthy that she can hardly believe that she's not here anymore; I somehow managed a response, when a lovely little bell rang.

"Time to go in." Opa clutched my arm. We winded our way to

our traditional seats, the rear of the orchestra, on the aisle, chosen
so Opa could spring to his feet and tear out should it become necessary. As the orchestra began its warm-up, just before the over-
ture, the prime nervous-making time it seemed to me, Opa pulled
a letter from his pocket.

"Here, darling, I've been carrying this around for days. A nice
fat-looking letter for you. Postmarked Los Angeles."

Billy's handwriting. How long had Opa had it? He was never
good about forwarding mail, it could have been there for a
month! Maybe it's a "Dear John" letter, so plump, so full of
explanation—"My dear, I have just met the love of my life
under a palm tree." Or perhaps it's just a listing of his musical adventures. A new record cut.

The lights went down and I shoved the letter into my bag.
Hardly the moment to read it anyway. "Producer Lawrence Wiltshire's daughter seen reading her mail during the first act of her
father's new production." Nonetheless, I felt my blood quicken.

Opa whispered, "You know who did some of the early arrangements for this show, don't you?"

"Who?"

"Your friend Bill Diamond."

I listened to the music for a minute, to the soft, swirling
sounds. Maybe he's coming home.

The house looked alive, even at four o'clock in the morning. In
fact every light in the place was on, as well as the radio in the
kitchen.

"Well, I don't know if these are box office reviews, Eva, but
I'm more or less satisfied."

"You should be. I thought everything went very, very well." I
was exhausted, my little silver boots pinched, but I picked up a little energy just from being back in the old house.

"I still think the first act drags; so did Frank Rich at the *Times*.
Sit and talk to me for just a minute, Eva." He poured himself a
brandy. "You like Noel and David Larkspur, do you, or are they
just too stylized?"

"No, not too stylized, but cool. A little too cool."

"True; oddly enough, the partnership seems to work very well."

We sank into chairs in Mother's study: it was smaller, more suitable for four o'clock in the morning.

"Well, it's over at last." Opa put his head back against the chair, closed his eyes for a long minute. "Everyone assumes, Eva, that I am lonely, at loose ends, without Mother, which is really not altogether true. Do you want to know why?" He looked at me. "She is still here with me. I know, of course, that she's not really here, but I haven't accepted her death in my entrails yet, you know that, don't you, Eva? I see her, I talk to her, I feel her presence—so much so that when I am here alone, I often don't feel badly. As you may notice, nothing of hers has been moved, not an inch. Does that seem spooky to you, Eva?"

"No. Perhaps it's just necessary."

"I'll tell you a little something about our marriage, Eva. We weren't very much alike—that's well known. I didn't follow every word she wrote, and some of my theater crowd irritated her. It wasn't a very practical relationship in many ways, and yet we very much needed each other. But we allowed ourselves to be romantic. Now this may be hard for you to imagine, but we liked to dance, late at night, in the living room, after all you children had gone to bed. No, of course we didn't understand every single thing about each other, there were even some wide gaps of understanding, but we let things go. We were gentle with each other; we didn't trample through the other's psyche with our boots on. Mother said that, Eva. We don't trample through each other's psyches with our boots on. Doesn't that sound just like her?" He shifted in his chair, shot me a quick smile.

"Now you go to bed, and I'll sit here and think about what she looks like in her funny evening dresses. You remember. I tried to get her to buy nice expensive ones, but to no avail. I'll let her come to me and reassure me that, yes, although the first act was too long, it still worked, and the play's probably going to run and that Venezuelan to whom I paid four thousand dollars to restore Martin's voice was worth it, and she'll tell me that the second act curtain needs restaging, despite what Noel says. So you see, I still have her with me, in my way."

"Good night, Opa." I kissed the top of his head.

Dear Missy,

Forgive me for being a lousy writer. I made a tape for you the other day, but I sent it to Chilmark, because I'm still not sure of the Edgartown address. Will you check at the Chilmark P.O. for it?

I have been so busy this last while. I thought California was for lying around in the sun, but I've been at recording studios for the last six weeks, both here and in San Francisco, and I don't remember seeing the sun. A record has been cut by a hot group called the Back Doors, terrific, with four of my songs, and I did most of the other arrangements. Another good break, Butch Holtzman, a great songwriter and bass player who I used to know in college, we've contracted to write the score for a fantastic thing that MCA is backing—hoping to open in New York next year. In other words, great things are happening.

I'd like to come back and see you, and more than that, if your house will hold me, I'd like to stay with you for a month or

A pencil line drawn lightly across the bottom. The letter ended. I'd like to stay with you for a month or—or what? There was no page two, no explanation for the sawed off thought. From the envelope fell a postcard wrapped in a piece of Kleenex. Pictured were the usual California oranges, looking huge and quite fake. On the back in his largest hand was written: "Coming home, Love, Billy."

XXV

I've come to love this porch. Mostly, I suppose, because I've spent much of the winter here, and now the winter is behind me, and we got through it together, me, Elizabeth, and the porch. I read out here, give harp lessons on this solid rectangle, the playpen is set up, I have meals and pay my bills here. Actually, it might have been a good deal easier if I just rented the porch instead of the whole house.

I sit here at night a lot and think about the year that has passed. I try to avoid evaluating my situation and certainly don't try to place events in their proper perspective, as I was constantly asked to do at college. No, I just digest things; digest that which has happened to me over the last year, Mother, Elizabeth, Billy, the diner. Even my two harp pupils, Mr. Crockett and Mrs. Danzig, could not have been imagined a year ago.

Today I sit on the porch scanning the cloudy sky like an old whaling wife, waiting for a ship to appear. Only in my case, it's the four-thirty boat from Woods Hole. Billy, after some delay, is on his way to me.

We are rested, brushed, and combed, Elizabeth and I. I have resisted the temptation to put a blue barrette in her wispy red hair. Too corny. "It would be awful nice, Elizabeth, if you'd behave perfectly for the next couple of days." From her playpen, she gives me a particularly blank look. I pick her up and give her a squeeze. "Okay. Just hold on through tonight."

It's hard to imagine what life was like when I didn't have her. I'm so used to carrying her. What did I carry last year, when I didn't have her?

I scrubbed her face. I am beginning to feel like one of those old-fashioned war brides, expecting her man back from battle, holding little Johnny Jr. in her arms. We are certainly done up accordingly. But this child has nothing to do with Billy, I remind myself. It wouldn't hurt if he liked her, though.

And if he doesn't? What if he's just one of those nice men who can't stand children? They do exist, nice men who can't stand children. Well, if he's like that, then to hell with him. I rammed an extra Pamper in my pocket and looked around.

The house is orderly, I have washed my hair, bought swordfish for dinner, put clean sheets on the bed, even cleaned out the jeep. I pinched Elizabeth's cheek and she returned me a crooked smile.

"Let's go, kid. There's nothing else to do now but go pick him up."

The ten-minute drive to Vineyard Haven along the ocean road takes us through the town of Oak Bluffs, where Billy played all summer. Stella's, closed through the winter, gives some signs of opening up. A piece of cardboard taped to the door says, "Opening June 1st." Will Billy want to play there again? Oak Bluffs has a kind of crowded charm; even in the rain the harbor is dense, vital, overloaded.

The salty air is touched with gentleness. It is May after all. There is a definite spring smell, a promise of warmth. Rain, blue-gray rain, has caused the landing dock and parking lot at Vineyard Haven to look glassy, to shine. This damp weather always makes my hair curl. I check in the car mirror to see if I could possibly look nice. Not bad. Not too bad. Certainly better than the last time we saw each other, standing in the driveway in Riverdale on that freezing cold day, me with my pear shape.

"Is the boat on time?" I ask a Steamship Authority figure with his orange slicker.

"Coming in now. But you can't leave your car here."

"I know." Of course I know. If I had a nickel for every boat I've met here I'd be rolling in money. I zipped up to the A & P market, parked underneath a sign which said, "For A & P customers only," and headed back to the dock.

The ferry, called the *Islander*, is rounding the bend toward the landing slip. The boat looks whiter and larger to me than before.

Elizabeth squirms in my arms.

At least twenty minutes seems to elapse from the first sighting of the *Islander* to its head-on approach into the slip to its final landing, oozing into the correct spot, connecting with a gentle thud. Suddenly cars and people belch forward from the boat, humans and dogs on leashes out the side ramp, cars piled high with camping gear and summer supplies out of the front of the boat, along with bicycles, trucks loaded with lumber, mail vans.

Where is Billy in this mayhem? My poncho has slipped down and off of one shoulder, my head is uncovered as a gentle rain continues to fall. Elizabeth is making little mewing noises. She is okay in the tumult of the diner. This is a little more than she's used to.

"You'll have to stand back, miss," speaks the orange-coated authority figure. "Move over to where the ropes are." I allow myself to be shoved over to the roped-off area. No sign of Billy.

I think, Well, if he doesn't come this afternoon, it will serve me right for being overprepared, the swordfish, clean sheets, and all.

"Missy."

A head is coming toward me, a funny-looking blond beard with a halo of hair. Yes, the eyes and the smile are the same.

"Oh, Billy."

His arms are around me so fast that I can't really see him or say anything.

I back up, still clutching Elizabeth. "Are you all right?"

"I am." He is smiling now, just the way I remember and I feel for one minute that we are right back in last summer, nothing has happened in between.

"What are you doing back behind these ropes?"

"They made us move."

"Dumbbells. So this is Elizabeth?"

"Yes."

"How are you, Elizabeth? You look like your mother." Elizabeth, ever a money player, beams. Billy looks drenched, rumpled, patches of sunburn cover his forehead.

"It's raining hard in New York, much worse than here, I thought the fucking bus wouldn't get us to Woods Hole on time. For Christ's sake, what's all this rain? It doesn't rain in California." He scans the sky with a grin.

I couldn't seem to make a sentence. Just standing there, rooted to the ground, nodding, I clutch Elizabeth.

"Well look, I brought a lot of gear, see this junk, what we'll do maybe is leave some of it here. Where are you parked?" He seems taller than I remember and his eyes dart everywhere, looking through the crowd, over the harbor.

"Up at the A and P."

"Good girl. All right now, I'll walk over with you, we'll put this stuff up against the post here, take this, this is my score, or the first part of it. You'll be glad to know that I dumped Frieda off with Ace Dukenney, miserable mutt. So how do you like this stupid beard?"

"Well . . ."

"I think I look like a fool, but, well, you have to do something when you're out there. I'll have it off in an hour." He is looking at me now, carefully. "You look fine, Eva."

"I feel fine," I managed.

"So how old is Elizabeth, four months?"

"Five months."

"Have I been gone that long?"

The beard is gone; the swordfish is gone; Elizabeth is asleep. The rain has stopped and left a damp, sweet smell to the air. We've opened all the windows.

"In California there's a plant called jasmine, and at night, when the jasmine is out, it has the greatest smell, you'd think you were in the most exotic place in the world."

"Maybe you were."

Billy leans back in the one big chair. We're both a little punchy from wine. "No. I don't think so." He smiles at me. "No. Missy, out there, the Coast, it's the land of freeways and great recording studios, and a lot of cocaine, lots of laid-back souls, but no, not quite exotic, not to me anyway."

"We don't have jasmine here though."

"Lilac. Lilac is just as good. Can I get a beer?"

He is altered, just a little. He looks thinner; that boyish, near angelic look about him is gone. I am trying not to stare but I actually see a line between the side of his mouth and cheek. We've not touched each other since he's been at the house.

He is standing in front of me now, pacing slightly. "It was worth it, Missy, those months out there. All the time, I often thought, why is this taking so long, why am I still here? I just thought I'd better wait until I heard back from this guy, or that office, and it kind of drove me crazy, but it was worth it. In that time, I made two records, and signed for the score for this show which is going to be fantastic, called *Blue Smoke,* or whatever the hell we're going to call it. The score is going to be wonderful, Missy. I'm going to make it wonderful. But I had to wait to get it. I really did." He looks at me with a question on his face. "You understand. Do you understand?"

"Yes. I guess so. Once you were there, and things started to move."

"I couldn't leave. I hated it at first, really, and I had the cast on my leg, and I never could find anything on the damn freeways. Then when I began to rehearse and get the musicians lined up and started to record and all, I got into it. Once I put things together, I certainly didn't want to stop." He sat near me now. "I lost touch with you for a while. I was never in the same place for more than two days. I'd fly up to San Francisco to work with Butch, and then grab a plane back down to L.A. to rerecord some damn thing, then we'd rehearse something else, then back up to San Francisco. It was madness, but I guess it was my kind of madness. I got a lot done."

"Then why did you come home? It certainly could have gone on, your kind of madness."

"I came home to see you. I don't want to lose you."

"Oh, Billy." I sat back in my chair. This is what I remember from before, those plain sentences: "good for you," "I don't want to lose you."

"Something else too, Eva. I began to feel as if I could fall into that whole California number. Musicians are superstars out there. But too much dope, too many dumb women. Too much sun."

"That sounds like a cheerful problem."

"But it isn't. I can take it, I could have taken it for longer, I suppose, but I began to feel as if I were losing my bearings. It's hard to describe. I missed Stella's." He laughed. "Can you imagine missing that dump?"

"It's opening again June first."

"But I'm not going back there. I've got to finish this score now. If you will have me I'd like to finish the score of *Blue Smoke* here."

"Okay." I smiled. The porch. The porch now takes on its third tenant.

We look at each other now, free of some of the earlier awkwardness. An arrangement has been made, a deal struck, he will stay here for a while, we'll swim in these waters now, with me no longer pregnant, we'll be just another couple, a man and his girl friend living together.

"Billy, I did think, once or twice, that you might stay in California. It is very seductive. I've been there, and I like it."

He shrugged. "No, Eva. Among other things, I find I can't compose very well out there. The recording studios are great, but writing, concentrating, was harder. Everybody talks too much."

"What?"

"There are so many clichés about the West Coast. One thing I'd always heard was that everybody is busy fucking away like jack rabbits. But that's not really so, at least not now. What they're doing is, they're all talking. Talking, group this, group that, talking about relationships, inner-personal weekends or whatever. Someone asked me to join a group of something, so I could relate better to something. I said shit no."

"That wasn't very nice."

He shifted. "Missy, did you have a hard time when the baby was born?"

"No, not when the baby was actually born, in fact I can hardly remember it. I had a hard time after. Mother died a week later."

"I spoke to you then."

"That's right. But then, those weeks after, when I was back in Riverdale, yes I did have a hard time then. Mother was just dead, and yet we all felt she was still somewhere, somewhere, maybe in the house, or coming up the driveway. And then there was this baby, and Opa wanted me to do this and that with him, and find his tuxedo and old telephone numbers. I wanted to get out but I had no place to go."

"Oh, Eva." He ran his hands through his hair. "I never thought you'd planned that out at all."

"How could I plan? When you're walking on a tightrope, you can't plan dinner."

"Sounds awful."

"I tried to call you a couple of times, those numbers you left me . . ."

"I know. I was never there, I guess."

"I came down here, stayed at the Chilmark house for a bit, and then we got lonely, just me and the baby, so we just moved into town and took the first house we could find. Things began to get better."

"See, I never knew you were down here. Then I called and your father told me he didn't have your address here, so I sent something to Chilmark."

"Well, I never got that. I got one letter later on."

"It's just as well. They were terrible letters anyway. Like letters from camp. This is what I did today. That kind."

"Not this is what I did last night, though."

"No." He shook his head. "No reason to talk about that. It doesn't matter anyway. When I was out there, I wasn't alone for five minutes, it seemed to me. I was always with Ace or Butch Holtzman, or Steve Markel, and two girls. I always seemed to move in fours. It was like high school. But I thought about you every day, Eva. I write lousy letters, I never say what I want. There were days when I didn't know where you were. But I did not forget about you." He is speaking slowly now, as if tired and a little drunk. "I have never not loved you."

I trembled slightly: I didn't expect him to say all these things, I thought we would be more cautious, more tentative. I have never not loved you?

"Tell me, is there a bedroom in this house? I don't see one."

"Upstairs."

"Can we go up there now?"

"Well, it's small, and a mess, and unheated . . ."

"So what?"

I stood up and moved back against the wall slightly. "I don't know, Billy, it's just that I . . . Billy, we haven't seen each other for a long time and perhaps it will be different."

"Won't matter," he murmured, looking at me. "Eva."

I turned out the one porch light and walked toward him.

Warm, solid Billy, his arms went around me, the same mouth, the same sweet chest. I could hear his heart beat as I held him, I could feel his heat, and although he seemed almost to weave on his feet, he looked at me with clear eyes.

"You look fine, Eva. You look just the way I hoped you would."

"I longed for you. I didn't admit it often, but I longed for you."

"Where is upstairs?"

We walked quietly, through the parlor, past the sleeping baby, upstairs.

By the pale light from the dormer window we undress and I see that he is thinner, that slightly hefty look of last summer is gone, his frame is almost lanky.

"You're thinner, Billy."

He came toward me and looked at me carefully. He reached over and touched my stomach. "You look thinner too, my girl."

True enough. He's never seen my stomach without a baby in it. I look down for a quick second. Yes, it's flat.

He looms over me now, powerful arms, his halo of hair, like before, and as I guide him toward me I think maybe I do really love him. Despite the still unfamiliar, unreunited corners of him, and the mysteries that separation introduces, he is with me now, in me now, and again, I feel swept away.

"Where are you going?" His tone was almost accusing.

"To work." I stood before him, half dressed, ready to dive down and get Elizabeth.

"What work?"

"I have a job at the SeaView Diner."

"Doing what?"

"Cooking breakfast."

"For who?"

"Anybody and everybody."

"You're kidding."

"No. Come down if you want. It's at the bottom of Main Street."

"Eva, what time is it?"

"Five thirty-five."

"You get up every morning at five thirty-five?" He was up on his elbows now. "To go to work?"

"See you later."

"We're busy this morning. Maybe because summer's almost here, and the crowds are starting, you know what I mean?" said Maureen.

"I know. I haven't stopped for one second since I got in." I was such an old hand by this time that a busy morning didn't bother me. In fact I preferred it. Time went faster. "Let's open the door. It's too steamy in here."

"Helen says not to."

"Open it until nine-thirty." I made up in insistence what I lacked in seniority.

Maureen shrugged. "Okay. If you say so."

The fresh air was welcome. Elizabeth, on her perch, looked a bit wilted. I picked her up and wiped off her face. Then I threw on four more omelets, zapped the toasters down, turned the sausages, prepared more sticky pancake batter, and watched more people line up for breakfast.

"Your boyfriend show up?" Maureen was never too busy to ask the important question.

"Yes, he did."

"And is he still . . . cute?"

"Well, actually he is still cute."

"You look a little tired."

"We stayed up late. Talking."

"Right. I don't think Helen's going to give you any time off. She says we're too busy and now her arthritis hurts."

"I don't really want time off. It's okay."

I was determined to maintain my schedule with or without Billy. Which meant Mrs. Danzig for her harp lesson at two o'clock this afternoon.

"Maureen, do you think that Betty can baby-sit a couple of nights this week?" Might as well show the old boy the town.

"I'll have her call you."

"Ma nee," cooed Elizabeth, as one of her favorite breakfast regulars, Harry Boyle who worked in the harbor, leaned over her. "Ma nee."

"What's she saying, Mommy or money?" he asked.

"I'd like to think it was Mommy, Harry. Do you want your usual?"

Because of the crowd we were a bit late in leaving the diner, and we didn't peel into the house until almost eleven. It was so still that for a brief moment I thought that maybe he hadn't been here at all, Billy, that I had had some kind of reverie. I dashed upstairs. He was draped across the bed, long and a little brown. The sun made patterns on his back.

I fed Elizabeth, changed her, and dropped her into her crib. "Sleep well. Sleep quietly, sleep long," I murmured.

"Good morning." I curled up next to him, gave him a little poke.

"Drummer here yet?" he mumbled.

"It's eleven-thirty, Billy. I just got back from the diner." He opened his eyes and smiled.

"Say it again," he ordered.

"I just got back from the diner."

"Okay." He rubbed his eyes. "I haven't really sort of registered that yet. You have a job at the diner. And what do you do with the baby these mornings?"

"She comes with me."

"What does she do, butter the toast?"

"She sits and coos at everybody."

"I see." He rolled over and sat up on his elbow. "Tell me something, Missy, does the baby really look like you, or like Hal?"

"Cal. Well, everyone thinks she looks like me."

"That's good. I'm glad. And is he ever going to come for little visits, or whatever?"

"Absolutely not."

"So he's not around. It's not like you're divorced, with the father showing up on weekends."

"No."

"Maybe it's more like you're a widow. Is that more like it?" he asked seriously.

"A widow. Yes. That's fine." I could scarcely control my enthusiasm. "Think of me as a widow. Can you?"

"I can until I look at you." He took me in his arms for the second time within the last twenty-four hours, and we had what is known in the trade as a nooner.

"Mrs. Danzig!"

"Mrs. who?"

"Billy, Mrs. Danzig is coming at two."

"So?"

"She's my pupil. My harp pupil."

"Eva, do you *give* harp lessons? I thought you *took* harp lessons."

"Give and take, Billy. What's the difference. It pays part of my phone bill."

"Do you know how to give a harp lesson?"

"Certainly." I was washed and dressed in minutes. Billy followed me downstairs, rumpled, in his chinos.

"Eva, how often does this woman come?"

"Once a week. And Mr. Crockett comes twice a week. And Betty the baby-sitter wants to take."

"To take what?"

"Harp lessons."

"It seems to me you've got a goddamn music school here."

"Don't wake the baby. You'll have to whisper."

"What happens if the baby wakes up during the lesson?" He looked genuinely concerned.

"I just hold her. Or she crawls around on the floor. You have to learn to do more than one thing at a time, Billy."

"Oh. Good." He rubbed his jaw. "Perhaps I'll just take a walk. Or maybe I'll go down to your diner and get some breakfast."

"Breakfast is from six-thirty to ten-thirty. Lunch is from eleven to two-thirty."

"What time might I come back and find you . . . free?"

"After three or so. I've asked Betty to come by this evening."

"For a harp lesson? At night?"

"No, to baby-sit. I thought we might go out to dinner or to a movie. Live it up a little."

"*Bien sûr*," he pronounced as he headed out the door.

He had asked a fair question. Can you give a harp lesson? My response, a solidly defensive one, was proving nonetheless to be almost accurate. I decided earlier this spring that my ability to play the harp was strictly limited. And I was simply too nervous to enjoy performing. But I found to my surprise that I could relay to others (two others) the essential instruction, a little sense of the music, and a fair amount of enthusiasm, which is really all a beginning harp student needs. God forbid that I draw a student who actually knew anything.

An island inhabitant for thirty years, my student Mr. Crockett observed and drew birds, particularly waterfowl. His fancy for the harp was born less out of a need to make music than to get away from Mrs. Crockett, a famous island sourpuss. He stretched the days of his lessons into near full-day sojourns, even hinted at one point that he might like to take me to "a nice lunch." Crockett once played the violin, which, he felt, gave him a leg up on the harp. Actually he did have a genuine ear for music, which is more than could be said for dear Mrs. Danzig.

They had come together, Mr. and Mrs. Danzig, to the interview preceding the first lesson, mostly to look me over. The Danzigs were recent, well-to-do emigrés to the island from New York, a worthy and tense couple who poorly tolerated the pressures of the Big Apple and came here to find "relaxation and peace." Mr. Danzig found vodka, and Mrs. Danzig, who did not touch liquor, remained unrelaxed. A scholar in European history, she was pleasant-looking, though woefully thin, and strung as tight as the high C string of my harp.

"We are hoping," said Mr. Danzig to me, that first day, "that

Bella will be able to relax with the harp. It's such a gentle and soothing instrument." Nothing but a hammer blow to the head could relax Bella Danzig, but I refrained from saying so.

She tried earnestly at her lessons and succeeded in part in the mastery of fingering, her knuckles inverted, tautly arched; she stroked the instrument as if it were a biting animal.

Nonetheless, the Crockett-Danzig team added thirty dollars a week to my coffers, and in their way, I liked them both. Mrs. Danzig sometimes brought me back copies of *Country Life*, a British magazine devoted to the joys of the English countryside, where I think she truly longed to be, as opposed to sitting on my porch off Pease Point Way in Edgartown, struggling with the harp.

XXVI

"What a sight, Missy."

We stood on the cliffs above Lucy Vincent Beach, the town beach, strictly off limits at night, and watched the waves roll in. It was the clearest evening in recent memory.

"Billy, we're the only people here. Makes you feel like some kind of potentate. Surveying our domain."

"It would be nice if it were ours."

The waves produced rhythmic, billowing sounds. Within the past minutes the sun had set, leaving a warm June glow at the horizon and little streaks of light across the top of the water.

"Let's go for a swim. Come on." Billy grabbed my arm. "There's a little bit of light. Come on."

We raced down the path from the top of the cliff to the beach, past the famous poison ivy patch, in our shorts and sneakers. "We'll pay for this escapade in poison ivy," I called.

"Well worth it," he shouted back. "A little poison ivy in exchange for a peak experience."

We undressed quickly, throwing clothes wherever they landed.

"It's going to be cold," Billy called over the din of the waves, "but the best thing to do is just run in. Just run in, Eva, and throw yourself in fast."

"Is there an undertow, do you think?"

"We'll swim near each other. We won't stay in long."

Following his own instructions, he ran and plunged and was

quickly lost in the gray-white tumult. Soon his head bobbed up.
"Holy shit," he cried. "Okay, Missy, it's your turn. You'll be
used to it in a minute."

Without allowing myself time to think about it, I ran, splash-
ing into the water, gritting my teeth, and falling forward, flopping
forward in a passive dive. The chill shot through me and gave me
a quick overall cramp, which went away as quickly as it came. I
made a halfhearted effort to swim toward Billy but almost immediately relaxed and allowed myself to be carried in toward the
shore by the tide. For a moment it seemed a relief, something that
was being done for me, swimming for me, carrying me. Within a
few seconds I was reversed, back out away from the beach, with a
feeling of tugging at my legs and thighs. The same confident motion that had carried me in now pulled me back out, the same
swift and insistent rhythm. I caught my breath and tried to swim
back in with it, the beach seemed so very near, almost within
grasp, and again the same tug pulled me down and sucked me
back and made the beach recede.

"Billy," I called.

"Hi." He was farther away than I expected, I could hardly hear
him.

I thought of Elizabeth now, Elizabeth without protectors, Elizabeth the baby, Elizabeth without me.

This time I started swimming hard before I had to, before the
reverse gear claimed me, I started swimming with a kind of fury.
At the point when the wave changed backwards, I changed forward, arms and legs thrashing, breathing like a horse, going forward blindly.

I felt rocks underfoot. Sharp, reassuring rocks. I stood up, and
the ocean was curling around my waist. I moved forward a few
steps, then turned and looked back. Innocent, those waves looked
innocent and almost cheerful, bobbing up and down. I only
wanted to be on land.

Shivering, I grabbed my few clothes, dried myself with the
shorts, and put on the sweater, trying to get my breathing back to
normal.

"Billy," I called.

He waved back, bouncing happily.

"There's an undertow."

"Hi."

Billy is a strong swimmer, I remember that, stronger than I am, but he doesn't realize what is between him and the beach.

I waved again.

But watching him carefully, I could see no pattern to his movements. He was not being brought in and back out like I was, in fact, he was happily bouncing around like a seal. Could I possibly have imagined my brief tussle with the undertow? If it was really undertow, maybe I couldn't have gotten in at all.

After a minute he started back, in a smooth, unencumbered swim, which landed him on the beach without effort.

"What's the matter, Missy?" He stood beside me, naked, glistening, hair matted down.

"I felt undertow, Billy, I was pulled back and off to the side, and I had a terrible time getting in."

"Really? I didn't feel anything at all. Undertow usually runs right along the beach. Come on in again and swim right next to me."

"No, I don't want to."

"Missy, the water is smooth as bath water. I'll stay right next to you. Come on, don't be a nervous Nellie."

I shook my head. "I am not a nervous Nellie."

The moon had gone down completely and the stars took on a bright, sharp glow. I walked up and down, around the rock, looking for my sneakers.

"All right, home we go," he sighed. He was dressed in a minute and we headed for the car.

Away from the roar of the waves he said, "Eva, there was no undertow there, I didn't feel it for a minute, and I was right near you."

"It scared me, Billy, that's all I can tell you."

"Sometimes when you first get in, and it's rough, sure the waves seem to toss you around a little bit, but that's not real undertow. I think you exaggerated, that's all."

"No I didn't. I did panic though, and I thought about Elizabeth." I could hear a slight shrillness in my voice.

"Elizabeth is fine. Maybe you're just getting paranoid."

"I worried about Elizabeth that one moment when I couldn't get in. People have drowned on this beach. Someone did last year. What would happen to her if I should drown?"

"Okay. I don't want to argue about it. It's just that this doesn't seem like you, that's all."

"It is like me, Billy, or it is like me now; and I bet it's like every other woman with children, maybe we all develop a case of paranoia in one form or another. It goes with the territory."

"Okay," he said. We drove home, feeling the beginning of soft summer air, not saying much.

What did he think of Elizabeth?

He seemed undisturbed by her, which at first relieved me. No, she was not going to drive him out of the house. And Billy occasionally looked at her with passing warmth. In the morning, for instance, when we got back from our session at the diner, ready for our eleven o'clock lunch, there would be Billy, starting his breakfast, so we'd all jockey for position, tuna fish sandwiches, Rice Krispies, and baby applesauce, around the kitchen table, and he might smile at Elizabeth, or he might run his hand over her wisps of red hair. But he never really focused on her.

He's not interested in her. Not even curious, I thought. I was used to the crowd at the diner, who gave her real (sometimes excessive) attention. Billy looked past her. I suspect Billy saw her as an appendage of me that had to be accepted, but he seemed to give her no human proportions. She might as well have been an overstuffed doll. I told myself that time was on our side, because after all she was not an overstuffed doll. He will fall prey to her at some point. Elizabeth is one hell of a flirt.

"When will you listen to my tapes?"

"As soon as I get back from taking Elizabeth to her doctor's appointment."

"Which will be when?"

"Around four."

"Okay, Missy. Come back soon. I want to know what you think."

Later, at early evening, I sat in the big chair on the porch watching the sun go down over Eel Pond, holding Elizabeth and her bottle while Billy tried to adjust the volume and the earphones he had just planted on my head.

"This is crazy," I murmured as Elizabeth sucked away at her bottle and Billy fiddled. "I feel like an astronaut."

"Want to just hear it without the earphones? It's okay with me."

"No, just let me finish with Elizabeth and put her in the playpen."

"She'll do better without earphones," said Butch Holtzman, sitting on the floor with part of Billy's score in front of him. "I think the sound is better."

Tiny, mustached, exuberant, Butch Holtzman moved through the house with kinetic energy, leaving in his wake half-empty beer bottles, uneaten sandwiches, a string of coffee cups. He had been with us for two days, and Billy said he would not be released until he finished lyrics begun in California and now in need of completion.

"Screw the earphones, man, just turn up the amps and let it fly."

"I'm not sure I can stand to hear it again, Butch, that's why I'm doing this," Billy grumbled. Butch made him cross.

"Oh shit, man, you're starting to turn on your own material, what do you expect Deke Wasserman to think. It's his nickel."

"Fuck him," murmured Billy, adjusting the earphones. "Okay, Missy, now we're set."

Butch had arrived at Vineyard Haven with a huge flat casket-like object which proved to be Billy's Fender Rhodes portable electric grand piano, a piece equal to my harp in terms of tonnage and awkwardness.

"What's that?" I had asked, as the two friends struggled toward the jeep suspending the black box between them.

"That's my piano, baby."

And now it sat, amplifiers connected, in the center of my porch. The harp was moved gently, respectfully to one side.

"Lookit here, Bill, just play the first song for her and I'll sing it."

"Oh Christ, no singing from you, man," Billy snapped.

"How's she going to know what the lyrics are?" squealed Butch.

"I'm giving them to her. Here." Billy handed me a sheet of paper on which were written some short repetitive phrases.

Butch was just going to stay overnight, but since he never seemed to sleep, I wasn't sure that he knew what overnight meant. But I liked him. He played with Elizabeth. Nonetheless, two straight days with him had made us all a little punchy.

"Okay. Eva, is it coming through?" I nodded.

Elizabeth whined from her playpen.

"Here, give me the goddamn baby." Butch leapt to his feet. "My sister has a baby, I know how to bounce them."

Billy sat back in the wicker chair, Butch bounced Elizabeth, and I listened.

Strong melodic sounds rushed through my ears, a fierce rhythm finally calming to a traceable, discernible theme.

"Here, now start here," shouted Billy, pointing to the top of the paper. I was lost but didn't say so, hoping to connect what I was hearing and what was written in front of me as the music went on. It was hardly soothing, but had a kind of compelling quality, these sounds, dominated by bass and guitar. Reminded me a little of some early Credence Clearwater numbers. I smiled at Billy.

Butch and Elizabeth stood next to me, their time run out, and Elizabeth, almost on the point of tears, dove into my arms, pulling the earphones off just as the music seemed to end. "Crash landing," cried Butch.

"What do you think?" Billy asked.

"I'll have to hear it again, but it sounded pretty good to me. How many instruments do you have there?"

"Six," said Billy, intense and unsmiling. "Did the sax really come through?"

"Why don't I sing the words for her, how can she follow what's on that dumb paper?"

"All right, all right," Billy gave in.

Butch reached into his pocket and pulled out a slightly bent joint, which he lit and passed on to Billy.

"Later," Billy snapped. "I'll record this, Butch. Let me get set up."

"Anything." Butch bounced up from the electric grand. "I could go for another tuna fish sandwich, how about you, Eva?"

"No thanks, but go ahead. Can you find the mayonnaise?"

"Right. I'll find it." He darted to the kitchen. "Mayo, mayo, where are you?" he screamed. "Come to me."

Billy said, "He's crazy, Missy, but there's no one like him in the business."

"I believe you."

"He understands how to put words and music together. Better than I do."

Butch reappeared and hit the piano keys like a cat pouncing on prey. Unlike Billy, who played the piano with a sense of kindred spirit, a near tenderness, Butch saw the piano as almost an adversary whom he hoped to outlast.

"My words now, folks," he announced, dropping his sandwich.

He sang like a drunk, but the words were oddly clear, madcap lyrics that still made sense and, unlike their author, betrayed a sense of order.

"Okay, now, here's the next one. Eva, where are you going?" Butch looked horrified as I prepared to leave the room.

"Elizabeth is jumpy. I'm going to try and put her to sleep. You guys be quiet for a minute."

I grabbed the bottle and took her upstairs, changed her and put her in a clean nightgown. "Enough is enough, right, Elizabeth?" I'd moved her upstairs into the nasty little second bedroom to give her some distance from the racket during this siege. But tonight, turned on by the amplified excitement from the porch, she was nowhere near sleep. I held her and rocked her for a few minutes, and slowly she calmed and her eyes began to close. The noises from downstairs had not decreased as much as I expected. "Never mind, Elizabeth. Try and sleep now," I whispered. "Think of the diner. It's quieter there." I turned on her toy music box. The Brahms lullaby sounded pretty good to me after two straight days and nights of Diamond and Holtzman's raucous music.

I stole downstairs. Billy was hunched over the tape recorder, Butch was stretched out on the day bed, earphones on, eyes closed.

"What's he doing?" I asked.

"I don't know. Maybe he's asleep. He just crashes when he wants to. He'll come to in a few minutes. Are you getting tired?"

"Not yet." I finished Butch's tuna fish sandwich.

"Now, Eva, listen to the 'Blue Smoke' song once more, with the new introduction."

I resumed my place under the second set of earphones, Billy at the controls, put my head back, and closed my eyes. "Blue Smoke," a witty, sultry song, flooded my system. It was a lovely song, really, and I recognized Billy's sure hand in its firm rhythm, its romantic fabric. It seemed to say, Relax and go with this for a while. Like Billy, the song seemed to have a kind of allure.

"I like it. There's a sort of Duke Ellington touch there," I told him as I handed back the earphones. "I think it's beautiful."

"Do you, you really do, now, you're not just saying that?" His eyes were wide, he was as eager as a schoolboy.

"No, I love it."

"Well, I love you," he said, nodding his head in that familiar way, "and not just because you like my music either."

But it helps. I curled up in the chair. It helps that I like that song, that I like other things he's written, because they are almost one, Billy and what he writes. Playing the piano is one thing, but his own songs, what *he* writes, is another, a more profound exposure.

"I love you too," I answered.

"Have the rest of this joint," he offered. "I hate to waste it just because Butch is asleep. Is the baby quiet?"

"She was just going off when I left her."

"Can I play the piano then, with the amps?"

"Try it. If she wakes up, I'll hold her for a while."

I took a drag on an almost gone joint and stretched my legs out in front of me and closed my eyes. There are worse ways to spend a Wednesday evening, I told myself, as a marijuana serenity captured my senses. I listened to Billy's fiddling, chords being reshuffled, breaks in the sound while he wrote things down or paced.

The house had been on a high for the last forty-eight hours. Since Butch and the piano arrived there had hardly been an unamplified moment. My little house, used to baby sounds and the six-thirty news. A blur, a drowsiness came over me, and I imagined for a moment that I was on a bicycle riding through a meadow.

"Well now, Miss Eva." Butch was on his feet, looking refreshed and alert. "Wake up now, no sleeping on the job."

"Oh, don't say the word job. My job starts at six-thirty tomorrow morning." I twisted in the chair, remembering the diner.

"I'll go to the village and bring back some pizza," said Butch, rubbing his hands together. "What do you all want?"

"No pizza for you, man, finish this piece right now, two-thirds of a lyric is worse than none."

"I must have pizza."

"There's nothing open," Billy argued.

"I'll open something," Butch shouted. He gave himself a quick slap on the face, shook his head like a wet dog just out of the water, and headed for the door.

"Pepperoni for everybody, right?" He was gone.

We stared at the door, then at each other. "See what I have to deal with?" Billy shook his head.

"I have Mrs. Danzig tomorrow. I'm going to bed." I felt as if tomorrow was another century away, as if the diner and Mrs. Danzig were some kind of joke that others were playing on me. "How can I rally for Mrs. Danzig?" I asked Billy.

He looked at me for a moment, gave me a smile. "You can and you will," he said softly.

"How much longer do we have Butch?"

"Another day. I've got to get him to finish one more thing. He's an unguided missile."

"Good night, Billy."

"You're made of stern stuff, Eva."

Wires and sheet music covered the floor, tapes were scattered on the day bed, the piano sat in bold relief, and Mrs. Danzig stood at the door.

"Good afternoon. I assume Eva is here?"

Billy stood before her in his underwear. She eyed him with suspicion.

"She's here. Please come in." My true love looked handsome in his rumpled boxer shorts, but Mrs. Danzig averted her eyes and sped past him.

"I'm a minute or two early for my lesson. I'll just wait on the porch."

Billy began to gather his tapes, stack his music, and de-amplify his piano as I tore downstairs from the bedroom, holding Elizabeth.

"Oh, here you are, Eva," murmured Billy as he dragged the harp from its station on the side of the porch to center stage. He nodded his head toward the figure staring out the window.

"Oh, Mrs. Danzig, am I late?" I unhooked Elizabeth, who had her little arms tight around me like a baby baboon.

"I'm early," she replied with a jittery smile. "This young man was kind enough to let me in."

"Mrs. Danzig, this is Bill Diamond."

Billy pulled up his shorts, which had slipped slightly, and smiled politely. "There you go, Eva. Your inning." He ambled toward the kitchen.

"Well, Mrs. Danzig, why don't we review the chords we did last week. Here, sit down."

I popped Elizabeth in her playpen. The sun shone through the porch windows, muted but clear, casting Mrs. Danzig in a pale religious light.

"Or would you like to begin with the Bach?"

"I'll begin with the chords."

She sat at the helm of the harp uneasily, braced as if for combat. Nonetheless, she managed to complete, in a somewhat tortured manner, most of the chords we'd been practicing for the past few lessons.

"Invert your fingers," I warned, ever the teacher.

"They are inverted." She was edgy, my pupil.

Elizabeth rustled in her playpen, thrashing and rolling, and managed to push her little top, which produced a quick kiddie rendering of "Twinkle, Twinkle Little Star."

"No, Elizabeth," I whispered, "play with *Pat the Bunny*."

"Yi yi noy," she called.

"I'll just hold her," I reassured Mrs. Danzig. "That way she won't make any noise."

From the seat at the harp, Mrs. Danzig shot me a desperate look. "I can't seem to concentrate today. All of this—other equipment, it seems to have gotten bigger than last time."

"It *is* distracting," I agreed. "Let's try the Bach."

A short Bach fugue, thirty-two bars, key of C, made for Mrs. D. She clutched the harp to her, fingers tense, her face bathed in anxiety.

"Yi noy," cried Elizabeth, as she pulled my hair.

"Goddamnit. Go find your ball," I whispered to her as I put her on the floor. "Why don't you begin then," I said smoothly to Mrs. Danzig, who was poised for the start.

She made up in determination what she lacked in skill. Without any regard to tempo of any sort, she inched through the fugue, just managing to find the right strings, forcing out the few notes, grim, leaden, but triumphant.

"That's good. Really fine," I said. "Now let's do it again, and this time count out loud. It's okay to count out loud. Really."

She took a deep breath.

"One, two, three, four," she measured her effort in four-part puffs. "One, two, three, four—"

Wheeze, rumble, bang! We froze as if a gun had gone off.

From across the room, at her post near the on button, Elizabeth gave a rueful smile. From the tape deck on the floor poured out one of Billy's more raucous, thumping songs, in a thin, high whine.

"Oh, dear God!" cried poor Mrs. Danzig. "It sounds like an air raid."

"Elizabeth!" I raced toward her. "Very, very naughty!" She wailed as I gathered her up.

"I'm so sorry, she pushed the on button by accident," I explained to the stricken Mrs. Danzig. Her curls seemed to stand up, her face was pale.

"I'm not sure I can go on," she said.

"I'm not surprised." I tried to sound soothing. "Why don't we schedule a make-up lesson."

"That would be fine," she said, and gathered her bag and her *Country Life*. "Perhaps under more peaceful circumstances." With dignity, she descended my rickety front steps.

The only good thing that could be said about the afternoon was that Butch didn't appear.

"We're going to have to clean up this joint or I'm going to lose one of my pupils," I said to Billy.

He shrugged. "What's the matter with her?"

"She's tense."

"We're all tense."

"She's trying to relax."

"Why don't you offer to give her a massage."

"It's my porch, Billy," I reminded him gently, "and my student."

He nodded. "True enough."

In the next few days order was partly, begrudgingly, restored. Butch returned to New York. For the part of the day of my lessons, the piano was placed on the side of the porch and the harp returned to center ring. The complex wiring and amplifiers did seem to take up a good deal of space, connected as they were to their mother electric piano, which looked unhappy in the corner. My harp, by comparison, seemed cool, independent, serene. The shifting of instruments, the changing of the guard, irritated Billy, but after a couple of weeks it became accepted routine.

"What's today?" he shouted.

"Tuesday."

"So neither of those creeps is coming, right?"

"Tomorrow. Mr. Crockett tomorrow." Mr. Crockett seemed to be able to absorb the new alignment of equipment and instruments on the porch. Either he was too tactful to say anything or, I suspect, he was mildly entertained by the leftover chaos of "young people," as he referred to us rather wistfully.

"So I'm going to spread out, okay?" Billy said.

Spread out he did. The porch shook with his spreading out. Elizabeth's playpen, the third component in our logistical struggle, was moved to the backyard, as the weather was warmer. It was not an unsatisfactory arrangement, but occasionally I longed for the days when the porch was all mine.

I began to dread the diner. Five-thirty A.M. (sometimes we'd go to six) seemed to arrive almost as soon as I'd fallen asleep at night, and Billy and I couldn't seem to manage to go to bed early the way any other pair of good citizens would do. Only a hardened sense of routine kept me from falling asleep at the grill.

"What's the matter with you?" hissed Maureen, seeing me drooping over my pancakes and omelets.

"Up late," I answered.

Of course, a logical thing to do was to quit. My romance with the diner, and it was that, had now been replaced by a real romance with a real man. But I didn't want to quit.

I did not want to quit just because my boyfriend had moved in with me and was keeping me up at night. I had found the damn job, I liked the people, it was my scene. The only danger was that I might die at the grill, aged by lack of sleep and steamy vapors from the torrid little place. I decided to hold on for a while.

Of course we stayed up late, because when the fits and starts and shifting and billowing and noise of the day drew to a close, the world was just us. We made love the way we had the summer before, without regard to time, tenderly, tirelessly, often reaching for each other in our sleep, murmuring love things, holding each other until morning.

I knew full well that although I might be exhausted on the surface, a sure energy came from the nights with Billy.

It was a kind of marathon. I was determined not to stop.

But in truth, it was often quite annoying to get home at ten-forty in the morning, the travail of the day behind me, only to find him just rising, or perhaps languishing at the piano, holding a bowl of Rice Krispies.

"It takes me a while to get going," Billy explained reasonably enough.

"We'll start lunch." I began to rustle Elizabeth's meal. "Are you getting anything done?" I asked, aware of what a potentially irritating question that was.

"Not as much as I'd like," he answered.

It was hard to tell what was really happening in those working sessions, piano sounds, tapes being played, occasional phone calls to Butch.

I loved to watch him at the piano, concentrating, grimacing, smiling occasionally. Can you love a man just because you like the way he sits at the piano?

I sat in the backyard (not yet a garden) and wondered what life with him might be like, Papa Bear in thumping on the piano, Mama Bear weaving her harp in and out and through the chaos, and Baby Bear—

She shrieked. I dropped my magazine and seized her from the playpen. Her face contorted, she held her plump right arm. A bee sting, round, red, and mean, its white center raised, staring up at me.

"Oh, Elizabeth," I cried holding her, "horrible bee."

Her howls were the kind that caused walls to crack, lamp shades to shudder. I raced her into the kitchen to get some ice.

"What's the matter?" Billy frowned, standing at the kitchen door. "Is she hurt?"

"Bee sting."

"Watch that she doesn't swell up. My brother used to do that. Dangerous."

He went back to the porch. A minute later, the chords began again, through Elizabeth's screams.

Summer was taking shape. The merchants in town, moving from a sleepy spring, began pulling their game up, responding to the influx of summer tourists, by-the-month renters, summer job seekers, and bicyclists. Hot days at last. Elizabeth and I headed out for the beach, with umbrella, towel, crackers, and a bottle. Knots of bathers, some nude, some clothed, gathered on the warm sand, with children running back and forth, happy to be barefoot. There was endless, familiar talk of beach permits.

"Come with us, Billy. Please. It's so nice."

"I can't, Eva, maybe tomorrow."

"I think you need a break. You're working too hard."

"Too hard but not very well, Missy."

"Why, what's wrong?" I stopped in the doorway, holding Elizabeth.

He looked disheveled, distracted, a man caught in the middle of something. "It's too fragmented, the score, so far. I can't seem to give it a central focus."

"I'd help you if I could," I offered.

"No, it's okay. I may ask you to listen to something later on." He looked up at me. "I love you anyway, Missy."

"I tell you. I'll pick some rose hip berries from those bushes on the path to the beach, and we'll make jelly, rose hip jelly. Would that cheer you?"

"No."

He was preoccupied by day, but often at night he stopped and then we'd ring in Betty to sit, and take off, sometimes just to drive up to Gay Head and walk around. The house at Chilmark had never really been closed for the winter, I had just shut the doors and left it last winter, so it was no big deal to open it, just a flick or two of the broom. One night we got some lobsters and drove out there, with Elizabeth in her port-a-crib, and made a little dinner and made a little love and got up with the dawn and drove back to town feeling splendid.

"Missy." Billy stood up in the center of the porch, restless, intense. "Missy, I need Butch."

"Well, I'm not sure I need Butch," I replied quickly, curled up in my chair.

"I've got to put some of these things together now, and I'm stuck. I'm stuck in a way that calls for Butch."

I had sensed for a while that he was stuck too, but I didn't want to press him on it. We could absorb Butch again, if I could lock him up during my harp lessons.

"I need some time from the lead guitar player, Al Crosby." He paced.

"Well, call them up."

Later that afternoon Trudy telephoned from Lambert's Cove, a particularly attractive part of the island, where she was spending a fancy weekend with some of her media crowd.

"I didn't know you were down here," I told her. "Who are you with?"

"The Freeds, and a few others. Can I come for lunch tomorrow? I haven't seen you in ages. I'd like to meet Billy, the composer."

"Well, he's not like Mozart or anything."

"I'd like to come for lunch and meet him anyway."

"We don't really have lunch, 'cause we're on different schedules, but come anyway. I get back from the diner just before eleven."

"You're not still doing that?" she cried.

"Sure."

"Really, Eva, how quaint. You can't keep that up forever, you know."

"I don't intend to keep it up forever."

"I think I can get you a job at NBC doing research."

"I don't want to do research. Come at twelve-thirty tomorrow then."

Billy stared out the window toward Eel Pond.

"What about Butch?" I asked. "I don't see Butch and Trudy crowding in together at our tiny kitchen table for one of our non-lunches. When is he coming?"

"I couldn't reach him." He turned to me. "Eva, I can't get any work done here."

"Where can you get work done?"

"In New York, at my own place."

We stopped for a minute, suspended, waiting for the other to speak.

I said quietly, "Then I think you should go back to New York and work with Butch down there."

He nodded.

"This house hasn't been right for you, Billy, this cramped little house and the harp lessons, and the playpen."

"I like it here though."

"But it's not a good enough working place."

"No. No it isn't. I need familiar ground. And, and I think I need New York, awful as it is. I do all right there."

I walked over to him, we both stood by the window. "I tell you what I think you should do, Billy."

He smiled. "Tell me, Eva."

"Go back to New York, sit down at your piano, and don't get up until you are finished with the score. And satisfied."

"And you?"

"I'll stay here. I'm used to being here in the summer."

"I don't want to leave you again. I did it before, and maybe it was necessary then, but I don't want to do it again."

"I'll be all right, Billy. Do you think I can't manage?"

"I'm beginning to think you can manage just about anything."

He looked sweet again, the look I loved, not the furrowed and preoccupied way he had been recently.

"I'm obsessed with this fucking music, but that's because it's giving me trouble. If I can get Butch to concentrate, and Deke to hear some of it, then I think I can solve it." He stood in front of me now. "Okay, okay, Eva. But I'll be here on weekends." He started to circle the room, gather his things.

"No, Billy. Don't do that. Don't come on weekends. Not until you're done. Musicians don't have weekends, as I understand it."

He stopped. "You do understand it. I think you do." He put his hand on my hair, an easy gesture, one that I loved, and I held his hand for a minute, pressing it to my cheek.

"Look, I may just come up when I feel I can, how's that?"

"That's fine." He stood quietly, holding the sheets of music from the piano. "You can call me up at night, too, Billy."

"Absolutely. I just don't know how long this will take, this final push. May not take too long."

I shrugged. "Most things worth doing take a while. For instance, it takes nine months to make a baby."

"You know, don't you."

"I know."

"Elizabeth's a good kid. I'll bring her a tamborine that I used to bang on when I was little. One of my favorite things. I have it in my apartment. What boat can I get tomorrow? Anything around noon?"

I moved to the phone to call Helen, to tell her that I would not be in the next day, that she would have to cover for me. She was grumpy as all hell, but agreed. "Just tomorrow, that's all," she rasped.

Tomorrow. One morning that's not going to begin at five-thirty.

I am beginning to feel like a professional dockside greeter and good-bye girl, counting last summer's traffic in and out to see Mother and this spring with Curtis and James and Billy, most of all Billy. He is organized now, standing on the edge of a wooden plank, organized around departure, hair combed, boat schedule in hand, wallet full of money, nervous. The boat is twenty feet out.

"Where are my sneakers, Missy?"

"I saw you put them in your knapsack."

He rummages through the blue knapsack. "They're not here. Damnit. I like those sneakers."

"They're probably in your suitcase." Elizabeth weighs a ton.

He is serious, edgy, as he faces me. "Look, Eva, let me just knock this thing together, and I'll be back. I'll be back before then probably. But this is the right thing to do. I'll get back to New York and nail it all down. I just know I will."

"I know you will too."

"It may not take too long."

"Don't hurry, Billy. It's too important. We've got plenty of time. After all, we're just 'young people,' as Mr. Crockett says."

"Mr. Crockett." He shakes his head. "You keep your lessons up now."

"Of course."

The ferry, looking fat, stuffed, and laden, discharges its load of cars and people. "You'd better get up there, Billy."

"Remember I love you, Eva, and Elizabeth too."

Elizabeth receives this news with a glassy stare.

"We love you."

We hug each other, a three-way squeeze in which we seem to find each other's lips for a minute. And he is gone.

"Well, I am disappointed."

"You'll meet him some other time." The sun warmed my shoulders.

Trudy held Elizabeth and munched on an egg salad sandwich. "Was it just that he . . . what, couldn't get his music written in this . . . foxhole?" She waved her hand in the direction of the house.

"That's right. He needed familiar ground."

She looked the perfect picture of a young professional on the rise, purple slacks that ballooned outward at the top, a crisp little Mary Jane blouse, huge shades. Pretty too. Healthy and pretty.

"It doesn't mean, then, that he's gone off into the wild blue yonder."

"Oh, I don't think of New York as the wild blue yonder."

"It has its temptations though."

"We'll survive it, Trudy."

"Maybe."

I shrugged. "Let's put Elizabeth in the playpen. I think she's drooling on your blouse."

"Oh God." She jumped up and we relocated Elizabeth in her square.

"She's getting a tooth I think, that's why all this drooling."

"A tooth, already? She *is* cute, Eva."

Trudy lit a cigarette. "Oh, I know I shouldn't smoke, Neddy sees these commercials and comes running in and tells me I'm shortening my life. It's really maddening."

"Don't let the kid bully you."

She poured herself some more Coke. "So what do you do all day, in this dear little place, you and Mr. Diamond. What do you talk about?"

"Oh, I don't know."

"What does he look like? Describe him."

"Well, Trudy, really, he's medium height, and very attractive . . ."

"Well, what does *he* do all day, let's start with that."

"Trudy, really, what he did all day was, he played the piano and from time to time he'd tell me he loved me."

She paused for a minute, considering this. "I see."

She leaned back in her chair. "Eva, there are not many people in the world who can do either; play the piano, or say I love you. If this is a man who can do both, maybe you'd better grab him."

"I don't really want to grab him. I might have been more inclined to do that a year ago, but now I don't really want to grab him, as you say."

"A good man is hard to find, Eva. And here you are with this child."

"He's just not ready for us yet, Trudy. Which doesn't mean he won't be. But he's not ready for us yet."

"Does that make you nervous?"

"No. I have my problems, but nothing about this man makes me nervous."

"I can't believe it."

"Sometimes I can't either." I reached for my yogurt. "Don't you want yogurt, Trudy? Here, I put this out for you."

She would not be put off the track. "What commitments have you to each other, what agreements have you made?"

"Well, we haven't written up a contract," I replied, a touch impatient. Trudy did run to inquisitions.

"You know what I mean. Have you talked about the future?"

"Not really."

"Eva, really, you should have an open discussion with him, share your feelings about each other, find out where you stand."

"It's not like that, Trudy. I think we love each other but we're not jockeying for position, or having open discussions. What's the opposite of an open discussion, by the way, a closed discussion?"

"Really, Eva, sometimes you are hard to deal with. Relationships are complex."

"I think relationships are complex too."

"Give me that yogurt, as long as you brought it out for me."

We allowed the warmth from the sun to soften what might have been edgy moods, as we sat in our dumpy little yard.

"So you'll just stay here." She indicated by her tone that she considered this to be a decidedly depressed area.

"Yes, and go out to the house in Chilmark some. James has a girl friend and he might be down with her, and Opa's in London now, but he said he'd like to be here most of August."

"His show is running."

"So he says."

"It will be queer, going there without Aunt Elizabeth. Maybe queer isn't the word."

"It's very different without her. And it will be more so in the summer. She never missed a summer in twenty years. It was so very much her place. Opa doesn't even like it that much, but he's coming anyway. It's a way of keeping her."

"What about Adrian?"

"Who knows. I wrote him a letter, and of course he didn't answer. I'll have to try and contact him again."

"What a nut."

"Funny, that's just the word Mother used."

She pulled her large straw bag from under her chair and ran a

brush through her hair. "I suppose I ought to go. I think Jack
Freed has a crush on me. He wants me to go rock climbing with
him. What do you suppose that means?"

I laughed. "Go and find out. It's possible that it may really just
mean rock climbing. At Gay Head or someplace. Let me know, in
any case."

"Oh, I will. Good-bye, Elizabeth." She bent down and gave the
child a quick kiss. "Let me see your face, Elizabeth."

Obediently Elizabeth turned toward the voice. Trudy gave her
close scrutiny. "Eva, I think she's beginning to look like Cal."

"Oh, you see it too!"

"Her mouth and nose—"

"You're the only one who has noticed. You met him so long
ago, I wouldn't think you could remember what Cal looked like."

"I remember him when I look at her. And so will you."

I sighed. "Oh dear. I was hoping to really put Cal out of my
mind."

"Well, you can't entirely. That's the price you pay for plunging
on and having Elizabeth. You're a lady with a past." She added,
"Just like the rest of us."

I gave my notice at the diner the following day. My love affair
with the SeaView Diner had run its course.

Helen snarled, "I just got you doing good, Eva. How come you
leave now?"

A HELP WANTED sign went up in the window.

Within three days a strapping student from Boston University
stepped into my place. I gave him a forty-minute introductory lesson to the grill section; he looked just as innocent and baffled as I
had three months ago.

"You'll get the hang of it in a couple of days," I assured him.

Thus the diner era came to a close. I celebrated this truly happy
experience by vowing never to eat a full breakfast again.

Maureen gave a little cook-out for me the night of my last day
at the grill, Helen and Al, Maureen and her husband and kids, a
couple of other regulars, and Betty the niece–baby-sitter.

"I'd like to take," Betty said quietly, as we finished our steaks.

"Take harp lessons? You've decided?"

"Yes. I think I can play as good as Mrs. Danzig."

"I suspect you can probably play as well as that right now. You can pay me in baby-sitting time."

"Cool." Thus my third harp pupil.

I slept late again for the second time in one week, late meaning seven o'clock. A few days later when Elizabeth adjusted to this new schedule we even graduated to eight A.M. I lay in bed in the mornings, waiting for her peep, aware of the fullness of the trees, the approaching warmth of the sun, the possibilities of a trip to South Beach, the smells of summer.

Billy called and woke our slumbering household at six-thirty one morning.

"Ah, Missy, I'm just going to bed, so I thought I'd call you and say good night."

"I just talked to you last night for an hour."

"Do you miss the diner?"

"Not much."

"Do you miss me?"

"Very much."

"I see, my girl, I'll call you later. Good night."

I did miss him. Restful as it was at first, the first couple of days without him, now time seemed a little flat without his mayhem, his body warmth.

Whatever profit he expected to make from the success of *Blue Smoke* was already spent in telephone bills, but I encouraged him. I honestly think we talked more on the phone than we did when he was here. I loved to feel him there on the other end of the line, to feel the progress of *Blue Smoke* through the telephone.

"Okay now, listen," he cried, that old (and ridiculous) business of playing a song on the telephone to me, while I struggled to sort it out, to see wherein it was different from the last telephone rendering. I listened.

"I'm worried about your not working, Eva," he told me one evening. "I don't want you to lapse back into—whatever it was—nondirection. I want you to have enough to do."

"Listen, Billy, I worked my head off at that job, and I can do it again if I want to and if I have to, but now, I'm just going to breathe for a while. Besides, I now have four harp pupils."

"Four? Who's the fourth?"

"Some sophomore from Radcliffe. The daughter of a friend of Mrs. Danzig's. She starts tomorrow. She looks like she really knows something."

"You'd better watch out then."

Those stretches of the day that I had free, I either went to the beach or roamed around Menemsha or Gay Head with Elizabeth on my back, with my binoculars, looking for shore birds by day and honking geese at dusk. It did not seem to bother me that I had no one to talk to. My four chatty pupils broke the quiet on a regular basis, an occasional old friend appeared, in for the summer.

A letter arrived from Opa one morning, from London, a fat, juicy-looking, handwritten letter, and I decided to stick it in my bag and head out to the Chilmark house and read it there. James and Laura Dash were due out there in a week or so, and I thought I'd better clean up from my last visit there with Billy, when we might have been a bit careless with the lobster shells.

I collapsed the playpen, put Elizabeth in her car seat, placed a bag full of groceries, a couple of new records, and my new bathing suit in the back of the jeep, and headed out for the house. A reprise, just like in Opa's musicals, where they play again a song from the first act in the second act, a reprise, time spent as before, back in the days when someone else, usually my mother, took responsibility for my happiness. The sky was overcast, but the air was warm. Not a good beach day, but a day to sit on the porch.

Each year the road to the house becomes more gnarled and tortuous; this summer was no exception. "Not welcoming," Opa used to say. Nonetheless we rocked down the quarter mile toward the house, the jeep absorbing each bump with a shimmy and a squeak.

I noticed the numbers of spiky Queen Anne's lace flowers and wild, pale rose bushes which had opened up since I was there last (by day). The property had a decidedly un-cared-for look. How could it be otherwise, since our central figure was not there?

Mother's garden was in disarray, weedy, overgrown, brown. There's my afternoon project—a renovation of her garden.

I put on my shorts, set up the playpen, made myself a tuna fish sandwich, and settled down with Opa's letter. A handwritten letter. Quite unlike him. With some eagerness I read:

Dear Little Eva:

Maybe I shouldn't call you Little Eva anymore, but old habits die hard. Forgive me. I am pleased for an evening more or less to myself—thus a chance to write to you. My London friends have made me something of a cause célèbre, and I've not had ten minutes to myself for the last three weeks.

I feel I must record to you, in prose instead of by my usual hot telephone, the circumstances of my meeting here with Adrian.

As you know, Mother's note to me at her death contained, among other things, a plea that I make an effort not to lose Adrian, to bring him back into the fold, so to speak. In that spirit I wrote to him at the old Nairobi address and asked him to meet me here in London for a few days with Inoye. Never one to turn down a free meal, Adrian accepted, and last Thursday, as I waited for his arrival from Nairobi in the lobby of the Dorchester, I braced myself for some kind of muted tense reunion, with each of us controlling ourselves to the point of suffocation (or not).

As Adrian and Inoye alighted from the cab, I thought I saw her carrying what appeared to be an extra-large handbag. We greeted each other quite warmly, given the cast of characters. While struggling with the delapidated luggage, Adrian took the bundle from Inoye and said, "This is your grandson, Arakaya," and handed me a babe in swaddling clothes! I peered in at the little creature who looked quite like a prune, and Eva, I can tell you I almost fainted. Where is Mother at these important moments? Can you imagine that Adrian has a child, and that he never told us anything? Little Arakaya is very cute. As you know I've always been terrified of babies, but I find I quite like holding him as long as Inoye is no more than six feet away.

We arranged through the good graces of the hotel to rent a crib and one of those collapsible strollers which I cannot for the life of me make collapse.

Between my illegitimate (but exquisite) granddaughter, Elizabeth, and the little black Arakaya, I do feel the breaking of new ground all around me, but no less content with it. I wonder what James will come up with?

To go on, after we got their ménage installed, we took a most agreeable short walk in Hyde Park. Spring flowers have passed for the most part, but the air is warm and fragrant and crowds swarmed past us and I felt part of the human race, Eva, a wonderful feeling. Adrian chatted about the new house that he is building, and the ever-ailing jeep (surely his favorite topic). Inoye smiled and cooed at the baby. We dined later at the hotel, Inoye holding the baby in her lap the whole time (mercifully she did not breast-feed him in the dining room).

After she and the baby left, I looked at Adrian for a minute, controlled the urge to demand an explanation from him for his total silence since Mother's death, particularly as he did have *some* news, after all. I wondered, "What am I to do with him now, at nine-fifteen in the evening?"

Well, we went to the bar, my dear Eva, and proceeded to tie one on, such as I haven't managed in quite a few years. And Adrian, who looks sort of drunk anyway, was worse off than I, as we lurched to our rooms some three hours later. I feel that we must have talked of important things, we couldn't have sat in silence for three hours, but I cannot for the life of me remember one word of it nor, I suspect, can Adrian. Suffice it to say that our subconsciouses must have recorded some kind of breakthrough, because the next day we were extremely cordial, if not downright palsy.

After a day of more promenades, lunch at Simpson's, high tea (I did buy Adrian a Burberry raincoat and Inoye a cashmere sweater), dinner with the Nigel Henshaws (at which Adrian talked the entire time), we fell into bed, quite exhausted from all of our good feelings. Adrian gave me an elephant tooth which he'd been wearing around his neck. As long as I don't have to wear it around *my* neck, I'm sure I will always treasure it.

But lo! There is more news. The next morning, I was waiting patiently at the elevator when Inoye came around the corner holding the baby. I saluted her, murmured, "Good morning," and as always, prepared to wait with her in silence. Then she said, "Where is the elevator?" She spoke in perfect English! "Where is the elevator," she said, with a hint of impatience. So stunned was I to hear the King's English from her, so *bouleversé* by this choice sentence—Where is the elevator—that I was rendered speechless. Now it was Inoye who murmured softly about the beautiful day, etc., while I stood, much as she had before, smiling, nodding; but dumbfounded.

As we sat waiting for Adrian in the lobby, I was seized with the temptation to grab this young woman by the shoulders and ply her with questions, such as 1) Why didn't you talk before? 2) When did you learn English? 3) Why didn't you tell us about the baby? 4) How can you stand Adrian? But no, Eva dear, you and Mother would have been proud of me, I sat passing the time of day, I believe the phrase is, and when Adrian appeared wearing a filthy pair of shorts under his new Burberry, we proceeded toward our morning walk, sedately, as if we'd never experienced anything but perfect harmony.

I don't know how to account for any of this. I guess you don't have to know everything about a son in order to love him, but I do have some questions I could pose here and there. Life is full of strange relationships, but I believe, instinctively, we all seek some form of reconciliation. I will learn to be more generous with Adrian, as your mother was generous with me. Remember that, Eva. Generosity with the other fellow makes life possible. Fun too.

And now, how are you? How is your love affair with Mr. Diamond? Are you going to marry him? I hope so.

I cannot imagine, Eva, that you are going to continue to work at that absurd diner, but perhaps I just don't understand what turns on your age group. In my day, we liked to go dancing at the Beekman Towers Roof Top and things like that.

I think about Mother without cessation. Keep *Little Elizabeth* well, darling.

                                                        Opa

So now it's Little Elizabeth, eh? (Underlined too!) Darling Opa, what did Kennedy say—A torch is passed to a new generation. No more Little Eva. Hail Little Elizabeth!

I could scarcely believe all this. Adrian and Opa strolling together in the park, exchanging elephant teeth, ah, what bliss! Mother, rest content. Opa, the least likely to succeed in the filial relations department, has put it together with Adrian, and they managed all this without the dubious help of (Little) Eva! The wonders of life.

I paced the porch, thinking of baby Arakaya. Arakaya Wiltshire.

"Hey, Elizabeth," I called to the sleeping child, "you have a cousin named"—I checked the letter for an exact reading—"Arakaya." Right the first time. She turned over in her playpen. I read again: "How is your love affair with Mr. Diamond? Are you going to marry him? I hope so."

(How are you getting along at camp? Are you learning to swim? I hope so.)

Does he like Billy, or is he just eager for me to make a legal union? Dear Opa, be patient with your children, we'll all get it right eventually. And Billy is my bright light. Just what you used to call me.

I gave Elizabeth a gentle nudge. She woke grudgingly, her face like a baby polar bear. "Come on, child. We'll walk to Menemsha. I won't make the car go over that road again."

I changed her quickly and saddled her upon my back. The aluminum frame of the Sears, Roebuck papoose was by this time molded to my back and quite comfortable. I laced my sneakers, grabbed a pair of shades in case the sun came out, and looked at my watch. Two-fifteen. It's just over a mile so we should make Menemsha in forty minutes or so, a challenge of sorts, reminiscent of the hikes we used to take at camp, a nice walk, a bit of a stretch, but hardly back-breaking. We started out.

As we bounced along I had a sudden clear memory of my girlhood camp, of not wanting to go, at age eleven, and then loving it, of course. I recalled the form that Mother had to fill out, a query from the camp concerning my virtues. I remember her showing it to me. In one question she was asked to describe my leadership abilities. She had replied, "Eva seems content to sing when the others sing."

What would she say now? I wonder. *Not necessarily* content to sing when the others sing? Dear God, I hope so. Or, No longer content to sing when the others sing? How would I ever know?

I looked back for a minute at the house, the porch bearing our junk, the playpen off to the side. And ever so briefly, I saw her, Mother, I saw her standing on the porch by the post, her faded jacket moving in the breeze. "Godspeed," she had said to me some months back; "Godspeed," she seemed to be saying now, with a slight wave of her hand. In an instant she was gone.

I stopped for a moment, then turned with Elizabeth and headed on up the road.

DATE DUE

FE 8 '90			
MY 10 '90			
FEB 10 199?